SURRENDER TO SEDUCTION

BY
ROBYN DONALD

MILLS & BOON®

All the characters in this book have no existence outside the imagination of the author, and have no relation whatsoever to anyone bearing the same name or names. They are not even distantly inspired by any individual known or unknown to the author, and all the incidents are pure invention.

*First published in Great Britain 1998
Harlequin Mills & Boon Limited,
Eton House, 18-24 Paradise Road, Richmond, Surrey TW9 1SR*

© Robyn Donald 1998

ISBN 0 263 81436 X

*Set in Times Roman 10 on 11 pt.
01-9901-56166 C1*

*Printed and bound in Norway
by AIT Trondheim AS, Trondheim*

She hugged her arms around herself.

She turned slightly so that she could see the face of the man silhouetted against the soft glow of the instrument panels; as well as the powerful contours, the faint light picked out the surprisingly beautiful, sensuous curve of his mouth.

Something clutched at her nerves, dissolved the shield of her control, twisted her emotions ever tighter on the rack of hunger. For the first time in her life she felt the keen ache of unfulfilled desire, a needle of hunger and frustration that stripped her composure from her and forced her to accept her capacity for passion and surrender.

Hair lifted on the back of her neck. This was terrifying; she had changed overnight, altered at some deep, cellular level, and she'd never be the same again.

'Why don't you go on down and sleep?'

Bryn's voice startled her. Had he noticed?

Robyn Donald has always lived in Northland in New Zealand, initially on her father's stud dairy farm at Warkworth, then in the Bay of Islands, an area of great natural beauty, where she lives today with her husband and an ebullient and mostly Labrador dog. She resigned her teaching position when she found she enjoyed writing romances more and has now written over fifty of them. She spends any time not writing in reading, gardening, travelling, and writing letters to keep up with her two adult children and her friends.

Recent titles by the same author:

THE NANNY AFFAIR
FORBIDDEN PLEASURE

CHAPTER ONE

GERRY DACRE realised that she'd actually heard the noise a couple of times before noticing it. Sitting on her bed to comb wet black hair off her face, she remembered that the same funny little bleat had teased her ears just before she showered, and again as she came back down the hall.

Frowning, she got to her feet and walked across to the window, pushing open the curtains. Although it was after seven the street-lamps were still struggling against a reluctant New Zealand dawn; peering through their wan light, she made out a parcel on the wet grass just inside the Cape Honeysuckle hedge.

The cry came again, and to her horror she saw movement in the parcel—a weak fluttering against the sombre green wall of the hedge.

'Kittens!' she exploded, long legs carrying her swiftly towards the front door.

Or a puppy. It didn't sound like kittens. How dared anyone abandon animals in her garden—anywhere! Anger tightened her soft mouth, blazed from her dark blue-green eyes as she ran across the verandah and down the wooden steps, across the sodden lawn to the parcel.

It wasn't kittens. Or a puppy. Wailing feebly from a shabby tartan rug was a baby. Little fists and arms had struggled free, and the crumpled face was marked with cold. Chilling moisture clung to its skin, to the knitted bonnet, to the tiny, aimlessly groping hands. So heart-breakingly frail, it had to be newborn.

'Oh, my God!' Gerry said, scooping up the baby, box and all, as it gave another weak wail. 'Don't do that, darling,' she soothed. 'Come on, let's get you inside.'

5

Carefully she carried it indoors, kicked the door closed behind her, and headed into the kitchen, at this time of day the warmest room in the old kauri villa. She set the box on the table and raced into the laundry to grab a towel and her best cashmere jersey from the hot water cupboard.

'I'll ring the police when I've got you warm,' she promised the baby, lifting it out and carrying it across to the bench. The baby let out another high-pitched wail.

Crooning meaningless words, Gerry stripped the clothes from the squirming body. It was, she discovered, a girl—and judging by the umbilical cord no older than a couple of days, if that.

'I'm going to have to find you some sort of nappy,' she said, cuddling the chilly baby against her breasts as she cocooned it first in cashmere and then the warm towel. 'I wonder how long you've been out there, poppet? Too long on a bitter winter morning. I hope your mother gave you some food before she abandoned you. No, don't cry, sweetheart, don't cry…'

But the baby did cry, face going alarmingly scarlet and her chest swelling as she shrieked her outrage.

Rocking and hushing, Gerry tried to lend the warmth of her body to the fragile infant and wondered whether she should bathe her, or whether that might make her colder. She pressed her cheek against the little head, relieved to find that it seemed marginally warmer.

The front door clicked open and the second member of the household demanded shrilly, 'What's on *earth's* going on?'

Two pairs of feet made their way down the hall, the busy clattering of Cara's high heels counterpointed by a long stride, barely audible on the mellow kauri boards.

It's not my business if she spends the night with a man—she's twenty, Gerry thought, propping the baby against her shoulder and patting the narrow back. The movement silenced the baby for a second, but almost immediately she began to cry again, a pathetic shriek that cut Cara's voice off with the speed of a sword through cheese.

She appeared in the doorway, red hair smoothed back from her face, huge eyes goggling. 'Gerry, what have you done?' she gasped.

'It's a baby,' Gerry said, deadpan, expertly supporting the miniature head with its soft dark fuzz of hair. 'Someone dumped her on the front lawn.'

'Have you rung the police?' Not Cara. The voice was deep and cool, with an equivocal note that made Gerry think of a river running smoothly, forcefully over hidden rocks.

Startled, she looked past Cara to the man who followed her into the room.

Not Cara's usual type, Gerry thought, her stomach suddenly contracting. Her housemate liked pretty television actors and media men, but this man was far from pretty. The stark framework of his face created an aura of steely power, and he looked as though he spent his life dealing with the worst humanity could produce. His voice rang with an authentic authority, warning everyone within earshot that he was in the habit of giving orders and seeing them obeyed.

'I was just about to,' Gerry said stiffly. Irritatingly, the words sounded odd—uneven and hesitant—and she lifted her chin to cover her unusual response.

Gerry had perfected her technique for dealing with men—a lazy, flirtatious approach robbed of any element of sexuality. Instinct warned her that it wasn't going to work with this man; flirting with him, she thought, struggling for balance, would be a hazardous occupation indeed.

A green gaze, clear and cold and glinting like emeralds under water, met hers. Set beneath heavy lids and bordered by thick black lashes, the stranger's eyes were startlingly beautiful in his harsh, compelling face. He took up far too much room in her civilised house, and when he moved towards the telephone it was with a swift, noiseless precision that reminded Gerry of the predatory grace of a hunting animal.

Lord, but he was big! Gerry fought back a gut-level appreciation of just how tall he was as he dialled, recounted the situation with concise precision, gave a sharp inclination of his tawny head, and hung up. 'They'll call a social worker and get here as soon as they can. Until then they suggest you keep it warm.'

'Her,' Gerry corrected, cuddling the baby closer. It snuffled into silence and turned its head up to her, one eye screwed shut, small three-cornered mouth seeking nourishment. 'No, sweetheart, there's nothing here for you,' she said softly, her heart aching for the helpless child, and for the mother desperate enough to abandon her.

'You look quite at home with a baby,' Cara teased, recovering from astonishment into her natural ebullience.

Gerry gave her a fleeting grin. 'You've lived here long enough to know that I've got cousins from here to glory, most of whom seem to have had babies in the past three years. I'm a godmother twice over, and reasonably hands-on.'

The baby began to wail again, and Cara said uncertainly, 'Couldn't we give it some milk off a spoon, or something?'

'You don't give newborn babies straight cows' milk. But if someone could go to the dairy—I know they sell babies' bottles there; I saw a woman buy one when I collected the bread the other day—we could boil some water and give it to her.'

'Will that be safe?' the strange man asked, his lashes drooping slightly.

Gerry realised that her face was completely bare of cosmetics; furthermore, she wore only her dressing gown—her summer dressing gown, a thin cotton affair that probably wasn't hiding the fact that she was naked beneath it. 'Safer than anything else, I think. Here,' she said, offering the baby to Cara, 'hold her for a moment, will you?'

The younger woman recoiled. 'No, I can't, I've never

held a baby in my life. She's so tiny! I might drop her, or break an arm or something.'

'I'll take her,' the green-eyed stranger said crisply, and did so, scooping the child from Gerry's arms with a sure deftness that reassured her. He looked at Cara. 'Put the kettle on first, then go to the dairy and buy a feeding bottle. My car keys are in my right pocket.'

She pouted, but gave him a flirtatious glance from beneath her lashes as she removed the keys. 'You trust me with your car? I'm honoured. Gerry, it's a stunning black Jag, one of the new ones.'

'And if you hit anything in it,' the man said, with a smile that managed to be both sexy and intimidating, 'I'll take it out of your hide.'

Cara giggled, swung the keys in a little circle and promised, 'I'll be careful. I'm quite a good driver, aren't I, Gerry?' She switched her glance to Gerry and stopped, eyes and mouth wide open. 'Gerry!'

'What?' she asked, halfway to the door.

Cara said incredulously, 'You haven't got any make-up on! I've never seen you without it before!'

'It happens,' Gerry said, and managed to slow her rush to a more dignified pace. At the door, however, she turned and said reluctantly, 'She hasn't got a napkin on.'

'It wouldn't be the first time a baby's wet me,' he said drily. 'I think I can cope.'

Oh, boy, Gerry thought, fleeing after an abrupt nod. I'll just bet you can cope with *anything* fate throws at you. Ruler of your destiny, that's you, whoever you are! No doubt he had another expensive dark suit at his office, just in case he had an accident!

In her bedroom she tried to concentrate on choosing clothes, but she kept recalling the impact of that hard-hewn face and those watchful, speculative eyes.

And that smile. As the owner of a notorious smile herself, Gerry knew that it gave her an undeserved edge in the battle of the sexes. This man's smile transformed his harsh features, honing the blatant male magnetism that came with broad shoulders and long legs and narrow hips and a height of close to six foot four.

It melted her backbone, and he hadn't even been smiling at her!

Where on earth had Cara found him?

Or, given his aura of masterful self-possession, where had *he* found *her*?

The younger woman's morals were no concern of hers, but for some reason Gerry wished that Cara hadn't spent the night with him.

Five minutes later she'd pulled on black trousers and ankle boots, and a neat pinstriped shirt in her favourite black and white, folded the cuffs back to above her wrist, and looped a gold chain around her throat. A small gold hoop hung from each ear. Rapidly she applied a thin coat of tinted moisturiser and lip-glaze.

Noises from outside had indicated Cara's careful departure, and slightly more reckless return. With a touch of defiance, Gerry delicately smoothed a faint smudge of eye-shadow above each dark blue-green eye. There, she told her reflection silently, the mask's back in place.

Once more her usual sensible, confident self, she walked down the hall to the living room. Previous owners had renovated the old villa, adding to the lean-to at the back so that what had been a jumble of small rooms was now a large kitchen, dining and living area.

The bookcases that lined one wall had been Gerry's contribution to the room, as were the books in them and the richly coloured curtains covering French windows. Outside, a deck overlooked a garden badly in need of renovation— Gerry's next project. It should have been finished by now, but she'd procrastinated, drawing endless plans, because once she got it done she might find herself restlessly looking around for something new to occupy herself.

Cara was sitting beside the man on one of the sofas, gazing into his face with a besotted expression.

Had Gerry been that open and easy to read at twenty? Probably, she thought cynically.

As she walked in the stranger smiled down at the baby lost in his arms. Another transformation, Gerry thought, trying very hard to keep her balance. Only this one was pure tenderness. Whoever he was, the tawny-haired man was able to temper his great strength to the needs of the weak.

The man looked up. Even cuddling a baby, he radiated a compelling masculinity that provoked a flicker of visceral caution. It was the eyes—indolent yet perceptive—and the dangerous, uncompromising face.

After some worrying experiences with men in her youth, Gerry had carefully and deliberately developed a persona that was a mixture of open good humour, light flirtation, and warm charm. Men liked her, and although many found her attractive they soon accepted her tacit refusal to be anything other than a friend. Few cared to probe beneath the pleasant, laughing surface, or realised that her slow, lazy smile hid heavily guarded defences.

Now, with those defences under sudden, unsparing assault—all the more dangerous because she was fighting a hidden traitor in her own body and mind—she was forced to accept that she'd only been able to keep men at a distance because she'd never felt so much as a flicker of attraction.

'Flicker' didn't even begin to describe the white-hot flare of recognition that had seared through her when she first laid eyes on the stranger, a clamorous response that both appalled and embarrassed her.

Hiding her importunate reaction with a slightly strained version of her trademark smile, she asked, 'How's she been?'

'She's asleep,' he said, watching her with an unfaltering, level gaze that hid speculation and cool assessment in the green depths.

Something tightened in Gerry's stomach. Most men

preened under her smile, wrongly taking a purely natural movement of tiny muscles in her face as a tribute to their masculinity. Perhaps because he understood the power of his own smile, this man was immune to hers.

Or perhaps he was immune to her. She wouldn't like him for an enemy, she thought with an involuntary little shiver.

The baby should have looked incongruous in his arms, but she didn't. Blissfully unconscious, her eyes were dark lines in her rosy little face. From time to time she made sucking motions against the fist at her mouth.

'We haven't been introduced,' Gerry said. Relieved that his hands were occupied with the baby, she kept hers by her sides. 'I'm Gerry Dacre.'

'Oh, sorry,' Cara said, opening her eyes very wide. 'Gerry's my agent, Bryn, and she owns the house—her aunt's my mother's best friend, and for her sins she said she'd board me for a year.' She gave a swift urchin grin. 'Gerry, this is Bryn Falconer.'

Exquisitely beautiful, Cara was an up-and-coming star for the modelling agency Gerry part-owned. And she was far too young for Bryn Falconer, whose hard assurance indicated that his thirty-two or three years had been spent in tough places.

'How do you do, Bryn?' Gerry said, relying on formality. 'I'll sterilise the bottle—'

'Cara organised that as soon as she came in,' he said calmly.

'Mr Patel said that the solution he gave me was the best way to disinfect babies' bottles,' Cara told her. 'I followed the instructions exactly.'

Sure enough, the bottle was sitting in a special basin on the bench. Gerry gave a swift, glittering smile. 'Good. How long does it have to stay in the solution?'

'An hour,' Cara said knowledgeably. She glanced at the tiny bundle sleeping in Bryn's arms. 'Do you think she'll be all right until then?'

Gerry nodded. 'She should be. She's certainly not hungry now, or she wouldn't have stopped crying. I'll make a much-needed cup of coffee.' Her stomach lurched as she met the measuring scrutiny of Bryn Falconer's green eyes. 'Can I get you one, or some breakfast?' Cara didn't drink coffee, and vowed that breakfast made her feel ill.

The corners of his long, imperious mouth lifted slightly. 'No, thank you.' He transferred his glance to Cara's face and smiled. 'Don't you have to get ready for work?'

'Yes, but I can't leave you holding the baby!' Giggling, she flirted her lashes at him.

Disgusted, Gerry realised that she felt left out. Stiffly she reached for the coffee and began the pleasant routine of making it.

From behind her Bryn said, 'I don't run the risk of losing my job if I'm late.'

Cara cooed, 'It must be wonderful to be the boss.'

Trying very hard to make her voice steady, Gerry said, 'Cara, you can't be late for your go-see.'

'I know, I know.' Reluctance tinged her voice.

Gerry's mouth tightened. Cara really had it bad; last night she'd been over the moon at her luck. Now, as though a chance to audition for an international firm meant nothing to her, she said, 'I'd better change, I suppose.'

Gerry reached for a cup and saucer. Without looking at him, she said, 'You don't have to stay, Mr Falconer. I'll look after the baby until the police come.'

'I'm in no hurry,' he replied easily. 'Cara, if you're ready in twenty minutes I'll give you a lift into Queen Street.'

'Oh—that'd be wonderful!'

Swinging around, Gerry said grittily, 'This is a really important interview, Cara.'

'I know, I know.' Chastened, Cara sprang to her feet. 'I'll wear exactly what we decided on.'

She walked around Bryn's long legs and set out for the door, stopping just inside it when he asked Gerry, 'Don't you have to work too?'

Cara said, 'Oh, Gerry's on holiday, lucky thing. Although,' she added fairly, 'it's her first holiday since she started up the agency three years ago.'

'You're very young, surely, to be running a model agency?'

Although neither Bryn's words nor his tone gave anything away, Gerry suspected he considered her job lightweight and frivolous. Her eyes narrowed slightly, but she gave him her smile again and said, 'How kind of you. What do you do, Mr Falconer?'

Cara hovered, her lovely face bemused as she looked from one to the other.

'Call me Bryn,' he invited, hooded eyes gleaming behind those heavy lashes.

'Thank you, Bryn,' Gerry said politely, and didn't reciprocate. His smile widened into a swift shark's grin that flicked her on the raw. In her most indolent voice Gerry persisted, 'And what do you do?'

The grin faded as rapidly as it had arrived. 'I'm an importer,' he said.

Cara interrupted, 'I'll see you soon, Bryn.'

Bryn Falconer's gaze didn't follow her out of the room. Instead he looked down at the sleeping baby in his arms, and then up again, catching Gerry's frown as she picked up the package of sterilising preparation.

'Gerry doesn't suit you,' he said thoughtfully. 'Is it your real name?'

Gerry's brows shot up. 'Actually, no,' she drawled, emphasising each syllable a little too much. 'It's Geraldine, which doesn't suit me either.'

His smile had none of the sexy warmth that made it so alarmingly attractive. Instead there was a hint of ruthlessness in it as his gaze travelled with studied deliberation over her face. 'Oh, I don't know about that. ''The fair Geraldine'',' he quoted, astonishing her. 'I think it suits you very well. You're extremely beautiful.' His glance lingered on the flakes of colour across her high cheekbones. Softly he said, 'You have a charming response to compliments.'

'I'm not used to getting them first thing in the morning,' she said, angry at the struggle it took her to achieve her usual poised tone.

His lashes drooped. 'But those compliments are the sweetest,' he said smoothly.

Oh, he knew how to make a woman blush—and he'd made the sexual implication with no more than a rasp in the deep voice that sent a shivering thrill down her spine, heat and cold intermingled. Into her wayward mind flashed an image of him naked, the big limbs slack with satisfied desire, the hard, uncompromising mouth blurred by kisses.

No doubt he'd woken up like that this morning, but it had been Cara's kisses on his mouth, Cara's sleek young body in his arms.

Repressing a sudden, worrying flare of raw jealousy, Gerry parried, 'Well, thank you. I do make excellent breakfasts, but although I'm always pleased to receive compliments on my cooking—' her voice lingered a moment on the word before she resumed, '—I don't know that I consider them the *sweetest*. Most women prefer to be complimented on more important qualities.' Before he had a chance to answer she switched the subject. 'You know, the baby's sleeping so soundly—I'm sure she wouldn't wake if I took her.'

It was the coward's way out and he had to know it, but he said calmly, 'Of course. Here you are.'

Gerry realised immediately that she had made a mistake. Whereas they'd transferred the baby from her arms to his in one swift movement, now it had to be done with slow care to avoid waking her.

Bryn's faint scent—purely male, with a slight, distasteful flavouring of Cara's favourite tuberose—reached right into a hidden, vulnerable place inside Gerry. She discovered that the arms that held the baby were sheer muscle, and that the faint shadow of his beard beneath his skin affected her in ways she refused even to consider.

And she discovered that the accidental brush of his hand against her breasts sent a primitive, charged thrill storming through her with flagrant, shattering force.

'Poor little scrap!' she said in a voice too even to be natural, when the child was once more in her arms. Turning away, she fought for some composure. 'I wonder why her mother abandoned her. The usual reason, I suppose.'

'Is there a usual reason?' His voice was level and condemnatory. 'How would you know? The mothers in these cases aren't discovered very often.'

'I've always assumed it's because they come from homes where being an unmarried mother is considered wicked, and they're terrified of being found out.'

'Or perhaps because the child is a nuisance,' he said.

Gerry gave him a startled look. Hard green eyes met hers, limpid, emotionless. Looking down, she thought, He's far too old for Cara! before her usual common sense reasserted itself.

'This is a newborn baby,' she said crisply. 'Her mother won't be thinking too clearly, and could quite possibly be badly affected mentally by the birth. Even so, she left her where she was certain to be noticed and wrapped her warmly. She didn't intend her to die.'

'Really?' He waited a moment—making sure, she wondered with irritation, that she knew how to hold the baby?—before stepping back.

Cuddling the child, Gerry sat down on the opposite sofa, saying with brazen nerve, 'You seem very accustomed to children. Do you have any of your own?'

'No,' he said, his smile a thin line edged with mockery. 'Like you, I have friends with families, and I can claim a couple of godchildren too.'

Although he hadn't answered her unspoken question, he knew what she'd been asking. If she wanted to find out she was going to have to demand straight out, Are you married?

And she couldn't do that; Cara's love life was her own business. However, Gerry wondered whether it might be a good idea to drop a few comments to her about the messiness of relationships with married men.

Apart from anything else, it made for bad publicity, just the sort Cara couldn't afford at the beginning of her career.

She was glad when the sudden movement of the baby in her arms gave her an excuse to look away. 'All right, little love,' she soothed, rocking the child until she settled back into deep sleep.

He said, 'Your coffee's finished percolating. Can I pour it for you?'

'Thank you,' she said woodenly.

'My pleasure.' He got to his feet.

Lord, she thought wildly, he towers! From her perch on the sofa the powerful shoulders and long, lean legs made him a formidable, intimidating figure. Although a good height for a model, Cara had looked tiny beside him.

'Are you sure you don't want one?'

'Quite sure, thanks. Will you be able to drink it while you're holding the baby?'

What on earth had she been thinking of? 'I hadn't—no, I'd better not,' she said, wondering what was happening to her normally efficient brain.

'I'll pour it, anyway. If it's left too long on a hotplate it stews. I can take the baby back while you drink.' He spoke pleasantly.

Gerry tried not to watch as he moved easily around her kitchen, but it was impossible to ignore him because he had so much presence, dominating the room. Even when she looked out of the window at the grey and grumpy dawn doing its ineffectual best to banish the darkness, she was acutely aware of Bryn Falconer behind her, his presence overshadowing her thoughts.

'There.' He put the coffee mug down on the table before her, lean, strong hands almost a dramatic contrast to its blue and gold and white stripes. 'Do you take sugar or milk?'

'Milk, thank you.'

He straightened, looking down at her with gleaming, enigmatic eyes. 'I'm surprised,' he said, his voice deliberate yet disturbing. 'I thought you'd probably drink it black.'

She gave him the smile her cousins called 'Gerry's offensive weapon'. Slow, almost sleepy, it sizzled through men's defences, one of her more excitable friends had told her, like maple syrup melting into pancakes.

Bryn Falconer withstood it without blinking, although his eyes darkened as the pupils dilated. Savagely she thought, So you're not as unaffected as you pretend to be, and then realised that she was playing with fire—dangerous, frightening, peculiarly fascinating fire.

In a crisp, frosty voice, she said, 'Stereotyping people can get you into trouble.'

He looked amused and cynical. 'I must remember that.'

Gerry repressed a flare of anger and said in a languid social tone, 'I presume you were at the Hendersons' party last night?' And was appalled to hear herself; she sounded like a nosy busybody. He'd be quite within his rights to snub her.

He poured milk into her coffee. Gerry drew in a deep, silent breath. It was a cliché to wonder just how hands would feel on your skin, and yet it always happened when you were attracted to someone. How unfair, the advantage a graceful man had over a clumsy one.

And although graceful seemed an odd word to use for a man as big as Bryn Falconer she couldn't think of a better one. He moved with a precise, assured litheness that pleased the eye and satisfied some inner need for harmony.

'I met Cara there,' he said indifferently.

Feeling foolish, because it was none of her business and she knew it, Gerry ploughed on, 'Cara's very young.'

'You sound almost maternal,' he said, his expression inflexible, 'but you can't be more than a few years older than she is.'

'Nine, actually,' Gerry returned. 'And Cara has lived in

the country all her life; any sophistication comes from her years at boarding school. Not exactly a good preparation for real life.'

'She seems mature enough.'

For what? Gerry wondered waspishly. A flaming affair? Hardly; it would take a woman of considerable worldly experience to have an affair with Bryn Falconer and emerge unscathed.

He looked down at the baby, still sleeping peacefully, and asked, 'Do you want me to take her while you drink your coffee?'

The coffee could go cold and curdle for all she cared; Gerry had no intention of getting close to him again. It was ridiculous to be so strongly aware of a man who not only indulged in one-night stands, but liked women twelve or so years younger than he was. 'She'll be all right on the sofa,' she said, and laid her down, keeping a light hand on the child as she picked up the mug and held it carefully well away from her.

Sitting down opposite them, he leaned back and surveyed Gerry, his wide, hard mouth curled in a taunting little smile.

I don't like you at all, Bryn Falconer, Gerry thought, sipping her coffee with feigned composure. The bite of the caffeine gave her the impetus to ask sweetly, 'What sort of things do you import, Mr Falconer?'

'Anything I can earn a penny on, Ms Dacre,' he said, mockery shading his dark, equivocal voice. 'Clothing, machinery, computers.'

'How interesting.'

One brow went up. 'I suppose you have great difficulty understanding computers.'

'What's to understand?' she said in her most come-hither tone. 'I know how to use them, and that's all that matters.'

'You did warn me about the disadvantages of stereotyping,' he murmured, green gaze raking her face. 'Perhaps I should take more notice of what you say. The face of an angel and a mind like a steel trap. How odd to find you the owner of a model agency.'

'Part-owner. I have a partner,' she purred. 'I like pretty things, and I enjoy pretty people.' She didn't intend to tell him that she was already bored with running the agency. She'd enjoyed it enormously while she and Honor McKenzie were setting it up and working desperately to make it a success, but now that they'd made a good name for themselves, and an excellent income, the business had lost its appeal.

As, she admitted rigorously, had everything else she'd ever done.

A thunderous knock on the door woke the baby. Jerking almost off the sofa, she opened her triangular mouth and shrieked. 'That's probably the police,' Gerry said, setting her cup down and scooping the child up comfortably. 'Let them in, will you?' Her voice softened as she rocked the tiny form against her breast. 'There, darling, don't cry, don't cry…'

Bryn got to his feet and walked out, his mouth disciplined into a straight line. Gazing down at the wrathful face of the baby, Gerry thought wistfully that although she didn't want to get married, it would be rather nice to have a child. She had no illusions—those cousins who'd embarked on marriage and motherhood had warned her that children invariably complicated lives—but she rather suspected that her biological clock was ticking. 'Shh, shh,' she murmured. 'Just wait a moment and I'll give you some water to drink.'

The baby settled down, reinforcing Gerry's suspicion that she'd been fed not too long before she'd been found.

Frowning, she listened as Bryn Falconer said firmly from the hall, 'No, I don't live here; I'm just passing through.'

Policemen were supposed to have seen it all, but the one who walked in through the kitchen door looked startled and, when his gaze fell on Gerry, thunderstruck.

'This,' Bryn said smoothly, green eyes snapping with

mockery, 'is Constable Richards. Constable, this is Geraldine Dacre, the owner of the house, who found the child outside on the lawn.'

'How do you do?' Gerry said, smiling. 'Would you like a cup of coffee?'

'I—ah, no, thank you, Ms Dacre.' His collar seemed to be too tight; tugging at it, he said, 'I was supposed to meet a social worker here.'

'She—or he—hasn't arrived yet.' Bryn Falconer was leaning against the doorpost.

For all the world as though this was his house! Smiling at the policeman again, Gerry said, 'If you have to wait, you might as well have something to drink—it's cold out there. Bryn, pour the constable some coffee, would you?'

'Of course,' he said, the green flick of his glance branding her skin as he strode behind the breakfast bar.

He hadn't liked being ordered around. Perhaps, she thought a trifle smugly, in the future he wouldn't be quite so ready to take over.

What the hell was she thinking? She had no intention of letting Bryn Falconer into her life.

CHAPTER TWO

HASTILY Gerry transferred her attention to the policeman. 'What do you want to know about the baby?' she asked. 'She's a little girl, and although I'm no expert I don't think she's any more than a day old, judging by the umbilical cord.'

He gave her a respectful look and rapidly became professional. 'Exactly what time did you first see her?' he said.

So, very aware of the opening and closing of cupboards in her kitchen, Gerry explained how she'd found the child, nodding at the box with its pathetic little pile of damp clothes. The policeman asked pertinent questions and took down her answers, thanking Bryn Falconer when he brought a mug of coffee.

The constable plodded through his cup of coffee and his questions until Cara appeared in the doorway, her sultry face alive with curiosity and interest.

'Hello,' she said, and watched with the eye of a connoisseur as the policeman leapt to his feet. 'I'm ready to go,' she told Bryn, her voice soft and caressing. 'Bye, Gerry. Have fun.'

Bryn smiled, the crease in his cheek sending an odd frisson straight through Gerry. Go now, she commanded mentally. Right now. And flushed as he looked at her, a hard glint in his eyes.

Fortunately the doorbell pealed again, this time heralding the social worker, a pleasant, middle-aged woman with tired eyes and a knack with babies. Cara and Bryn left as she came in, so Gerry could give all her attention to the newcomer.

'I'm rather sad to see her go,' Gerry said, watching as

the woman efficiently dressed the baby in well-worn but pretty clothes, then packed her into an official carrycot while the policeman took the box and its contents. 'For what it's worth, I think her mother fed her before she put her behind the hedge—she's not hungry. And she wasn't very cold when I picked her up, so she hadn't been there long.'

The social worker nodded. 'They usually make sure someone will find them soon.'

Gerry picked up her towel and the still dry cashmere jersey. 'What will happen to the baby?'

'Now? I'll get her checked over medically, and take her to a family who'll foster her until her mother is found.'

'And if her mother isn't found?'

The social worker smiled. 'We'll do our best for her.'

'I know,' Gerry said. 'I just feel a bit proprietary.'

'Oh, we all do that.' The woman gave a tired, cynical smile. 'When you think we're geared by evolution to respond to a baby's cry with extreme discomfort, it's no wonder. She'll be all right. It's the mother I'm worried about. I don't suppose you've seen a pregnant woman looking over the hedge this last couple of weeks, or anything like that?'

'No, not a glimpse.'

The policeman said, 'I'd say she's local, because she put the baby where she was certain she'd be found. She might even have been watching.'

Gerry frowned, trying to recall the scene. 'I don't think so. Apart from the traffic, I didn't see any movement.'

When they'd gone she lifted the cashmere jersey to her face. It smelt, she thought wryly, of newborn baby—that faint, elusive, swiftly fading scent that had probably once had high survival value for the human race. Now it was just another thing, along with the little girl's heart-shaking fragility and crumpled rose-petal face, to remind Gerry of her empty heart.

'Oh, do something sensible instead of moping,' she advised herself crisply, heading for the laundry.

After she'd dealt with the clothes she embarked on a brisk round of necessary housework that didn't ease her odd flatness. Clouds settled heavily just above the roof, and the house felt chilly. And empty.

Ruthlessly she banished the memory of wide shoulders, narrow masculine hips and a pair of gleaming green eyes, and set to doing the worst thing she could find—clearing out the fridge. When she'd finished she drank a cup of herbal tea before picking up the telephone.

'Jan?' she said when she'd got through. 'How are you?'

'I'm fine,' said her favourite cousin, mother of Gerry's goddaughter, 'and so are Kear and Gemma, but why aren't you at work?'

'How do you know I'm not?'

'No chaos in the background,' Jan said succinctly. 'The agency is mayhem.'

'Honor persuaded me to take a holiday—she said three years without one was too long. And she was right. I've been a bit blasé lately.'

'I wondered how long you'd last,' Jan said comfortably. 'I told Kear a month or so ago that it must be time for you to look around for something new.'

'Butterfly brain, that's me.'

'Don't be an idiot.' For a tiny woman Jan could be very robust. 'You bend your not inconsiderable mental energy to mastering something, and as soon as you've done it you find something else. Nothing butterfly about that. Anyway, if I remember correctly it was your soft heart that got you into the modelling business. You left the magazine because you didn't agree with the way it was going—and you were right; it's just appalling now, and I refuse to buy it—and Honor needed an anchor after she broke up with that awful man she was living with. Whatever happened to him?'

'He died of an overdose. He was a drug addict.'

'What a tragedy,' Jan sighed. 'If you're on the lookout for another job, will you stay in the fashion industry?'

'It's a very narrow field,' Gerry said, wondering why she now yearned for wider horizons. She'd been perfectly happy working in or on the fringes of that world since she'd left university.

'Well, if you're stuck you can take over from me.'

'In which capacity—babysitter, part-time image consultant, or den mother to a pack of wayward girls?'

Several years previously Jan had inherited land from her grandfather in one of Northland's most beautiful coastal areas, and had set up a camp for girls at risk. After marrying the extremely sexy man next door, she'd settled into her new life as though she'd been born for it.

Jan laughed. 'The camp is going well,' she said cheerfully, 'but I don't think it's you. I meant as image consultant. You'd be good at it—you know what style means because you've got it right to your bones, and you like people. I've had Maria Hastings working for me, but she, wretched woman, has fallen in love with a Frenchman and is going to live in Provence with him! And I'm pregnant again, which forces the issue. I sell, or I retire. I'd rather sell the business to you if you've got the money.'

'Well—congratulations!' It hurt. Stupid, but it hurt. Jan had everything—an adoring husband, an interesting career, a gorgeous child and now the prospect of another. Quickly, vivaciously, Gerry added, 'I'll think about it. If I decide to do it, my share of the agency should be enough to buy you out.'

'Have you spoken to Honor? Does she mind the thought of you leaving?'

'No. Apparently she's got a backer, and she'll buy my share at a negotiated price.'

'I don't want to over-persuade you,' Jan said quickly. 'I know you like to develop things for yourself, so don't feel obliged to think about it. Another woman wants it, and she'll do just as well. You're a bit inclined to let the people you like push you around, you know. Too soft-hearted.'

'You're not over-persuading.' Already the initial glow of enthusiasm was evaporating. What would happen when she got tired of being an image consultant? As she would. A shiver of panic threaded through her. Surely that wasn't to be her life? Her mother had spent her short life searching for something, and had failed spectacularly to find it. Gerry was determined not to do the same.

'Something wrong?' Jan asked.

'Nothing at all, apart from an upsetting start to my day.' She told her about the abandoned baby, and they discussed it for a while, until Gerry asked, 'When's your baby due?'

'In about seven months. What's the matter, Gerry?'

'Nothing. Just—oh, I suppose I do need this holiday. I'll let you know about the business,' Gerry said.

'Do you want to come up and stay with us? We'd love to see you.'

'It sounds lovely, but no, I think I want to wander a bit.'

Jan's tone altered. 'Feeling restless?'

'Yes,' she admitted.

'Don't worry,' Jan said in a bracing voice. 'Even if you don't buy my business a job will come hopping along saying, Take me, take me. I'm fascinating and fun and you'll love me. Why don't you go overseas for a couple of weeks—somewhere nice and warm? I don't blame you for being out of sorts; I can't remember when New Zealand's had such a wet winter.'

'My mother used to go overseas whenever life got into too tedious a routine,' Gerry said.

'You are *not* like your mother,' Jan said even more bracingly. 'She was a spoilt, pampered brat who never grew up. You are a darling.'

'Thank you for those kind words, but I must have ended up with some of her genes.'

'You got the face,' Jan said drily. 'And the smile—but you didn't get the belief that everyone owed you a life.

According to my mama, Aunt Fliss was spoilt stupid by her father, and she just expected the rest of the world to treat her the way he did. You aren't like that.'

'I hope not.'

'Not a bit. Gerry, I have to go—your goddaughter is yelling from her bedroom, and by the tone of her voice it's urgent. I'll ring you tonight and we can really gossip. As for a new job—well, why not think PR? You know everyone there is to know in New Zealand, and you'd be wonderful at it. One flash of that notorious smile and people would be falling over themselves to publicise whatever you want.'

'Oh, exaggerate away!' Gerry laughed, but after she'd hung up she stood looking down at the table, tracing the line of the grain with one long finger.

For the last year she'd been fighting a weariness of spirit; it had crept on her so gradually that for months she hadn't realised what it was. The curse of my life, she thought melodramatically, and rolled her eyes.

But it terrified her; boredom had driven her mother through three unsatisfactory marriages, leaving behind shattered lives and discarded children as she'd searched for the elusive happiness she'd craved. Gerry's father had never got over his wife's defection, and Gerry had two half-brothers she hardly ever saw, one in France, one in America—both abandoned, just as she'd been.

She sat down with the newspaper, but a sudden scatter of rain against the window sent her fleeing to bring in the clothes she'd hung on the line an hour before.

A quick glance at the sky told her they weren't going to get dry outside, so she sorted them into the drier and set it going. Staring at the tumble of clothes behind the glass door, she wondered if perhaps she *should* go overseas.

Somewhere warm and dry, she thought dourly, heading back to pick up the newspaper from the sofa. The model disporting herself beneath palm trees was one she had worked with several occasions in her time as fashion editor; Gerry was meanly pleased to see that her striking face was at last showing signs of the temper tantrums she habitually engaged in.

'Serves her right, the trollop,' she muttered, flicking the pages over before putting the newspaper down.

No, she wouldn't head overseas. She couldn't really afford it; she had a mortgage to pay. Perhaps she should try something totally different.

She read the Sits Vac with mounting gloom. Nothing there. Well, she could make a right-angle turn and do another degree. She rooted in a drawer for the catalogue of extension courses at the local university, and began reading it.

But after a short while she put it to one side. She felt tired and grey and over the hill, and she wondered what had happened to the baby. Had she been checked, and was she now in the arms of a foster-mother?

Gerry decided to clean the oven.

It was par for the course when halfway through this most despised of chores the telephone beeped imperatively.

An old friend demanded that Gerry come to lunch with her because she was going through a crisis and needed a clear head to give her advice. Heaving a silent sigh, Gerry said soothingly, 'Yes, of course I'll have lunch with you. Would you like to eat here?'

Her hopes were dashed. 'We'll go to The Blue Room,' Troy said militantly. 'I've booked. I'll pick you up in half an hour.'

'No, I'll meet you there,' Gerry said hastily. Troy was the worst driver she knew.

Coincidences, Gerry reflected gloomily, were scary; you had no defence against them because they sneaked up from behind and hit you over the head. Bryn Falconer was sitting at the next table.

'And then,' Troy said, her voice throbbing as it rose from an intense whisper to something ominously close to a screech, 'he said I've let myself go and turned into a cabbage! *He* was the one who *insisted* on having kids and *insisted* I stop work and stay at home with them.'

Fortunately the waiter had taken in the situation and was already heading towards them with a carafe of iced water, a coffee pot and a heaped basket of focaccia bread.

Very fervently Gerry wished that Bryn Falconer had not decided to lunch at this particular restaurant. She was sure she could feel his eyes on her. 'Troy, you idiot, you've been drinking,' she said softly. 'And don't tell me you didn't drink much—it only takes a mouthful in your case.'

'I had to, Gerry. Mrs Landless—my babysitter—had her thirtieth wedding anniversary party last night. Damon wouldn't go so she saved me a glass of champagne.'

'You could have told her that alcohol goes straight to your head. Never mind—have some coffee and bread and you'll soon be fine, and at least you had the sense to come by taxi.'

Her friend's lovely face crumpled. 'Oh, Lord,' she said bitterly, 'I'm making a total *idiot* of myself, and there's bound to be sh-someone who'll go racing off to tell Damon.'

Five years previously Gerry had mentally prophesied disaster when her friend, a model with at least six more years of highly profitable work ahead of her, had thrown it all away to marry her merchant banker. Now she said briskly, 'So, who cares? It's not the end of the world.'

'I *wish* I was like you,' Troy said earnestly and still too loudly. 'You have men falling in love with you all the time, and you just smile that *fabulous* smile and drift on by, breaking hearts without a second thought.'

Acutely aware that Bryn Falconer was sitting close enough to hear those shrill, heartfelt and entirely untrue words, Gerry protested, 'You make me sound like some sort of *femme fatale,* and I'm not.'

'Yes, you are,' Troy argued, fanning her flushed face with her napkin. 'Everyone expects *femmes fatale* to be evil, selfish women, but why should they be? You're so *nice* and you never poach, but *nobody* touches your heart, do they? You don't even *notice* when men fall at your feet. Damon calls you "the unassailable Gerry".'

Gerry glanced up. Bryn Falconer wasn't even pretending not to listen, and when he caught her eyes he lifted his brows in a cool, mockingly level regard that sent frustration boiling through her.

Hastily Gerry looked back at Troy's tragic face. Tamping down an unwise and critical assessment of Damon's character, she said firmly, 'He doesn't know me very well. Have some coffee.'

But although Troy obediently sipped, she couldn't leave the subject alone. 'Have you ever been in love, Gerry? I mean really in love, the sort of abject, dogged, I-love-you-just-because-you're-you sort of love?'

Gerry hoped that her shrug hid her burning skin. 'I don't believe in that sort of love,' she said calmly. 'I think you have to admire and respect someone before you can fall in love with them. Anything else is lust.'

It was the wrong thing to say, and she knew it as soon as the words left her mouth. Bryn Falconer's presence must have scrambled her brain, she decided disgustedly.

Troy dissolved into tears and groped in her bag for her handkerchief. 'I know,' she wept into it. 'Damon wanted me and now it's gone. He's breaking my heart.'

Gerry leaned over the table and took her friend's hand. 'Do you want to go?' she asked quietly.

'Yes.'

Avid, fascinated stares raked Gerry's back as they walked across to the desk. She'd have liked to ignore Bryn Falconer, but when they approached his table he looked up at her with sardonic green eyes. At least he didn't get to his feet, which would have made them even more conspicuous.

Handsome meant nothing, she thought irrelevantly, when a man had such presence!

'Geraldine,' he said, and for some reason her heart stopped, because that single word on his lips was like a claiming, a primitive incantation of ownership.

Keeping her eyes cool and guarded, she sent him a brief smile. 'Hello, Bryn,' she said, and walked on past.

Fortunately Gerry's custom was valuable, so she and the desk clerk came to an amicable arrangement about the bill for the uneaten food. After settling it, she said, 'I'll drive you home.'

'I don't want to go home.' Troy spoke in a flat, exhausted voice that meant reality was kicking in.

'How long's Mrs Landless able to stay with the children?'

'Until four.' Troy clutched Gerry's arm. 'Can I come with you? Gerry, I really need to talk.'

So sorry for Troy she could have happily dumped a chained and gagged Damon into the ocean and watched him gurgle out of sight, Gerry resigned herself to an exhausting afternoon. 'Of course you can.'

Once home, she filled them both up on toast and pea and ham soup from the fridge—comfort food, because she had the feeling they were going to need it.

And three exhausting hours later she morosely ate a persimmon as Troy—by then fully in command of herself—drove off in a taxi.

Not that exhausting was the right word; gruelling described the afternoon more accurately. Although Troy was bitterly unhappy she still clung to her marriage, trying to convince herself that because she loved her husband so desperately, he had to love her in return.

The old, old illusion, Gerry thought sadly and sardonically, and got to her feet, drawing some consolation from her surroundings. She adored her house, revelled in the garden, and enjoyed Cara's company as well as her contribution to the mortgage payments.

But restlessness stretched its claws inside her. Gloomily she surveyed the tropical rhododendrons through her window, their waxy coral flowers defying the grey sky and cold wind. A disastrous lunch, a shattered friend, and the prospect of heavier rain later in the evening didn't mean her holiday was doomed. She wasn't superstitious.

But she wished that Bryn Falconer had chosen to eat lunch anywhere else in New Zealand.

Uncomfortable, jumpy—the way she felt when the music in a horror film indicated that something particularly revolting was about to happen—Gerry set up the ironing board. Jittery nerves wouldn't stand up to the boring, prosaic monotony of ironing.

She was putting her clothes away in her room when she heard the front door open and Cara's voice, bright and lively with an undercurrent of excitement, ring around the hall. The masculine rumble that answered it belonged to Bryn Falconer.

All I need, Gerry thought with prickly resignation.

She decided to stay in her room, but a knock on her door demanded her attention.

'Gerry,' Cara said, flushed, her eyes gleaming, 'come and talk to Bryn. He wants to ask you something.'

Goaded, Gerry answered, 'I'll be out in a minute.'

Fate, she decided, snatching a look at the mirror and despising the colour heating her sweeping cheekbones, really had it in for her today.

However, her undetectable mask of cosmetics was firmly in place, and anyway, she wasn't going to primp for Bryn Falconer. No matter that her dark blue-green eyes were wild and slightly dilated, or that her hair had rioted frivolously out of its usual tamed waves. She didn't care what he thought.

The gas heater in the sitting room warmed the chilly air, but the real radiance came from Cara, who lit up the room like a torch. Should I tell her mother? Gerry thought, then dismissed the idea. Cara was old enough to understand what she was doing.

But that little homily on messing around with married men might be in order.

Not that Bryn looked married—he had the air of someone who didn't have to consider anyone else. Forcing a smile, Gerry said, 'Hello, Bryn. Did you have a good lunch?'

His eyes narrowed slightly. 'Very.'

Gerry maintained her hostess demeanour. 'I like the way they do lunch there—sustaining, and it doesn't make you sleepy in the afternoon.'

'A pity you weren't able to stay long enough to eat,' he said blandly.

Despising the heat in her skin, Gerry kept her voice steady. 'My friend wasn't well.' Before he could comment she continued, 'Cara tells me you want to ask me something?'

'I'd like to offer you a very short, one-off project,' he said, and without giving her time to refuse went on, 'It involves a trip to the islands, and some research into the saleability—or not—of hats.'

Whatever she'd expected it wasn't that. 'Hats,' she repeated blankly.

The green gaze rested a moment on her mouth before moving up to capture her eyes. 'One of the outlying islands near Fala'isi is famous for the hats the islanders weave from a native shrub. They used to bring in an excellent income, but sales are falling off. They don't know why, but I suspect it's because they aren't keeping up with fashion. Cara tells me you have a couple of weeks off. One week at Longopai in the small hotel there should be ample time to check whether I'm right.'

No, she wanted to say, so loudly and clearly that there could be no mistaking her meaning. No, I don't want to go to a tropical island and find out why they're no longer selling their hats. I don't want anything to do with you.

'*I'd* love to go,' Cara said eagerly, 'but I'm booked solid for a couple of months. You're a real expert, Gerry—you style a shoot better than anyone, and Honor says you've got an instinct about fashion that never lets you down. And you'd have a super time in the islands—it's just what you need.'

Gerry looked out of the window. Darkness had already fallen; the steady drumming of rain formed a background to the rising wail of wind. She said, 'I might not have any idea why they aren't selling. Marketing is—'

'Exactly what you're good at,' Bryn said smoothly, his deep voice sliding with the silky friction of velvet along her nerves. 'When you worked as fashion editor for that magazine you marketed a look, a style, a colour.' He looked around the room. 'You have great taste,' he said.

As Gerry wondered whether she should tell him the room was furnished with pieces from her great-grandmother's estate, he finished, 'I can get you there tomorrow.'

Gerry's brows shot up. It was tempting—oh, she longed to get away and forget everything for a few days, just sink herself into the hedonism of a tropical holiday. Lukewarm lagoons, she thought yearningly, and colour—vivid, primal, shocking colour—and the scent of salt, and the caress of the trade winds on her bare skin...

Aloud, very firmly, she said, 'If you got some photographs done I could probably give you an opinion without going all the way up there. Or you could get some samples.'

'They deal better with people,' he said evenly. 'They'll take one look at you and realise that you know what you're talking about. A written report—or even a suggestion from me—won't have the same impact.'

'Most people,' Cara burbled, 'are dying to get to the tropics at this time of the year. You sound like a wrinklie, Gerry, hating the thought of being prised out of your nice comfortable nest!'

And if I go, Gerry thought with a tiny flash of malice, you'll be alone here, and no one will realise that you're spending nights in Bryn's bed. Although that was unkind;

Cara knew that Gerry wouldn't carry tales to her parents. And she honestly thought she was doing Gerry a favour.

Hell, she probably was.

Green eyes half-closed, Bryn said, 'I'd rather you actually saw the hats. Photographs don't tell the whole story, as you're well aware. And of course the company will pay for your flights and accommodation.'

She was being stupid and she knew it; had any other man suggested it she'd have jumped at the idea. Striving for her usual equanimity, she said, 'Of course I'd like to go, but—'

Cara laughed. 'I told you she wouldn't be able to resist it,' she crowed.

'Where is this island?' Gerry asked shortly.

'Longopai's an atoll twenty minutes by air from Fala'isi.' All business, Bryn said, 'A taxi will pick you up at ten tomorrow morning. Collect your tickets from the Air New Zealand counter at the airport. Pack for a week, but keep in mind the weight restrictions.'

What did he think she was? One of those people who can't leave anything in their wardrobe when they go overseas?

Cara headed off an intemperate reply by breaking in, 'Gerry can pack all she needs for three weeks in an overnight bag,' she said on an awed note.

Bryn's brow lifted. 'Clever Gerry,' he said evenly, his voice expressionless.

So why did it sound like a taunt?

CHAPTER THREE

IT DIDN'T surprise her that Bryn Falconer's arrangements worked smoothly; he'd expect efficiency in his hirelings.

Everything—from the moment Gerry collected her first-class ticket at Auckland airport to the cab-ride through the hot, colourful streets of Fala'isi with the tall young man who'd met the plane—went without a hitch.

'Mr Falconer said you were very important, and that I wasn't to be late,' her escort said when she thanked him for meeting her.

A considerable exaggeration, she thought with a touch of cynicism. Bryn liked her as little as she liked him. 'Do you work for the hotel on Longopai?'

He shook his head. 'For the shipping company. Mr Falconer bought a trader to bring the dried coconut here from Longopai, so it is necessary to have an office here.'

Bryn had said he was an importer—clearly he dealt in Pacific trade goods.

At the waterfront Gerry's escort loaded her and her suitcase tenderly into a float plane. Within five minutes, in a maelstrom of spray and a shriek of engines, the plane taxied out, broke free of the water and rose over the lagoon to cross the white line of the reef and drone north above a tropical sea of such vivid blue-green that Gerry blinked and put on her sunglasses.

She'd forgotten how much she loved the heat and the brilliance, forgotten the blatant, overpowering assault on senses more accustomed to New Zealand's subtler colours and scents. Now, smiling at the large ginger dog of bewildering parentage strapped into the co-pilot's seat, she relaxed.

36

Between the high island of Fala'isi and the atoll of Longopai stretched a wide strait where shifting colours and surface textures denoted reefs and sandbanks. Gazing down at several green islets, each ringed by blinding coral sand, Gerry wondered how long it would take to go by sea through these treacherous waters.

'Landfall in distant seas,' the pilot intoned dramatically over the intercom fifteen minutes later.

A thin, irregular, plumy green circle surrounded by blinding sand, the atoll enclosed a huge lagoon of enchanting, opalescent blues and greens. To make it perfect, in the centre of the lagoon rested a boat, white and graceful. Not a yacht—too much to expect!—but a large cruiser, some rich man's toy.

Gerry sighed. Oh, she wouldn't want to live on a place like this—too cut off, and, being a New Zealander, she loved the sight of hills on the horizon—but for a holiday what could be better? Sun, sand, and enough of a mission to stop her from becoming inured to self-indulgence.

After a spray-flurried landing in the deeper part of the lagoon, Gerry unbelted as a canoe danced towards them.

'Your transport.' The pilot nodded at it.

Glad that she'd worn trousers and a T-shirt, she pulled on her hat. The canoe surged in against the plane, manned by two young men with dark eyes and the proud features of Polynesians, their grins open and frankly appreciative as they loaded her suitcase.

Amused and touched by the cushion that waited on her seat, Gerry stepped nimbly down, sat gracefully and waved to the pilot. The dog barked and wagged its tail; the pilot said, 'Have a great holiday.'

Yes, indeed, Gerry thought, smiling as the canoe backed away from the plane, swung around and forged across the glittering waters.

New Zealand seemed a long, long way away. For this week she'd forget about it, and the life that had become so terrifyingly flat, to wallow in the delights of doing practi-

cally nothing in one of the most perfect climates in the
world.

And in one of the most perfect settings!

Following the hotel porter along a path of crushed white
shell, Gerry breathed deeply, inhaling air so fresh and lan-
guorous it smelt like Eden, a wonderful mixture of the un-
matched perfumes of gardenia and frangipani and ylang-
ylang, salted by a faint and not unpleasing undernote of
fish, she noted cheerfully. Her cabaña, its rustic appearance
belying the luxury within, was one of only ten.

'*Very* civilised,' she said aloud when she was alone.

A huge bed draped in mosquito netting dominated one
end of the room. Chairs and sofas—made of giant bamboo
and covered in the soothing tans and creams of tapa cloth—
faced wide windows which had shutters folded back to reveal a deck. Separated from a tiny kitchen by a bar, a
wooden table and chairs stood at the other end of the room.
Fruit and flowers burst from a huge pottery shell on the
table.

Further exploration revealed a bathroom of such unas-
hamed and unregenerate opulence—all marble in soft sunrise hues of cream and pale rose—that Gerry whistled.

Whoever had conceived and designed this hotel had had
a very exclusive clientele in mind—the seriously rich who
wanted to escape. Although, she thought, eyeing the toiletries laid out on the marble vanity, not too far.

The place was an odd but highly successful blend of
sophisticated luxury and romantic, lazy, South Seas sim-
plicity. Normally she'd never be able to afford such a place.
She was, she thought happily, going to cost Bryn Falconer
megabucks.

Half an hour later, showered and changed into fresh
clothes, she strolled down the path, stopping to pick a hibiscus flower and tuck it behind her ear, where its rollicking
orange petals and fiery scarlet throat would contrast splen-
didly with her black curls. Only flowers, she decided, could
get away with a colour scheme like that! Or silk, perhaps…

According to the schedule her escort in Fala'isi had given her, she'd have the rest of the day to relax before the serious part of this holiday began. Tomorrow she'd be shown the hats. As the swift purple twilight of the tropics gathered on the horizon, she straightened her shoulders and walked across the coarse grass to the lounge area.

And there, getting up from one of the sinfully comfortable chairs and striding across to meet her, was Bryn Falconer, all power and smooth, co-ordinated litheness, green eyes gleaming with a metallic sheen, his autocratic features only hinting at the powerful personality within.

Gerry was eternally grateful that she didn't falter, didn't even hesitate. But the smile she summoned was pure will-power, and probably showed a few too many teeth, for he laughed, a deep, amused sound that hid any mockery from the three people behind him.

'Hello, Geraldine,' he said, and took her arm with a grip that looked easy. 'Somehow I knew just how you'd look.'

As she was wearing a gentle dress the dark blue-green of her eyes, with a long wrap skirt and flat-heeled sandals, she doubted that very much. Flattering it certainly was— the straight skirt and deep, scooped neckline emphasised her slender limbs and narrow waist—but fashionable it was not.

Arching her brows at him, she murmured, 'Oh? How *do* I look?'

His smile hardened. 'Rare and expensive and fascinating—perfect for a tropical sunset. A moonlit woman, as shadowy and mysterious as the pearls they dive for in one small atoll far to the north of here, pearls the colour of the sea and the sky at midnight.'

Something in his tone—a disturbing strand of intensity, of almost-hidden passion—sent her pulse skipping. Automatically, she deflected.

'What a charming compliment. Thank you,' she returned serenely, dragging her eyes away from the uncompromising authority of his face as he introduced his companions.

Gone was the lingering miasma of ennui; the moment she'd seen him every nerve cell had jolted into acute, almost painful alertness.

Narelle and Cosmo were an Australian couple—sleek, well-tanned, wearing expensive resort clothes. Lacey, their adolescent daughter, should have been rounded and sturdy; instead her angular figure indicated a recent illness.

After the flurry of greetings Gerry sank into the chair Bryn held for her, aware that Lacey was eyeing her with the yearning intensity of a hungry lion confronted by a wildebeest. Uncomfortably, Gerry waited for surnames, but none were forthcoming.

'Isn't this a wonderful place for a holiday?' Narelle, a thin, tanned woman with superbly blonded hair and a lot of gold chains, spoke brightly, her skilfully shaded eyes flicking from Gerry to Bryn.

'Ideal,' Gerry answered, smiling, and was about to add that she wasn't exactly on holiday when Bryn distracted her by asking her what she'd have to drink.

'Fruit juice, thanks,' she said. After the fiasco with Troy she wasn't going to risk anything alcoholic in her empty stomach. She smiled at the waiter who'd padded across on bare feet, and added, 'Not too sweet, please.'

'Papaya, madam? With passionfruit and lime?'

'That sounds wonderful,' she said.

She was oddly uneasy when Lacey said loudly, 'I'll have one of those too, please.'

Her mother gave her a sharp look. 'How about a diet soft drink?' she asked.

'No, thanks.'

Narelle opened her mouth but was forestalled by Bryn, who said, 'Did you have a good flight up, Geraldine?'

Why the devil didn't he use her proper name? 'Geraldine' sounded quite different from her normal, everyday self. 'Yes, thank you,' she said, smiling limpidly.

If he thought that one compliment entitled him to a more intimate footing, he was wrong. All right, so her heart was still recovering from that first sight of him, and for a moment she'd wondered what it would be like to hear that deep voice made raw by passion, but she was strong, she'd get over it.

'We've been here several times,' Narelle said, preening a little. 'Last year Logan Hawkhurst was here with the current girlfriend, Tania Somebody-or-other.'

Logan Hawkhurst was an actor, the latest sensation from London, a magnificently structured genius with a head of midnight hair, bedroom eyes, and a temper—so gossip had it—that verged on molten most of the time.

'And was he as overwhelming as they say?' Gerry asked lightly.

Narelle gave an artificial laugh. 'Oh, more so,' she said. 'Just gorgeous—like something swashbuckling out of history. Lacey had a real a crush on him.'

The girl's face flamed.

Gerry said cheerfully, 'She wasn't the only one. I had to restrain a friend of mine when he finally got married—she wept half a wet Sunday and said she was never going to see another film of his because he'd break her heart all over again.'

They dutifully laughed, and some of the colour faded from the girl's skin.

'Don't know what you women see in him,' Cosmo said, giving Bryn a man-to-man look.

His wife said curtly, 'He's very talented, and you saw quite a lot in his girlfriend, whose talent wasn't so obvious.' She laughed a little spitefully. 'He must like fat women.'

Fortunately the waiter returned with the drinks just then, pale gold and frosted, with moisture sliding down the softly rounded glasses.

Gerry had seen more than enough photographs of the woman Logan Hawkhurst had wooed all over the world and finally won; a tall, statuesque woman, with wide shoulders, glorious legs and substantial breasts, she'd looked as though she was more than capable of coping with a man of legendary temper.

Whatever, Gerry didn't want to deal with undercurrents and sly backbiting. Blast Bryn Falconer. This was not the way she'd envisioned spending her first evening on the atoll.

Even more irritating, Narelle set out to establish territory and pecking order. Possibly Bryn noted the glitter in Gerry's smile, for he steered the conversation in a different direction. Instead of determining who outranked whom, they talked of the latest comet, and the plays on Broadway, and whether cars would ever run on hydrogen. Lacey didn't offer much, but what she did say was sharply perceptive.

Gerry admired the way Bryn handled the girl; he respected her intelligence and treated her as an interesting woman with a lot to offer. Lacey bloomed.

Which was more than Gerry did. Infuriatingly, the confidence she took for granted seemed to be draining away faster than the liquid in her glass. Every time Bryn's hooded green gaze traversed her face her rapid pulse developed an uncomfortable skip, and she had to yank her mind ruthlessly off the question of just how that long, hard mouth would feel against hers...

How foolish of Narelle to try her silly tests of who outranked whom! Bryn was the dominant male, and not only because he was six inches taller than Cosmo; what marked him out was the innate authority blazing around him like a forceful aura, intimidating and omnipresent.

Dragging her attention back, she learned that Cosmo owned a chain of shops in Australia. Narelle turned out to be a demon shopper, detailing the best boutiques in London for clothes, and where to buy gold jewellery, and how wonderful Raffles Hotel in Singapore was now it had been refurbished.

Lacey relapsed into silence, turning her glass in her hand, drinking her fruit juice slowly, as Gerry drank hers, occasionally shooting sideways glances at Bryn. Another crush on the way, Gerry thought, feeling sorry for her.

Politeness insisted she listen to Narelle, nodding and putting in an odd comment, but the other woman was content to talk without too much input from anyone else. From the corner of her eye Gerry noted Bryn's lean, well-shaped hands pick up his beer glass. So acutely, physically aware of him was she that she fancied her skin on that side of her body was tighter, more stretched, than on the other.

'You've travelled quite a bit,' Lacey said abruptly, breaking into her mother's conversation.

'It's part of my job,' Gerry said.

'What do you do?'

She hesitated before saying, 'I work in fashion.'

Lacey looked smug. 'I thought you might be a model,' she said, 'but I *knew* you were something to do with fashion. You've got that look.' She leaned forward. 'Do models have to diet all the time to stay that slim?'

'Thin,' Gerry said calmly. 'They have to be incredibly thin because the camera adds ten pounds to everyone. Some starve themselves, but most don't. They're freaks.'

'F-freaks?' Lacey looked distinctly taken aback.

Bryn asked indolently, 'How many women do you see walking down the street who are six feet tall, skinny as rakes, with small bones and beautiful faces?'

Although the caustic note in his voice stung, Gerry nodded agreement.

'Well—not many, I suppose,' Lacey said defensively.

'It's not normal for women to look like that,' Bryn said with cold-blooded dispassion. 'Gerry's right—those who do are freaks.'

'Designers like women with no curves,' Gerry told her, 'because they show off clothes better.'

Narelle laughed a little shrilly. 'Oh, it's more than that,' she protested. 'Men are revolted by fat women.'

'Some men are,' Bryn said, leaning back in his chair as though he conducted conversations like this every day, 'but most men like women who are neither fat nor thin, just fit and pleasantly curvy.'

So she was not, Gerry realised, physically appealing to him. Although not model-thin, she was certainly on the lean side rather than voluptuous. His implied rejection bit uncomfortably deep; she had, she realised with a shock, taken it for granted that he found her as attractive as she found him.

Lacey asked, 'Are you in fashion too, Mr Falconer?'

'I have interests there,' he said, his tone casual.

Did he mean the hats?

With a bark of laughter Cosmo said, 'Amongst others.'

Bryn nodded. Smoothly, before anyone else could speak, he made some remark about a scandal in Melbourne, and Lacey listened to her parents discuss it eagerly.

Illness or anorexia? Gerry wondered, covertly taking in the stick-like arms and legs. Lacey had her father's build; she should have been rounded. Or just a kid in a growing spurt? Sixteen could be a dangerous age.

Had Bryn discerned that? Why else would he have bothered to warn her off dieting? Because that was what he'd done, in the nicest possible way.

Gerry drained her glass and settled back in her chair, watching the night drift across the sea, sweep tenderly through the palms and envelop everything in a soft, scented darkness. The sound of waves caressing the reef acted as a backdrop; while they'd been talking several other people had come in and sat down, and now a porter was going around lighting flares.

If she were alone, Gerry thought, she'd be having a wonderful time, instead of sitting there with every cell alert and tense, waiting for something to happen.

What happened was that a waiter came across and bent over Bryn, saying cheerfully, 'Your table is ready, sir.'

'Then we'd better eat,' he said, and got to his feet, towering over them. 'Geraldine,' he said, holding out his hand.

Irritated, but unable to reject him without making it too

obvious, Gerry put hers in his and let him help her up, smiling at the others. He kept his grip until they were half-way across the room, when she tugged her fingers free and demanded, 'What on earth is going on?'

'I'd have thought you'd know the signs,' he said caustically. 'If she hasn't got anorexia, she's on the brink.'

'I didn't mean Lacey,' she snapped. 'What are you doing here?'

'I discovered I had a few days, so I decided it would be easier for you if I came up and acted as intermediary.'

Impossible to tell from his expression or his voice whether he was lying, but he certainly wasn't telling the whole story.

'Just like that?' she said, not trying to hide her disbelief. 'You didn't have this time yesterday.'

'Things change,' he told her blandly, pulling out a chair.

He was laughing at her and she resented it, but she wasn't going to make a fool of herself by protesting. So when she'd sat down she seized on the comment he'd made. 'What do you mean, you thought I'd have been able to recognise anorexia?'

'You deal with it all the time, surely?' he said.

She replied bluntly, 'Tragically, anorexic young women who don't get help die. They don't have the stamina to be models.'

'I know they die,' he said, his face a mask of granite, cold and inflexible in the warm, flickering light of the torches. 'How many do you think you've sent down that road?'

His grim question hurt more than a blow to the face.

Before she could defend herself he continued, 'Your industry promotes an image of physical perfection that's completely unattainable for most women. From there it's only a short step to eating disorders.'

'No one knows what causes eating disorders,' she said, uncomfortable because she had worried about this. 'You make it sound as though it's a new thing, but women have always died of eating disorders—they used to call it green sickness or a decline before they understood it. Some psychologists believe it's psychological, to do with personality types, while others think it's caused by lack of control and power. If you men would give up your arrogant assumption of authority over us and appreciate us for what we are—not as trophies to impress your friends and associates—then perhaps we could learn to appreciate ourselves in all our varied and manifold shapes and sizes and looks.'

'That's a cop-out,' he said relentlessly.

She lifted her brows. 'I'm always surprised how responsibility for this has been dumped onto women—magazine editors, writers, models.'

'Are you a feminist, Geraldine?'

The surprise in his voice made her seethe. 'Of course I am,' she said dulcetly. 'Any woman who wants a better life for the next generation of girls is a feminist.'

'Don't you like men?'

'Of *course* I do,' she retorted even more sweetly. 'Some of my best friends are men.'

His smile turned savage. 'Are you trying to be provocative, or does it come naturally to you?'

The taunting question hit her in a vulnerable place. Her father's voice, ghostly, earnest, echoed in her ear. 'Don't tease, Gerry, darling. It's not fair—men don't know how to deal with a woman who teases.'

Banishing it, she counter-attacked. 'Do you think you're the only person who's ever accused me of forcing women into a strait-jacket? Sorry, it happens all the time. Interestingly, no one ever accuses me of forcing the male models into one, or the character models. Just the women.'

He didn't like that; his eyes narrowed to slivers of frigid green.

Strangely stimulated, she went on, 'And with interests in clothing, as well as computers and coconut, don't you think you're being just the tiniest bit hypocritical? After all, some of the money that pays for this fantasy of the South

Pacific—' her swift, disparaging glance scorched around
the area '—comes from the women you're so concerned
about...those so-called brainwashed followers of fashion.'

As a muscle flicked in the arrogant jaw she thought re-
signedly, Well, at least I've had half a day in the sun!

But it was something stronger than self-preservation that
compelled her to lean forward and say, 'Let's make a bargain, Bryn. You work to stop all the actors and politicians
and big businessmen from arming themselves with pretty,
slaves-to-fashion trophy women, and I can guarantee that
the magazines and fashion industry will fall neatly into line
behind you.'

'Are women so driven by what men want?' he asked
idly, as though he wasn't furious with her.

A hit. She laughed softly. 'Give us a hundred years of
freedom and things will probably be different, but yes, men
are important to us and always will be—just as men are
affected by women. After all, nature set us up to attract
each other.'

'So the desire to find a male with money and prestige is
entirely natural, whereas a man's search for a mate who
will enhance his prestige is wrong?'

Amusement sparkled in her voice. 'A woman's desire for
wealth and prestige is linked, surely, to her instinctive
knowledge that her children will have a better chance of
surviving if their father is rich and has power in the com-
munity? Whereas a man just likes to look good in the eyes
of other men!'

Since her university days, Gerry realised, she'd forgotten
the sheer pleasure of debating, the swift interchange of
ideas intended to provoke, to make people think, not necessarily meant to be taken seriously. Then she made the
mistake of looking across the table, and wondered uneasily
if for him this was personal. Behind the watchful face she
sensed leashed emotions held in check by a formidable will.

'Women want a man who looks good in the eyes of other
men,' he retorted. 'You've just said they see losers as bad

bets for fatherhood. Besides,' he added silkily, 'surely the reason some men seek younger mates is *their* instinctive understanding that to perpetuate as many of their genes as possible—which is what evolution is all about—they need to mate with as many women as possible? And that young women are more fertile?'

'So men are naturally promiscuous and women naturally look for security?' she challenged. 'Do you believe that, Bryn?'

'As much as you do,' he said ironically, looking past Gerry to the waitress.

Gerry chose fish and a salad; she expected Bryn to be a red meat and potatoes man, but he too decided on fish. She must have looked a little startled because he explained, 'The fish here is one of the natural wonders of the world. And they cook it superbly.'

Those green eyes didn't miss a trick.

From now on she'd be more cautious; no more invigorating arguments or discussions. Even if he was one of the few men who made her blood run faster, she'd be strictly businesslike. She certainly wasn't interested in a man who'd slept with Cara. And who'd then, she realised far too late, had the nerve to trash the modelling industry.

Unless he'd been being as provocative as he'd accused her of being? She shot him an uneasy look, and wondered whether that strong-framed face hid a devious mind.

Possibly. So over a magnificent meal she firmly steered the conversation into dinner-party channels, touching on art, books, public events—nothing personal. Bryn followed suit, yet Gerry found herself absorbed by that intriguing voice with its undercurrent of—what?

It made her think of secrets, his voice—of violent emotions held under such brutal control that the prospect of releasing them assumed the prohibited glamour of the forbidden. It made her think all sorts of tantalising, exciting things.

Fortunately, before she got too carried away, a glance at

his harsh face with its uncompromising aura of power banished those nonsensical thoughts.

This man had no time for subtlety. He probably hadn't been deliberately winding her up with his contempt for models; he'd slept with Cara because he wanted her, and he wouldn't see any contradiction between his words and his behaviour.

Her appetite suddenly leaving her, Gerry looked down at her food.

Bryn Falconer fascinated her, but she knew herself too well—had dreaded for too long the genes that held the seeds of her destruction—to allow herself to act on that excitement.

'Did you see the baby in the newspaper?' he asked.

'Yes, poor wee love, while I was in the first-class lounge waiting for the plane.' And had slipped into sentimentality at the photograph of the crinkled little face, absorbed in sleep. Turning her half-empty glass, she kept her eyes fixed on the shimmering play of light in the crystal. 'The social worker said they'll do their best to find her mother and help her make a home for the child, but if that isn't possible the baby will be adopted. In the meantime she'll be with a foster family.'

'Clock ticking, Geraldine?' he asked. His eyes mocked her.

Repressing the swift, raw antagonism detonated by his lazy percipience, she parried lightly, 'Babies are special. I just hope she has a happy life, and that her mother is able to deal with whatever made her abandon her.'

'You have a kind heart.' An enigmatic note in his dark voice robbed the words of any compliment.

'I am noted for my kindness,' she said evenly. Putting the glass down, she pretended to hide a yawn. 'I'm sorry, I'm tired. Do you mind if I go now?'

'Am I so dull?' he asked with a disconcerting directness.

Startled, she looked up, to be pierced by glinting, sardonic green eyes. 'Not at all,' she said abruptly, antipathy prickling through her veins. Any other man would have accepted her face-saving explanation instead of challenging it.

'It's only nine o'clock. Cara tells me you've been known to stay out all night.'

'Staying out doesn't mean staying up,' she returned tartly, so irritated that Cara should gossip about her that she only realised what she'd implied when his mouth tightened. Almost immediately those firm lips relaxed into a smile that sent complex sensations snaking down her spine.

'Of course not,' he said, drawling the words slightly.

Oh, great, now he thought she was promiscuous. Well, she wasn't going to explain that because she disliked driving at night she tended to borrow a bed when the party looked like running late—and she certainly wasn't going to tell him that she spent the night in those beds alone!

This was a man who'd slept with a woman at least ten years younger than he was. He had no right to look at her like that, with lazy speculation narrowing his eyes.

Getting to her feet, she donned her most serene expression. 'Thank you very much for a lovely meal.'

He rose with her. 'I'll walk you to your room.'

'You don't need to,' she said steadily. 'I'm sure I'm perfectly safe here.'

'Absolutely, unless you consider the flying foxes. They tend to swoop low over the paths and some people find them scary.'

'I don't,' she said, but he came with her anyway.

After a silent walk along the sweet-smelling paths, lit by flares and the moon, he stopped at the door of her chalet while she unlocked it, and said, 'Goodnight, Geraldine.'

'Gerry,' she said before she could stop herself. 'Nobody calls me Geraldine.'

In the soft, treacherous moonlight his face was all angles and planes, an abstract study of strength emphasised by his eyes, their colour bleached to silver, hooded and dangerous. 'Who named you Geraldine?'

Startled, she gave him a direct answer. 'My mother.'

'Did she die young?'

'Oh, yes,' she said flippantly. 'But she'd left me long before she died. She was a bolter, my mother—she got bored easily. She died in a car crash, running away from her third husband to the man who was going to be her fourth.'

'How old were you when she left?'

Past pain, Geraldine had learnt, was best left to the past, but by telling him she'd opened the way for his question. 'Four. That was pretty good, actually. She left my half-brothers before they were able to recognise her.'

'Yet you can find sympathy for the woman who abandoned the baby?'

She shrugged. 'It's always easier to forgive when it's not personal. Besides, my mother made a habit of it, and she left chaos behind her. She had a talent for wrecking lives.'

'Did she wreck yours?' His voice was reflective.

Gerry lifted her head. 'No. I couldn't have asked for a happier childhood—my father devoted himself to me. But he never married again.'

'Then she only wrecked one life,' he pointed out objectively. 'If you don't include hers, of course.'

Reining in a most unusual aggression, Gerry retorted, 'She didn't do much for my half-brothers or their fathers.'

'She sounds more disturbed than malicious.' He stopped abruptly, as though he'd said more than he'd wanted to.

Looking up, Gerry caught the sudden clamping of his features. 'You're right,' she said lightly, mockingly. 'There are always two sides to every question, and we will never know what drove my mother headlong to destruction.'

He said brusquely, 'Thank you for your company at dinner. I'll see you at breakfast.'

'I always have breakfast in my room,' she said calmly. 'I'm not at my best in the mornings.'

'You coped very well with a totally unexpected incident

yesterday morning. I'm sure you'll manage a working breakfast.'

'In that case, of course,' she said in her briskest, most professional tone. 'What time would you like me to be there?' She didn't say sir, but the intimation of the word hung in the air.

'Eight o'clock,' he drawled.

'Then I'll say goodnight.' Gerry tossed him a practised smile and went inside, closing the door behind her with a sharp, savage little push.

But once inside she didn't turn the light on. From a shuttered window, she watched as Bryn Falconer strode along the path between hibiscuses and the elegant bunches of frangipani. Light fell through the slender trunks of the coconuts in lethal silver and black stripes.

He looked so completely at home in these exotic, alien surroundings. It would be easy to imagine him as a sandalwood trader or a pearl entrepreneur two hundred years ago, fighting his way through a region noted for its transcendent beauty and its dangers, taking his pleasures as seriously as he took its perils.

And because that sort of fantasy was altogether too inviting she made herself note the unconscious authority in his face and air and walk. Lord of all he surveyed she thought with an ironic smile.

An intriguing man—and one who was sleeping with Cara.

She shouldn't forget that just because she hated the thought of it. And while she was about it, why not remind herself that although she found him fascinating now, it wouldn't last.

There had been other men. She'd had two serious relationships, and although she'd honestly believed she loved both men, too soon the attraction had died like a flash of tinder without kindling, leaving her with no self-respect.

Because she hated hurting anyone she'd eventually given up on this man-woman thing.

This fiery, dramatic attraction would pass. She just had to keep her head while she waited it out.

CHAPTER FOUR

MORNING in the tropics was always a time of ravishingly fresh beauty. It would have been perfect if Gerry had been able to eat her breakfast alone on the small balcony with its view of the sea.

Nevertheless, she smiled as she showered and dressed. One of the exasperating things about winter was the extra clothes needed to keep warm, so she revelled in the freedom of a sundress and light sandals.

Not that she'd skimp on her make-up; painting up like a warrior going to battle, she thought with a narrow smile as she opened her cosmetics kit. She'd learned from experts how to apply that necessary mask so skilfully that even in the penetrating light of the sun she looked as though she wore only lip colouring.

And she'd be especially careful now, for reasons she wasn't prepared to go into. Frowning a little, she smoothed on tinted moisturiser with sunscreen; and the merest hint of blusher to give lift and sparkle to her olive skin.

Bryn had made it obvious that this was business, so he'd get the works—subtle, understated eyeshadow to deepen the intensity of her dark blue-green eyes, and two shades of lipstick, carefully applied with a brush and blended, blotted, then applied again.

Grateful that, as well as a tendency to restlessness, her mother had bequeathed her such excellent skin, Gerry slid into a gauzy shirt the exact blue of her sundress. She did not want her shoulders exposed to Bryn Falconer's unsettling green gaze.

Sunlight danced through the whispering fronds of the palms, and close by a dove cooed, a sound that always

54

lifted her heart. Cynically amused at the anticipation that seethed through her, she picked a frangipani blossom and tucked it into the black curls behind her ear.

In the dining area Bryn rose from a chair as the waitress showed her to his table. Gerry recognised excellent tailoring and the finest cloth in both his trousers and the short-sleeved shirt. Clearly his business paid him very well.

And she'd better stop admiring those wide shoulders and heavily-muscled legs, and collect her wits.

'Good morning,' he said, eyeing her with a definite gleam of appreciation.

'It's a magnificent morning,' she said, squelching the forbidden leap of response as she allowed herself to be seated. 'What happens today?'

'Eat your breakfast first.' He waited a second, then added, 'If you have breakfast.'

She concealed gritted teeth with a false, radiant smile. 'Always,' she returned.

She chose fruit and yoghurt and toast, watching with interest as he ordered a breakfast that would have satisfied a lumberjack.

He looked up, and something in her face must have given her away, because that gleam appeared in his eyes again. 'There's a lot of me to keep going,' he said smoothly.

Unwillingly she laughed. 'How tall are you?'

'Six feet three and a half,' he said, deadpan.

'I thought so. Are your family all as big as you?'

Not a muscle moved in the confident, striking face, but she got the distinct impression of barriers clanging down. 'My mother was medium height. My father was tall,' he said, 'and so was my sister. Tall and big.'

All dead, by the way he spoke.

'You,' he resumed calmly, 'are tall, but very feminine. It's those long, elegant bones.' He paused, his eyes sliding over her startled face. 'And you walk like a breeze across the ocean, like the wind in the palms, graceful and unselfconscious. You don't look as though you know how to make a clumsy movement. Feminine to the core.'

He put his hand beside hers on the table. Emphasised by crisp white linen, the corded muscles of his forearm exuded an aura of efficient forcefulness. In the dappled light of the sun the glowing vermilion and ruby hibiscus flowers in the centre of the table seemed to almost vibrate against his golden-brown skin.

Beside his, her slender fingers, winter-pale, looked both sallow and ineffectual. And out of place.

Gerry gave herself a mental shake. Stop it, she commanded; you're competent enough.

Lean, blunt fingers rested a fraction of a moment on the shadowed veins at her wrist; his touch went through her like fire, like ice, speeding up the pulse that carried its effects in micro-seconds to the furthest part of her body. Dry-mouthed, a sudden thunder in her ears blocking out the mournful calling of the doves, she quelled an instinctive jerk. Even though he lifted his hand immediately, the skin burnt beneath his touch.

If his plan had been to show her how fragile she was against his strength he'd succeeded, but she saw no reason to let him know.

'Thank you,' she said. Thank heavens her voice didn't betray her. It sounded the same as it always did—cool, a little amused. 'But all women are feminine, you know, just as men are masculine. It goes with the sex.'

And could have bitten her tongue. Why did everything she said to him, everything he said to her, seem imbued with an undercurrent of innuendo, an earthy sensuality that neither of them would acknowledge?

'Some women seem to epitomise it,' he said drily, and glanced up with a smile for the waitress arriving with coffee.

Feeling as though she'd been released from some kind of hypnotic spell, Gerry filled her lungs with fresh, salt-tinged air, and studiously applied herself to getting as much caffeine inside her as she could.

Not that she needed any further stimulus. Her nerves were jumping beneath her skin, and thoughts skittered feverishly through her mind.

Nothing like this, she thought distractedly, had ever happened to her before. Still, although it would be foolish to pretend she was immune to Bryn's dark magnetism, she had enough self-discipline to wait it out. If she deprived this firestorm of fuel, it would devour itself until it collapsed into ashes, freeing her from his spell.

All she had to do was behave with decorum and confidence until it happened. And whenever she felt herself weakening, she'd just recall that he'd slept with Cara.

Yes, that worked; every time Gerry's too-pictorial brain produced images of them in bed together, she felt as though someone had just flung a large bucketful of cold water across her face.

Uncomfortable, but exactly what she needed.

'So what are your plans for this morning?' she asked when her leaping pulses had steadied and she was once more sure of her voice.

'We go for a walk,' he told her.

Gerry allowed her brows to lift slightly. 'A walk?'

'Yes. You do walk, I assume?'

She refused to acknowledge the taunt. 'Naturally,' she said graciously.

'Good. There are only three vehicles on the island.' He smiled. 'Nobody knows who you are, and nobody will expect anything more than a hotel guest's interest in the handicrafts.'

'We're keeping this a secret now?' she asked directly.

'I'd prefer no one to know what you're here for.' He met her gaze with a bland smile that set her teeth on edge.

Shrugging, she looked away. 'You're the boss.'

He was partly right—nobody knew who Gerry was. However, the people they met certainly knew who he was, and they did not view her as a casual hotel guest. They thought she was Bryn Falconer's woman.

He added fuel to their speculation by his attitude, a cool attentiveness that had something possessive about it.

She should have been profoundly irritated. Instead, her body tingled with life, with awareness, with a charged, vital attention, so that even when he was out of her direct sight she knew where he stood, felt him with a sixth sense she'd never experienced before.

Before long she realised the islanders' smiles and open interest meant they approved. The women who sat in groups plaiting the fine fibre greeted Bryn with pleasure and a familiarity that surprised her. Perhaps he was related to them; that would explain his concern.

On the floor of one of a cluster of thatched houses, incongruous beneath corrugated iron roofs, one old woman grinned at Bryn and made a sly comment in the local tongue, a little more guttural than the Maori spoken in New Zealand. He laughed and said something that set her rolling her eyes, but she retorted immediately, her dark eyes flicking from Gerry's set face to Bryn's.

Bryn shot back an answer that had everyone doubling over with mirth. Night school, Gerry decided with a flash of anger; as soon as she got back home she'd register in a Maori conversation class. For years she'd intended to, and now she was definitely going to do it.

'Sorry,' Bryn said, making no attempt to translate.

'That's all right,' she said too sweetly, her smile as polished and deadly as a stiletto. 'I'm a humble employee— it's not for me to show any offence.'

Mockery glinted in his eyes. 'I like a woman who knows her place. Let's go and see how they make the hats.'

As she watched the skilled, infinitely patient fingers weaving fine strands of fibre, Gerry said, 'They do need updating. Are you serious about increasing exports?'

'This is all the islanders have got,' he said. 'They use

the income from the industry to pay for secondary and tertiary education for their children and for health care. Fala'isi provides primary education and a nurse and clinic, but anything else they have to work for themselves. And this is the only export they have.'

'I thought you said they had pearls.'

He shook his head. 'Not here. We're negotiating to set up a pearl industry, but that's a long-term project. The hats are an assured market—if we can keep and expand it.'

'If I sent some photographs, could they copy them?'

Bryn asked the old woman, who was working with two small, almost naked children playing around her feet. Clearly the leader of the group, she frowned and answered at length.

'Yes,' Bryn said, 'they could do that.'

After a round of farewells they left the village behind and walked on beneath the feathery, rustling crowns of coconut palms. The heat collected there, intensifying, thick. Eventually Gerry gave in and eased her shirt off.

Bryn didn't even look at her.

So much, she thought acidly, for not wanting to expose myself. Aloud she said, 'I can find photographs of hats that will sell much better than these. Luckily everyone in the world wants to keep the sun off their face now. But to make it work properly, they need an agent to keep them in contact with what's going on in fashion. There'll always be a small market for the classic styles, but if they want to expand they need someone with a good knowledge of trends.'

Bryn nudged a thin black and white dog out of his way. Fragments of white shell clattered as the dog scrambled up and slouched towards a large-leafed bush. Once in the shade, it gave itself a couple of languid scratches and yawned fastidiously before settling to sleep. Three hens and a rooster clucked amiably by, ignoring the dog, which pricked its ears although it didn't lift its head from its paws.

Gerry laughed softly. 'I'll bet he'd give one of his teeth to chase them.'

'Not if he wants to live. All food is precious here.'

Something oblique in his voice caught her attention. She gave him a sharp sideways glance. 'I suppose it is,' she said, because the silence demanded a response.

'Are you thirsty?' he asked abruptly.

His words suddenly made her aware that her throat was dry. 'Yes, actually I am.'

'Why didn't you say?'

She reacted to the irritation in his voice with a snap. 'There's no shop close by, so what's the use?'

'Dehydrating in this climate can be dangerous. And drinks are all around us. If—' with an intolerable trace of amusement in the words '—you like coconut milk.'

'I do, but I certainly don't want you going up there,' she answered, tipping back her head to eye the bunches of nuts, high above them at the top of the thin, curved trunks.

'It's not dangerous.'

A boy with brilliant dark eyes and a ready smile came swinging through the palms, armed, as many of the children were, with a machete half as tall as he was. After he and Bryn had conducted a cheerful conversation, the boy used a loop of rope to climb the palm with verve and flair. Trying to tell herself he'd probably done it a hundred times before, Gerry watched with anxiety.

'He's an expert,' Bryn reassured her with a smile. 'All the boys here can climb a coconut palm—it's a rite of passage, like learning to kick a football.'

'No doubt, but at least when you play rugby you're on the ground, not a hundred feet above it,' she said, breathing more easily when she saw the boy cut a green nut from the bunch at the crown of the palm and begin swinging down.

Back on the ground, he smiled bashfully at Gerry's thanks, sliced the top off the green nut with a practised flick of the machete, and presented it to her with a gamin grin, before disappearing through the palms towards the beach.

'Mmm, lovely,' Gerry said when she'd drunk half of the clear, refreshing liquid. 'Do you want some?'

She didn't expect Bryn to say yes, but he did, and drank the rest of the liquid down. Strangely embarrassed, she looked away. It seemed such an intimate thing, his mouth where hers had been, the coconut milk going from her lips to his.

You're being stupid, her common sense scolded. Just because he makes your skin prickle, because he has this weird effect on you, you're concocting links. Stop it this minute. Right now. And don't start it again.

'We'd better go back,' Bryn said. 'We've come quite a way and it's starting to get hot.'

On the way back she asked casually, 'When did you learn to speak Maori?'

'I grew up speaking it,' he said drily.

Not exactly a mine of information. Perversely, because it was clear he had no intention of satisfying her curiosity, she pursued, 'You're very fluent.'

'I should be. I lived here until I was ten.'

The depth of her need to know more startled her. It was this which silenced her rather than his brusque answer. Staring through the sinuous grey trunks of the coconut palms to the dazzle of sea beyond, she thought, I'm not going to try to satisfy such a highly suspect curiosity.

'My father,' he said coolly, 'was a beachcomber. It's not a word used much nowadays; I think he felt it had a romantic ring to it.'

Surprised at her sympathy, Gerry said, 'I don't suppose they were particularly good specimens of humanity, but there's a tang of romance to the term.'

'Not for me,' he said. 'He and my mother eloped from New Zealand and eventually made their way to Longopai. They sponged off the islanders until she died having my sister when I was five. After a few months my father drifted on without us, leaving us with a family here. He never came back.'

'That,' she said in a voice few of her friends had heard, 'was unforgivable.'

'Yes.' He looked down at her, eyes as transparent as green glass, but she had the feeling that he wasn't actually seeing her. 'You know what it's like.'

'At least I had a father who loved me,' she said fiercely. 'You were alone.'

'I had my sister. We weren't unhappy; in fact, we probably led a more idyllic life than most children. Our foster family accepted us completely, and we went to school and played and worked with the other kids until I was ten. My mother's parents discovered that we existed, so they sent someone up to collect us and take us back to New Zealand.'

'That would have been a difficult adjustment.'

He was silent for a moment, then said, 'We weren't the easiest of children to deal with, but our grandparents did their best to civilise us.'

'They succeeded,' she said promptly.

His laugh sent a shiver down her spine. 'In all outer respects,' he said. 'But for the first ten years of my life I ran wild. It's not an easy heritage to outgrow.'

It sounded like a warning, yet why should he warn her— and of what?

She asked, 'Was it difficult to adapt to life in New Zealand?'

'I loathed it.' He spoke reflectively, but beneath the smooth surface of his voice Gerry heard raw anger.

'It must have been terrible,' she said quietly.

'They sent me to a prep school to be beaten into shape. Fortunately I have a good brain, and I played rugby well enough to be in the first fifteen.'

A picture of the young boy, dragged away from the only home he'd ever had, pitched into a situation he had no knowledge of or understanding for, transmuted her sympathy into something more primitive—outrage. 'Your sister?'

'Didn't fare so well,' he said roughly. 'As I said, she was

a big girl, nothing dainty about her. She liked to play rugby too, but our grandparents didn't approve of that. In fact, they didn't approve of her at all, especially when she reached adolescence and shot up until she hit six feet.' He surveyed her with hard, unsparing calculation. 'She wasn't like you—she had no inborn style. She was plain, and because she wasn't valued she became clumsy. By the time she was fifteen she was utterly convinced that she was ugly and uncouth and worth nothing.'

Gerry dragged in a deep breath, fighting back the primal fury that coursed through her. 'Your grandparents have a lot to be ashamed of,' she said, thinking of her cousin Anet, another big, tall woman.

But Anet had been born into a family that loved her, and urged her to make the most of her natural athletic ability. After winning a gold medal in the javelin at the Olympics, she'd settled down to married life with a magnificent man who adored her.

Even after three children, the way Lucas Tremaine looked at his wife sent shivers down Gerry's spine. 'Children should be cherished,' she finished curtly.

A car came chugging down the narrow track towards them, if car it could be called. It might have originally been covered in, but consisted now of four wheels, a bonnet and the seats. When the elderly grey-haired driver saw them he slowed down and stopped.

'Message for you, Bryn,' he shouted above the sound of the engine, 'back at the hotel. They want you now.'

Bryn nodded. 'Hop up,' he said to Gerry.

Gerry was sorry the apology for a car had arrived just then. She hadn't satisfied that ravenous curiosity to know more about Bryn, but she understood now why he despised fashion magazines. No doubt his sister had yearned to look like the models in their pages.

What had happened to her? She cast a glance up at Bryn's implacable profile and as swiftly looked away again.

He'd put her so far out of his mind that she might as well not be there.

Trying not to resent his withdrawal, she leapt down when the car halted in front of the high, intricately thatched building that housed the office and the manager's quarters.

'I'll see you at lunchtime,' Bryn said curtly, and strode into the office.

As Gerry walked to her chalet, sticky and slightly salt-glazed, the taste of green coconut milk still faint on her tongue, she decided it didn't take much intuition to guess that he probably owned the hotel. He certainly organised the sale of the hats, and from what he'd said he was the person who was negotiating the pearling project. It was clear that he felt a profound obligation to the islanders who had given his sister her happy, early years.

Gerry admired that.

'Did you get your message?' she asked during lunch, looking up from her salad.

'Yes, thank you.'

She hesitated, then decided to go ahead with the decision she'd made while showering before the meal. 'Now that I've worked out what the problem is with the hats, there's no need for me to stay. It must be costing you a packet for my accommodation.'

'A week,' he said calmly, his eyes very keen as he studied her face. 'You can stay for the week you were hired for. Besides, you haven't seen much of the hat-making industry.'

Made uncomfortable by his concentrated scrutiny, she shrugged. 'Very well,' she said lightly. 'I'll do that tomorrow.'

His smile was narrow and cutting. 'Bored, Geraldine?'

'Not in the least,' she said truthfully. This seething, elemental attraction was about as far removed from boredom as anything could be. And it didn't help that she was terrified he'd notice its uncomfortable physical manifesta-

tions—the increased pulse-rate beating in her throat, the
heat in her skin, the darkening of her eyes.

If he had noticed, he didn't remark on it. Irony charged
his voice as he said, 'After that you can lie in the sun and
gild those glorious legs until the week is up.'

'Tanning is no longer fashionable, I'm afraid.' Her smile
was syrupy sweet.

Although he didn't rise to the bait, the hooded, predatory
gleam of green beneath his lashes sent a sizzle of sensation
down the length of her backbone.

She'd leave the day after tomorrow, but because she
liked to keep things as smooth and amicable as possible
she wasn't going to make a point of it. Bryn was a man
accustomed to getting his own way, and she'd always found
it simpler not to oppose such people head-on. She just ignored them and did what she wanted to. As a strategy, it
usually worked very well.

He insisted she rest in the heat of the day, and because
she was surprisingly tired she lay on the chaise longue in
her suite and watched the tasselled shadows of the coconut
palms on the floor. She did try to read one of the books
she'd brought with her, but when her eyelids drifted down
she allowed her fantasies to break through the bounds her
conscious mind had set on them.

Later, under another cool and reviving shower, she tried
to persuade herself that she must have been asleep, because
her thoughts had run together and blurred, just like dreams.
But they were all of the same man: Bryn Falconer, with
his ice-green eyes and hard, strong face, its only softening
feature lashes that were long and thick, and curled at the
tips.

Gerry's mother had taught her too well that when you
fell in love you created mayhem; you left shattered souls
behind. Her father had taught her that falling in love meant
unhappiness for the rest of your life. He'd taken one look
at her mother and wanted her, and when she left him he'd
been broken on the wheel of his own passion.

As his daughter grew into a mirror image of the beautiful, flighty, selfish woman who had abandoned them both, he'd warned her about the impact of her beauty. Gerry had seen it herself; men liked her and wanted her without even knowing her, because she had a lovely face and a way of flirting that made them feel wonderful.

So she'd grown up distrusting instant attraction.

Had some cynical fate made sure it had happened to her—a clap of thunder across the sunlit uplands of her life, dark, menacing and too powerful to be ignored?

For a lazy hour she'd lain in the soothing coolness of the trade winds and listened to the waves purring onto the reef, and slipped the leash on her imagination. She'd drowned in the sensuous impact of images of Bryn smiling, talking, of Bryn holding the baby...

Sheer, moony self-indulgence, she thought crossly.

All right, so she was physically attracted to the man— he was sexy enough to be a definite challenge, and that aura of steely power set her nerves jumping and her pulses throbbing—but she wasn't going to get carried away on a tide of imagination and wish herself into disillusion.

Armed with resolution, she went down to the lagoon and swam for twenty minutes in a sea as warm as her bath. She was wringing out her hair as she walked up the beach— swiftly, because the sand burned the soles of her feet— when her skin tightened in a reaction as primitive as it was involuntary.

Tiger-striped by shadow, Bryn stood beneath the palms. His eyes were hidden by sunglasses, and for a moment her heart juddered at his patient, watchful stance. Face bare of cosmetics, she felt like some small animal caught in the sights of a hunter, vulnerable, naked. Her legs suddenly seemed far too long, far too bare, and her bathing suit, sedate and sleek though it was, revealed too much of her body.

He didn't smile, and when he said, 'Hello,' an oblique

note in his voice sent something dark and primitive scudding through her.

'Hello,' she replied, keeping her eyes fixed on her small cache of belongings on the sand only a couple of feet away from him. He looked like some golden god from the days when the world was young, imperious and incredibly, compellingly formidable.

Furious with herself, she forced her shaking legs to walk up to her bag. She grabbed the towel from beneath it, and ran it over her shoulders, then dropped it to pick up a pareu. One swift shake wrapped it around her sarong-fashion. She secured it above her breasts with a knot, and anchored back the wet strands of her hair with two combs.

'Good swim?' His voice was gravelly, as though he'd been asleep.

At least he still wore his shirt. 'Glorious. The water's like silk,' she murmured, banishing images of him sprawled across a bed from her treacherous mind.

'That has to be the most interesting way to wear a length of cotton,' he observed gravely.

'Take your sunglasses off when you say that,' she growled in her best Hollywood cowboy manner.

He removed the sunglasses and stuffed them into his pocket. 'Sorry,' he said, a slow smile lingering as he surveyed her with open appreciation. 'I hope you put sunscreen on.'

She could feel his gaze travel across her shoulders, dip to the delicate skin of her cleavage, the smooth length of her arms. Pinned by that too-intimate survey, she thought confusedly that one of the reasons tanning had been so popular was that, like her cosmetics, it gave the illusion of a second skin; exposed under Bryn's questing scrutiny, she felt vulnerable.

With stiff reserve Gerry said, 'Naturally I take care of my skin.'

He seemed fascinated by the pearls of sea water on her shoulders, each cool bubble falling from her wet hair. One lean finger skimmed the slick surface. Such a light touch, and so swiftly removed, yet she felt it right to the pit of her stomach. Her body shouted *yes,* and melted, collapsed in a wave of heat, of painfully acute recognition.

'Oh, you do that,' he said, his voice a little thicker. 'And very well, too. Your skin's flawless—shimmering and seductive, with a glow like ripe peaches. What Mediterranean ancestor gave you that colouring?'

'My mother left before I had a chance to ask her about her ancestors, but one of them was French,' she said harshly, hearing the uneven crack in her voice with horror.

And she forced herself to step away from the tantalising lure of his closeness, from the primal incitement of his touch. Dry-mouthed, her brain cells too jittery to frame a coherent thought, she blundered on, 'However, that's a nice line. I'm sure Cara liked it.'

Something colder than Saturn's frozen seas flickered within the enigmatic depths of his eyes. 'She'd giggle if I said that to her.'

No doubt, but Cara clearly wasn't too young or unsophisticated to sleep with. Gerry shrugged and turned towards the path to the hotel.

Bryn said coolly, 'She spent the night at my place. Not, however, in my bed.'

Gerry made the mistake of glancing back. 'It's none of my business what Cara—or you—do,' she said, struggling to hold her voice steady in the face of the level, inimical challenge of his gaze and tone.

'Do you believe me?' he asked.

'Is it important that I do?'

He smiled, and his gaze lingered on her mouth. 'Yes,' he said levelly. 'Unfortunately it is.'

CHAPTER FIVE

GERRY hesitated, aware that she was about to step into the unknown, take the first, terrifying stumble over a threshold she'd always evaded before. Every instinct shouted a warning, but even a faint, cautionary memory of her mother, and the damage she'd caused in her pursuit of love, couldn't dampen down the fever-beat of anticipation.

'I do believe you,' she said slowly, her fingers tightening on the knotted cotton at her breast. 'I hope you don't hurt her. Although she thinks she's very sophisticated, she's a baby.'

'She knows she's in no danger from me.'

'That's not the point. She's very attracted to you.'

Frowning, he said abruptly, 'I can't do anything about that.'

If she had any intelligence she'd shut up, but something drove her to say, 'You *are* doing something about it. You're encouraging it.'

Broad shoulders moved in a slight shrug. Coldly, incisively, his eyes as hard as splintered diamonds, he said, 'I met her at a dinner party, saw that she was a little out of her depth, and watched her drink too much. I didn't trust the man hovering around, so I offered her a bed for the night.' He repeated with a dark undertone of aggression, of warning, 'A bed, not *my* bed.'

Gerry's humiliating resentment wasn't appeased. 'I know I shouldn't worry about her,' she said, trying to sound as though she were discussing a purely maternal instinct instead of a fierce, female possessiveness unrecognised in her until she'd met Bryn. 'It's just that she's such a kid in some ways.'

One brow lifted slightly as he said, 'You're also her role model, her idea of everything that's sophisticated and successful.'

'I know,' she said, wishing they could talk about someone other than Cara. 'She'll grow out of it.'

'Oh, I'm sure she will. Hero-worship is an adolescent emotion.' Voices from behind made him say with a caustic flick, 'And here is someone else all ready to worship at the shrine of high fashion.'

It was the Australian family—slightly overweight father, artificial wife and the too-thin daughter with the seeking eyes and vulnerable mouth. Although they were all smiling as they came up, their body language gave them away; they'd been quarrelling.

Gerry tamped down her guilty exasperation at their intrusion.

'Had a good day?' Cosmo asked heartily.

'Lovely, thank you.' Gerry smiled at him and saw his eyelids droop. By now thoroughly irritated, she transferred the smile to his wife and daughter. 'What have you been doing?'

'Swimming,' Narelle said with a little snap.

Lacey eyed Gerry. 'I've been diving,' she offered. 'Did you know that when you go down a bit everything turns blue? Even the fish and the coral? It's nothing like the wildlife documentaries.'

Gerry nodded sympathetically. 'They're specially lighted in the documentaries. Still, the ones close to the surface where the sunlight reaches are gorgeous.'

'It's not the same, though,' Lacey said with glum precision.

'It just shows how careful lighting can glamorise things,' Bryn observed.

Gerry kept her countenance with an effort. 'Exactly,' she said drily.

The younger woman shrugged. 'Oh, well, there's a lot

to look at down there, even if it is all blue. I saw a moray eel.'

Narelle pulled a face. 'Ugh.'

Without looking at her, Gerry said, 'In some places they tame them by feeding them.'

'I wouldn't want to get too close to one.' Lacey shuddered, an involuntary movement that turned into a sudden stumble. She flung out a thin arm and clung for a moment to Gerry, fingers bruising her arm. After a moment she straightened and stepped back, face pasty, her angular body held upright, Gerry guessed, by sheer will-power.

Narelle had been laughing at something Bryn said. She turned now, gave her daughter a swift, irritated glance and said, 'Let's go up and shower. All that lying on the beach is exhausting.'

Lacey's eyes wrung Gerry's heart. Adolescence could be the cruellest time; she herself would have suffered much more if she hadn't had a father who loved her, good friends, aunts who'd listened to her and taught her what to wear, and a plethora of cousins to act as sisters and brothers.

This girl seemed acutely alone, and beneath the prickly outer shell Gerry discerned a kind of numb, stubborn fear. She walked up to the cabañas beside her, talking quietly about nothing much, and slowly a little colour returned to Lacey's face.

An hour later, when they met again in the open-air bar, Gerry was glad to see that Bryn was with the younger woman, and that she was laughing. She had, Gerry realised, the most beautiful eyes—large and grey, and when she was amused they shone beneath thick lashes.

Did she remind Bryn of his sister, who'd been awkward and unhappy? What had happened to her?

Gerry chose a long, soothing glass of lime juice to drink, oddly touched to have Lacey follow suit. Bryn's gaze moved from Lacey's face to Gerry's; she almost flinched at the nameless emotion chilling the crystalline depths.

'So what did you two do today?' Narelle asked flirtatiously.

'Checked out hats,' Bryn said.

'Oh, did you? I saw some in the shop here, but they're
hopelessly old-fashioned. Quite resolutely unchic.' She dismissed the subject with a wave of her ringed hand. 'We
bought pearls. They're good quality.'

And sure enough, around her throat was a string of
golden-black pearls, the clasp highlighted with diamonds.

'They're very pretty,' said Gerry politely, and listened as
Narelle told her how much they were worth and how to
look after them.

A little later, when Narelle suggested that they eat together, Gerry smiled but said nothing. For a moment it
seemed that Bryn might refuse, but after a keen glance at
Lacey, silent in loose jeans and a white linen shirt, he
agreed.

Gerry enjoyed her usual substantial meal, and wondered
as Lacey demolished a much bigger one. In spite of
Narelle's protests she even ate dessert.

As they drank coffee in the scented, flower-filled night,
Lacey made an excuse and left them. A few moments later
Gerry followed her to the restroom, slipping quietly in to
the sound of retching.

'Lacey, are you all right?' she asked.

Silence, and then a shocked voice. 'I—ah—think I must
have a bug,' Lacey muttered from behind the door.

'I'll get your mother.'

'No!' Water flushed. Loudly Lacey said, 'She's not my
mother; she's my stepmother. My mother lives in Perth
with her new husband.'

Gerry said, 'You shouldn't have to suffer through a
stomach bug; I'm sure the hotel will have medication.'

'I'm all right,' Lacey said sullenly.

But Gerry waited until eventually Lacey opened the door
and glowered at her. Then she asked, 'How long have you

been throwing up after each meal? Your teeth are still all right, so it can't have been going on for long.'

'What do you mean?' the younger girl demanded belligerently, turning her back to wash out her mouth.

Remorselessly Gerry asked, 'Didn't you know that your teeth will rot? Stomach acid strips the enamel off them.'

Colour burned along the girl's cheekbones. Her hands moved rhythmically against each other in a lather of foam.

Gerry pressed on. 'Does your stepmother know?'

'No,' Lacey blurted. 'And she wouldn't care. All she's ever done is pick at me for being fat and greedy and clumsy.'

'Your father will certainly care.'

Doggedly, Lacey said, 'I should have been like my mother instead of like him.' She eyed Gerry. 'She's tall too.'

I hope to heaven this is the right way to tackle this, Gerry thought. Her hands were damp and tense, but she took a short breath and ploughed on. 'You're never going to be tall. Even if you kill yourself dieting—and that's entirely possible—you'll never look like your mother. She's a racehorse; you're a sturdy pony. Each is beautiful.'

Lacey glared in the mirror at her with open dislike. A stream of water ran across her writhing hands, flooding away the bubbles. 'It's not fair,' she burst out.

Leaning over to turn off the tap, Gerry said, 'Life's not fair, but you're stacking the odds against yourself. If you don't get help, all your potential—all the essential part of you that's been put on earth to make a difference—will be wasted trying to be something you're not.'

'That's easy for you to say!' Lacey flashed. 'You eat like a horse and I'll bet you don't put on a bit of weight.'

Gerry said calmly, 'That's right. But when I was fourteen I was already this tall, and so thin one of my uncles told me I could pass through a wedding ring. I hated it. I towered over everyone in my class, and I was teased unmercifully.'

'I wouldn't mind,' Lacey muttered.

'Do you like being teased?'

The younger woman bit her lip.

Hoping desperately she wasn't making things worse, Gerry went on, 'You have to find some sort of defence against it, but trying to turn yourself into the sort of person an aggressor thinks you should be is knuckling under, giving up your own personality, becoming the slave of their prejudices.'

Lacey frowned. 'It's fashionable to be thin,' she objected.

'In ten years' time the fashion will have changed. It wouldn't surprise me if it swung back to women like you, women with breasts and thighs and hips. Don't you want to get married?'

'Who'd have me?' she snapped, drying her hands without looking at Gerry.

'A man like the actor who was here last time, whose girlfriend caught your father's eye. I'll bet she wasn't skinny and smelling of vomit all the time.'

Lacey's shoulders hunched. 'She had big boobs and too much backside,' she mumbled, 'but she had long legs.'

'Are you sliding into bulimia because you want to attract boys? Because if you are I can tell you now they don't like women who throw up after every meal, whose skin goes pasty and coarse, whose teeth rot, who smell foul and who look like death.'

'Someone said I was fat,' Lacey muttered, a difficult blush blotching her face and neck. 'A boy I like.'

'So you're putting yourself into death row because someone with no manners—an adolescent dork—makes a nasty, untrue remark?' Brutal frankness might work if the girl wasn't too far down the track. Whatever, she couldn't just stand by and do nothing. 'You're letting someone else force you into his mould.'

'I—no. It's not like that.' But Lacey's voice lacked conviction.

'Is that how you'll go through life? Not as an intelligent person, which you are—you showed that the other night— with valuable talents and ideas and gifts, but a tadpole in a flooded creek, tossed every which way by other people's opinions?'

Open-mouthed, Lacey swung around to stare at her. 'A t-tadpole?' She started to laugh. 'A *tadpole*? No, I d-don't want to be a tadpole!'

'Well, that's where you're heading.' Gerry grinned. 'Instead of being a very self-possessed woman, with confidence and control over your own life. If you give up on yourself you risk losing everything that makes you the individual, unique person you are.'

'I wish it was that simple!' But a thoughtful note in Lacey's voice gave Gerry some hope.

'Nothing's ever simple,' she said, thinking of her reluctant, heated attraction to Bryn Falconer.

'I suppose you think I'm stupid,' Lacey said defensively.

'I told you what I think you are—intelligent, aware, with a sly wit that is going to stand you in good stead one day.'

'And fat,' Lacey finished cynically.

Gerry frowned. 'Promise me something.'

'What?'

Gerry chose her words with care. 'Promise me that when you go home you'll see a counsellor or a woman doctor you trust.' *Or I'll tell your parents.* The unspoken words hung in the scented air.

Lacey bit her lip, then blurted, 'If I do, will you write to me?'

'Yes, of course I will.' Gerry said, 'Are you on e-mail? I'll give you my address.' She hooked a tissue from her small bag and scribbled her address and telephone number on it. 'There. Ring me if you need to talk to someone. And, Lacey, you've got the most beautiful eyes.'

Scarlet-faced, the younger girl ducked her head and stammered her thanks.

'Right, let's go,' Gerry said, still worried, but hoping that somehow she'd managed to get through to the girl.

Apart from Bryn, who gave them both a swift, keen glance, no one seemed to have noticed that they'd been gone quite a while; Narelle was trying covertly to place someone on the other side of the room, and Cosmo was looking at his empty glass with the frown of a man who wonders if it would be sensible to have another.

As Gerry picked up her coffee cup Bryn's dark brows drew together into a formidable line and he looked over her head. From behind came a cheerful voice, 'A telephone call for Ms Dacre.'

'Thank you,' she said, taking the portable telephone from the tray and getting back to her feet. She walked across to the edge of the dining area and said, 'Yes.'

'Gerry, oh, thank God you're there, it's Cara.'

'What's happened?'

'M-Maddie—Maddie Hopkinson—is in hospital.'

Maddie, an extremely popular model who'd come back to New Zealand after three years based in New York, was to have left for Thailand for a shoot the day after next. An important shoot—the start of a huge, Pacific-wide campaign. She'd been through a difficult period, getting over the American boyfriend who'd dumped her when she insisted on coming home, but over the past month or so she seemed to have recovered her old fire and sparkle.

Icy tendrils unfolded through Gerry's stomach. 'In *hospital*? What's the matter with her?'

'She OD'd.' Cara sounded scared.

'*What?*'

'Drugs—her flatmate thinks it might have been heroin.'

Gerry had worried about Maddie, talked to her, suggested counselling, but had never suspected the model was taking drugs. Glancing automatically at her watch—silly, because Langopai was in the same time zone as New Zealand, so it was eight o'clock there too—she asked, 'When was this?'

'Last night.' Cara hesitated, then said in a voice that had horror and avidity nicely blended, 'Sally—the girl she shares a flat with—rang me this morning. Gerry, I went to see her this afternoon—there were police at her door and they wouldn't let me in.'

Shock stopped Gerry's brain. She drew in a deep breath and forced the cogs to engage again, logic to take over from panic. 'Why hasn't Honor contacted me?'

'Because she doesn't know anything about it,' Cara said. 'I've been ringing and ringing her flat, but all I get is the answer-machine. And it's Queen's Birthday weekend, so she won't be back until Tuesday.'

Blast Honor and her habit of taking off for weekends without letting anyone know where she was! Striving very hard to sound calm and in control, Gerry said, 'All right, I'll get a plane out of here as soon as I can. In the meantime, look in my work diary and get me the phone number of—' Her mind went blank. 'Maddie's booker.' The bookers at the agency organised each model's professional appointments.

'Jill,' Cara said. 'All right, I'll be back in a moment.'

While Cara raced off to get her diary from her bedroom Gerry gnawed on her lip and tried to work out what to do next. From the eight or nine guests enjoying the ambience of the communal area came a low, subdued hum of conversation punctuated with laughter. Lights glowed, dim enough to give the soft flattery of candles; she noted with an expert's eye the line and drape of extremely expensive resort wear, the glimmer of pearls, the sheen of pampered skin, the white flash of teeth.

Hurry up, Cara! And hang in there, Maddie, she mentally adjured, thinking of the exquisite, fragile girl lying in her hospital bed with a police guard at the door. Lately there had been a lot of publicity about heroin being chic amongst models and photographers. Oh, why hadn't she noticed something was wrong?

And how would this affect the agency? Her head

throbbed, and she had to take another deep breath. Swinging away to look out over the lush foliage beyond the public area, she scrabbled in her evening bag and found a ballpoint pen.

'I've got it.' Cara's voice wobbled, then firmed. 'Here's Jill's number.' She read it off.

Gerry wrote it on another tissue. 'OK.' She gave Cara the name of the advertising agency in charge of Maddie's shoot. 'Get me the art director's number—it's there.'

'She won't be at work now,' Cara said. 'It's Friday night.'

'She might be. Her home number's there as well, so get it too.'

'Gosh, you're so organised.' Sounds of scrabbling came through the static, until Cara said in a relieved voice, 'Yes, here they are.'

'Let's hope to heaven she either works late or stays home on a Friday night.' Gerry spread out the tissue and began to copy the numbers down as Cara read them out.

When the younger woman had finished she said, 'Gerry, it took me ages to get through to you so you might have trouble ringing New Zealand. Do you want me to ring Jill and tell her what's happened?'

Gerry hesitated. 'Good thinking. And if I haven't got hold of her, ask her to track down the art director and tell her that I suggest Belinda Hargreaves to take Maddie's place. I know she was second choice, and if I remember right she hasn't got anything on at the moment. Jill's her booker too, so she'll know.'

'What if the ad agency or the client doesn't want Belinda?'

Gerry said, 'I'll deal with it when I get back. Don't worry. Many thanks for ringing me. Cara, how is Maddie?'

'She's alive, but that's all I've been able to find out. The hospital won't tell me anything because I'm not a relation, and apparently her brother is still on his way back from Turkestan or somewhere.'

Gerry twisted a curl tight around one finger. Pushing guilt to the back of her mind, she said, 'Send her flowers from us all. And get me the number of the hospital, will you?'

Where the *hell* was Honor? Probably spending the weekend with a man; she had a cheerful, openly predatory attitude where the other sex were concerned, swanning unscathed through situations that would have scared Gerry white-haired.

Why couldn't she have waited until Gerry got back before going off like this? And why, when she knew Gerry would be away, hadn't she left a contact number?

But of course she hadn't known that Gerry was coming up to Longopai. Clearly she'd believed that if anything needed attending to, Gerry would do so, even though she was on holiday.

After soothing Cara some more, Gerry said goodbye, dropped the telephone at the main desk and organised to pay for all phone bills with her credit card, then went back to the table, composing her expression into blandness.

'Problems?' Bryn said, getting to his feet. The ice-green gaze rested on her face, expressionless, measuring.

Damn, how did he know? 'I have to make a few calls,' she said lightly, avoiding a direct answer.

It was none of his business, and she refused to give him a chance to make more comments about her agency exploiting young women. She was feeling bad enough about Lacey and Maddie. Summoning her best smile, she said to the table at large, 'If you'll excuse me, I'll leave you now.'

'That's all right,' Cosmo said breezily. 'See you tomorrow, then.'

She smiled and said goodnight, startled when Bryn said, 'I'll walk you up to your cabaña.'

After a moment's silence she said, 'Thank you.'

He took her arm in a grip that had something both predatory and possessive about it. Back erect, head held high, she smiled at the Australian family and went with him.

When they were out of earshot he said, 'What problem?'

Steadily she said into the sleepy heat of the night, 'I'm sorry, I can't tell you. It's important and urgent—I need to get back to New Zealand as soon as possible.'

'Someone ill?' His voice was cool.

She dithered. 'I—no, I don't think so. I'm needed back at the agency—there's an emergency. I'm sorry about the hats—but I do know now what the problem is, and I'll send you recommendations. If that's not enough, I will, of course, repay the money you've spent—'

'Don't be an idiot.' Although his voice was crisp and scornful, he continued, 'If you have to go, you have to go.'

Surprised that he didn't try to hold her to their agreement, she asked, 'Is there any chance of leaving the island tonight?'

'No,' he said abruptly. 'The seaplane's not authorised for night flights.'

Stopping, she said, 'I'll see if the desk clerk can organise a seat for me on the first flight tomorrow.'

'I'll do it,' he said, urging her on. 'And get you onto a flight out of Fala'isi tomorrow.'

He was being kind, but something drove her to say, 'I can't put you to all that trouble.'

'I have more pull here than you,' he said coolly.

There was no sensible reason why she shouldn't accept his help. Struggling with an inconvenient wariness, she said, 'Thanks. I'd be very grateful.'

'What's happened?'

Gerry resisted the temptation to tell him everything and let him take over. So this, she thought, trying for her usual pragmatism, is the effect a pair of broad shoulders and an air of competence have on susceptible women. Odd that she, who prided herself on being capable and practical and the exact opposite of susceptible, should want to succumb like a wilting Victorian miss.

'Just some trouble at the agency. It's nothing you can help with,' she said woodenly, 'but thank you for offering.'

'You don't know what I can help with.'

Beneath the smooth, amused surface of his voice a note of determination alerted her senses. 'I do know you can't do anything about this,' she said.

He left it at that, although she thought she could sense irritation simmering in him. 'I'll organise your flights to New Zealand and be back in half an hour,' he said.

'Thank you very much.' She made the mistake of glancing upwards. In the soft starlit darkness his face was a harsh sculpture, all tough, forceful power. Sensation slithered the length of her spine, melting a hitherto inviolate impregnability.

It would be easy to want this man rather desperately—so easy, and so incredibly perilous. He was no ordinary man; her cousin Anet's husband had something of the same sort of hard, contained intensity.

No, that was silly. Lucas had fought in a vicious and bloody guerrilla war; he wrote books about conspiracies and events that shook the world. Bryn was an importer. A successful businessman could have nothing in common with a man like Lucas.

After she'd closed the door behind her she exhaled soundlessly. It had been surprisingly difficult to turn down Bryn's offer of a listening ear. He hadn't liked it—no doubt he was accustomed to being the person everyone relied on.

Gerry had never relied on a man in her life, and she wasn't going to start now.

With a swift shake of her head she dialled the hospital, who would only tell her that Maddie was as well as could be expected. After thanking the impersonal voice, Gerry hung up and began damage control.

Jill, the booker who managed Maddie's professional life, already knew of Maddie's illness—although not, Gerry deduced, its nature—and was doing her best to tidy up the situation; she agreed that Belinda was the best replacement they could offer, and had already got in touch with her. Belinda was ready to go.

'Oh, that's great,' Gerry said, breathing a little more easily. 'Now I have to convince the art director at the ad agency that Belinda can do it.'

'I could do that,' Jill said.

'I'm going to have to crawl a bit—it should be me. Still, if you don't hear from me within the hour, start ringing her.'

'Will do. What are her numbers?'

'Bless you,' Gerry said, and told her. Hanging up, she breathed a harassed sigh.

It wasn't going to be easy.

After a frustrating and infuriating twenty minutes she gave up trying to contact the art director, who didn't even have an answering machine. It was useless to keep trying; she needed a good night's sleep, so she'd try again the next morning. And if she still couldn't get her, Jill would.

Swiftly, efficiently, she began to pack.

Half an hour to the minute later there was a knock on the door. Bracing herself, she opened it.

Bryn said, 'I've booked you on a flight from Fala'isi at six o'clock tomorrow morning.'

'But the seaplane—'

'I'll take the cabin cruiser and get you to Fala'isi before then.' His gaze took in her suitcase. 'Good, you're ready. Let's go.'

Taken aback, she protested, 'But—'

He interrupted crisply, 'I thought you wanted to get back to New Zealand in a hurry?'

'Yes! I—well, yes, of course I do.' Yet still she hesitated. 'I presume you know how to get from here to Fala'isi in a strange cabin cruiser?'

His mouth curved. 'The cruiser's mine. And with radar and all the modern aids, navigation's like falling off a log. Besides, I do know these waters—I come up here quite often.'

Feeling stupid, she said, 'Well—thank you very much.'

He lifted her case and she went with him through the

palms, past the public area, out onto the clinging, coarse white coral sand of the beach, where the hotel's outrigger canoe was ready. The two men who'd picked her up from the plane were there; they said something in the local Maori to Bryn, who answered with a laugh, and before long they were heading across the lagoon, the only sound a soft hissing as the hulls sliced through the black water.

Gerry had a moment of disassociation, a stretched fragment of time when she wondered what she was doing there beneath stars so big and trembling and close she felt she could pick them like flowers. The scents of sea and land mingled, the fresh fecundity of tropical vegetation balanced by the cool, salty perfume of the lagoon.

Thoughts spun around her brain, jostling for their moment in the light, then sliding away into oblivion. She should be trying to work out how to help Maddie. Bryn would be disgusted if he knew; poor Maddie's condition would be another nail in Gerry's coffin, another thing to despise her for.

Was he right? Was her career one that drove young women down Lacey's path? Would Maddie have begun using heroin if she hadn't been a model? Would Lacey be bulimic if she hadn't longed to be thin?

Stricken, she pushed the thoughts to the back of her brain and looked around.

The starlit silence, the swift flight of the canoe, the noiseless islanders and the awe-inspiring beauty of the night played tricks on her mind. She wondered if this was what it would be like to embark on a quest into the unknown, a quest from which she'd return irrevocably transformed. Her eyes clung to Bryn's profile, arrogant against the luminous sky. Something tightened into an ache inside her; swallowing, she looked hastily away.

You've been reading too much mythology, she told herself caustically. What you're doing is catching a plane home to Maddie's personal tragedy, and there's nothing remotely magical about that!

Paddles flashed, slowing the canoe's headlong flight; carefully, precisely, they eased up to the white hull of the cruiser. Bryn stood up, and in one lithe movement hauled himself up and over the railing. Within two minutes he'd unzipped the awning and lowered steps from the cockpit. Gerry climbed up and waited while Bryn stooped to take her case from the hands of one of the men.

'Thank you,' she said.

They smiled and waved and sped off into the darkness.

CHAPTER SIX

FEELING oddly bereft, Gerry said, 'What happens now?'

Bryn gestured at a ladder and said, 'I'm going up to the flybridge because I can see better from up there. You might find it interesting to watch as we go out.'

'Can I do something?'

'No.'

The surprisingly large flybridge was roofed in and furnished with comfortable built-in sofas. One faced a bank of intimidating gauges and switches and dials beneath what would have been the windscreen in a car. There was even, Gerry noted, what appeared to be a small television screen. The other sofa was back to back with the first, so that it faced the rear of the boat where awnings blocked out the night. There was enough seating for half a dozen people.

Without looking at her, Bryn sat down in front of the console and began to do things. The engine roared into life and small lights sprang into action.

Wishing that she knew more about boats, Gerry perched a little distance from him and wrinkled her nose at the hot, musty air. Presumably the awnings at the back were usually raised—lowered? removed?—while the boat was in use.

As though she'd spoken, Bryn pressed a button and two of the side awnings slid to one side, letting in a rush of fresh air.

Desperately worried though she was about Maddie, Gerry couldn't entirely squelch a humiliating anticipation. A lazy inner voice that came from nowhere, all purring seductiveness, murmured, Oh, why worry? A few moments of fantasy can't do any harm.

Turning his head, Bryn asked, 'Will you hold her steady

while I haul up the anchor? Keep her bow pointed at the clump of palms on the very tip of the outer passage. You won't have to do anything more than that, and it's so calm you won't have any trouble.'

Her stomach lurched slightly, but he made the request so casually that she said, 'Fine,' and got to her feet, gripping the wheel tightly while he disappeared. She stared at the graceful curves of the palms until her eyes started to blur. She rested them by watching Bryn down on the deck in front.

He began to haul on the anchor chain, bending into the task with a strength that sent an odd little flutter through her. Broad shoulders moving in a rhythm as old as time, he pulled with smooth precision, power and litheness combining in a purely masculine grace.

He'd be a magnificent lover, prompted that sly inner voice.

A sudden rattle, combined with the stirring wheel in her hands, persuaded her to shut off the tempting images conjured by that reckless inner voice. Guiltily she looked back at the palm trees, breathing her relief that the bow still pointed in the right direction

'Good work,' Bryn said, coming up noiselessly beside her and taking over. 'Are you tired?'

'A bit.' She moved aside to gaze out across the water, smooth and dark as obsidian, polished by the soft sheen of the tropical stars. Heat gathered in her veins, seeping through her like warmed honey. She felt like a woman from the dawn of time, aware yet unknowing, standing on the edge of the first great leap into knowledge. 'It's a wonderful night.'

'Tropical nights are known for their seductive qualities,' Bryn agreed, his voice pleasant and detached.

It sounded like a warning. Gerry kept her gaze fixed on the lagoon. 'I'm sure they are,' she said drily.

'But you don't find them so.'

She shrugged. 'They're very beautiful. So is a summer's night at home—or a winter's one, for that matter.'

'A dyed-in-the-wool New Zealander,' he jibed.

'Afraid so. I think if you've been happy in a place you'll always love it.'

'And in spite of growing up motherless you were a happy child?'

'I was lucky,' she said. 'I had innumerable relations who treated me like their own child. And my father was very devoted.'

'His death must have hit you hard,' he said, looking down at the instruments behind the wheel.

'Yes.' Four years previously her father's heart had finally given up the struggle against the punishing workload he'd been forced to take on in his retirement years.

'I liked him,' Bryn said.

Gerry nodded, not surprised that they had met. New Zealand was small, and most people in a particular field knew everyone in it. Her father had earned his position as one of New Zealand's most far-sighted businessmen, building up his small publishing business into a Pacific Rim success.

She'd mourned her father and was over his death—or as over it as she'd ever be—but because the memory still hurt she asked, 'Did you ever try to find out what happened to *your* father?'

If he snubbed her, she wouldn't blame him.

But he answered readily enough, although a stony undernote hardened his words. 'He'd been hired as crew on a yacht headed for Easter Island. He died there in an accident.'

'A lonely place,' she said, thinking of the tiny, isolated island, the last outpost of Polynesia, so far across the vast Pacific that it was ruled from South America.

'Perhaps that's what he wanted. Loneliness, oblivion.' His voice was coolly objective. 'He didn't even have a headstone.'

For some reason the calm statement wrung Gerry's heart. 'Have you been there?'

'A year ago.'

She stared at the white bow wave chuckling past. 'Did you find anyone who knew him?'

'Several remembered what had happened. Apparently he got drunk and set out to swim ashore. He was washed up on the beach the following day. I tried to trace the yacht, but to all intents and purposes it sailed over the edge of the world. It certainly didn't turn up in any of the registers after that.'

At least she had been loved and valued! Tentatively she asked, 'He must have been shattered by your mother's death. Do you remember him?'

'Only that he was a big man with a quick, eager laugh. The islanders called him a starchaser, because you can never catch a star.'

'Like my mother,' she said softly, warmed by a sense of kinship. 'I don't know whether she ever knew what she wanted, but she certainly never got it.'

'Damaged people, perhaps. Both of them unable to accept responsibility for themselves or their children.'

Gerry nodded, watching as the bow swung, steadied, headed towards the black gap in the reef that was the channel. 'That passage looked very narrow from the air. Is it difficult to take a boat through?'

'Not this one. Longopai's trading vessel has to stand off and load and unload via smaller boats, but a craft this size has no trouble.' She looked up and saw a corner of his mouth lift, then compress. He went on, 'I know the channel as well as I know the way I shave. Besides, with the equipment on the *Starchaser* it would take an act of God or sheer stupidity to get us into any sort of trouble. Relax.'

Why had he called his boat after his father? Some sort of link to the man who'd abandoned him and his sister— or a warning? A glance at his profile, all hard authority in the greenish light of the dials and screens, destroyed that idea. No hint of sentiment or whimsy in those harsh male angles and lines. A warning, then.

Aloud, Gerry said lightly, 'I trust you and the *Starchaser*'s instruments entirely.'

He sent her a sharp glance before saying equivocally, 'Good.'

Nevertheless she didn't distract him with conversation while he took the cruiser through the gap, admiring the efficient skill with which he managed the craft in a very narrow passage. Once through, the boat settled into a regular, rocking motion against the waves.

'I forgot to ask,' Bryn said. 'Do you get seasick?'

'I haven't ever done so before.'

'There's medication down in the head if you need it.'

'The head?' she asked, smiling.

He turned the wheel slightly. In an amused voice he said, 'The bathroom. There are three on board, one off each of the staterooms and another for the other cabins.'

'Such opulence,' she said lightly.

'Never been on a luxury cruiser before?' he asked, the words underlined with a taunt.

'Quite often,' she said, then added, 'But always as a mere day passenger. And for some reason I assumed that luxury didn't mean much to you.'

He shrugged. 'I like comfort as much as the next man,' he said. 'But I can do without it. The boat is used mostly by guests from the hotel, and as they're brought here by the promise of luxury—and pay highly for it—the boat has to follow suit. There's no luxury at all on Longopai's trading vessel.'

'Does the vessel belong to the islanders?'

'Yes. They had no regular contact with the rest of the world. The trader has made quite a difference for them.'

Had he bought it for them?

Somewhere to the south lay Fala'isi, lost for now in the darkness. With a throb of dismay Gerry thought that she could stand like this for the rest of her life, watching the stars wheel slowly overhead in a sky of blue-black immensity, and listening to Bryn.

As soon as she realised where it was leading, she banished the delusion.

She was not, she told herself sternly, falling even the tiniest bit in love with Bryn Falconer. 'Do you know Lacey's address?' she asked, filling in a silence that was beginning to stretch too long.

'I could find out. Why?'

'I want to send her a photograph of my cousin and her husband,' she said. 'Anet threw the javelin for an Olympic gold; she's as tall as me and about three sizes bigger—a splendid Amazon of a woman.'

'Anet Carruthers? I saw her win. She threw brilliantly.'

'Didn't she just! One of my most exciting experiences was watching her get the gold. Her husband is gorgeous, and I think it might cheer Lacey up if she could see them together.'

'You continually surprise me,' he said after a moment.

'People who make incorrect assumptions based solely on physical appearance must live in a state of perpetual astonishment,' she returned evenly.

He laughed quietly. 'How right you are. I'm sorry.'

'You judged me without knowing anything about me,' she said, the words a crisp reprimand.

'Admitted. First appearances can be deceiving.'

When he strode into her house Gerry had thought him a hard man, exciting and different and far too old for Cara. Certainly she'd not suspected him to be capable of tenderness for a baby, or such kindness as this trip to Fala'isi. A little ashamed, she said, 'Well, anyone can make a mistake.'

She fought back a bewildering need to ask him more about his life, find out who his friends were and whether they shared any. Pressing her lips firmly together, she forced herself to think of other, far more urgent matters.

How was Maddie? And why—*why*—did someone with her advantages throw everything away in servitude to a drug?

When she recovered—Gerry refused to think she might not—they'd do their best for her, see that she got whatever help she needed to pull her life together. Honor would know what to do; she'd spent four years with a heroin-addicted lover. In the end she'd escaped with nothing but her dream of opening a modelling agency.

Frowning, Gerry wondered again whether Bryn was right. Did the constant pressure of unrealistic expectations lead young women into eating disorders and drug abuse?

She hugged her arms around her, turning slightly so that she could see the face of the man silhouetted against the soft glow of the instrument panels; as well as the powerful contours, the faint light picked out the surprisingly beautiful, sensuous curve of his mouth.

Something clutched at her nerves, dissolved the shield of her control, twisted her emotions ever tighter on the rack of hunger. For the first time in her life she felt the keen ache of unfulfilled desire, a needle of hunger and frustration that stripped her composure from her and forced her to accept her capacity for passion and surrender.

Hair lifted on the back of her neck. This was terrifying; she had changed overnight, altered at some deep cellular level, and she'd never be the same again.

'Why don't you go on down and sleep?'

Bryn's voice startled her. Had he noticed? No, how could he? 'I think I will,' she returned.

'The bed in the starboard cabin won't be made up, but the sheets are in the locker beside the door.'

'Is starboard left or right? I can never remember.'

'Right,' he said. Amused, he continued, 'Starboard and right are the longer words of each pair—port and left the shorter.'

'Thanks. Goodnight, Bryn. And thank you. This is wonderfully kind of you.'

'It's nothing.' He sounded detached.

Rebuffed, she made her way down to the cockpit, and then down three more steps to the main cabin. At the end a narrow door opened into an extremely comfortable little cabin, with a large double bed taking up most of the floor space. Close by, her suitcase rested on a built-in bench beneath a curtained band of windows.

After making the bed and discovering the secrets of the tiny *en suite*—only here it was a head, she reminded herself—Gerry slipped off her shoes and lay down. Soon this would be over. She'd fly back to New Zealand, and after that she'd make sure she didn't see much of Bryn. He was too dangerous to her peace, too much of a threat. And banishing the treacherous little thought that he'd never bore her, she courted sleep.

She woke to the gentle rocking of the boat, a bar of sunlight dazzling her closed eyes. For several moments she lay smiling, still mesmerised by dreams she no longer remembered, and then as her eyes opened and she stared through the gap in the curtains she gasped and shot upright.

Daylight here was just after six, so by now she should be high on a jet, heading back to New Zealand. A startled glance at her watch revealed that it was nine minutes past eight. No, she should be landing in the cold grey winter of Auckland. Jolted, she leapt off the bed and ran from the cabin.

Bryn was stretched out on a sofa, but his eyes were open, densely green and shadowed in his grim face. As Gerry skidded to a halt and demanded breathlessly, 'What's going on? Why are we stopped?' he got up, all six feet three and a half of him.

Tawny hair flopped over his forehead; raking it back, he said, 'The bloody electronics died, so I can't get the boat to go—or contact anyone.'

Her stomach dropped. Taking a short, involuntary step backwards she asked, 'Where are we?'

'I used the outboard from the inflatable to get us inside

a lagoon, so we're safe enough, but it won't take us to Fala'isi.'

A swift glance revealed that they were anchored off a low, picture-postcard atoll. Blinking at a half-moon of incandescent white sand, Gerry concentrated on calming her voice to its usual tone and speed. 'Can the islanders get us to Fala'isi? It's really important that I get back as soon as I can.'

'There are no islanders.' At her blank stare he elaborated. 'It's an uninhabited atoll about a hectare in extent.'

'Flares,' she urged. 'Distress flares—haven't you got any?'

'Five. I plan to fire them if we hear a plane or see a boat. It's our best chance of being found.'

'You don't sound very hopeful,' she said tautly.

Wide shoulders moved in the slightest of shrugs. 'The plane to Longopai flies the shortest route, and we're well off his track, but if he's looking in the right place at the right time he'll see a flare. The same goes for boats.'

While she stood there, scrabbling futilely for a solution, he asked without emphasis, 'Why is it so important for you to get back?'

'There's a problem with the agency,' she evaded woodenly.

'Surely you have someone in charge while you're away?'

'Honor McKenzie—my partner—but they can't get hold of her.'

He frowned. 'Why?'

'She's gone away without leaving a contact number,' Gerry snapped.

'Is that usual?'

She moved edgily across to the window, staring out. The boat rocked in the small waves; somewhere out there a fringing reef tamed the huge Pacific rollers. On the atoll, three coconut palms displayed themselves like a poster for a travel agency, and several birds flashed silver in the sun as they wheeled above the vivid waters of the lagoon. The sky glowed with the rich, heated promise of a tropical day.

It's not the end of the world, she told herself, taking three deep breaths. Even if I don't get back today or tomorrow it's not the end of the world. Jill will contact that wretched art director at the ad agency, and organise Maddie's replacement—the bookers know their stuff so well they can function without Honor.

Even if the art director or the client throws a tantrum and refuses to use Belinda, *it's still not the end of the world.*

But her body knew better. The last—the very last!—thing she wanted to do was spend any time shut up in a boat—however luxurious—with Bryn Falconer. An hour was too much.

Stomach churning, she said, 'Every so often Honor likes to get away from everything.'

'When you're not there?'

The dark voice sounded barely interested, yet a whisper of caution chilled her skin.

'She'll probably be back on Tuesday, but I need to get back *now*.' Her voice quavered. Gamely, she snatched back control and, because anything seemed better than letting him know that she was acutely attracted to him and terrified of it, she added, 'One of our models is ill, and there are things to be organised. I told Cara I'd be back today. She'll worry.' Quickly, before he had a chance to probe further, she asked, 'How on earth could everything fail on the boat? Surely the engine isn't run by electronics?'

'I'm afraid that it is,' he said. 'Just like your car—if the computer dies, it won't go.'

'Why can't you fix it? You're supposed to be an expert on computers, aren't you?' Shocked outrage shimmered through her voice, putting her at a complete disadvantage.

'Geraldine, I import them,' he said, as though explaining something to a child. 'I don't make them, and when my computers go down I call in professionals to fix them. I'm sorry, but I can't find out what the problem is.'

'So that means we have no facilities—we're not able to cook—'

'Calm down,' he said easily. 'The kitchen and heads are powered by gas. There's a small auxiliary engine that I can use to charge the generator with, so we'll have light. You're not going to be living in squalor, Geraldine.'

The taunting undernote irked her, but she ignored it. 'Can't you use that other engine to fix the electronic system? No, that wouldn't work.'

'Electronic systems don't run on fossil fuels,' he agreed tolerantly. 'Besides, the fault is in the electronics themselves, not the power.'

She cast a glance at his face with its shadow of beard. Although he didn't look tired, he might have been up all night getting them to safety. Dragging in another breath, she asked more moderately, 'How long do you think we'll have to wait here?'

His eyes were hooded and unreadable. 'I have no idea. Until someone comes looking for us.'

'When will they miss you?'

'They won't,' he told her. 'The islanders are accustomed to me taking off whenever I feel like it. But if you told Cara you'd be back today I'd say it will be tonight or tomorrow.'

Relief flooded her. 'Yes,' she said slowly. 'Yes, of course.'

'As soon as you don't turn up she'll alert people, and we'll be found.'

Gerry sank down onto the leather sofa. 'I'm sorry,' she said after a moment. 'I don't usually fly off the handle like that.'

'Everyone involved in a shipwreck is entitled to a qualm or two.'

Damn him, his mouth quirked. She bared her teeth in what she hoped looked like a smile. 'I suppose it is a shipwreck,' she said. 'On a desert island, of all places. How fortunate there are no pirates nowadays.'

'The world is full of pirates,' he said. His tone was not exactly reassuring, and neither were his words.

Gerry stared at him. 'What do you mean?' she asked uncertainly.

'Just that there are people around who would steal from you,' he said. 'If for any reason I'm not on board, be careful who you let in. Not that you're likely to have to face such a situation, but Fala'isi—and Longopai too—have their share of unpleasant opportunists.'

If that was meant to be reassuring, he should take lessons. A stress headache began to niggle behind one eye. Straining for her usual calm pragmatism, she said, 'Then I hope we get away before the local variety turns up. I have to tell you that although it sounds really romantic, being stranded has never appealed to me. And a steady diet of fish and coconuts will soon get boring.'

'There are staples on board,' he said casually. 'Plenty of water and tinned stuff. With fish and coconuts we have enough for a couple of weeks.'

'A couple of weeks!' she repeated numbly.

'Cheer up, we won't be here for that long. Would you like some breakfast?'

Gerry suddenly realised that she was still wearing the crumpled clothes she'd slept in. Worse, she hadn't combed her hair or cleaned her teeth.

Or put any make-up on.

Abruptly turning back to her cabin, she said, 'Thanks— just toast, if we've got bread. And coffee. I'll go and tidy up first.'

In the luxurious little bathroom Gerry peered at herself in the mirror, hissing when she saw a riot of black hair around her face, and eyes that were three times too big, the pupils dilated enough to make her look wild and feverish. Hastily she washed and got into clean clothes before reducing her mop to order and putting on her cosmetics.

When at last she emerged Bryn was making toast in the neat kitchen. A golden papaya lay quartered on the bench, its jetty seeds scooped from the melting flesh. Beside a hand of tiny, green-flecked bananas stood a bowl of oranges and the huge green oval of a soursop.

'Where did you get all this?' she asked.

'No sensible person travels by sea without loading some food,' he said evenly. 'It's a huge ocean, and every year people die in it, some from starvation. How many pieces of toast do you want?'

'Only a couple, thanks. I'm not very hungry.'

'You have a good appetite for someone so elegant.'

Sternly repressing a forbidden thrill of pleasure at the off-hand compliment, Gerry said, 'Thank you. Perhaps.'

He gave her a narrow glance, then smiled, reducing her to mindlessness with swift, intensely sexual charm. 'You're right,' he said blandly. 'Commenting on someone's appetite is crass. And you must know that you're not just elegant; you have the sort of beauty that takes the breath away.'

Shaken by her clamouring, unhindered response, Gerry said unevenly, 'From one extreme to the other. You're exaggerating—but thank you.'

'There should be a tablecloth in the narrow locker by the table,' Bryn told her. 'Plates and cutlery in the drawers beside it.'

Still quivering inside, she set the table, using the familiar process to regain some equilibrium.

By the time she sat down to fruit and toast she'd managed to impose an overlay of composure onto her riotous emotions. To her surprise she was hungry—and that bubble in her stomach, that golden haze suffusing her emotions was expectation.

Worried by this insight, she looked down at the table. In the morning sunlight the stainless steel knives and forks gleamed, and she'd never noticed before how pristine china looked against crisp blue and white checks, or how clean and satisfying the scents of food and coffee were.

Bryn was wearing a pale green knit polo shirt that emphasised the colour of his eyes and his tanned skin. He looked big and dangerous and powerfully attractive. Fire ran through her veins; resisting it, she forced herself to butter her toast, to spread marmalade and to drink coffee.

'I'll clean up in the kitchen if you want to go and fiddle with the electronics,' she offered when the meal was over.

'Sea-going vessels don't have kitchens.' He sounded amused. 'You come from the country with the biggest number of boats per person in the world, and you don't know that a boat's kitchen is called a galley?'

She shrugged. 'Why should I? My family ski and play golf in the winter, and play polo and tennis and croquet in the summer.'

'I'm not surprised,' he said, and although there was almost no inflection in his voice she knew it wasn't a compliment.

Smiling, each word sharpened with the hint of a taunt, she returned, 'All the yuppie pastimes.'

'But your family aren't yuppies,' he drawled. 'They're the genuine twenty-four-carat gold article, born into the purple.'

'Hardly. Emperors of Byzantium we're not!'

'No, just rich and aristocratic for generations.'

She lifted her brows, met gleaming eyes and a mouth that was hard and straight and controlled. Some risky impulse persuaded her to say, 'Do I detect the faint hint of an inferiority complex? But why? If your grandparents sent you to a private school they had money and social aspirations.'

The moment the words left her mouth she wished she'd kept silent. Instinct, stark and peremptory, warned her that this man didn't take lightly to being taunted.

'My maternal ones did. The other two lived in a state house with no fence and no garden, and a couple of old cars almost buried in grass on the lawn.' His voice betrayed nothing but a cool, slightly contemptuous amusement. 'Don't worry, Geraldine, I won't tell your family and friends that you've been slumming it.'

Damn, she'd hit a nerve with her clever remark. Beneath the surface of his words she sensed jagged, painful rocks...

Stacking her coffee mug onto her bread-and-butter plate, she said, 'I'm not a snob. Like most New Zealanders with any intelligence, I take people as I find them.'

'And how do you find me?'

Something about the way he spoke sent slow shivers along her spine, summoned that suffocating, terrifying intensity. Prosaically she said, 'A pleasant, interesting man.'

'Liar,' he said uncompromisingly. 'You find me a damned nuisance, just as much a nuisance as I find you. And you're every bit as aware of me as I am of you. The moment I walked into that pretty, comfortable, affluent house and saw you, tall and exquisite and profoundly, completely disturbing, I knew I wasn't going to find it easy to forget you.'

The startled breath stopped in her lungs; she sat very still, because he'd dragged her reluctant, inconvenient response to him from behind the barriers of her will and her self-discipline, and mercilessly displayed it in all its sullen power.

After swallowing to ease her dry throat, she said huskily, 'Of course I found you attractive. I'm sure most women do.'

'I'm not interested in most women.'

Gerry's heart lifted, soared, expanded. Ruthlessly she quelled the shafting pleasure, the slow, exquisitely keen delight at his admission that he wanted her with something like the basic, undiluted hunger that prowled through her veins.

But she couldn't allow it to mean anything. She said, 'I don't think now is a good time to be discussing this.'

'Look at me.' The words were growled as though compelled, as though they'd escaped the cage of his self-control.

Caught unawares, Gerry lifted her lashes. A muscle flicked in his autocratic jaw, and the beautiful sculpture of his mouth was compressed. But it was his eyes that held her captive, the pure green flames so bright her heart jumped in involuntary, automatic response. For a tense, stretched moment they rested with harsh hunger on her mouth.

And then he broke contact and said roughly, 'I agree. It's the wrong time. But it's not going to go away, Geraldine, and one day we're going to have to deal with it.'

Struggling to regain command of her emotions, she said in her most composed, most off-putting voice, 'Possibly. In the meantime, forgive me if I point out that while I tidy up here, you could employ your time better by trying to find out exactly what has gone wrong with your boat.'

He laughed and got to his feet, towering over her. 'Of course,' he said, and left the cabin.

Half an hour later she pulled the bed straight and stood up, frowning through the window. The dishes were washed and stacked away in their incredibly well-organised storage. She'd firmly resisted the urge to explore more of the kitchen. Her cabin was tidy. The bathroom had been cleaned. She didn't know what was behind the door into the other stateroom, and she wasn't looking.

So what could she do now? Apart from fret, of course.

Consciously, with considerable effort, she relaxed her facial muscles, drew in a couple of long, reviving breaths, and coaxed every tense muscle in her body to loosen.

Only when she was sure she had her face under control did she walk through the luxurious main cabin and up the short flight of stairs.

Bryn had pulled off a panel and was staring at a bewildering series of switches and wires. Although he didn't show any signs of knowing she was there, she wasn't surprised when he said shortly, 'Sometimes I think the old-fashioned ways were the best. I could probably do something about a simple engine failure.'

His tone made it obvious that it galled him to have to

admit to ignorance. In spite of her frustration, Gerry hid a smile. 'Complexity—the curse of the modern world,' she said.

Clearly he wasn't going to allude to that tense exchange over the breakfast table; it hurt that he could dismiss it so lightly and easily.

'Don't humour me,' he said abruptly, and pushed the panel back into place, screwing it on with swift, deft movements. When it was done he looked up, green eyes speculative. 'Well, Geraldine, what would you like to do? You'll get bored just sitting on the boat.'

'It depends how long we stay here,' she said coolly, not responding to the overt challenge. She looked across at a life preserver; written in red on it was the name *Starchaser*, and under it 'Auckland New Zealand', for its port of registration. 'It's a lovely boat,' she said kindly.

Bryn laughed at her. 'Thank you. Do you want to go ashore?'

The sun was too high in the sky, beating down with an intensity that warned of greater heat to come. 'Not just yet,' she said politely. 'There doesn't look to be much shelter there. I'd sooner stay on board until it cools down.'

'Then I'll show you the library.'

The books, kept in a locker in the main cabin, were an eclectic collection, ranging through biographies to solid tomes about politics and economic theory. Not a lot of fiction, she noted, and—apart from a couple of intimidating paperbacks probably left behind by guests—nothing that could be termed light. Or even medium weight.

'It doesn't look as though you read for entertainment,' she observed.

He gave her a shark's grin. 'I don't have time. I'm sorry there's nothing frothy there.'

'That,' she returned sweetly, 'sounds almost patronising, although I'm sure you didn't mean it to.'

'Sorry.'

She didn't think he was, but at least she hoped he

wouldn't make any more cracks like that. 'Readers of froth are not invariably dumb. People who like to read—real readers—usually enjoy variety in their books, and froth has its place,' she said acidly. Just to show that she wasn't impressed by his outmoded attitude, she added, 'Stereotyping is the refuge of the unreasonable.'

A swift flare of emotion in the clear green eyes startled her. 'You're the first person to ever accuse me of being unreasonable,' he said, the latent hardness in his voice very close to the surface.

'Power can isolate people.' Rather proud of the crisp mockery that ran beneath her statement, she picked up a book and pretended to read the blurb.

The written words made no sense, because Bryn was deliberately surveying her face, the enigmatic gaze scanning from her delicately pointed chin to the black lashes hiding her eyes before returning to—and lingering on—her mouth. Something untamed and fierce flamed through every cell in Gerry's body, but she bore his scrutiny without flinching. Yet that forbidden joy, that eager excitement, burst through the confines of her common sense once more.

'So can outrageous beauty,' he said.

Gerry knew that men found her desirable, and other women envied her the accident of heritage that gave her a face fitting the standards of her age. She had turned enough compliments, refused enough propositions, ignored enough gallantries, to respond with some sophistication.

Now, however, imprisoned in the glittering intensity of Bryn's gaze, her breath shortened and her heart picked up speed, and—more treasonable than either of those—heat poured through her, swift and sweet and passionate, setting her alight.

He recognised it. Harshly he said, 'I'm no more immune than any other man to the promise of a soft mouth and eyes the blue-green of a Pacific pearl, skin like sleek satin and a body that would set hormones surging through stone. If you want a quick affair, Geraldine, over as soon as we leave here, I'll be more than happy to oblige you, but don't go getting ideas that it's going to last, because it won't.'

Unable to hide her flinch, or the evidence of fading colour and flickering lashes, she kept her head high. 'No, that's not what I want, and you know it,' she said. 'I don't do one-night stands.'

CHAPTER SEVEN

BRYN'S eyes darkened and held hers for a fraught, charged moment before he said in a voice that betrayed no emotions, 'Good. It makes things much cleaner.'

He turned, and as though released from a perilous enchantment Gerry picked up a book and walked across to the stairs, hoping her erect back and straight shoulders minimised the visible effects of that excoriating exchange.

Anger swelled slow and sullen; Gerry, who hadn't lost her temper for years, had to exert her utmost will to rein it in. Because although Bryn had been unnecessarily brutal, he'd seen a danger and scotched it, and one day she'd be relieved by his cold pragmatism.

The last thing she wanted was to fall in love—or even in lust—with this man. Bryn Falconer wasn't the sort of lover a woman would get over quickly; indeed, Gerry suspected that if she let down her guard he'd take up residence in her heart, and she'd never be able to cut herself free from the turbulent alchemy of his masculinity.

And that would be ironic indeed, because by her twenty-fourth birthday she'd given up hope of finding a lasting love, one that would echo down the years.

Retreating to the shade of the canvas shelter he'd rigged over the cockpit, she sat down—back stiff, shoulders held in severe restraint, knees straight, ankles crossed—and pretended to read. The words danced dizzily, and eventually she allowed her thoughts free rein.

How many times had she thought herself in love, only to endure the death of that lovely excitement, the golden glow, with bitter resignation? At twenty-three, after breaking her engagement to a man who was perfect for her, she'd realised she was tainted by her mother's curse. After that she'd kept men at a distance. Her mother's endless search, the pain she'd caused her husbands and her children, had been a grim example, one Gerry had no intention of following.

In spite of the intensity of her infatuation for Bryn, it would die.

And she was happy with her life, apart from her dissatisfaction with her career. She loved her friends and cousins, loved their children, was loved and valued by them.

Movement from the main cabin, and the sharp click of a closing door, indicated that Bryn had gone into his stateroom; Gerry wondered why he'd slept on the sofa the previous night. Had he wanted to know when she woke so that he could tell her of their situation? A treacherous warmth invaded her heart.

He emerged almost immediately and came into the cockpit. Gerry pretended to be deep in the pages of her book, but beneath her lowered lashes her eyes followed him as he went up the stairs to the flybridge.

She could hear him moving about up there, and to block out the graphic images that invaded her mind she concentrated on reading. At first her eyes merely skipped across the pages, but eventually the written word worked its magic on her and she became lost in the book, an account of a worldwide scam that had ruined thousands of lives.

'Interesting?' Some time later Bryn's voice dragged her away from the machinations of the principal characters.

Frowning, she put the book down. 'Fascinating,' she said levelly. 'One wonders how on earth criminals can ignore the agonies of the people whose lives they're shattering.'

'One does indeed,' he said, his voice almost indifferent. 'One also gathers that you hate being interrupted when you're reading.'

Colour heated her skin. Irritated with herself for being rude enough to reveal her annoyance, and with him for being astute enough to pick it up, she said wryly, 'I do, but there's no excuse for snarling. I'm sorry.'

'I like your honesty,' he surprised her by saying, 'and you didn't snarl—you have beautiful manners which you use like a shield. When you're angry you hide behind them, and then you retreat.'

Shocked, she stared at him and felt heat flame across her cheekbones. 'Well, that's put me well and truly in my place,' she said uncertainly.

He gave her that narrow-eyed, sexy smile. 'I didn't intend to do that,' he said. 'Just a clumsy attempt to analyse what it is about you I find so intriguing. If you need anything in the next half hour or so, call out. I'm going to have a look at the engine to see if there's anything I can do.'

And he turned and went below.

Determinedly Gerry returned to her book; determinedly she followed the twists and turns of the scam, the links with drug lords, the whole filthy odyssey from genteel white-collar crime to dealing in sex and slavery and obsession. Yet as she read she was acutely aware of Bryn's movements, of the gentle swaying of the deck beneath her as he walked around below. When, some time later, he arrived in the doorway, every sense sprang into full alert.

'You'd better have something to drink,' he said. 'It's easy to dehydrate in this heat.'

Reluctantly she uncurled from the chair and followed him into the cabin. 'I'll make a pot of tea. How are we off for water?'

'There's enough if you don't spend hours in the shower.'

'No more than three minutes at a time, I promise.'

'Good.' His unsmiling look lifted the hairs on the back of her neck. 'Are you enjoying the book?'

'Not exactly *enjoying*. It's absolutely appalling, but riveting.'

He began to discuss it as though he assumed she had the intelligence to understand the complicated financial manoeuvring. So he didn't entirely think she was a flippant, flighty halfwit. And she shouldn't be comforted by this thought.

After they'd drunk the tea Bryn disappeared once more into the bowels of the boat, presumably to see whether he could find anything there that had failed. Freed from the driving necessity to appear calm, Gerry fretted about Maddie, hoping to heaven the girl was recovering, wishing that she'd seen what the problem was.

Maddie had come back from New York saying that she needed to take time to reconsider her life. Perhaps she had been trying to kick a drug habit; if only she'd said something about it, they could have helped.

It was utterly wicked that all that youth and intelligence and promise could be wiped out in the sick desire for a drug! Gerry didn't normally worry about things she couldn't change; over the years she'd learned to cultivate a practical, serene outlook. Now, however, she sat stewing until Bryn reappeared.

Her attempt to reimpose some sort of control over her features failed, for after one swift, hard glance he demanded abruptly, 'What's the matter?'

Trust him to notice. 'You mean apart from being stranded?' She relaxed her brows into their normal unconcerned arch.

'Don't worry, someone will find us soon.'

'But first they have to miss us.'

'I assume that will happen as soon as you don't arrive back in New Zealand.' He spoke patiently, as though they hadn't already had this conversation.

Gerry bit her lip. 'Of course it will. I'm sorry, I'm not helping the situation.'

Cara would begin to worry by evening. No doubt she'd ring the airline; they'd have noticed that Gerry hadn't arrived for the flight Bryn had booked for her, and as soon as they contacted the hotel on Longopai they'd realise what had happened. They'd have search parties out by tomorrow morning at the latest.

Which wouldn't be too late, if Jill, Maddie's booker, had managed to contact the ad agency...

Bryn said, 'Of course you're concerned, but you're in no danger.'

Taking refuge behind her sunglasses, Gerry gave him a collected smile. 'I know,' she said obligingly.

He'd noticed the hint of satire in her tone because his mouth tightened fractionally, but he didn't comment.

They ate lunch—a light meal of salad and fruit, and crusty bread he must have swiped from the hotel kitchen— and then Gerry tried to ease the tension that had gathered in a knot in her chest by retiring to her cabin to rest through the heat of the afternoon.

To her astonishment she slept, not waking until the sun had dipped down towards the horizon. After washing her face she combed her hair into order, pinning it back behind her ears to give her a more severe, untouchable look, then reapplied her make-up.

The main cabin was empty, but a glance up the stairs revealed Bryn standing beside the railings. Something about his stance made her skin prickle; he looked aggressive, all angles and bigness and strength.

She thought she moved as silently as he did, but his head whipped around before she'd come through the door. He surveyed her with eyes half-hidden by thick lashes.

'Good sleep?' he asked.

'Great.' She walked across to the side of the craft, stopping a few feet away from him to peer down through the crystal water. A battalion of tiny fish cast wavering shadows on the white sand beneath them. 'No signs of any rescuers?'

'No.'

Still staring at the pellucid depths, she said casually, 'So we sit and wait.'

'Basically, yes.' He sounded aloof, almost dismissive. 'I'm taking the dinghy onto the island. Want to come?'

'I'd love to. I'll just go and get my hat.'

After anchoring it to her head with a scarf around the brim she rejoined him, sunglasses hiding her eyes, her armour in place. Although he didn't look at her long, bare legs as she got into the dinghy, as she sat down on the seat she wondered uneasily whether she should have put on a pair of trousers.

Awareness was an odd thing; both of them kept it under iron control, but no doubt he could sense the response that crackled through her, just as she knew that he was acutely conscious of her, that those green eyes had noticed her feeble attempts at protection.

He moved a vicious machete well away from her feet, and began to row the inflatable across the warm blue waters of the lagoon.

'Don't tell me there's anything dangerous on the island,' she commented brightly, trying to ignore the steady, rhythmic bunching of muscles, the smooth, sure strokes, the purposeful male power that sent the small craft surging through the water.

'Not a thing. This is a foraging expedition. Note the bag to put coconuts into.'

'I thought you had an outboard motor for this dinghy?' she asked, more to keep her thoughts away from his virile energy than because she wanted to know.

'I'd rather not use it. It's unlikely, but we might need it.'

If they weren't rescued. Chilled, she nodded.

The inflatable scraped along the sand as they reached the beach. Hiding her sharp spurt of alarm with a frown, Gerry waited until the craft had come to a halt, then stepped out into water the texture of warm silk and helped Bryn haul the dinghy out of the reach of the waves. He didn't need her strength, but it gave her a highly suspect pleasure to do this with him.

Looking around, she asked, 'Do we really need coconuts?'

'Not now.' His voice was cool and judicial. 'But we

might if we don't get rescued straight away. I believe in minimising risks, so we'll drink as much coconut milk as we can bear and save the water.'

Gerry believed in minimising risks too, but at the moment all she could think of was the possibility of him falling. 'Do you know how to get up there?'

'Yes.' He gave her a brief, blinding smile. 'Don't worry, I spent a lot of time climbing coconut palms when I was a kid.'

'I didn't spend any time splinting broken limbs—as a kid or when I grew up—so you be careful,' she told him briskly.

He laughed. 'It's amazing what you can do if you have to. I could probably splint my own if it comes to that, but it won't. Don't watch.'

She should go for a walk around the island—she knew that he wouldn't do anything unless he was convinced he could. But she said, 'And miss something? Never!'

'You'd better get into the shade then.'

Retreating into the welcome coolness of the sparse undergrowth, she watched as he looped a rope around a palm bole. He certainly seemed to know what he was doing. With an economy of movement that didn't surprise her, he used the loop of rope to support him while he made his way rapidly to the tufted crown of the palm.

He was back on the ground in a very short time, nuts in a bag he'd tied around his shoulders, not even breathing heavily.

Gerry strolled across and eyed them as he dumped them in the shade. 'Now all we have to do is catch some fish and we'll really be living naturally.'

His brow lifted. 'We?'

She grinned. 'Normally I'd be squeamish,' she admitted, 'but when it comes to a matter of life and death I'm prepared to do my bit. And it's all right to kill something if you actually use it.'

'Well, that makes living on a desert island much easier,'

he said, not trying to hide the slightly caustic note in his voice. 'But we won't catch much at this time of the day. Wait until the evening. Do you want to walk around the island?'

'Yes, I'd like that.'

He smiled at her, his eyes translucent in their dark frame of lashes. 'Let's go,' he said.

The island was tiny, a dot of sand in a maze of reefs and other islets, all with their crown of palms, all too small and lacking in food and water to have permanent settlers. 'But the people from Longopai come down in the season to fish and collect coconuts,' Bryn told her. 'I've been here often. That's how I knew how to get in last night.'

Gerry looked respectfully at the reef. 'We were lucky,' she said. 'Are coconuts native to the Pacific?'

'No one knows, although most authorities believe they came from Asia. The palm's certainly colonised the tropics; in fact, if it hadn't, these islands of the Pacific could never have been settled. The Polynesians and Micronesians would have died of starvation before they reached any of the high islands where they could grow other foods. Coconuts and fish; that's what the Pacific was founded on. And that's what many live on still.'

'But it's no longer enough,' she said, thinking of the islanders who needed the money from the hats they exported to provide for their children's education.

'It never was—why do you think the Polynesians became the world's greatest explorers? But the islanders certainly want more than any atoll can provide now.'

Gerry looked around at the huge immensity of sea and sky. 'And that's unfortunate?'

He shrugged. 'No, it's merely a fact of life. The world is going to change whether I agree with it or not. Anyway, I'm glad I live now. We have great challenges, but great advantages as well.'

They walked across the thick, blinding sand, talking of the scattered island nations of the Pacific and their problems: the threat of a rising sea level, desperate attempts to balance the disruptive effects of tourism, the almost empty exchequers of many of the little countries.

It took less than twenty minutes to circle the islet. As Bryn hefted the coconuts onto his shoulder, Gerry eyed the cruiser, so big and graceful in the lagoon, and smiled ironically at its impotence.

'"How are the mighty fallen",' she quoted. 'If *Starchaser* had been a yacht we could have sailed it to Fala'isi. As it is, until it's fixed it's just a splendid piece of junk.'

'It provides us with shelter, and gas for cooking,' he said.

'True, but I'm sure you'd have been able to make some sort of shelter here on the atoll. And build a fire for cooking.'

One brow shot up. 'Yearning for the romance of a desert island?' he asked derisively. 'You wouldn't like it, Geraldine. There's no water, and you'd hate getting dirty and sweaty and hot.'

'I could do what the islanders do, and swim,' she pointed out crisply. 'You're not a romantic.'

'Not in the least.'

When he stooped to pull the little craft into the water she grabbed a loop of rope and yanked too.

'I can do it,' he said.

Strangely hurt, she stood aside until the dinghy bobbed on the surface.

'In you get,' Bryn told her. He waited until she was seated before heaving the inflatable further out into the water. Without fuss he got in himself, picked up the oars and sent the dinghy shooting through the calm, warm lagoon. 'I've lived on atolls like this and it's a lot of hard work. At least on the boat I can pump water up from the tanks manually, and we don't have to find timber for a fire every day.'

Gerry nodded. She should, she thought, looking back at the palms bending towards their reflections, be still worried sick, struggling to get back to New Zealand. But although one part of her remained anxious and alarmed, the other, seditious and unsuspecting, was more than content to be stranded in the sultry, lazy ambience of the tropics, safe with Bryn.

And that should be setting off sirens all through her, because Bryn Falconer was far from safe. Oh, he'd look after her all right, but his very competence was a threat.

In spite of that secret yearning for a soul-mate, common sense warned that loving a man as naturally dominant as Bryn would not be a peaceful experience, however seductive the lure. Her glance flashed back to Bryn's harsh-featured face and lingered for several heart-shaking moments on the subtle moulding of his mouth before returning to the shimmering, glinting, scalloped waves.

The lure, she admitted reluctantly, was *very* seductive. A forbidden hunger rose in her; she had to spurn the impulse to lean across and wipe the trickle of sweat from his temple, let her fingers tarry against the fine-grained golden skin and smooth through the tawny hair...

In other words, and let's be frank here, she told herself grimly as she swallowed to ease her parched mouth and throat, you want him.

So powerfully she could taste the need and the desire with every breath she took. This was something she couldn't control, a primeval gut-response, lust on a cellular level.

She'd fallen in love before, only to have time prove how false her emotions had been. It would happen again.

And yet—and yet there *was* a difference between the way she'd felt with other men, and the way Bryn affected her. This couldn't be curbed by will or determination; it had its own momentum, and, although she could leash any expression of it, she couldn't stifle the essential wildness of passion.

It would have been easier to deal with if he'd been Cara's lover. Oh, she'd still want him like this—no holds barred,

a violent, simple matter of like calling to like—but she'd
have an excellent reason for not acting on that hunger.

A gentle bump dragged her mind back from its racing
thoughts to the fact that they'd reached the cruiser again.
The long, corded muscles in Bryn's arms flexed as he held
the dinghy in place while Gerry got shakily to her feet and
climbed the steps into the cockpit.

'Catch,' he said, throwing her the rope before coming up
after her, lean and big enough to block the sun.

'Give me the painter,' he commanded.

Handing the rope over, she drawled, 'Painter? Why not
call it a rope, for heaven's sake?'

'Because that's not its name.'

She watched carefully as he wound the rope around the
cleat. 'It doesn't look very safe,' she said, her voice sharp-
edged because she hated the way he made her feel—like a
snail suddenly dragged from its shell, naked and exposed.
'Shouldn't you do an interesting knot—a sheepshank, or a
Turk's Head, or something Boy Scouts do?'

'Trust me,' he said on a hard note, 'it'll keep the dinghy
tied on.'

'I trust you.' She turned towards the steps down to the
cabin and asked over her shoulder, 'Do you want anything
to drink? Tea? Coffee?'

'Something cold,' he said. 'Check out the fridge.'

His retreat into detachment was a good thing—on the
boat there was little hope of avoiding each other.

Yet it stung.

Telling herself not to be a fool, Gerry extracted glasses
from their cupboard—as cleverly constructed as everything
else on the boat, so that even in the worst seas nothing
would break—and poured lime juice over ice before carrying them up to the cockpit. Bryn was staring at the horizon, watchful green eyes unreadable beneath the dark
brows.

'Here,' she said, offering the glass.

He turned abruptly and took it, careful not to let his fingers touch hers, and drank it down. 'Thanks,' he said, handing over the glass without looking at her.

Rebuffed, Gerry went back to the kitchen and drank her juice there.

Let someone find them soon, she prayed, before she did something stupid like letting Bryn see just how much she wanted him.

CHAPTER EIGHT

To HER relief they spent the rest of the day at a polite distance. While Bryn poked about the internal regions of the boat, Gerry wondered about washing her clothes, finally deciding against it. She didn't know how much water the tanks held, and she had enough clean underwear for three days. They certainly wouldn't take long to dry in the minuscule bathroom.

The afternoon sun poured relentlessly in through the cabin windows. Although she opened them, in the hope of fresh air, eventually the heat drove her into the cockpit where, still hot under the awning, she read, keeping her attention pinned very firmly to the printed page.

Towards sunset Bryn got out fishing lines from lockers in the cockpit.

Looking up, Gerry asked, 'Can I help?'

'No, I'll take the dinghy out into the centre of the lagoon.'

He didn't ask her to go with him, and she didn't offer. In the rapidly fading light Gerry kept her eyes on the western sky, watching the sun silkscreen it into a glory of gold and red and orange, until with a suddenness that startled her the great smoky ball hurtled beneath the horizon. As the last sliver disappeared a ray of green light—the colour of Bryn's eyes—stabbed the air, a vivid, astonishing flash that lasted only a second before dusk swept across the huge immensity of sky, obliterating all colour, cloaking everything in heated velvet darkness.

Gerry stared into the dense nothingness until her eyes adjusted to the lack of light. A few hundred metres away she could see the outline of the dinghy with Bryn in it—

patient, predatory, still—and was amazed by her sudden atavistic fear at the contrast between that stillness and his usual vital energy. A moment later she detected a swift movement, and shortly afterwards the dinghy headed back towards the cruiser.

Determined not to spend the rest of the evening in the same silence as the afternoon, Gerry met him with a smile. 'And what, oh mighty hunter, did you catch?'

He laughed shortly. 'A careless fish.'

She'd expected a whole fish, but he'd already filleted and scaled it. 'Will it be all right fried?' she asked.

'Unless you have more exotic ways of dealing with it.'

'I'm your basic cook—and that's probably overstating the case—so I'll stick to the tried and true,' she said, adding with a hint of mischief, 'Of course, you could cook it.'

His eyes gleamed in the starlight. 'I think the traditional division of duties is that I catch and kill, you cook.'

'You Tarzan, me Jane,' she said, laughing. 'That went out with the fifties.'

'Not entirely.'

'In any civilised country,' she retorted, heading down the companionway and thence into the kitchen. Perhaps she should try to think of it as the galley. You're getting used to this lazy life out of life, she warned herself severely. Be careful, Gerry.

'We're not in a civilised country here,' he said, following her.

'So it's lucky that I'm quite happy to cook,' she parried, aware of something else running through the conversation, a hidden current of provocation, of advance and retreat, of unspoken challenge.

Too dangerous.

She made the mistake of looking up at him. He was smiling, a mirthless, fierce smile that didn't soften his face at all.

Gerry's heart gave a wild thump; without volition she took a step backwards, and although she held her head high and kept her gaze steady she knew he'd seen and noted that moment of weakness.

'*Can* you cook it?' he asked, lounging against the bar that separated the galley from the main cabin.

She took the fish and slid it onto a plate and into the fridge. 'I'll manage,' she said evenly.

'Then I'll leave you to get on with it.'

Gerry's breath came soundlessly through her lips as he straightened up and walked towards his cabin. 'Damned arrogant man,' she muttered as she pulled out a tin of coconut cream. She didn't like arrogance; both the men she'd thought she'd loved had been kind and pleasant and intelligent and tolerant.

Nothing like Bryn Falconer.

Banishing him from her mind, she wondered whether perhaps she should use the coconut he'd got that day. Except that she didn't know how you turned the milk in it into the cream you bought in tins—suitable for delicious oriental-style sauces that were especially suitable for fish.

'Give me modern conveniences every time,' she muttered as she found the tin opener in its special slot in a drawer.

Bryn emerged as she was lowering the floured fish fillets into the big frying pan. Through the delicate sizzle she heard him close the door; she didn't look over her shoulder, but as he went past she thought she smelt his clean, just-washed fragrance.

'Would you like some wine?' he asked.

Then she did look up, and once more her heart lurched. He'd changed into a short-sleeved shirt and fine cotton trousers. Lean-hipped, long-legged, he moved with a smooth grace that pulled at her senses.

'Yes, thank you,' she said simply. Keep it light, her common sense warned her. Pretend that this is just another man, just another occasion.

He reached into what she'd assumed to be another cupboard. It was a bar fridge, from which he pulled out a bottle of wine. Once more everything was stored so carefully that it was safe whatever the height of the waves.

'All mod cons on this boat,' she teased as he removed the cork in one deft movement and poured the subtly coloured, gold-green vintage into two elegant glasses. 'It's more luxurious than my house.'

He picked up a glass, set it down close to her. 'Even you,' he said calmly, 'must know that boats are referred to as women, so she's she, not it.'

'All these funny traditions! Why?'

'Perhaps because they're inherently beautiful,' he said, his voice a blend of whisky and cream, of honey and dark, potent magic. 'And dangerous. And therefore profoundly attractive to men.'

Gerry turned the fillets of fish with great care before she could trust herself to answer. Picking up the glass of wine, she lifted it to her lips and took a small, desperate sip. Then she set it down and allowed herself a smile, although it felt cold and stiff on her lips. 'An interesting theory,' she said lightly, dismissively, 'but I think it's just part of the desire to confuse the uninitiated—which is why the kitchen is a galley and a rope is a painter. It's jargon, and it connects people with the same interests so that they can feel part of a common brotherhood, shutting others out.'

'Feeling lost and alone, Geraldine?'

Ashamed at the snap in her words, she shrugged. 'I suppose I am.'

'Don't you trust me to look after you?' A steely thread of mockery ran beneath the words.

She bit her lip. 'Of course I do,' she said, keeping her voice steady.

'Then it must be the situation back in Auckland.'

Shocked by the strength of her temptation to tell him all about it, she poked gingerly at the fish fillets. Bryn was a hard man, and sometimes she could kick him, but he would know how to deal with almost anything that came his way. However, the problem wasn't hers to tell. Maddie had a future—Gerry refused to believe otherwise—and the fewer people who knew about her addiction the better.

Even though Cara would probably tell Bryn once they got back to Auckland.

No, not if she was asked not to. Cara was young, and she could be foolish, but she was trustworthy.

'Partly,' Gerry said coolly, 'but there's nothing I can do about that so I'm trying not to worry. Besides, Honor McKenzie, my partner, is probably back by now and dealing with it.'

'A very pragmatic attitude.'

'My father was big on being sensible.'

'If I had a daughter who looked like you I'd do my best to bring her up to be sensible,' Bryn agreed lazily.

Yet James Dacre had worked himself into the grave saving a business that had been run into the ground by a greedy manager, who'd then decamped into the unknown with everything James had spent his lifetime building. He hadn't been sensible, but he'd been honourable.

Tight-lipped, Gerry said, 'He was a man who believed in responsibility.'

'I know.'

Gerry pulled the frying pan from the gas ring and lifted each perfect, golden piece onto a plate, warm from the oven. Picking up the plates and heading towards the table, which she'd set while Bryn was showering, she said, 'He paid back every last dollar the firm owed before he died.'

He carried a bowl of pasta salad across to the table. 'Leaving you with nothing.'

If he'd sounded curious, or even sympathetic, she'd have been short with him, but his voice revealed nothing more than a cool impersonality. 'That wasn't important,' she said crisply as she set the plates down. 'I can make my own way. But it'll be a cold day in hell before I forgive the man who sent my father to an early grave. I just wish I knew where he is now.'

Bryn's enigmatic glance lingered on her angry face. 'Do you have a taste for vengeance?'

She sat down. After a moment she said flatly, 'No. I'd like to, because nothing would give me greater pleasure than to see the man who killed my father in exactly the same situation—sick, tired, so exhausted that in the end nothing mattered any more. Dad used to say that eventually you reap what you sow. He didn't, but it gives me some comfort to believe that of the man who drove him to his death.'

'Eat up,' Bryn said, his voice unexpectedly gentle.

Obeying, Gerry was eventually able to taste the food she'd prepared. She finished her glass of wine a little more quickly than was wise, so refused another, and was oddly pleased when Bryn only drank one too.

Over the meal they spoke of impersonal things; Bryn's attitude reminded her of the day they'd met. He'd been gentle then too, holding the baby with strength and security and comfort. He'd be a good father.

What would he be like as a husband?

'That's an odd smile,' he said idly.

'I was hoping that the baby is all right.'

'Unfortunately that's all you can do—hope.' He'd helped her clean up and wash the dishes, then banished her while he made coffee. Now he came from behind the bar and handed her a cup and saucer. 'What made you think of her?'

'I don't know.' She put the coffee down on the table in front of her and frowned. 'Bryn, why on earth should everything die on the boat? Surely the communications and the engine don't work off the same systems?'

'No.'

He sat down beside her, alarming her. She could cope when he was opposite her—she was fine with the table between them, or a metre or so of space. But the sofa seemed very small suddenly, and his closeness stifled every ounce of common sense. Swallowing unobtrusively, she sat up straighter, trying to keep her eyes on the steam that swirled up from her coffee.

'Occasionally kids from Longopai get into the *Starchaser*,' he said. 'I can't say it was definitely them, but someone removed most of the diesel; that same someone left the communications system on so that the batteries are completely drained.'

'I'm surprised you're not furious,' she said, ironing out the husky note in her tone into a somewhat clipped curtness.

His crystalline gaze flicked across her face and his smile sizzled right through her. It was, she thought, as elemental as a force of nature. Did he know its effect on susceptible women?

Almost certainly. He was too intelligent not to.

'I can remember what I was like at ten,' he said, wry laughter in his words. 'All devilry and flash, keen to see how things worked; I'd have examined *Starchaser* from bow to stern, from propeller to aerial, and I'd probably have drained the battery as well.'

'And stolen the diesel?' she asked.

He shrugged. 'You know as well as I do that to Polynesians what belongs to a brother belongs to you, and on Longopai I'm everyone's brother. Someone needed it. They'll replace it. If we hadn't had to get away so quickly I'd have been told there wasn't enough fuel to get me to Fala'isi.' Unsmiling, he added, 'In fact, they're probably out looking for us now.'

God, Gerry thought, drinking her coffee too fast, I hope they find us first thing tomorrow.

He asked suddenly, 'What have you done to your finger?'

'Cut it while I was chopping the onions. It's nothing.'

He held out an imperative hand. 'Let me see.'

While she hesitated he took her hand and turned it over, examining the small cut with frowning eyes. 'It looks deep.'

'It's fine,' she said quickly, tugging away.

To no avail. Bryn ran the tip of a finger across the cut and then, without pausing, down and across her palm. The touch that had been comforting changed in a few short centimetres to wildly sensuous.

He must have heard the sharp, indrawn breath she couldn't control, but he lifted her hand to his mouth and kissed the small cut, and the palm of her hand before saying harshly, 'I'll get some antiseptic. Cuts can become badly infected in the tropics.'

Numbly, fingers curling, she watched him head towards a drawer. The place he'd kissed burned, echoing the fire that swept through her blood.

He took a tube from the drawer and tossed it to her with the curt command, 'Rub it well in, and put it on several times a day.'

Eagerly Gerry bent her head and unscrewed the cap, and smoothed the pale ointment onto her finger.

It stung a little, but she ignored the pain to babble into the tense silence, 'It's nice that you're still so close to the islanders you grew up with. I have a vast number of cousins, but I always wanted real brothers and sisters.'

'Don't you have two brothers?'

'Half-brothers,' she said. 'From different fathers—one in America, one in France. I've met them occasionally, and we have nothing in common. My father did his best to turn me into a lady, but I'd have liked brothers to be mischievous with.'

'You have enough of an advantage now,' he said harshly.

Startled, she looked up, into eyes as unfathomable as the wide ocean. Her breath came quickly. 'I don't know what you mean,' she said stupidly.

'I think you do,' he said, irony underscoring each word. 'You know how you affect men. The first time I saw you I thought you were a dark-eyed witch—half-devil, half-angel, all woman—with a smile that promised the delights of paradise. And then I realised that your eyes are a fascinating, smoky mixture of blue's innocence and green's provocation, and I was lost...'

Spellbound by the gathering passion that roughened his voice, she let him pull her up and into his arms. She had known he was strong—now she felt that strength, the virile force and power, and her immediate, ardent response sang through her like a love song as Bryn's mouth found her lashes and kissed them down, traced the high sweep of each cheekbone, the square chin. Bryn's scent—fresh, fiercely male—filled her nostrils, and his mouth on her skin was heaven, gentle and powerful and agonising. Dazed, she heard her own wordless murmur as she lifted her face in supplication.

Yet he didn't take the gift so freely offered. Instead his lips found the pulse-point beneath her ears, the soft, vulnerable throbbing in her throat, and each time he touched her fire licked through her veins.

It stunned her with its heat, with its intensity. The only point of contact was his mouth, a slow, potent pledge of rapture against her waiting, welcoming skin. It was insulting, this deliberate display of control when Gerry was rapidly losing the ragged threads of hers. Harried by desperation, she wanted to feel his hands on her—had been wanting that ever since she'd met him, even though she'd believed he was Cara's lover.

For a moment she held back, remembering that she should be worrying about Maddie, and then he kissed the corner of her mouth, tormenting her with a promise of passion, a compulsion of desire such as she'd never experienced before.

She didn't hear his laugh; she felt it, a quick brush of air against her skin, a recognition that he knew what he was doing to her. Splintered by a sudden, dangerous fury, she forced her heavy lids upwards and clenched her hands on his arms.

'Wait,' she commanded.

'Why?' he asked, narrowed eyes green diamonds set in thick black lashes. A smile curled the ruthless mouth.

Swift shock ran the length of Gerry's spine, but she tried again. 'Stop teasing me,' she said, hearing the helpless, hopeless note of need in her voice.

'How am I teasing you?'

Still angry, she reached up and kissed him boldly on his taunting, beautiful mouth.

She wanted to pull back immediately, to show him that she wasn't completely mesmerised, but it was too late. When her lips met his he laughed again and crushed her to him, strong hands moulding her against his body, his mouth ravishing every thought from her brain.

It was like being taken over, she thought just before she succumbed to the hunger that had been building in her ever since she'd looked over a baby's downy head and met his eyes.

He no longer kept up the farce of gentleness, of tenderness. He kissed her with the driving determination of a man who had finally slipped the leash of his will-power and allowed his desire free rein. Gerry's curbed hunger exploded, overwhelming every warning, every ounce of common sense her father had tried to drum into her.

With molten urgency she returned Bryn's kiss. Her pulses galloped as he lifted her and sat down on the sofa with her in his arms, and without taking his mouth from hers pulled her across his knees and slid his hand beneath the wrap-around front of her blouse, fingers cupping her breast.

Sensation rocketed through her. Her mouth opened and he took swift advantage, thrusting deep in a blatant simulation of the embrace both of them knew was coming. Gerry twisted under the remorseless lash of desire; every sense was overloaded. Bryn's experienced caress was transformed into an unbearably stimulating friction that smashed through the remaining fragile barriers of her will.

His taste was pure male, exotic, stimulating, his arms a

welcome, longed-for prison, the surface texture of his chest exquisitely erotic to the tips of her fingers as she unsteadily pulled the buttons of his shirt free and ran her hand across the heated skin below.

Gerry felt his shudder like a benediction.

'Yes, you like that,' he said, lifting his head so that the words touched her lips, to be drunk in without too much attention to meaning. 'You like the power your beauty gives you, the way men respond to the primitive allure beneath that sophisticated, glossy outer appearance. I'm just like all the rest, Geraldine—I want you. But what do you want? Because if this keeps on for much longer I'm not going to be able to stop.'

She lifted weighted eyelids, met the blazing green of his eyes with a slow smile. 'You,' she said, and because her voice shook, she tried again. 'I want you.'

Something perilously close to satisfaction flared in his eyes. 'Good.'

Her lashes drifted down, but instead of kissing her eager mouth he shocked her by pushing back the lapel of her shirt and kissing the soft skin his hand so possessively caressed.

Fire seared away everything but the hunger that shattered her last vestige of composure. Her legs straightened, and she stiffened, blind to everything but the savage need to take and be taken.

When his mouth closed around the tip of her breast a hoarse, low sound was torn from her throat, to be lost in the conflagration of her senses. He began to suckle and she gasped again, splaying her hands over his chest, blindly seeking satisfaction. The delicate friction of his body hair against her hot skin shivered from her fingers to the pit of her stomach.

On impulse she turned her head and sought the small male nipple and copied his actions, an intimacy she'd never offered before, never known. Under her cheek his chest wall lifted, and she heard the beat of his heart, heavy, demanding.

'Geraldine,' he muttered, his voice reverberating through her.

And when he got to his feet and carried her into her cabin she made no protest.

Stranded in the dazzling, shape-shifting haze he'd conjured around her, she lay back against the pillows and watched with unsated eyes while he tore off his shirt and the trousers she'd admired earlier. No hesitation spoiled the moment, no fear—nothing but a glowing anticipation that wrapped her in silken fur, clawed at her with primal, eager hunger.

With the light from the main cabin reflecting lovingly on Bryn's golden skin, he came down beside her and said with an odd thickness in his voice, 'I seem to have thought of nothing but this since I first saw you—lovely, elusive Geraldine, lying in my bed, waiting for me...'

Deft hands slipped her shirt from her, smoothed her shorts down. She shivered at the skill with which he undressed her, shivered again—and for a different reason—when the long fingers stroked down her legs, lingering across the smooth skin on the inside of her thighs before moving to her calves.

'Fine-boned and elegant,' he said, and found her ankles and her feet.

She had to clear her throat to say, 'I've never thought of my calves and feet as erotic zones.'

'Haven't you?' He sounded amused, and bent and kissed the high arch. As her foot curled in involuntary reaction he said in a deeper voice, 'Every part of a responsive woman is an erotic zone. If you don't know that it's high time you learned.'

She learned. Where Bryn wanted to go was where she wanted to be, and he wreaked such dark havoc with his mouth and his enormously skilled, knowledgeable hands that in a few minutes he'd proved his statement and she was begging for mercy, her body craving the consummation only he could give her.

'Not yet,' he said huskily. 'Not yet, little witch.'

In self-defence she tried to turn the tables by caressing him, but perhaps she lacked the experience, for when she had completely unravelled he was still master of himself—and of her body's responses.

By then, wild-eyed and panting, she didn't care.

'Now,' she gasped, almost sobbing as she finally pulled at his broad shoulders.

Later she would remember that they were slick with sweat, and that his eyes were hooded slivers of glittering emerald, so focused that she thought they burned wherever they rested. But at that moment she was completely at the mercy of her body's need for completion, torn by this unfamiliar passion.

In answer he came over her and entered her violent, supplicating body in one strong thrust.

Gerry gasped. He froze, the big, lithe body held in stasis. 'You should have warned me that it's been a long time for you,' he said, his voice raw with barely maintained control.

He was going to leave her. He thought he'd hurt her so he was going to abandon her to this savage, unfulfilled need.

'It's all right—it doesn't matter,' she said, her voice thready in the quiet cabin.

He said something so crude she flinched. 'It matters,' he growled. Beneath her importuning hands she felt the swift coil and bunching of muscles as he prepared to get up.

She looked up into a face stripped of everything but anger. Driven by a merciless compulsion, she fastened her arms across his broad back and offered herself to him, arching beneath him, flexing muscles she hadn't known she had, moving slowly, sensuously against him.

'No!' he commanded.

Gerry thought she'd lost, but within seconds she saw her triumph in his eyes as the anger prowling in the metallic opacity was joined by a consuming hunger, basic, white-hot.

Her heart jerked within her chest. Bryn withdrew, but only to bury himself again to the hilt in her, and as she enclosed him in her heated flesh, tightening her arms around his back to pull him down against her, he said, 'This is what you want, isn't it?'

She couldn't answer, and he demanded, 'Gerry?'

'Yes, damn you!' she shouted, twisting her hips against him.

He curled his fingers in her hair, holding her face back so that he could see it. This was not satisfaction—that was far too weak a term to use. On his face was exultation, pure and simple, and she couldn't deny him it because it was her victory too.

With deliberation, with authority and steady male power, he began to move in her. Holding his gaze, she locked her feet around his calves and returned movement for movement, passion for passion, until the knot of pleasure inside her began to unravel, sending her soaring, hurtling over some distant edge and into a world where nothing existed but she and Bryn, and the boat moving slightly, peacefully beneath them in the embrace of the Pacific.

A starburst of rapture tore a cry from her and she imploded into ecstasy, stiffening into rigidity, and then, when the exquisite savagery began to fade, responding anew to Bryn's desire.

And soon, even as the fresh nova ripped through her, she saw his head go back and a fierce, mirthless grin pull his lips into a line as he too found that place where nothing else mattered.

Like that, they lay until their breaths slowed and their hearts eased and sleep claimed them.

Much later, after she'd slept in his arms and they'd woken and made love again—love that had started slow and lazy, without the edge of unsated desire, and then exploded into incandescent passion, desperate and all-consuming—Gerry yawned, a satisfying gape that almost cracked her face in two, and eased herself free.

'Where are you going?' he asked, his voice husky.

'Bathroom,' she muttered.

'Head,' he said lazily. 'On a boat it's called the head.'

He was laughing at her, and she laughed too, and kissed the curved line of his mouth and said, 'Whatever, I need to shower. I'm sticky.' A thought struck her. 'Have we enough water and power for frivolous showers?'

'Plenty, if we shower together.'

'It's too small,' she protested.

'We'll fit.'

They did—just. Bryn laughed at her shocked face.

'It's not decent,' she said demurely, 'and it's too hot.'

'The water will cool us down.'

Green eyes gleamed as he soaped her, became heavy-lidded and purposeful when she insisted on doing the same for him.

'You're as sleek as a panther,' she said from behind him, sliding wet hands across his back.

'Panthers have fur.'

Gerry linked her hands across his chest and pressed her cheek against his shoulderblade. 'Mmm,' she said slowly, 'I'd like that.'

Beneath her palms she felt his chest lift as he laughed.

The water sputtered and she let him go so that he could turn around and rinse the soap off. A lean hand turned the shower off, then he looped an arm around her and kissed her, hard and fast, before picking her up. As he edged by the rack he grabbed a towel and tossed it onto the bed, and her in the middle of it, and came down and made love to her with a ferocity that blew her mind.

Gerry woke to a voice, a low murmur that teased the edge of her hearing. Almost as soon as her tired brain registered what was happening, the sound died into silence, and before she had a chance to get up Bryn came in through the door. Opening her eyes, she saw that it was dawn, a still, soft light that held the promise of delight.

But not as much as Bryn's slow, possessive survey.

'Who were you talking to?' she asked, smothering a yawn with the back of her hand.

His brows rose. 'Talking? No—oh, I did express my opinion of his thieving habits to a gull that tried to snatch the bait from my line.'

'Did you catch any fish?'

'I lost the urge,' he said gravely, sitting down on the bed.

Colour leaped again through her skin. He was wearing a terrible old pair of shorts, but he at least had some clothes on whereas she had nothing.

'You blush from your heart upwards,' he said, a dark finger tracing the uppermost curves of her breasts.

Drugged with satiation, she said languidly, 'I suppose everyone does.'

'I don't blush,' he said.

'Neither do I, normally.'

'And we established very effectively last night that this isn't normal behaviour for you,' he said without much expression.

'I wasn't a virgin,' she said, 'but I don't make a habit of—' her skin warmed again when he moved a curl back from her cheek and tucked it behind her ear '—of sleeping with men I barely know.'

'At first I thought you were—a virgin, I mean.'

'It had been a long time.'

'We didn't get much sleep,' he said absently. 'You must be tired.'

Raising her head, she bit his shoulder, quite hard, then licked the salty skin. She could hear the sudden harshness of his breathing.

'I'm hungry,' she said demurely.

He laughed deep in his throat and turned her towards him, his eyes fierce and primal. 'So am I,' he said, taking her with him as he slid down onto the tumbled sheets. 'Let's see what we can do about it, shall we?'

Later—an hour or so later—Gerry yawned prodigiously and muttered, 'You're insatiable.' Each word slurred off her tongue.

Bryn kissed her. 'Apparently,' he said lazily.

Something in his tone alerted her, but her eyes were heavy and she could feel waves of exhaustion creeping up from her toes, dragging her further and further into unconsciousness. Although she tried for clearer pronunciation, her words ran together again. 'What bothers me is that I seem to be too...'

He said something, but she couldn't fathom it out, didn't even want to. The rumble of his voice was the last sound she heard before sleep, voracious and draining, claimed her.

CHAPTER NINE

GERRY woke to find the sun high in the sky. Dry-mouthed, filmed with sweat, she stretched, aware of the change in Bryn's breathing as he too woke. Her body ached pleasantly, and when she moved she felt a slight tenderness between her legs.

And although she'd spent the night in his arms, now, more than ever, she craved the protection of her cosmetics.

She croaked, 'I need another shower and a large glass of water. I think I'm dehydrated.'

He laughed. 'I've got a better idea.'

Naked and entirely confident, he got to his feet and stooped over her, eyes glittering, dark face intent. Gerry's heart leapt in her breast, but he picked her up and carried her through the cabin and out into the cockpit. She smiled as she realised what he planned to do. No man had ever carried her around before, no man had ever made her so sure of herself, so positive in her sexuality.

He jumped with her still in his arms. Supple and languid from the night, Gerry welcomed the cool embrace of the sea, an embrace that soon turned warm. They sank down through the water; opening her eyes, Gerry squinted at the sun-dazzle above, and the harsh lines of Bryn's face, arrogant, tough, exultant.

As his legs propelled them towards the surface she wondered how such a man could be as tender as he was fiery, both gentle and ruthless, a dominant male who refused to take his own satisfaction until his lover had reached the peak of her ecstasy. Her previous lover had been considerate, but nothing she'd experienced came anywhere near the transcendent sensuality of Bryn's lovemaking.

Chilled, she realised that he'd set a benchmark; when this idyll was over she might never find another man who could love her as he had. Was this aching sense of loneliness and incompletion the goad that had spurred her mother on her futile search?

In an explosion of crystals they burst through the surface into the kiss of the sun, and she broke away from him, striking out for the island.

It was further than she thought. Although a good swimmer, she was tired when she got there. Not so Bryn, who kept pace easily with her. As they walked through the shallows and side by side across the white unsullied sand, Gerry thought they were like Adam and Eve, and wished futilely that they didn't have to return to their responsibilities.

He waited until they'd reached the shelter of the palms before asking, 'Do you want to eat breakfast here?'

It would be a perfect way to end this time out of time. Today someone would come looking for them and they would go their separate ways. Oh, in spite of his specific denial, they might resume their affair in Auckland, but it would never again be like this. The mundane world had a habit of tarnishing romance.

And that belief too she'd probably inherited from her mother.

Gerry pushed her hair back from her face. 'I'd love to.'

'OK, stay here in the shade. I'll swim back to the boat and load up the dinghy.'

'What if you get a cramp?' Stupid, she thought despairingly. Oh, that was stupid. Why fuss over a man so obviously able to look after himself?

'I know how to deal with it,' he told her calmly, his eyes transparent as the water, cool and limpid and unreadable. 'And if a shark comes by I'd be much happier knowing you weren't in the water with me.'

She cast a startled glance around. 'Are there sharks here?'

'It's not likely.' He set off towards the water.

Gerry watched while his strong tanned arms clove the water, only relaxing when he hauled himself up into the cruiser and waved.

Swimming had cleared some of the sensuous miasma from her brain, but she needed to think about the fact that during the night she had surrendered much more than her body to Bryn—she had handed over a part of her heart.

It terrified her.

Biting her lip, she stared down at the strappy leaves of a small plant, tough and dry on this waterless island, a far cry from the usually lush tropical growth. Idly she began to plait the leaves together.

Long ago she'd become reconciled to the fact that she was like her mother. Oh, she fell in love—no problem there. Only then, inevitably, she fell out of love. Sooner or later her dreaded boredom crept in, draining each relationship of joy and interest.

This time it might be different; Bryn was nothing like the other men she'd loved.

'No,' she muttered. She'd gone through this exercise before—tried to convince her sensible inner self that what she felt was real and true, an emotion enduring enough to transcend time and familiarity.

A stray breeze creaked through the fronds of the coconut palms above. Frowning, she rubbed her eyes. Last night Bryn had kissed her lashes down; her breath came quickly as she recalled things he'd said, the raw, rough sound of his voice, the sinfully skilled hands...

Impossible to believe that she'd ever grow tired of him!

But that was just sex, and Bryn was a magnificent lover. Gerry might not be experienced—her second love affair, six years ago, had been her only other physical relationship—but she recognised experience and, she thought grimly, a great natural talent. Bryn knew women.

Surely she'd never be able to look at him without responding to his heart-jolting impact!

And it wasn't just sex. He was sharp and tough and intelligent, he made her laugh, he refused to let her get away with using her charm instead of logic—oh, he fascinated her.

Would that last? Perhaps. She knew couples who still preferred each other's company after years of marriage.

Emotionally, however, he was uncharted territory.

Appropriate, she thought, her fingers stilling as she looked around the tiny islet. Bryn was a desert island—she understood nothing of his emotions, his feelings. And so, she thought painfully, was she. She had never known the particular power of transformation that accompanied such unselfconscious selflessness.

Even if he was the one man who could fix her wayward emotions—he'd shown no signs of loving her. Oh, he'd enjoyed taking her, and he'd met and matched her gasping, frenzied response with his own dynamic male power—but he didn't know her, so how could he love her? And in spite of the dark sexual enchantment that bedazzled them both, she suspected that he didn't like her much.

Even if he hadn't stated that it wouldn't last, they had no future.

It hurt even to think it, but Gerry fought back an icy pang of desolation to face facts squarely. And once she'd forced herself to accept them, her way was clear.

She'd enjoy this passionate interlude and then she'd end it before it had a chance to fizzle into damp embers. That way they'd both keep their dignity.

Some unregenerate part of her wondered just how Bryn would take a dignified dismissal. That bone-deep assurance indicated a man unused to rejection. Perhaps he'd pursue her, she thought with a flash of heat.

Why should he? cold logic demanded mockingly. He'd understand. What they shared was sex, and Bryn could get that from almost any woman he wanted. Why should he care if she turned him down? Beyond a momentary blow to his ego it wouldn't mean a thing.

She gazed at the pattern she'd made with the long leaves

of the plant. An ironic smile hurt her mouth. Somehow she'd managed to weave them together into a lopsided heart. Swiftly, deftly, she separated them, straightened out a couple she'd twisted, and turned back to the beach.

Bryn was almost there, the sun gilding his skin as he rowed the dinghy in. Until then Gerry hadn't bothered about her nakedness, but now she felt conspicuous and stupidly shy.

'Stay in the shade,' he called as the dinghy grounded on the glaring sand. 'I'll bring the stuff up.'

She waited in the shade, absently scratching a runnel of salt on her forearm. Naked, moving easily and lithely around the small craft, Bryn's sheer male energy blazed forth with compelling forcefulness. Incredibly, desire clutched her stomach, ran like electricity through her nerves, sparked synapses through her entire body. All that strength, she thought dizzily, all that power, and for a short time—for a few racing hours—it had been hers.

A hamper under one arm, something that turned out to be a rolled up rug under the other, he strode across the sand like a god worshipped by the sun, muscles moving with unstudied litheness beneath the mantle of golden skin.

Erotic need turned into a ripple, a current, a torrent of hunger. Gerry drew in a deep, ragged breath. Damn it, she'd never been at the mercy of her urges, and she wasn't going to start now!

She'd thought she'd succeeded in controlling her reaction, but Bryn took one look at her set face and asked, 'What's the matter?'

'Nothing.'

Although he wasn't satisfied, he didn't pursue it. Handing her the rug, he said, 'Spread this out, will you?'

She found a spot between bushes, shaded and secluded, yet with enough breeze for comfort. Bryn set the hamper down and helped her with the rug, then tossed her a length of cotton coloured in startling greens and blues and an intense muted colour halfway between them both.

'I thought you might want a pareu,' he said drily as he wound another length, in tans and ochres and blacks, around his lean hips.

With shaking fingers Gerry wrapped herself in the cotton, tucking two corners in just above her breasts to make a strapless sundress. Keeping her face turned away from him, she knelt on the rug to examine the contents of the hamper.

'My grandfather used to say,' Bryn told her as she took the lid off the hamper, 'that only a fool allowed himself to be manoeuvred into an untenable situation. If someone finds us while we're eating breakfast, I'd rather be clothed.'

'Me too,' she said fervently, looking up.

He smiled, and it was like being hit in the heart with a cannonball of devilish, sexually-charged charm. No man, she thought, setting out delicious slices of pawpaw and melon, should be able to do that. It gave him a totally unfair advantage.

'Here,' he said, offering her a tube of sunscreen. 'I didn't bring your make-up, but this will give you some protection.'

'Thank you,' she said stiltedly, wishing that he wasn't so astute. Of all her acquaintanceship only Bryn seemed to have realised that cosmetics were the shield she donned against a prying world.

Hastily she spread the lotion onto her face and arms and legs, on the soft swell of her breast above the cotton pareu, and as far down her back as she could reach.

When she'd finished, he said, 'Turn around, I'll do the rest.'

Even slick with sunscreen, the power and strength of his hands set her nerve-ends oscillating, sending tiny shocks through her body.

'You have such an elegant back,' he said evenly. 'But then, you're elegant all over, from the way you walk, the way you hold your head on that slim, poised neck, to the graceful, spare lines of your face and throat and body, the narrow wrists and fragile ankles—and that air of fine, steely strength and courage.' His hands swept up across her shoulders and fastened loosely around her throat, his fingertips resting against the turbulent pulse at its base. 'A true thoroughbred,' he said, the latent harshness in his voice almost reaching the surface.

She had to swallow, and his fingers would have felt her tense muscles. 'A fortunate genetic heritage,' she said. 'Like yours.'

He laughed and withdrew his hands. 'From a beach bum and a spoilt, frail little rich girl?' he asked sardonically.

Reaching for the tube, she said, 'Turn around and I'll put sunscreen on you.' She was playing with fire, but she didn't care. Some note in his voice had made her wince, and she needed to try and make things better for him.

For a moment she thought he'd refuse, but almost immediately he presented his back to her, the smooth golden skin taut and warm over the muscles beneath—the shape of a man, she thought fancifully, cupping her palm to receive the sunscreen. Her hands tingled as she spread the liquid.

'Even if your father wasn't the most responsible man in the world,' she said, 'he had the guts to actually do what many men only dream of. And so did your mother. Has it ever occurred to you that your father knew you'd be well looked after when he left Longopai? Or that he probably intended to come back?'

'An optimist as well,' he jeered. 'No, it hasn't.'

Aware that she'd trespassed onto forbidden ground, she massaged the lotion into his skin. 'Then at least you should take credit for overcoming your heredity.'

His shoulders lifted as he laughed, deep and low and humourless. 'Perhaps I should thank heaven that I had such a brilliant example of what not to do, how not to be. At least I accept responsibility for my actions. And for my mistakes. Have you finished there?'

'Yes.' She recapped the tube and gave it to him to pack, then poured them both coffee.

With little further conversation they ate breakfast, a feast of fruit, plus rolls he'd taken from the freezer and heated in the oven. Passionfruit jelly oozed across the moist white bread, tangy and sweet, and the coffee he'd carried in a Thermos scented the salt-laden air.

'A truly magnificent repast,' Gerry sighed, sucking a spot of jelly from the tip of one finger. Looking up, she caught Bryn's green gaze on her mouth, and grinned. 'And don't tell me your grandfather used to insist on table napkins at all times. So did my father, but I still lick the occasional finger.'

'You shouldn't be allowed to,' he said.

Eyes widening, she stared at him.

'It's all right,' he said roughly. 'I do have some self-control. We'd better get back on board.'

It was an excuse to move, and she leapt to her feet with alacrity. Although desire pulsed through her with swift, merciless power, making love again would stretch already over-strung muscles and tissues.

Working swiftly, they repacked the hamper and folded the rug. Swiftly they walked across the scorching sand, and swiftly made their way across the peacock water to the sleek white cruiser.

Once she was aboard, Bryn handed up the hamper. 'Leave it there, I'll carry it below,' he said. 'Here, take the painter and cleat it.'

Gerry took the rope—the painter, she corrected herself—and wound it around a horizontal bar of metal bolted to the deck as Bryn stepped aboard. The boat lurched a second under the transfer of weight, and she mis-stepped and tripped. Lightning-fast, he reached for her, but in her efforts to save herself from hitting the deck she slammed her arm across the instrument console. As she staggered, some of the levers moved.

To her astonishment an engine roared into life.

'What—?' Stunned, she stared at the lever she'd clutched, and then at Bryn as he got there in two swift strides and turned the engine off. Silence echoed around them, broken only by the drumming of her pulse in her ears.

'Why didn't you tell me you'd got the engine going?' she asked, racked by an enormous, unwanted sadness. It had come so quickly, the end of a fragile, beautiful dream.

Had he too not wanted this to end?

One glance at him put paid to that wistful hope. The bone structure of his face had never been so prominent, never seemed so ruthless.

'I didn't,' he said.

Chilled, she shook her head, every uneasy instinct springing into agitated life. 'Then why did it start just then and not when you tried it yesterday?' she asked, watching the play of reflection from the water move across the brutal framework of his face.

He surveyed her with hard eyes that gave nothing away, opaque and green and empty. In a level voice he said, 'Because you turned it on.'

'What?' She blinked, unable to believe that she'd heard correctly.

Bryn looked like something carved out of granite, the only warmth the red gleam summoned by the sun from his tawny hair. Calmly, without inflection, he said, 'I brought us here deliberately. We're staying until I decide to take you back to Fala'isi.'

She spluttered, 'What the hell do you mean?'

'Just that.'

'Are you saying you've *kidnapped* me?'

'No,' he said, eyes steady as they rested on her face. 'You came with me of your own free will so I think the technical term is probably imprisonment.'

By now a whole series of minor questions and queries had jelled. Anger bested fear as adrenalin accelerated her heart, iced her brain. 'You lured me away from New Zealand,' she said, never taking her eyes from his face. 'You made up some specious reason to get me to the hotel, and then you deliberately marooned us here. I gather the boat isn't disabled?'

'No.'

'And the communications system works too?'

'Yes.'

Her knees gave way. Collapsing into one of the chairs, she fought back rage and a bitter, seething disillusionment. When she could trust her voice again she asked, 'Why?'

'If you don't know, you're better off not knowing,' he said with deadly detachment. 'As for luring—no, you came to Longopai on a legitimate mission.'

'A photograph would have been enough to solve that,' she said with bared teeth. She'd been so stupid, allowing herself to be tempted by a week in the islands! Drawing in a ragged breath, she promised, 'But it won't solve your problems when I go to the police once I'm back in New Zealand.'

His smile sent a shudder through her. 'I don't think you will,' he said calmly. 'Who'd believe you? They'd assume that you came to Longopai of your own free will to join me. In fact, they'd know it—why do you think I asked you in front of Cara?'

Gerry said shakily, 'If you don't let me go—today—I'll see you in every court in New Zealand.'

'And if you do that,' he said ruthlessly, 'I'll tell them that you wanted to come, that you wanted to stay, and that your charge is a malicious fabrication because I refused to marry you. It will be my word against yours, because you'll have nobody to back you up.'

'If you think that you can—that you can get away with raping me—'

'Raping you?' His voice roughened, became thick and furious.

Shocked, she realised that she'd almost pushed him into losing control. Gerry wouldn't have believed it to be possible, but his face hardened even further.

However, he pulled back from the brink. 'That wasn't

rape,' he said with calculated indifference. 'I took nothing you weren't willing—eager—to give. I must admit I was flattered to realise that you hadn't slept with anyone for some time. I should have remembered that your friend in Auckland called you unassailable.'

Troy and her drunken ravings, Gerry thought explosively, so angry she could barely articulate the thought.

Gritting her teeth, she said, 'I'd have thought you were sophisticated enough to understand that you can't trust anyone in their cups.'

'Oh, you have a reputation extending well past old friends who ingest mind-altering substances,' he said. 'Didn't you know that, Geraldine? She only said what everyone else says behind your back. The unassailable Gerry! When you smile you make the sun come out, you dazzle with your warmth and your beauty and your laughter, you promise all delight but it's a promise you never keep.'

To the sound of her heart breaking, she asked, 'So what was last night, then?'

His contempt had sliced through the thin shield of her composure, but it was nothing to the wound his smile inflicted. In a deceptively indolent voice he said, 'Oh, you make love like Aphrodite, but it didn't really mean much, did it? You're not grieving now—you're furious.'

Thank God he couldn't read her heart; she'd get out of this with her pride reasonably intact. And because it was so appalling that she should be thinking of pride when every instinct was mourning, she remained silent, lashes lowered as she stared stubbornly at the deck. On her deathbed, she thought, she'd remember the pattern of the boards.

Casually, dismissively, Bryn went on, 'Don't worry, Geraldine, you're quite safe as long as you behave nicely and don't try to run away.' He paused, and then finished, 'I won't sleep with you again.'

'Why did you sleep with me last night?' She tried to speak as easily as he had.

'You were beginning to ask questions,' he said. 'It seemed a good idea to cause a diversion.'

The frail edifice of the night's happiness shattered around her. She ground out, 'What the hell is going on?'

'If you're as innocent as you seem to be, nothing that need concern you,' he said dismissively.

Her hands clenched. Not now, she thought, fighting back the red tide of fury and pain to force her brain into action. After a rapid, painful moment of thought, she said, 'Cara.'

'What about her?'

Think, she commanded. Damn it, you have to think, because he's not going to tell you anything. Perhaps if you make him angry...

Steadying her voice, she said scornfully, 'She's in love with you and you used her to get to me.'

His expression didn't change at all, and when he spoke his voice was amused, almost negligent. 'Cara's dazzled, but her heart won't be dented.'

'God, you're a cold-hearted sod!' The words exploded from her, filled with the fear she refused to accept. 'Why are you keeping me here? What is going on?'

'I can't answer that,' he said, and turned away.

Rage gripped her. 'You mean you won't answer.'

'It doesn't make any difference.'

Finally overwhelmed by anger and pain, she hurled herself forward and hit him, using the variation of street fighting she'd been taught in self-defence lessons years ago.

He was like steel, like rock, but she got in one kidney punch that should have laid him low. He staggered, then rounded on her. Although big men were usually slow, she'd known Bryn was not. However she hadn't been prepared for the lethal speed of his response.

Oddly enough, it gave her some satisfaction. She struck out again, fingers clawing for his eyes, and he parried the blow with his forearm, face blazing with an anger that matched hers.

What followed was an exhausting few minutes of vicious

struggle. Eventually she realised that he wasn't trying to hurt her; he was content to block her every move. She slipped several blows past his guard, but he kept them away from every vulnerable part, until at last, sobbing with frustration, she gave up. Then he locked her wrists together in a grip as tight as it was painful.

'Feel better?' he asked silkily.

As the adrenalin faded into its bitter aftermath, she gained some consolation from the fact of his sweating. Meeting his narrowed, glittering eyes defiantly, she gasped, 'I wish I could kill you.'

'You had a bloody good try. Where did you learn to fight like that?'

'I took lessons years ago.' Her heart threatened to burst through her skin, and the corners of her pareu had loosened, so that she was almost exposed to him. Panting, she said, 'Let me go. I won't try it again.'

'You'd better not.'

He meant it. Shivering, she pulled away, and this time he let her go, watching her while he wiped his hands on the cloth around his hips as though she had contaminated him.

Yanking the ends of her pareu together, she breathed in deeply until she was confident enough of her voice to say, 'For an importer you know how to handle yourself.'

'For a woman who works in high fashion you know some remarkably lethal moves.'

In spite of the heat she felt deathly cold. Swallowing, she said, 'I'd like to go to my room, thank you.'

He went with her—standing guard, she thought with a flash of anger. At her door he said, 'Give me a call when you want to come out and I'll unlock the door.'

In the flat tone of exhaustion she said, 'Let's hope the boat doesn't sink.'

'You should have thought of that before you attacked me.'

Without looking at him, Gerry went inside and listened to the key turn in the lock.

Numbly she walked across to the windows and pushed the glass back. For a moment she wondered whether she should try to get out of a window, but the ones that opened were far too small to take her. Pulling the curtains would stop some of the fresh air, but she couldn't bear the possibility of Bryn checking on her through the window, so she dragged them across.

Then, refusing to think, refusing to feel, she lay down on the big bed and by some kind miracle of sympathetic fate went almost immediately to sleep.

The curtains shimmered gold when she woke, telling her it was late afternoon. She lay for long minutes on the bed, lethargic and aching, trying to work out why Bryn had kidnapped her and was intent on keeping her here.

It had to be something in New Zealand. What? Had Cara's telephone call given him an excuse, or had it been the trigger? Perhaps he'd have suggested a trip in the boat anyway, hiding his purpose with a fake affair.

The thought ached physically through her. But it could wait; she'd deal with it when she knew what was going on.

Cara was the only link, and Gerry's decision to go back to New Zealand had precipitated this abduction, if abduction it could be called when the abductee had co-operated so eagerly.

No, she wouldn't think of that. Please God, Honor would soon arrive back from wherever she'd been to look after the agency, and Maddie—

Maddie.

Gerry's heart stopped. Maddie had overdosed on heroin. Was that—could that be—the link? Had Cara rung Bryn to tell him about it?

No. Why would she? And what would it mean to him?

She could have, Gerry's rational brain said relentlessly.

Or Bryn could have monitored the calls Gerry made in her cabaña after she'd left him.

An importer with a legal business and impeccable credentials as a businessman—a man like Bryn Falconer—would find it quite easy to set up an illicit organisation to ship in drugs.

Nausea made Gerry gag, but she rinsed out her mouth and washed her face and sat down again. If that unscrupulous importer could persuade a credulous young girl like Cara, who had contacts with people going overseas, that he needed to bring stuff in without Customs knowing—then perhaps the agency could be used as a distributing point.

An island like Longopai would be very useful too, she thought, remembering the trading vessel he had bought for the islanders so that they wouldn't be dependent on the schedules of others.

Such a man could probably persuade Cara to store the stuff in her house; grim logic reminded Gerry he'd wanted Cara's landlady away from Auckland.

No, it was impossible. She'd been watching too many late-night television shows.

Yet here she was, caged in a boat on the Pacific, an almost-willing prisoner who'd swallowed everything Bryn told her because she was attracted to him. Oh, she'd been a fool!

Common sense should have told her that it was highly unlikely—to say the least!—that every system on a boat like *Starchaser* would fail together. Yet she'd been so mesmerised by Bryn's physical magnetism that she'd swallowed his sketchy explanation hook, line and sinker.

A blast of fury surged through her, was suppressed; it clouded the brain. What she needed was clear-headed logic. Unclenching her teeth, she wooed calmness.

From now on she wasn't going to take anything for granted. 'Think,' she muttered. 'Stop wailing and think!'

Could Cara be so criminally naive as to fall in with a scheme like that? Probably not, but she was easily dazzled—and Gerry had first-hand experience of just how plausible Bryn could be.

No, it was utterly ridiculous! Gerry got to her feet and paced through the stateroom, shaking her head. She was spinning tales out of shadows.

She had absolutely no proof, nothing but the wildest speculations.

Yet Bryn had lied about the boat, and kept her prisoner. And he'd made love to her because she'd asked questions—what questions? Was it when she asked who he'd been talking to? He must have been using the radio. Humiliation stung through her but she ignored it.

Also, he certainly hadn't been fooling when he'd locked the door behind her.

Unless he was a psychopath he must have good reasons for his actions.

Psychopath or drug importer—both seemed so unlikely she couldn't deal with them. Yet she would have to accept that she might well be in danger—in such danger that her only hope of saving herself lay in pretending she was the stupid piece of fluff he clearly thought her to be.

Adrenalin brought her upright, but before it had time to develop into full-blown terror a flash of memory made her sink back down again. The first time they'd met, Bryn had held a baby in his arms, and smiled at it with tenderness and awe and a fierce protectiveness.

That had been when she fell in love with him, Gerry thought now. Could a man who'd looked at a child like that cold-bloodedly sleep with a woman and then murder her?

Her heart said no, but she'd already found out she couldn't trust that unwary organ. She'd have to work on the assumption that Bryn Falconer was exactly that sort of man.

She rubbed a shaking hand across her forehead. Why did he need to keep her out of the way now?

Because Maddie had overdosed?

No, it was too far-fetched, too much like some thriller. She was overwrought, and so stressed by his betrayal that her mind was running riot.

But why else would he be keeping her here incommunicado? Obviously he hadn't booked her plane seat to New Zealand, so no one except Cara and Jill were expecting her. With bitter irony, Gerry realised that he'd probably rung Cara and reassured her, giving her some excellent reason why Gerry wasn't coming home. A tropical fever perhaps, she thought wearily. Not dangerous, but debilitating. And perhaps he'd asked Cara to tell Jill that everything was all right.

Gerry tried to remember whether she'd told him about her conversation with the booker. No, she wouldn't have, but if he'd monitored her calls from Longopai he'd know Jill wouldn't be sending off search parties.

He really didn't have anything to worry about. The islanders were his—if he asked them not to speak they wouldn't.

And if he wanted to kill her then he'd probably find a way to get rid of Cara too.

Panic clawed at her gut. She rested her hands on her diaphragm and concentrated on breathing, slow and easy, in and out, in and out, until her racing brain slowed and the terror had subsided.

Ridiculous; it was all ridiculous. This was Bryn who made love like a dark angel, Bryn who'd been gentle when she needed gentleness, fierce when she needed ferocity, Bryn who had made her laugh and talked to her with intelligence and a rare, understated compassion.

Unfortunately history was full of women who had been betrayed by the men they'd loved, men they'd given up everything for.

So she was going to take any chance she could to get away. She'd never forgive herself if she didn't do something to protect Cara.

First, she'd try to use the communications system and send out an SOS.

If she got out of this unscathed, she promised herself grimly, she'd not only take those Maori classes, she'd do a course in maritime navigation and communications.

Or perhaps it would be simpler never to set foot off dry land again.

CHAPTER TEN

WHEN Bryn opened the door some hours later Gerry was sitting on her bed, hands folded in her lap, face carefully blank, while the flicker of fear burnt brightly in her mind.

'You look like a good little girl,' he said, a smile just touching the corners of his mouth.

Gerry's heart leapt frantically. No, she thought gratefully, she couldn't believe he had any connection to the wild concoction of ideas she'd dreamed up.

'I always try to please kidnappers,' she said with a slight snap.

His mouth tightened. 'Come out and have a drink.'

He looked dangerous, but not murderous. Still buoyed by that spurt of relief, she knew that of course he wasn't a murderer! He had, however, lied to her and abducted her, and he wouldn't tell her why.

So she had to work on the assumption that he was up to something that was not for her good.

Getting to her feet, she picked up the letter she'd written to keep her mind from tearing off into ever wilder shores of conjecture, then preceded him into the main cabin.

Once there, she said, 'I've written to Lacey. I'd like to send it to her if you have her address.'

'Send it to the hotel and ask them to forward it,' he said coolly.

'It's not sealed. Do you want to read it?' She held it out to him.

His brows drew together. 'Stop pushing,' he commanded softly.

But she couldn't. 'I haven't written anything that might lead her to think I'm in dire danger.'

'Keep on like that, and you might be. If you send it to the hotel they'll make sure Lacey gets it.'

Gerry said chattily, 'I made her promise to contact a doctor when she gets back home. I thought I'd better remind her of it just in case I go missing.'

'You won't go missing,' he said between his teeth. 'How did you extract a promise like that from her?'

'I threatened to tell her parents. Oh, I didn't say so, but she knew I would. She wants to stop; the bulimia terrifies her but she's also determined not to put any weight on. She needs professional help, and I more or less blackmailed her into seeing someone she trusts when she gets home.'

He said nothing, and she went on abruptly, 'I'm beginning to wonder whether there might not be some truth in what you said about magazines sending all the wrong messages.'

'Guilty conscience, Geraldine?'

She shrugged moodily, trying to sound and look normal, trying to reassure herself that a man who worried about the messages high fashion was sending to young women couldn't possibly be a drug peddler. 'No. The magazine I worked for concentrated on style rather than fashion, and we did a lot with models who weren't size eights. As for the agency, we represent all sorts—character as well as fashion—and I can assure you that none of our models are anorexic or bulimic.'

But one was a drug addict. Just how much did she know about the models?

Swiftly she went on, 'Lacey worries me. She's big-boned, the sort of build with no middle ground between gaunt and voluptuous. She's also bitterly unhappy with her stepmother, and I gathered that her mother doesn't want her living with her and her new husband. I don't entirely believe that the fashion business is to blame for the increase in eating disorders. There are millions of women throughout the world who read fashion magazines, and although they're nothing like the models they're happy with their lot.'

Bryn walked across to the drinks fridge. 'I know.'

He caught her surprised glance. A cynical lift of his mouth made him look suddenly older. 'Wine?' he asked.

'No, thank you. Something with fruit in it.'

He poured her pineapple juice, and lime and soda for himself. If he'd chosen beer she might have had a chance to try and get him drunk.

Hardly. Bryn Falconer was a very controlled man; it was difficult to imagine him drinking to excess.

Silence stretched between them. Refusing to show how intimidated she was, Gerry sipped her drink. Outside the sun had set; as the darkness thickened a bird flying overhead gave a strange, wild cry, and she only just prevented herself from jumping.

'Relax,' he said, something like irritation flicking through his voice. 'I told you before, you're in no danger. Stop looking at me as though you expect me to leap on you.'

'I'm not accustomed to being held prisoner,' she returned crisply. 'It makes me angry.'

'You're not just angry,' he said. 'You're scared.'

Damn. She made her muscles respond in a smile, packed though it was with irony. 'You must forgive me, but in spite of all your protestations about not wanting to harm me, you are holding me here for reasons I'm not allowed to know. I think a certain amount of wariness is normal in such situations. Of course I *believe* you when you say I'm safe,' she finished, her voice dripping polite sarcasm. 'How long will I be forced to stay here?'

'Until I'm told it's safe to let you go.'

So he wasn't doing this on his own. Well, she'd realised that there had to be other people in it with him, whatever *it* was!

Feeling her way, she said, 'A week? A month? A year?'

But of course he wasn't goaded into revealing anything. 'Until I let you go,' he repeated levelly, his face impassive, as though they'd never looked at each other with naked lust, never made love, never slept a long night in each other's arms.

'What excuse did you give Cara for my not coming back?'

'I told her you had a very mild case of dengue fever. She said that you weren't to worry, she and Jill would cope,' he told her, and before she had a chance to say anything more went on, 'I'll get dinner.'

He'd cooked steak, and served it with potatoes and taro leaves cooked in coconut milk. Gerry had no appetite, but she forced as much as she could down because she wasn't going to weaken herself by starving.

After the meal she said, 'I'd like to go back to the cabin now.'

Hot anger glittered in Bryn's gaze, was immediately extinguished. 'Of course,' he said courteously.

So Gerry sat in the small room, nerves taut, and listened to the sound of the waves on the reef. Towards ten o'clock she heard his voice drift in through the open windows. It was impossible to make out individual words, but from his tone—crisp, businesslike, resolute—it was clear that he was using the radio.

She was never going to trust any other man, no matter how attractive she found him and how tenderly he looked at babies.

Thoughts prowled through her mind, rattling the bars and poking hideous faces as the slow tropical night wheeled through its cycle, splendid, indifferent, majestically beautiful. Lying tense and fully-clothed on the bed, Gerry spent hours trying to convince herself that the man who had made love to her with such fiery tenderness couldn't possibly want to harm her.

Dawn came as a surprise. Yawning, she rubbed her eyes and realised that somehow she'd managed to fall asleep.

A glance in the mirror revealed dark circles under her eyes, and sallow, colourless skin. Hastily she showered before making up with every ounce of skill and care she could call on, not satisfied until her face gazed back at her—smooth and unmarked by betrayal, the sleepy eyes and full mouth delicately enhanced so that no one could guess how much time it had taken to manufacture that discreet, inconspicuous mask.

She dressed in white linen trousers and a muted silk shirt in her favourite shades of blue and green, slid her narrow feet into blue sandals, and straightened her shoulders and lifted her chin. With her best model gait she walked across to the door.

It was unlocked. Hardly daring to breathe, she slipped through it.

Bryn looked up from the galley. 'Good morning,' he said, scanning her with half-closed eyes that sent a shiver from the top of her head to the base of her spine, so masculine and appreciative was that swift, hot glance. It disappeared in the length of a blink; he lifted his brows and said easily, 'Ah, the exquisite, sophisticated, aloof Ms Dacre once more! It's almost a pity; I've grown to like the slightly tousled Geraldine who lurks beneath the cosmetics.'

Smiling, showing her teeth, she murmured, 'How sweet.'

He laughed. 'Come and have some breakfast.'

No, she thought hopefully, whatever the reason he kept her here, it couldn't possibly be because he was smuggling drugs. That had been a fevered figment of her imagination; he couldn't look at her like that, or tease like that—couldn't *laugh* like that—and wish her any harm.

With a cautiously lifting heart, she sat down at the table and began to eat.

He didn't lock her into her cabin again; as though they'd silently negotiated a truce they tidied the boat and repaired to the cockpit, sitting out of the sun. Bryn read what looked like business papers from a locked briefcase, and Gerry tried to concentrate on a book.

With very little success. A volatile cocktail of emotions—raw fury and desolation and pride mixed with a persistent, stubborn hope—washed through her like rollers pounding the shore. Ignore the hope, she told herself, it will weaken you. Polish up that pride.

And look for an opportunity to get to the instrument console and radio for help, even though you have no idea how to use it.

However, he'd placed himself between her and the console, and during the long morning he made sure she didn't have a chance to get near it.

The sun was high in the sky when something beeped from the panel. Bryn looked up. 'Would you mind going below?' he asked pleasantly.

'Not at all,' Gerry replied with steely composure, gathering up the unread book as she got to her feet.

Of course she couldn't settle; clutching the book, she stood in the main cabin and stared blindly through the windows while Bryn's voice echoed in her ears.

Should she be frightened?

No.

However hard she tried to see him as a criminal, she couldn't. Oh, she could imagine Bryn killing a man in self-defence, but even in her most paranoid fears she hadn't been able to be afraid of him. A deep-seated instinct told her he was a man with his own strict code of honour.

Her lips stretched in a painful, wry smile. In spite of everything her foolish heart trusted him. Nevertheless that same organ gave an enormous jump when he appeared in the doorway, brows drawn together, face grim.

'Well?' she demanded.

He came down the last step. 'Tell me about your partner in the agency,' he commanded.

'Honor?' Totally bewildered, Gerry stared at him. 'What's happened? Is she all right?'

'As far as I know she's fine,' he said. 'How long have you known her? Where did you meet her?'

She asked, 'Do you know whether a model called Maddie Ingram is all right? She was in hospital.'

It was a test. If he knew about Maddie, he knew too much.

He paused a second before saying, 'She's recovering.'

A clutch of terror diluted Gerry's relief. Yet her voice

stayed steady when she asked, 'Why do you want to know about Honor?'

'Because it's important.' The relentless note in his voice warned her that she wasn't going to be able to stall.

Feeling oddly disconnected, she said slowly, 'She used to be a model—I've known her for years.'

'Is she a friend?'

She gave him a startled look but could read nothing from the harsh face or hooded eyes.

'Not exactly a friend,' she answered slowly. 'We get on well together, and she's an excellent partner.'

'What made you decide to go in with her?'

He sounded like a policeman—polite, determined, relentless. The hairs on the back of her neck stood up. 'After my father died I was restless, and when the magazine I worked for was taken over, and the new owners put in an editor who took it down a path I despise, I started looking around for another job. Honor had just broken up with the man she'd been living with.'

Drugs, she recalled sickly. He'd been a heroin addict. She cast a swift glance at Bryn's stone-featured face and continued, 'He'd run through all her money and she was desperate. The only thing she knew was modelling, so she suggested we open an agency. At the time it seemed a good way of getting over my grief. A model agency is the next best thing to chaos that you've ever come across—you don't have time to think.'

'How was the agency set up?'

'On a shoestring. Neither of us had any money—what we did have were contacts. And I have a reputation for seeing promise in unlikely people.'

'Who actually runs the agency?'

Gerry said crisply, 'In an agency as small as ours we can all do everything. We've got bookers, of course—they organise the models' bookings—but Honor and I do almost everything else, and we take the responsibility for planning careers.'

'All right,' he cut in. 'Who deals with the finances?'

Frowning, Gerry said, 'We have an accountant.'

'Who is sleeping with Honor McKenzie.'

She looked up sharply. There had been no inflection in his tone, but something warned her that she wasn't going to like what was coming. 'I hope not,' she said just as brusquely. 'He's married to a very nice woman.'

'He's been your partner's lover since before the agency opened.'

Gerry said quietly, 'I didn't know that.'

'Do you know where Honor was when Cara rang you in a panic about Maddie Ingram?'

Who the *hell* was he? Or rather, *what* was he? He certainly didn't sound like your average rich importer. And where was this all heading? Chilled by nameless fear, Gerry shook her head. 'Cara said she couldn't contact her, but that's not unusual. She takes the occasional long weekend off.'

In an expressionless voice he told her, 'She was in Tahiti.'

Tahiti? Six hours away from New Zealand by air? Her expression must have revealed Gerry's astonishment, but she said evenly, 'I don't understand why this is important.'

'She was meeting an emissary from a Colombian cocaine-trafficking cartel.'

Gerry's jaw dropped.

Calmly, mercilessly, Bryn went on, 'Colombians made the big time with cocaine but now they're moving into heroin—it's easier to transport and yields far higher profits. In New Zealand, what heroin comes in—and that's not been much until recently—has been sourced in Asia.'

'From the Golden Triangle,' Gerry said dully. She'd read about the wild region on the border of Thailand and Myanmar where drug lords ruled an empire based on misery.

Although she knew now what he was going to tell her, she was gripped by an overwhelming relief, a giddy sense of being reprieved from something too dreadful to contemplate because her suspicions of Bryn were baseless.

'Yes. The Colombians want this traffic; using New Zealand as a staging post, they can move into Australia and Asia.' Sources say they have over forty thousand acres of opium poppy under cultivation, and they're planting more. They're also aggressive marketers. Their product is cheaper and purer than the Asian stuff, and they're "double-breasting''—offering a free sample of heroin to each buyer of cocaine.'

She said, 'You think there's a connection between Maddie's overdose and Honor.'

He frowned. 'There's certainly a link with the agency.'

'How do you know?'

'There have been whispers about the agency for a year or so, but nothing tangible, nothing the police could put a finger on. However, Maddie told a friend she had a contact there, and the friend, thank God, told Maddie's brother. He went to the police, and your agency has been under investigation since then.'

'How do I know that you're not lying, that this isn't some elaborate scam?' Gerry couldn't believe it. She knew Honor much better than she knew him, and she'd never suspected her partner of any connection with drug-dealing. 'And why did you stop me from going back to New Zealand?'

'The police asked me to keep you away from the agency for as long as possible.'

'Why?'

'They were still not entirely convinced that you weren't part of the drug ring.' He spoke unemotionally, but she realised he was watching her with an intense, unnerving concentration, dispassionate and intimidating. 'Although they had a search warrant they needed time to get into your computers and drag everything out. They've been there since half an hour after Cara rang you.'

'I see,' she said in a stifled monotone. Thoughts barged around her head, colliding, melding in turmoil. She drew a deep breath and said harshly, 'Why do the police think Honor had something to do with Maddie's OD? And how—how do you know who she met in Tahiti? You can prove that, I assume?'

'She's been under surveillance, and, yes, it can be proved.'

Sweat sprang out across her skin in great beads as she closed her eyes, but blocking him out didn't help. 'Who are you? Apart from being an importer?'

Eyes as cold as quartz, he told her, 'I'm not—I lied to you. I own a construction company. We do projects all around the Pacific Rim, and the company was used in a smuggling racket some years ago. I worked closely with Customs and the police to get to the bottom of that, so I have contacts within each department.'

Frowning, Gerry asked, 'And how did you get mixed up with this?'

After an infinitesimal pause he answered, 'I'm a good friend of Peter Ingram, Maddie's brother. He contacted me a couple of months ago, after he'd found out she was back on heroin. He had to leave for Turkestan and I promised I'd keep an eye on her. I also went to the police. They contacted me a few weeks ago to see if I could get you out of the way for a few days.'

'So you set out to find some dimwitted person with a connection to the agency and picked up Cara, who led you to me.' Her voice was brittle, as brittle as her heart.

His mouth tightened but he said evenly, 'Yes. You were the most likely suspect.'

'Why?' Her emotions were lost in a hollow emptiness.

'A tip-off.'

She stared at him. 'A tip-off?' she said numbly. 'Who from?'

He was still watching her with cool, unsparing assessment. 'A long-time drug user. The police suspect that he mistook you for Honor. Or she might have used your name occasionally.'

Sinking down onto the sofa, she looked down at her feet.

Nausea made her swallow. Bryn had believed this; he'd been sure that she was a prime mover in this trade, and he'd slept with her, made love to her...

It was only marginally less shattering than if he'd been the dealer of death. Her throat ached with tears, tears she'd never be able to shed. She said, 'And on that basis, a tip from a known drug user, you assumed that I ran a drug ring.'

'There were other factors. When the police began investigating, a trail led them to a Swiss bank account, supposedly set up by you.'

With a sense of complete unreality, Gerry noticed that her hands were trembling. Sweat collected across her shoulders, ran the length of her back. Her arid throat prevented her from speaking until she'd swallowed again, and even then her voice emerged thin and shaken. She could discern nothing in Bryn's hard face, nothing in his tone, to tell her whether he believed this or not.

'No,' she said.

'It certainly gave credence to the tip-off,' he said neutrally.

Had Honor done this? Gerry had always been reasonably confident about her judgement of character until then; now she realised that the woman she'd worked with and trusted could have plotted to send her to prison, to ruin her life. She shook her head.

'It made sense,' Bryn went on with grim persistence. 'Although your father had indulged you all your life, his insistence on paying back his creditors left you penniless.'

'I had a salary,' she flared.

'Peanuts to what you'd been accustomed to. Before he divested himself to pay off his creditors your father was a rich man.'

Gerry said tautly, 'My father stopped supporting me when I left university, and since then I've lived off my income. I agreed wholly with him when he decided to pay back the money his manager had taken.'

'It seemed likely that you might look for a way to up

your income to that level again. Also, you'd done a lot of travelling when you were with the magazine, especially in Asia and the Pacific. Plenty of chances to make contacts there. And then there was the friend I saw you eating lunch with the day I met you. She'd taken something.'

'She'd had less than a glass of wine. Troy's very susceptible to alcohol—it makes her drunk so quickly she can't even eat a sherry trifle.' With an effort that took all of her nervous energy, she steadied her voice. 'So when we made love you really thought that I was running a smuggling ring. Not only that, but that I was introducing my models to heroin.'

'By then I was almost convinced that you were innocent.'

His impersonal, judicial tone fired her anger to fury—a fury mixed with weary disillusion.

'Almost.' She straightened her spine. 'Go on,' she said tonelessly. 'Tell me how you decided that it was Honor.'

'You don't seem surprised,' he observed shrewdly.

Slowly Gerry said, 'I am—but not shocked. In some ways she's surprisingly amoral, so perhaps I should have wondered if that extended into other areas of her life. But she didn't try to fiddle the books—I learned from my father's experience, and I go over the records regularly.'

'You went over the records she wanted you to see. There were others, but she kept her illegal activities totally separate from the agency.'

'Except for Maddie,' she said bitterly.

He shrugged. 'Except for Maddie. Nevertheless, the police realised that, in spite of the tip-off, Honor McKenzie had just as many chances as you to travel, she had as little money as you, and she'd also lived with a man who was deep in the drug culture.'

'She isn't a user,' Gerry said, adding wearily, 'at least, I don't think she is.'

'She isn't, and neither is her lover, who actually set this whole thing up. The people who sell rarely are. They know what damage their wares cause.'

'If there was a bank account in my name, how did the police decide that it was Honor who organised the trade, not me?' Her cool voice hid, she hoped, the intense desolation that racked her.

'It all seemed just a little too pat—especially when it was discovered that the accountant and Honor were lovers. He was a suspect in a fraud case five years ago—they couldn't pin anything on him, but the Fraud Squad were convinced that he was not only guilty but the organiser of the scam. A month ago your accounting department hired a clerk, an undercover agent who's a computer expert. If you know what you're doing you can find anything that's ever been on a computer, even if it's been dumped in the trash. She was surprised to find security so tight in your accounting department, but she dug away discreetly, only to be even more surprised to find a not too difficult trail leading to a Swiss bank account—in your name.'

Gerry licked dry lips. 'I see,' she said quietly. 'You mean the agency has been used to launder money?'

'No, but the agency's computers had been used to organise it all. Apparently by you. And that increased the police suspicions, because the trail was a little too clear, a little too obvious. So they began looking into Honor's affairs, and they found that she'd gone to Thailand earlier this year, and while she was there she'd met a couple of extremely unsavoury characters. The New Zealand police liaise very closely with the Thai drug squad, and they'd been watching these men.'

Thank heavens for suspicious police. Gerry's shoulders ached with the effort it took to keep them straight.

To her astonishment Bryn asked, 'Do you want a drink— a cup of tea, something?'

Her stomach roiled at the prospect. 'No thanks. Go on.'

'Honor has been living just above her income; she seems to be taking great care not to exceed it by enough to cause suspicion. But even then you weren't entirely in the clear. They were certain Honor was guilty, but your status was problematical. She and her lover might well have intended to use you as a scapegoat, hence the nice clear trail to the Swiss account.'

'So the police decided that you should sniff around much more closely,' she said, not even trying to inject some emotion into the words. 'What a pity I'm not good at pillow talk.'

Although green fire smouldered in the depths of his eyes, his voice remained level. 'In the end they decided to apply a little pressure.'

'How?'

'You were got out of the way and put in a situation where any calls could be monitored.' His voice was hard. 'Honor was contacted by someone who told her he could sell heroin at a cut rate—much better heroin than she was getting from Asia. He sent her a sample which had been tagged.'

'Tagged?'

'Treated so that it is easily identifiable. She didn't even try to contact you; instead, she and the accountant took off for Tahiti after they'd sold the heroin on. It was traced through several people, including the person who'd named you. He's been taken into custody, and he talked enough to convince the police he'd never met the woman he called Gerry. The accountant and Honor were arrested half an hour ago as they landed from Tahiti.'

Gerry couldn't bear to look at him, couldn't bear to think of Honor, peddling beauty and death. Reining herself in, she asked, 'It still isn't conclusive proof that I'm in the clear?'

He frowned. 'The police have been through your affairs with a fine-tooth comb, and nothing but the tip-off connects you to the smuggling. You live within your income, you have no secret assets, and the hidden bank account has been examined by the Swiss—although it was set up under your name, the beneficiaries turned out to be Honor and the accountant. That's proof enough, Geraldine.'

'Why?' Gerry asked harshly. She should be relieved, but

she was too shattered to feel anything. 'What made her do it?'

'She's in it for the money.' Contempt seared the words. 'She met the accountant, and the two of them set it up; you were the perfect scapegoat.'

'So you did your duty as a good citizen and got me out of the way while they investigated Honor. I admire your dedication to the cause.'

He shrugged. 'By then I was as certain as anyone could be without proof that you were in the clear.'

'But you needed that proof,' she said, her quiet comment hiding, she hoped, the pain behind it. 'And you made love to me to stop me from making any connections. You must think I'm a total fool. I must *be* a total fool.'

'I made love to you because I couldn't help myself,' he said roughly.

Why did he lie? Did it matter? Driven by the need to escape, to lick her wounds in private, she said, 'It seems you make a habit of using women. First Cara, then me—'

He said ferociously, 'Will you stop saying that? I haven't even kissed Cara, and as for you—doesn't it tell you something that when I should have kept you at arm's length I couldn't wait to get into bed with you?'

'It tells me that—' She stopped, twisting her head. 'What's that? It sounds like a plane.'

Bryn swore under his breath, but didn't try to stop her when she brushed past him and ran up the steps. The seaplane headed towards them and came in slowly, settling into the lagoon in twin feathers of spray.

Bryn said, 'I called him up half an hour ago, but he said he'd be at least an hour.'

'You can't trust anyone nowadays, can you?' Gerry said bitterly.

'I'll get your luggage,' he said tightly, disappearing down the steps.

Biting her lip, Gerry walked across to the railing, watching through a mist of tears as the plane taxied to a stop. What had she expected? Making love to her had been hardly honourable, but then, he had done it for the good of the country, she thought tiredly.

And she was not in love with him.

Not even one tiny bit.

It was a silent trip in the dinghy to the plane. All Gerry had to rely on now was her dignity. She forced a smile for the pilot and his hairy, enthusiastic co-pilot, who barked a greeting and had to be restrained from hurtling into the lagoon. Without hearing the pleasantries Bryn and the pilot exchanged, she clambered in.

Bryn looked up, green eyes burning in the emphatic framework of his dark, autocratic face. 'Goodbye, Geraldine,' he said, and expertly backed the dinghy away, rowing steadily towards the *Starchaser*.

She couldn't summon a reply; instead she nodded and settled back into her seat.

'Put your seatbelt on,' the pilot yelled.

She did up the clasp and turned her head resolutely away, watching the island skim past until the engine noise altered and they lifted above the vivid lagoon. As soon as they were in the air she allowed herself to wipe her eyes and blow her nose, and watched steadfastly as the water fell away beneath them and the bright, feathery crowns of the coconut palms dwindled into a fringe within the protective white line of the reef, and then were left behind.

CHAPTER ELEVEN

'ALL right,' Gerry said with a sigh, 'let's call it a day.'

Troy covered a yawn. 'It's been a long one,' she said with a grimace, looking at the cluttered circular table with its central rack of files.

Gerry got to her feet and stretched. 'Oh, well, it's over now.'

The past six months had been horrendous, with Honor in prison awaiting trial, and then the trial itself, culminating in long sentences for both her and her lover. Gerry had been appalled to discover how cleverly the whole operation had been managed. Honor had targeted the rich and the famous—people who'd wanted to avoid any sleaze or violence or danger.

The agency had been thoroughly compromised, but although they had lost models, many had stuck by Gerry. Which was surprising, as Honor's defence had suggested with infinite delicacy that Gerry had been the prime mover in the heroin ring and that Honor had been framed.

Gerry thought drearily that her models' loyalty had been virtually the only good thing about these last six months.

No, that was untrue. She'd learned enough basic Maori at night classes to make herself understood, and Lacey hadn't vomited for three months. She and the Australian girl kept in close touch with e-mail, and it certainly sounded as though Lacey was getting her life together.

Abruptly Gerry said, 'I'm going to sell the agency.'

Troy stared. 'Why? You've worked like a slave to control all the damage, and now that things are going smoothly again you want to leave. It doesn't make sense. What will you do?'

It was impossible to tell her the real reason—that Gerry was heartsick for a man who hadn't been near her since, grim-faced and impervious, he'd watched her leave him. Bryn hadn't appeared in any of the court proceedings; for all she knew, he could have disappeared off the face of the earth.

She said, 'I'm going to have a holiday. And I think I might learn to cook. Properly.'

Troy's mouth opened, then closed on her unspoken comment. After a moment, she nodded. 'Good idea. And after you've learned to cook properly—what then?'

'I'm going to write a column for one of the magazines— personal style, to thine own self be true, where to shop for good, elegant, stylish clothes that suit and don't break the budget—that sort of thing. Under a pseudonym, of course. The editors think—and I agree—that it would be better to lie low for a while until the stink from this has died down, if it ever does. Mud sticks.'

Troy said briskly, 'Don't be an idiot. Anyone who knows you knows you had nothing to do with Honor and her rotten get-rich-quick scheme.' She paused before asking, 'Are you going to be able to earn enough to live on?'

'I should get a decent sum for the agency. It's worth quite a bit, so I'll pay off the mortgage on the house, repay the bank loan that I took out to buy Honor's share of the agency, and invest any money left over. I won't be able to live on that, but as well as the magazine column, I've been thinking about going back to journalism—freelancing.' She gave a wry smile. 'There'll be enough variety in that to stop me getting bored. I used to enjoy writing articles, and I was good at it.'

'You were brilliant at it,' Troy said, eyeing her thoughtfully. 'I think it's a wonderful idea. Have you got a buyer for the agency?'

'The first person with the money,' Gerry answered cynically. 'No, it'll have to be someone I trust. I haven't got it back into running order to sell it to anyone I don't like. I probably haven't thanked you for coming in as assistant and general dogsbody, either. Honestly, Troy, it's made all the difference.'

'I've loved doing it.'

'How does Damon feel about it?'

Her friend set two pens carefully down on the table. 'At first he hated it, and whined about how bad a wife and mother I am, even though the new nanny is working out brilliantly—the kids love her, and she's so good with them.' She picked up a pen and fiddled with it. 'Anyway, it doesn't matter what he thinks. I've left him.'

Gerry landed limply in the chair beside her. 'Oh,' she said inadequately.

Troy flushed, but held her head high. 'And it's not because he's having an affair with one of his executives, either. I'd decided before I knew about that. I just looked at him and thought, Would anyone who really loved me treat me the way he does? And I thought, No, if you love someone you want them to be happy, instead of making them miserable as sin. So I got my lawyer to draw up a separation agreement. Damon's flounced off to live with his dark-haired, clever girlfriend, and the kids and I are in the house with the nanny.'

'I'm sorry,' Gerry said. Sorry, she meant, for shattered illusions and broken dreams, not sorry that Damon had gone. 'Why didn't you tell me?'

Troy looked self-conscious. 'Well, you've been so busy with the agency, and so worried about the court case, I didn't want to add to your woes. And I needed to do this on my own. I've always turned to you and cried all over you and generally leaned on you; I thought it was about time I grew up and made some decisions for myself, and carried through on them.'

'You've certainly done that,' Gerry said, feeling oddly abandoned.

Troy shook her head. 'Yes, well, it hasn't been easy,' she admitted, 'but really I've known ever since we got married that I'd been a fool—I just didn't want to admit it. You know me, stubborn as hell. This job has been a lifesaver, and I've loved it.' She looked around the office with its posters of models on the walls, its air of being in a continual state of chaos, and said, 'And I'd have to talk it over with my financial advisers, but I'd like to buy the agency very much. I know you bought Honor out—she hasn't any other claim on it, has she?'

'No,' Gerry said shortly. She'd gone to the finance company expecting to be turned down, but it had been no problem, and Honor, needing the cash for lawyers, had been eager to be rid of her share.

'Good.' Troy put the pen down. She looked eager and excited, more like the woman who'd been a very successful model than the overwrought wife who'd wept in the restaurant six months ago. 'Do you remember Sunny Josephs, who used to be booker for me in the days when I was setting the catwalks on fire? She went off to Chicago just after I married, and did really well there, but she wants to come home. She wrote to me a couple of months ago and asked if there was something she could buy into here. There wasn't at the time, but if she's interested in coming in as my partner, it would be perfect. She knows more about the industry than anyone else, and having her here would give me more time with the kids.'

'It sounds ideal,' Gerry said.

'It does, doesn't it?' Her friend smiled. 'OK, then, I'll get my financial person to talk to yours.'

Troy had worked hard, earning trust and respect from the models. Her background had helped, but it was her driving desire to succeed that would make her a success. If she wanted to put the small fortune she'd earned from her days as a model into the agency, she'd do well.

Gerry drove home through a late summer dusk, enjoying the incandescent colours of sunset staining the western sky. Auckland had wound down for the day, but there were still too many cars on the roads and plenty of people on the streets. Through her windows floated that indescribable mixture of flowers and car fumes and salt and barbecues— the scents of Auckland in summer.

But in her heart it was always winter, and even as she scoffed at herself for being melodramatic she accepted that the interlude with Bryn had altered her life, changed something basic in her soul.

She couldn't have fallen in love so quickly, so what she felt for him had to be sheer, teeth-clenching frustration, an intense, unsatisfied desire. If they'd had a torrid affair she'd be restless by now, seeking ways to be free of him without hurting him.

Turning into her gate, she hit the button for the garage and watched the door fold upwards. As she nudged into place beside the empty space where Cara's sporty little model usually sat, she smiled. After a couple of edgy months pining for Bryn, Cara had found herself a boyfriend. Simon played professional rugby and had been picked for the All Blacks, New Zealand's national team.

It had to be true love, Gerry had decided, because although he was a dear, and very intelligent, with a degree in history, he was a far cry from the handsome models and television stars Cara had preferred before him. In spite of this, Cara seemed totally besotted, and although Simon viewed his love with a slightly sardonic gaze, he clearly loved her deeply. Gerry hoped it would last, especially as Cara was talking about moving in with him.

Her new housemate wasn't home either. Improbably named Alfred, he was six feet two of impossibly gorgeous male with shoulders as wide as barn doors. He drove a beat-up Falcon with rusty doors and a hood that rattled, in which he'd been living until Gerry offered him a room and bed, and was headed for super-stardom as a model. So far he'd stuck close to home because his father was ill, but it wouldn't be long before he was snapped up by the overseas market.

She'd miss him. Not only was he funny and a good cook, but he'd provided eager muscle when she'd remodelled the garden that spring.

The prospect of finding another housemate was depressing. But then, she thought, walking between banks of cosmos to the door, everything depressed her this golden summer. Since she'd flown away from an unnamed atoll and left Bryn Falconer behind, life had seemed too much trouble.

She'd hoped that when she sent a carefully selected folder of photographs of hats for the Longopai islanders to copy he might contact her, but he hadn't, unless you counted a formal, perfectly phrased letter written by his secretary to thank her for her efforts on the islanders' behalf.

Even now that Gerry had secured the future of her models and cleared her name as far as it could be cleared, and was confident the agency would be in good hands, she couldn't summon much enthusiasm for either a holiday or her latest venture into journalism.

She stooped to smell a heavy peach and yellow Abraham Derby rose, losing herself in its intense, heady fragrance. As she stood up and walked towards the front verandah a blackbird, deciding she was an imminent threat to avian life, flew screaming across the lawn towards the hedge.

'Oh, grow up!' Gerry told it crisply, and bent to examine the round, glossy leaves of her Chatham Island forget-me-nots. It was a gamble, growing them this close to the equator, but given the right place they could thrive even in Auckland's warm, humid, maritime climate. These ones looked all right so far, but getting them through the summer would be tricky.

As a car stopped outside the hedge a latent, atavistic intuition pulled her skin taut. Every sense on full alert, she straightened, staring at the house, unable to swivel around.

'Geraldine.'

How had she known? She hadn't seen him, certainly hadn't heard him, and yet from the moment the car drew to a halt she'd known it was Bryn.

Gathering her inner resources, she slowly turned. As he came towards her, her heart contracted fiercely, squeezing her emotions into one solid, unreachable ball. 'Hello, Bryn,' she said quietly. 'How are you?'

'I'm well, thank you. And you?'

He looked good. Green eyes gleaming, golden skin glow-

ing in the apricot light of dusk, white shirt open at the neck
and with the sleeves rolled back to reveal his muscular forearms, dark trousers cut with the spare, unforgiving elegance
of English tailoring—oh, yes, he looked more than good.

Gerry felt tired and grubby.

'I'm well too,' she said courteously. She most emphati-
cally did not want him inside her house again, and yet she
could see that he wasn't going to go until he'd got whatever
it was that had brought him there.

Sure enough, he said quietly, implacably, 'Invite me in,
Geraldine.'

'Come inside, Bryn.' Her voice was flat, composed.

'Thank you.'

She led him to the kitchen and asked, 'Would you like
a beer?'

'If you're having one.'

'I'll have juice.' Stooping, she picked up a bottle of
Alfred's ice beer and a jug of grapefruit juice before closing
the fridge door.

'Can I get down some glasses?' Bryn said.

'Unless you drink it from the bottle?' She winced as the
glass bottom of the bottle rang against the stainless steel
bench.

Black brows lifting, he shook his head. 'Do you?'

'No. My father had very strong ideas on how a young
lady should behave—feminism passed him by completely.'
She indicated a cupboard door, and as Bryn reached for
two heavy-based glasses she opened the drawer and took
out a bottle-opener. 'Drinking anything from the bottle was
about as low as you could go and still call yourself human.'

'Let me do that,' Bryn said.

Gerry set her jaw. He certainly could; then he might not
notice her shaking hands.

His were perfectly steady, as steady as his voice. 'Your
father was a gentleman of the old school.'

Her heart thudded with erratic impatience; deliberately,
carefully, she armoured herself against the pulsing, driving
need he'd brought with him.

'Yes,' she said.

He gave her a glass and lifted his own. 'So here's to the future,' he said pleasantly, and drank.

Gerry looked away. The future. Yes, she could drink to that. 'The future,' she echoed, and took a tiny mouthful of juice. 'Come and sit down,' she urged in her most gracious, hostessy voice.

His mouth twisted slightly, but he stood back to let her lead the way to the sitting area. Once there, however, he stayed standing and surveyed the room with a long, considering gaze. 'When I walked in here the day we met,' he said, 'I thought how warm and welcoming, how serene and elegant and mischievous this room was.'

'Mischievous?' she echoed warily.

He smiled. 'It's decorated with an impeccable eye for colour and proportion but a closer look reveals the quirky things that save it from stultifying good taste. Like the glass frog on the table, and the clock.'

'It's an American acorn clock,' she said, trying to stifle the warm glow caused by his appreciation, 'about a hundred and fifty years old. I fell in love with its shape and the lovely little picture on glass, and the dealer let me pay it off by instalments, bless her.' She couldn't stop babbling. 'It was a bargain too—I got it for about half what it's worth.'

He looked at her with an enigmatic smile. 'You're nervous,' he said. 'Why?'

Gerry fought for self-possession, and managed to produce a fairly good approximation. With a faint snap in her tone she said, 'I didn't expect to see you again.'

He drank half the beer and set it down. 'I stayed away,' he said calmly, 'because I was warned that it might compromise the case if I saw you while it was in progress. And because I had a couple of things I wanted to do, and something I had to come to terms with.'

Her breath stayed locked in her chest. 'Such as?' she asked, almost dizzy with expectation too long denied.

'I had to track down the man who duped your father.'

He spoke equably, as though this was just another task ticked off.

'How did you know who he was?'

'Everyone in New Zealand knew who he was. We're too small a country for that sort of thing not to get around.'

Gerry's mouth dried. 'And did you find him?'

'In Australia, living a comfortable life in Perth.' His voice was considered, but when she stole a look at him she drew in a jagged breath at the cold glitter in his eyes.

She said, 'What happened?'

'I confronted him. He did a lot of wriggling, but in the end we came to an understanding. He agreed that you should be reimbursed, and what's left of the money is now waiting in a holding account. I know that nothing can repay you for your father's pain and death, but at least you have what is rightfully yours and the cause of it has been punished.'

'I don't believe it,' Gerry said numbly. 'How did you do it?'

His smile was sardonic. 'You don't want to know. It was legal, if a trifle unethical.'

'And will he find someone else to steal from?'

His face hardened. 'Not for some years, anyway. He's now in prison.'

She drank some of the juice, welcoming the sharp, tangy taste. 'Did you put him there?' she asked.

'I gave him a choice,' he said calmly. 'He chose what he felt was the lesser of two evils.'

She stole a careful look. 'What was the alternative?'

'Extradition to New Zealand.'

Gerry met his eyes. They were flat and deadly and opaque; he looked a very formidable man indeed. Her stomach performed a few acrobatics and she said mutedly, 'I'm very grateful.'

'You're not, you're worried, but it will be all right.' He smiled ironically. 'He didn't deserve to get away with it.'

'No, he didn't, but I don't want you doing my dirty work for me. And revenge is never a good basis for action.'

'This wasn't revenge,' he said coolly. 'It was justice.'

Still troubled, she moved to look out of the window at the new garden. Angular rust-red flowers of kangaroo paw lifted towards the sky, the spiky leaves reflected in the still, smooth water of the pool. Nosing its way slowly from beneath a waterlily leaf, the biggest and reddest of the goldfish headed across towards the other side, then gave a flick of its long white tail and disappeared into the depths.

Gerry's galloping heartbeat had eased into something like its normal speed, but she could taste the awareness on her tongue, feel Bryn's presence on her skin. Was informing her of the incarceration of her father's manager all he'd come back for? Caution clogged her tongue as she said, 'Thank you.'

'If you don't mind,' he said, 'I'd like to tell you about my sister.'

She almost held her breath. 'No, I don't mind at all.'

He looked down at his empty glass and said austerely, 'I told you that she was tall.'

'And unhappy.'

He nodded. 'Yes. It was all right while we both went to primary school, but when I was sent away to boarding school she lived for the times I came home. After I'd finished school I took an engineering degree at Christchurch, and when I came home the last time she was so thin and ill I was horrified. I took her to the doctor; he diagnosed anorexia. Apparently she'd been tormented at school about her height and her size. My grandmother was also ill, so I can't entirely blame her for not noticing what was going on.'

Gerry had guessed—of course she'd guessed—but she was horrified just the same. 'I'm so sorry,' she said, feeling wretchedly inadequate.

'I stayed with her, but it was too late. She died of heart failure.' His voice thickened. 'She was seventeen.'

She went across and wrapped his hands in both of hers. 'Oh, Bryn,' she said.

His fingers tightened on hers. 'I should have noticed.'

'How could you? You weren't there. And ten years ago people didn't know much about eating disorders.'

He let her hands go. Rebuffed, she stepped back, watching him reimpose control over his features. 'I blamed everyone—my grandparents, popular culture, the fashion magazines Anna used to pore over—but I've realised it was to hide my own guilt.'

Gerry said quietly, 'It's a normal reaction. And perhaps you were right. Our preoccupation with thinness is unhealthy.'

'I blamed you too,' he said.

'I know.'

He paused, then said deliberately, 'When I saw you with that baby in your arms I thought, Damn it all to bloody hell, there she is. My woman. It was as simple and inevitable as that, a sudden, soul-deep recognition. You were everything I thought I despised—fashionable, elegant, well-bred, beautiful, working in a career I loathed. And possibly an importer of heroin. I had to manufacture reasons for disliking you, for stopping you from affecting me, but you cut straight through into my heart and took up residence there.'

Her stomach dropped. He waited, but when she couldn't speak he said coolly, 'I soon found out that you weren't superficial and foolish; you had a natural kindness that made you take poor Lacey under your wing, and you tolerated being stranded with grace and fortitude.'

'It had to be one of the most luxurious strandings anyone's ever had,' she said huskily.

'I should have kept my distance. I'd never been at the mercy of my hormones before, but every time I saw you my gut clenched and I wanted you. I had no intention of making love to you,' he said curtly. 'I couldn't believe that you could be connected with the heroin ring, but it was a measure of how far I'd fallen in love with you that I let my passion override my common sense.' When she remained silent he added harshly, 'That had never happened to me before.'

Head bent so that he couldn't see her face, she asked, 'If you loved me, why didn't you tell me? We might not have been able to meet during the trial, but I'd have known.'

He waited so long to answer that she looked up swiftly, and saw the autocratic features set in lines of self-derision and irony. 'I was afraid to put it to the test. You gave me no indication that you wanted me for anything other than a lover.'

Gerry had lived with the knowledge of her love for so long that she couldn't believe her ears. While impetuous words clogged her tongue, he went on.

'You can't know how it felt to put you on the plane and let you go when every instinct was hammering at me to keep you with me by whatever means I had to use.'

She drew in a deep, impeded breath. The first wild delight at seeing him, at hearing him tell her what she'd only ever imagined in fantasy, was fading, leaving her fearful and tense. She asked, 'What were the other things you wanted to do?'

'I needed to see Lacey. I was determined that she wasn't going down the same road as Anna.'

'She didn't tell me,' she said in surprise.

'I asked her not to. I had to persuade her father to let her see a counsellor. She's helped, but it was your letters and your encouragement that pulled her back from the brink. She's going to be all right.'

'And the thing you had to come to terms with?'

He walked across to the French windows and stood looking out over her newly revamped garden. It had been a good summer and the plants were growing apace, lush and vigorous. On the edge of the wide deck a large pot held a tumble of petunias in soft lilacs and white and pinks.

Bryn turned away and said quietly, 'I've fought against loving anyone ever since my mother died and my father abandoned us. It hurt too much. I didn't rationalise like that, of course, when I was a kid, but I made sure I only loved Anna. And then she died. When I met you I resented what I felt for you and I was scared. Loving you—needing you—

gave you power that I was intensely reluctant to yield. It took me some time to accept that when you love someone as much as I love you, there is no capitulation. Or, if there is, it's surrender to all that's good, to a happiness I've never expected, never hoped for because I didn't think it existed. Even though I suspected you, I learned to love you. I need you, Geraldine, and I think you need me too.'

A volatile mixture of joy and dread filled her. Almost whispering, she said, 'Bryn—I must—'

Two strides brought him back to stand in front of her. For the first time, she could read what lay in the clear, glimmering depths of his eyes. Her heart turned over and agony gripped her, froze the words on her tongue, speared through her in an unrelenting torment.

With the rough note in his voice more pronounced than she'd ever heard it, he said, 'So, Geraldine, now that you're in the clear and your life's back on track, will you marry me?'

She allowed herself one radiant moment of pure, keen happiness, sharp and penetrating as a knife-blade, and then, because she didn't dare hope for more, she said, 'I'm not in the clear—I probably never will be. After the defence's insinuations plenty of people think I was in it up to my neck and managed to frame Honor. Or, if not that, that I knew what she was doing and condoned it.'

'That's stupid—'

She gave him a tight smile. 'I've been asked if I can get the stuff,' she said without bitterness.

'By whom?' There was no mistaking the lethal intentness in the quiet voice.

'It doesn't matter.'

'It matters,' he said, that menacing silky note back in his words. 'I want to know so that I can tell whoever did that they'd better back off or they'll have me to deal with.'

Gerry managed to say on a half-sob, 'It wouldn't help, Bryn. And having a wife who's been mixed up in a very unsavoury case isn't going to help your reputation.'

'If you don't want to marry me, just say so,' he said. 'Don't make excuses.'

'I don't want to marry you,' she said, listening to the sound of her heart shattering.

To her astonishment he laughed. 'Good,' he said outrageously. 'I'm going to have a wonderful time changing your mind.'

She looked at him—indomitable, tall and strong and tough—and knew that she wouldn't win. While she searched for ways to handle this—and to fight the insistent whispering from her treacherous heart that this time it might be the true, the real thing—he took her glass and raised her shaking hands to his mouth and kissed her fingertips.

In a dark, smoky voice he said, 'Marry me, Geraldine, and I'll do my utmost to make you happy, I swear it.'

'No,' she said, unshed tears burning behind her eyes. 'You don't understand, Bryn. I can't promise you that—or anything. I fall in love, but it never lasts. Eventually I get bored, or irritated, or desperate—or all three. My self-esteem takes a beating every time it happens, and you'll end up hating me. Even if you're willing to take the chance, I'm not.'

'How long does it usually last?' he demanded, not giving an inch.

She shook her head, but he lifted her chin with a hand that wouldn't be denied, and stared into her eyes as though trying to force her surrender. 'How long, damn you?'

'It's useless. I won't do this to you.'

'I won't let you go. I've been looking for you all my life and I'm not going to give up now.'

She read the truth in his eyes. Concentrated purpose blazed there, masterful, unsparing. Joy battled with terror in her heart. Summoning her utmost strength of will, she said, 'I'll be your mistress—live with you—but I won't marry you. I won't ask anything of you at all except that when I want to go you let me.' Her eyes were as hard as his; she should be sending him away, but she was racked by love, by her need for what he alone could give her.

She expected him to refuse. Bryn wasn't a man who surrendered to another's will; he'd said he was possessive, and she believed him, and the only thing she could offer him would be sheer torture for both of them.

As well as an insult.

But after staring at her for several heart-racking moments he demanded, 'What's the longest you've ever stayed in love?'

'A year,' she said, closing her eyes. 'Not more than a year.'

Silence, taut and terrifying, crackled between them. She couldn't look at him, couldn't bear the sound of her heart thudding unsteadily, painfully, in her ears.

At last he said heavily, 'All right. If that's what it takes. Only I'm setting a condition too. Two, in fact.'

'What?'

'That we don't refer to this again, and that if we're still together after two years you marry me.'

Tears roughened her voice as she said, 'All right. We'll do that.'

Gerry walked towards the front door. Yes, there he was, smiling, the green eyes lit with the secret flame that was for her and her alone, the autocratic face intent only on her.

'Good day?' he asked, shrugging off his jacket.

She smiled and reached up to kiss him briefly. 'Great. At ten o'clock this morning—just as I was driving over the Harbour Bridge—I finally got a handle on the article about computers, and I've just about finished it.'

'Of course you have,' he said.

'You must have begun to wonder, especially when you found me fretting at the laptop at three o'clock this morning,' she teased against his mouth.

'I can think of much more interesting things to do at three in the morning than obsess over an article.' His arms tightened around her and he kissed her again, his mouth demanding, seeking, a potent, heated promise.

Gerry's heart sped up. 'Mmm,' she breathed when his head lifted, 'you did. Much more interesting...'

She'd never get used to seeing him like this, eyes gleaming, all tension gone from his face.

After dropping a hard, swift kiss on her mouth, he straightened, saying, 'What are we doing tonight?'

'Nothing.' She said the word casually. Not that he'd be fooled; during the past two years he'd learned to read her most guarded tone and expression. Yet in many ways he was still an enigma to her. Oh, she understood the imperatives that drove him, and she had come to appreciate his standards and values, but although he was a tender, fierce, sensual lover, and a man she could rely on utterly, she had no idea whether he wanted to change things now that the two-year period was over.

'What are we eating?' he asked cautiously.

Laughing, she hugged him. 'I ordered in,' she said promptly. 'It'll be here in three-quarters of an hour.'

He didn't open champagne, but as she sat on the bed and talked to him while he changed from dark suit to trousers and shirt that showed off his broad shoulders and long legs so well, she told herself that she didn't care. What they had was precious enough for her; in fact, if she was any happier she might well explode with it.

The meal—prepared by one of Auckland's best restaurants—was superb, and the wine Bryn chose magnificent, a wonderful New Zealand white. At last, when they were both replete, Bryn asked, 'Brandy?'

'No, thank you.' She was curled up on the huge sofa, watching him with heavy eyes, anticipation licking feverishly through her veins. Light shimmered in a tawny aura around his head, played across the authoritative features, the arrogant nose, the strong line of jaw, the beautiful sculpture of his mouth.

He looked up and his mouth hardened. 'When you look at me like that, I want you,' he said deliberately. 'In fact, when I'm with you I'm in a constant state of arousal, but all it takes is one sleepy glance from those blue-green eyes and my body springs into violent life.'

Although his deep voice was slow and tranquil and composed, sensation sky-rocketed through her.

She smiled, and he laughed under his breath. 'Sheer magic. That smile's enough to charm the birds from heaven. I think I must be addicted to you.'

'It works both ways,' she said, aware of a faint disappointment, knowing that she had no right to be disappointed; she had set the parameters of their relationship. If he didn't want to change them she'd accept his decision, because she knew now that she loved him with a love that would last all her life.

'Addiction?' He walked across to the sofa, smiling with a set, savage movement of his mouth as she made room for him and held out her arms. Softly he said, 'Let's see if we can appease this addiction a little, shall we?'

During their time together he had introduced her to ways of making love that had thrilled and shocked her, but this time he took it very tenderly, very gently, as though she were still a virgin and this was their first time.

'It has to be addiction,' he said much later, when they were lying together, heart pressed to heart, 'because I can never get enough of you, never satisfy this need to take you. You walk ahead of me, just out of reach, too much your own woman to ever become wholly mine.'

Muscles flexed beneath skin sheened slightly with sweat as he sat up and reached for his trousers on the floor. Gerry ran an indolent finger down his spine, smiling when she felt the skin tighten beneath her fingertip. 'I am yours,' she said lazily. 'You know that.'

He smiled grimly and turned back to her. 'I know you like what you can do to me.'

From his hand dropped a shower of pearls, darkly peacock blue as a tropical lagoon at twilight, rounded and gleaming and luminous, landing on her sensitised skin with gentle impact, sliding coolly across her breasts and stomach and waist.

'Oh, darling,' she said, her voice velvet and replete, 'what on earth are these for?'

Casually pushing them aside, Bryn dropped a kiss on the slight curve of her stomach. 'It's our anniversary,' he said.

Although the vow he'd extracted from her two years ago had been uppermost in her mind for the past couple of weeks, she was filled with a quite ridiculous apprehension.

'And so?' she asked.

He scooped up a handful of pearls and spread them across her skin. 'Satin against satin. You haven't left me,' he said, not looking at her.

'No.'

'Do you want to?' His voice was level and detached, almost indifferent.

'No,' she said again, her heart pounding so heavily she thought he must be deafened by it. And because she owed him this surrender, she added jaggedly, 'Not ever.'

'In that case, I suppose the only decision we have to make is where we get married.'

Vast, consuming relief—and a strange, superstitious pang—shot through her. 'If you think,' she said forcefully, 'that that is any sort of proposal, you'd better think again.'

'Do you want me to go down on my knees?' His mouth was taut, and still he wouldn't look at her. 'I will if you want me to. You know that I'd do anything to keep you, anything at all.'

She wound her arms around him, pulling his lean, naked body down to her. 'All you need to do is say that you forgive me for thinking that what I feel for you was anything like the way I felt for any other man,' she said unevenly. 'These past two years have been the happiest in my life. I don't ever want to leave you—sometimes I wake up in the middle of the night terrified that it's all been a dream, that you don't love me, that I drove you away because I was stupid enough to think that I was like my mother. And I stare into an empty world, dark and hopeless.'

His mouth touched her trembling one, stifling the feverish words.

'Hush,' he murmured, 'there's nothing to forgive. Nothing. I love you, and I'd follow you to the ends of the earth, give you anything you ever asked for, even if it was a life together with no formal ties.'

'I was frightened when I made that stipulation,' she admitted.

'I know. But I was almost convinced that you loved me. I have no idea what drove your mother, but you're not like her. Along with the passion and the fire and that keen, astute brain, you're sane and kind and loving—all I'll ever want. And I knew it the moment I walked into the kitchen in the villa and saw you cuddling that baby—even though I still thought you were mixed up with the drug ring.'

'The sight of me holding a baby convinced you I wasn't?' she asked, running her fingertips over the smooth swell of his shoulder.

'Yes. Even though I knew of that trail to Switzerland, neatly labelled with your name. You were so concerned about the child. It didn't jell with Geraldine the smart, sophisticated woman of the world, or Geraldine the drug smuggler. But it wasn't faked. After that, although I struggled hard to keep an unbiased mind, in my heart I knew you couldn't have done it, because you valued life too much to be caught up in a filthy trade like that.'

She kissed the side of his throat and said, 'Maddie's all right now. I had lunch with her today.'

'Good.' But he spoke absently. His mouth touched a certain spot below her ear and she shivered. 'Speaking of babies,' he said huskily, 'how do you think I'd be as a father?'

She smiled dreamily. 'You'll be a wonderful father,' she whispered. 'But we'd better get married first because children need stability. They need to know that their parents are going to be there for them. They need to know that their parents care enough about each other to get married.'

Although they'd decided on a small wedding, somehow it turned into a huge one, a riotous affair with cousins and children and friends mingling in a day-long summer celebration. Afterwards they went to Longopai, their honeymoon interrupted only by a visit to the atoll where they'd first made love, and first known that they loved.

It was there, lying in the shade of the palms, that Bryn said, 'By the way, I've found the baby.'

'What?'

He opened a sleepy eye and smiled into her puzzled face. 'The abandoned baby. The one you found outside your house.'

Against his chest she asked, 'How did you find her? The social welfare wouldn't tell you.'

'I sent someone to dig deep. She's been adopted. Would you like to see her?'

'Could I?'

'We wouldn't be able to tell them who we are. And I think it should only be the once.'

She nodded. 'Yes, they have their lives,' she said slowly, reluctantly. Then she smiled. They hadn't used any precautions at all since the wedding. With any luck she might be pregnant herself.

A month later she walked across the crisp green grass of the Domain in Auckland towards a hillside seething with excited children and parents. A cool wind blew, but the children in their vivid clothes lit up the glowing green hillside as vividly as the array of kites.

'Over there,' Bryn said, nodding at a couple. The woman, young and slightly overweight, bent to tie up the laces of a child, while a thin young man looked up from a kite laid out on the ground and said something that made both mother and daughter laugh.

Gerry looked at the child. Chubby, rosy in the crisp air, she had candy-floss hair and big blue eyes. Her mother straightened the hood of her anorak, and picked her up. The child snuggled against her mother's shoulder, and both watched as her father lifted the kite and began to run with it. The gusting wind caught it, snatched it and tossed it high into the sky on the end of its string.

The child laughed and clapped her hands, and her mother smiled at her. Another facet of love, Gerry thought.

Quietly she said, 'Goodbye,' and added as mother and daughter followed the man and the kite, 'I didn't even realise that I needed to see her—just to make sure.' She raised a radiant face and said, 'You know me better than I do myself.'

Bryn hugged her and turned her around, walking her back to the car. 'Underneath that elegant mask you're as soft as butter,' he teased.

'So are you.'

He laughed. 'Where you're concerned, yes. But then, why wouldn't I be? You make my life complete.'

'Not just me,' she said demurely. 'I hope not, anyway, because in eight months' time there's going to be another of us.'

His arm tightened around her. When she looked up she saw the sudden intense glitter of tears in his eyes, and then he said, 'Geraldine.'

In that word, said with such raw need, such tenderness, she heard everything she'd ever want to hear. Hand in hand, they walked down the hill and into their future.

MILLS & BOON®

Next Month's Romance Titles

♡

Each month you can choose from a wide variety of romance novels from Mills & Boon®. Below are the new titles to look out for next month from the Presents™ and Enchanted™ series.

Presents™

THE PERFECT LOVER	Penny Jordan
TO BE A HUSBAND	Carole Mortimer
THE BOSS'S BABY	Miranda Lee
ONE BRIDEGROOM REQUIRED!	Sharon Kendrick
THE SEXIEST MAN ALIVE	Sandra Marton
FORGOTTEN ENGAGEMENT	Margaret Mayo
A RELUCTANT WIFE	Cathy Williams
THE WEDDING BETRAYAL	Elizabeth Power

Enchanted™

THE MIRACLE WIFE	Day Leclaire
TEXAS TWO-STEP	Debbie Macomber
TEMPORARY FATHER	Barbara McMahon
BACHELOR AVAILABLE!	Ruth Jean Dale
BOARDROOM BRIDEGROOM	Renee Roszel
THE HUSBAND DILEMMA	Elizabeth Duke
THE BACHELOR BID	Kate Denton
THE WEDDING DECEPTION	Carolyn Greene

On sale from 5th February 1999

H1 9901

Available at most branches of WH Smith, Tesco, Asda, Martins, Borders, Easons, Volume One/James Thin and most good paperback bookshops

MILLS & BOON®
Presents™

Next month, **Sharon Kendrick** *delights us with the first story of her brand new trilogy where three brides are in search of the perfect dress—and the perfect husband!*

Look out for:

One Bridegroom Required!
On sale 5th February '99

One Wedding Required!
On sale 2nd April '99

One Husband Required!
On sale 4th June '99

4 FREE

books and a surprise gift!

We would like to take this opportunity to thank you for reading this Mills & Boon® book by offering you the chance to take FOUR more specially selected titles from the Presents™ series absolutely FREE! We're also making this offer to introduce you to the benefits of the Reader Service™—

- ★ FREE home delivery
- ★ FREE gifts and competitions
- ★ FREE monthly Newsletter
- ★ Books available before they're in the shops
- ★ Exclusive Reader Service discounts

Accepting these FREE books and gift places you under no obligation to buy, you may cancel at any time, even after receiving your free shipment. Simply complete your details below and return the entire page to the address below. *You don't even need a stamp!*

YES! Please send me 4 free Presents books and a surprise gift. I understand that unless you hear from me, I will receive 6 superb new titles every month for just £2.30 each, postage and packing free. I am under no obligation to purchase any books and may cancel my subscription at any time. The free books and gift will be mine to keep in any case.

P9EA

Ms/Mrs/Miss/Mr.................................Initials ....
BLOCK CAPITALS PLEASE

Surname ....

Address ....

....

....Postcode..............................

Send this whole page to:
THE READER SERVICE, FREEPOST CN81, CROYDON, CR9 3WZ
(Eire readers please send coupon to: P.O. BOX 4546, DUBLIN 24.)

Offer not valid to current Reader Service subscribers to this series. We reserve the right to refuse an application and applicants must be aged 18 years or over. Only one application per household. Terms and prices subject to change without notice. Offer expires 31st July 1999. As a result of this application, you may receive further offers from Harlequin Mills & Boon and other carefully selected companies. If you would prefer not to share in this opportunity please write to The Data Manager at the address above.

Mills & Boon Presents is being used as a trademark.

PENNILESS AND SECRETLY PREGNANT

JENNIE LUCAS

STEALING THE PROMISED PRINCESS

MILLIE ADAMS

MILLS & BOON

First Published in Great Britain 2020
by Mills & Boon, an imprint of HarperCollins*Publishers*
1 London Bridge Street, London, SE1 9GF

Penniless and Secretly Pregnant © 2020 Jennie Lucas

Stealing the Promised Princess © 2020 Millie Adams

ISBN: 978-0-263-27834-7

MIX
Paper from
responsible sources
FSC® C007454

PENNILESS
AND SECRETLY
PREGNANT

JENNIE LUCAS

To Pete—Then, Now and Always

CHAPTER ONE

HE COULDN'T AVOID it any longer. He had to tell her the truth.

From the bed, Leonidas Niarxos looked out the window. Across the river, on the other side of the bridge, Manhattan skyscrapers twinkled in the violet and pink sunrise.

Taking a deep breath, he looked down at the woman sleeping in his arms. For the last four weeks, he'd enjoyed the most exhilarating affair of his life. After years of brief, meaningless relationships with women who had hearts as cold as his own, Daisy Cassidy had been like a fire. Warming him. *Burning him*.

For weeks now—from their very first, accidental, surprising night—he'd been promising himself he would end their affair. He would tell her who he really was.

But he'd put it off, always wanting one more day. Even now, after a night of lovemaking, Leonidas wanted her. As he looked at her, feeling her soft naked body pressed so trustingly against his, his willpower weakened. Perhaps he could put off his confession one more day. Until tomorrow.

No, he thought furiously. No!

He had to end this. Daisy was falling in love with him. He'd seen it in her lovely face, in her heartbreakingly luminous green eyes. She believed Leonidas to be Leo Gianakos, a decent, kindhearted man. Perfect, she called him. She thought he was a store clerk without a penny to his name.

Lies, all lies.

Maybe if he took her to his house in Manhattan first, it might soften the blow, he argued with himself. Maybe

Daisy would be more likely to forgive him in his fifty-million-dollar mansion, while he offered her a life filled with luxury and glamour…

Forget it. Did he really believe that either love or money would make Daisy forgive what he'd done? After he revealed his real name, the only emotions she'd ever feel for him again would be horror and hate.

It had all been stolen time.

She sighed in his arms. Looking down, he saw her dark eyelashes flutter in the gray dawn.

He had to tell her. Now. Get it over with. For her sake. For his own.

"Daisy," he said quietly. "Are you awake?"

Stretching her limbs out luxuriously between the soft cotton sheets, Daisy blinked dreamily in the pale light of dawn. Her naked body was filled with the sweet ache of another night of lovemaking. She felt delicious. She felt cherished. She felt like she was in love.

Was she also in trouble?

Her eyes flew open. *You don't* know *anything's wrong*, she told herself fiercely. *It might be nothing. It* has *to be nothing.*

But her ridiculous fear had already ruined their date last night, when Leo had gone to tremendous expense to take her to a way too fancy French restaurant in Williamsburg. She'd been miserable—not just afraid of using the wrong fork, not just uncomfortable in the formal setting, but haunted by a new, awful suspicion.

Could she be pregnant?

"Daisy?" Leo's voice was a husky growl, his powerful body exuding heat and strength as he wrapped one muscular arm around her in the large bed.

"Good morning." Pushing away her fears, she smiled up at his darkly handsome face, silhouetted by the rising dawn.

He hesitated. "How did you sleep?"

Daisy gave him a shyly wicked grin. *"Sleep?"*

Leo gave her an answering grin, and his gaze fell slowly to her lips, her throat, her breasts barely covered by the sheet clinging to her nipples. Over the sheet, his hand brushed her belly, and she wondered again if she could be pregnant. No. She couldn't be. They'd used protection, even that first wild night four weeks ago, when he'd taken her virginity.

But as he softly stroked her body, her breasts felt strangely tender, swollen, beneath his sensual hands...

A sigh rose from the back of his throat as Leo reluctantly pulled away. "Daisy, we need to talk."

Never a phrase anyone wanted to hear. She swallowed. Did her body feel different to him? Had he already guessed her fear? "Talk about what?"

"There's something I need to tell you," he said in a low voice. "Something you're not going to like."

His grim black eyes met hers, over his cruel, sensual mouth and hard jaw, dark with five o'clock shadow.

An awful new fear exploded in the back of her mind.

How much did she really know about him?

After a hellish year, Leo Gianakos had wandered into her life last month like a miracle, like a dream, all dark eyes, tanned skin, sharp cheekbones and a million-dollar smile. From the moment Daisy had first looked at his breathtaking masculine beauty, at his powerful shoulders in that perfectly tailored suit, she'd known he was a thousand miles out of her league.

Yet somehow, they'd ended up in bed. Since that magical day, they'd spent nearly every night together, whenever she wasn't at work.

But it was strange to realize how little she actually knew about him. She didn't know where he worked, or where he lived. He'd always evaded personal questions.

There were all kinds of good reasons why, she'd told herself. Perhaps Leo shared a tiny rat-infested studio with three roommates and was self-conscious about it. After all, not everyone had a wealthy artist friend, as Daisy did, who'd asked them to house-sit. If not for Franck's generosity, Daisy would undoubtedly be sharing a studio with three people, too.

She hadn't pushed Leo for details about his life. They were happy; that was enough.

Now, for the first time, a horrible idea occurred to her. Could there be some other, more sinister reason why he hadn't told her where he worked, or invited her to his apartment? What if—could he possibly be—

"Are you married?" she blurted out, her heart in her throat.

Leo blinked, then gave a low laugh. "Married? If I were married, could I be here in bed with you?"

"Well, are you?" she said stubbornly.

He snorted, his black eyes glinting. "No. I am not married. And for the record, I don't ever intend to be. Ever." His voice dropped to a husky whisper. "That's not the problem."

Daisy stared at him. She was relieved he wasn't married, but...

Leo didn't want to get married? Ever?

She took a deep breath. "I just know so little about you," she said in a small voice. "I don't know where you work, or where you live. I've never met your family or friends."

Pulling away from her, Leo pushed off the sheets and abruptly stood up from the bed. She enjoyed the vision of his powerful naked body in the rosy morning light. She drank in the image of his muscular backside, the strong muscles of his back.

Without looking at her, he reached down to the floor, and started putting on his clothes. Finally, as he pulled on his shirt, he turned back to face her. She was distracted by the brief vision of his muscular chest, laced with dark hair, before he buttoned up the shirt. He looked down at her. "Do you really want to see where I live? Does it matter so much?"

"Of course it matters!" Sitting up in bed, holding the sheet over her breasts with one hand, she motioned around the spacious bedroom with its view of the Manhattan skyline. "Do you think I'd be living in a place like this if my dad's oldest friend hadn't taken pity on me? So please don't feel self-conscious, whatever your apartment is like. Or your job. Whatever it is, I will always think you're perfect!"

Leo stopped buttoning up his shirt. Dropping his hands to his sides, he stared at her across the bedroom, silhouetted by the view of the East River and Manhattan beyond.

She realized he was going to break up with her. She could see it in his grim expression, in the tightness of his sensual lips.

She'd always known this day would come. Leo was ten years older, sexy, tall, broad shouldered and darkly handsome. Daisy had never quite understood what he'd seen in her in the first place. She was so…ordinary. How could a badly dressed, not very interesting waitress from Brooklyn possibly keep the attention of a man like Leo Gianakos?

And if she was pregnant…

No. She couldn't be. *Couldn't*.

Leo took a deep breath. "Would you like to come to my house? Right now? And then…we can talk."

His voice was so strained, it took several seconds for Daisy to realize he was inviting her to his apartment, not breaking up with her.

"Sure." She realized she was smiling.

No, quick, don't let him see; he can't know I'm falling in love with him.

It had been only a month. Even Daisy, with her total lack of romantic experience, knew it was too soon to confess her feelings. Turning her face away, she rose from the bed. "I'll go take a shower…"

She felt Leo's gaze follow her as she walked naked across the luxurious bedroom. Entering the lavish en suite bathroom, she tossed him back a single glance.

Before she'd even had time to turn on the water in the enormous walk-in shower, Leo had caught up with her, already rapidly pulling off his clothes. He kissed her passionately as she pulled away from him with a light laugh, drawing him into the hot, steamy water. They washed each other, and he stroked every inch of her. She leaned back her head as he washed her long brown hair. After she'd rinsed, she straightened, and saw the dark heat of his gaze.

Pushing her against the hot, wet tiled wall, he kissed her, and she nearly gasped as her sensitive, swollen nipples brushed against his muscular chest, laced with rough dark hair. She felt the hardness of him pushing against her soft belly, and yearned. Finally, he wrenched away from her with a rueful growl. "No condom," he sighed.

As he turned off the water, and gently toweled her off with the thick cotton towels, in the back of her mind Daisy wondered nervously if it was already too late for that, if she could be pregnant in spite of their precautions.

Taking her hand in his own, he pulled her back to the bed and made love to her, gently, tenderly, after a night during which they'd already made love twice. She told herself it was their lovemaking which caused her breasts to feel so heavy, her nipples so sensitive that she gasped as he suckled her. That had to be the reason. There could be lots of reasons why her cycle, normally so predictable, was two weeks late… She couldn't be pregnant. *Couldn't.*

She pushed the thought away as Leo lightly kissed her cheeks, her forehead. Smoothing back her unruly brown hair, he cupped her jawline with his powerful hands, and lowered his lips to hers. His kiss was hot and sweet against her lips, so, so sweet, and she was lost in the breathless grip of desire. As he pushed inside her, she cried out with pleasure, soaring to new heights before he, too, exploded.

Afterward, Leo held her tight against his powerful body, the white cotton sheets twisted at their feet. Blinking fast, Daisy stared out the window toward the unforgiving Manhattan skyline, and heard the grim echo of his words.

I am not married. And for the record, I don't ever intend to be. Ever.

His hands tightened around her. "I don't want to lose you," he said in a low voice.

"Lose me?" She peeked at him in bed. "Why would you?"

He gave a low laugh. It had no humor in it. "Let's go to my house. And talk."

"Talk about what?"

"About…me." His serious expression as he got dressed sent panic through her. Nervously, she pulled on clothes in turn, a clean T-shirt and jeans.

"I'm not scheduled to work today. Are you?"

"I can be late," he said flatly.

"Don't clerks need to be at the store when it opens at ten?" When he didn't respond, she tried again. "You won't be fired if you're late?"

"Fired?" Leo sounded grimly amused. "No." He gave her a smile that didn't meet his eyes. "Shall we go?"

As they left the apartment, he held the door open for her, as usual. He was always gallant that way, making her feel cherished and cared for.

When she was younger, and even now that she was twenty-four, boys her age always seemed to want quick, meaningless hookups, without bothering with old-fashioned niceties like opening doors, bringing flowers, giving compliments or even showing up on time. No wonder Daisy had been a virgin when she met Leo. Ten years older, powerful, and handsome like a Greek god, no wonder she'd fallen into bed with him the first night!

Now, as they left the co-op building, going out into the fresh October morning, Daisy glanced at him out of the corner of her eye. She should have been thrilled he was taking her to his apartment. Instead, she had a weird sense of foreboding. What did Leo want to talk about? And which of her own secrets might tumble from her mouth—her love for him, her possible pregnancy or even the fact that she was the daughter of a convicted felon?

As they walked, sunshine sparkled across the East River with the enormous bridge and Manhattan skyline beyond. She started to head for the nearest subway entrance, two blocks away, when he stopped her.

"Let's take a car."

He seemed strangely tense. Smiling, she shook her head. "You can't seriously want to get a rideshare, after all the expense of that fancy dinner last night. The subway is fine. You don't need to bankrupt yourself trying to impress me." She couldn't help thinking how much she loved him for trying. "You're already perfect."

"I didn't mean a rideshare."

She heard a noise behind him. Frowning, she tilted her head. "Did you hear that?"

"Hear what?"

She looked around. "Sounds like a baby crying."

"I'm sure there are children everywhere here. Its mother will take care of it."

A baby was an *it*? Daisy's forehead furrowed. Then she heard the soft cry again. Weak. More like a whine, or a snuffle. She turned toward the alley behind the gleaming waterfront co-op.

"Where are you going?" he asked.

"I just need to make sure…"

"Daisy, it's not your problem—"

But she was already hurrying toward the alley, following the sound. There had been a newspaper story just the month before about a baby abandoned in an alley in New Jersey. Thankfully that child had been found safely, but Daisy couldn't get the story out of her mind. If she didn't investigate this, and something bad happened...

She followed the sound down the alley and was only vaguely aware of Leo behind her. She saw a burlap bag resting on the top of a dumpster. The sound seemed to come from that. It was wiggling. She heard a weak whine. Then a whimper.

"Daisy, don't," Leo said sharply behind her. "You don't know what it is."

But she was already reaching for the bag. It weighed almost nothing. Setting the burlap bag gently on the asphalt, she undid the tie and opened it.

It was a tiny puppy, a fuzzy golden-colored mutt, maybe two months old, wiggling and crying. She stroked it tenderly. "It's a dog!" Sudden rage filled Daisy. "Who would leave a puppy in a dumpster?"

"People can be monsters," Leo said flatly. She looked back at him, bemused. Then the puppy whined, weakly licking her hand, taking all her attention.

"She seems all right," Daisy said anxiously, petting the animal. "But I'd better take her to the vet to make sure." She looked up at Leo. "Do you want to come?"

He looked grim. "To the vet? No."

"I'm so sorry. Could we maybe get together later? You could show me your apartment tonight?"

"Tonight?" His jaw set. "I'm having a party."

She brightened. "How fun! I'd love to meet your friends."

"Fine," he said shortly. "I'll send a car to pick you up at seven."

"I told you, a car's not necessary—"

"Wear a cocktail dress," he cut her off.

"All right." Daisy tried to remember if she even owned a cocktail dress. Carrying the puppy carefully in her arms, she reached up on her tiptoes and kissed Leo's scratchy cheek. "Thanks for understanding. I'll see you at your party."

"Daisy—"

"What?"

She waited, but he didn't continue. He finally said in a strangled voice, "See you tonight."

And he turned away. She watched him stride down the street, his hands pushed in his pockets. Why was he acting so weird? Was he really so embarrassed of where he lived? Embarrassed of his friends?

She looked down at the puppy in her arms, who whined weakly. Turning on her heel, she hurried down the street, going to the veterinary office owned by one of her father's old friends.

"Dr. Lopez, please," she panted, "it's an emergency..."

The kindly veterinarian took one look at the tiny animal in Daisy's arms and waved her inside his office. After an exam, she was relieved to hear the mixed breed puppy was slightly dehydrated, but otherwise fine.

"Someone must have just wanted to get rid of her. She must have been dumped sometime during the night," Dr. Lopez said. "It's lucky the weather isn't colder, or else..."

Daisy shivered. It was heartbreaking to think that while she'd been snuggled warm in bed in Leo's arms, some awful person had been dumping an innocent puppy in the alley, leaving her to die in a burlap bag.

People can be monsters. Leo was right. All Daisy had to do was remember those awful lawyers who'd vindictively harassed her innocent father into prison on those trumped-up forgery charges. Her tenderhearted, artistic-minded father had collapsed in prison, surrounded by strangers. He'd had a stroke and died—

"What are you going to name her?" the vet asked, mercifully pulling her from her thoughts. Daisy blinked.

"Me?"

"Sure, she's your dog now, isn't she?"

Daisy looked down at the puppy on the examining table. She couldn't possibly own a pet. She didn't even rent her own apartment. Franck Bain was due to return from Europe soon, and she'd need to find a new place to live. With her meager income, it was unlikely she'd be able to afford an apartment that allowed a pet. Just thinking of the cost in dog food alone—

No. Daisy couldn't keep her.

But someone had left this puppy to starve. A sweet floppy mutt who just needed a loving home. Could Daisy really abandon her?

Uncertainly, she reached out and softly stroked the dog's head. The animal's big dark eyes looked up at her, and she licked Daisy's hand with a tiny rough tongue.

No. She couldn't.

"You're right. I'm keeping her." She pushed away the worry of expensive vet bills and dog food. "I'll think about a name."

Dr. Lopez tried to wave off her offer of payment, but she insisted on paying. She couldn't live off the charity of her father's friends forever. It was bad enough she'd lived in Franck's apartment for so long, even if he insisted *she* was the one doing him a favor by house-sitting.

She wondered if the gray-haired artist would still think so, after he discovered she'd brought a puppy home.

Leaving the vet's, she went to the nearest bodega and bought puppy food and other pet supplies. Passing another aisle in the store, she hesitated, then furtively added a pregnancy test into her basket, too. Just so she could prove her fears were ridiculous.

After Daisy got the puppy back home and fed, she

stroked her fur. "How could anyone have thrown you away?" she whispered. "You're perfect." Finally, gathering her courage, she left the tiny dog to drowse on the fluffy rug in front of the gas fire and went into the elegant modern bathroom to take the pregnancy test. *Just get it over with*, she told herself. Once she took the test, she would be able to relax.

Instead, she found out to her shock her fears were right. *She was pregnant.*

Pregnant by a man she loved, though she barely knew him.

Pregnant by a man who would never marry her.

Daisy didn't have any money. She didn't have a permanent home. She didn't have a family. Soon, she'd be raising both a puppy and a baby, utterly alone.

She couldn't do it alone. She *couldn't*.

Could she?

She had to tell Leo at the party tonight. The idea terrified her. What would he do when he found out she was pregnant? What would he say? Fear gripped Daisy as she looked at herself in the bathroom mirror.

What had she done by following her heart?

Leonidas Niarxos was in a foul mood as he arrived at his skyscraper in Midtown Manhattan, the headquarters of his international luxury conglomerate, Liontari Inc.

"Good morning, Mr. Niarxos."

"Good morning, sir."

Various employees greeted him as he stalked through the enormous lobby. Then they took one look at his wrathful face and promptly fled. Even his longtime chauffeur, Jenkins, who'd picked him up in Brooklyn—around the corner from Daisy's building, so she wouldn't see the incriminating Rolls-Royce—had known better than to speak as he'd driven his boss back across the Manhattan Bridge.

Leonidas was simmering, brooking for a fight. But he had only himself to blame.

He hadn't been able to tell Daisy his real name.

She'd looked at him with her mesmerizing green eyes, her sensual body barely covered by a sheet, and she'd hinted that seeing where Leonidas lived might make a difference—might give them a future.

At least, that was what he'd wanted to hear. So he'd given in to the temptation to postpone his confession. He'd convinced himself that pleading his case in the private luxury of his mansion, later, after he'd made love to her one last time, might lead to a different outcome.

Now he was paying for that choice. Leonidas Niarxos, billionaire playboy CEO, had just been upstaged by a dog. And he would be forced to confess his true identity in the middle of a political fundraiser, surrounded by the ruthless, powerful people he called friends. Besides, did he honestly think, no matter where or when he told Daisy the truth, she'd ever forgive what he'd done?

Standing alone in his private elevator, Leonidas gritted his teeth, and pushed the button for the top floor.

Daisy was different from any woman he'd ever met. She loved everyone and hid nothing. Her emotions shone on her face, on her body. Joy and tenderness. Desire and need. Her warmth and goodness, her kindness and innocent sensuality, had made him feel alive as he'd never felt before. She'd even been a virgin when he'd first made love to her. How was it possible?

Leonidas never should have sought her out a month ago. But then, he'd never imagined they would fall into an affair. Especially since he'd sent her father to prison.

A year ago, Leonidas had heard a small-time Brooklyn art dealer had somehow procured *Love with Birds*, the Picasso he'd desperately sought for two decades. His lawyer, Edgar Ross, had arranged for Leonidas to see it in his office.

But he'd known at first sight it was fake. He'd felt heartsick at yet another wild-goose chase, trying to recover the shattered loss of his childhood. He'd told his lawyer to press charges, then used his influence with the New York prosecutor to punish the hapless art dealer to the fullest extent of the law.

He'd found out later that the Brooklyn art dealer had been selling minor forgeries for years. His mistake had been trying to move up to the big leagues with a Picasso—and trying to sell it to Leonidas Niarxos.

The old man's trial had become a New York sensation. Leonidas never attended the trial, but everyone had known he was behind it.

It was only later that Leonidas had regrets, especially after his lawyer had told him about the man's daughter, who'd loyally sat behind her elderly father in court, day after day, with huge eyes. He'd seen the daughter's stricken face in a poignant drawing of the courtroom, as she'd tearfully thrown her arms around her father when the verdict had come down and he'd been sentenced to six years. She'd clearly believed in Patrick Cassidy's innocence to the end.

A few months ago, on hearing the man had died suddenly in prison, Leonidas hadn't been able to shake a strange, restless guilt. As angry as he'd been at the man's deceit, even *he* didn't think death was the correct punishment for the crime of art forgery.

So last month, Leonidas had gone to the Brooklyn diner where Daisy Cassidy worked as a waitress, to confirm for himself the girl was all right, and anonymously leave her a ten-thousand-dollar tip.

Instead, as the pretty young brunette had served him coffee, eggs and bacon, they got to talking about art and movies and literature, and he was amazed at how fascinating she was, how funny, warm and kind. And so damn beautiful. Leonidas had lingered, finally asking her if she wanted to meet after her shift ended.

He'd lied to her.

No. He hadn't lied, not exactly. The name he'd given her was a nickname his nanny had given him in childhood, Leo, along with his patronymic, Gianakos.

Leo, Daisy called him, her voice so musical and light, and hearing that name on her sweet lips, he always felt like a different person. A better man.

No woman had ever affected him like this before. Why now? Why her?

He'd never intended to seduce her. But Daisy's warmth and innocent sensuality had been like fire to someone frozen in ice. For the first time in his life, Leonidas had been powerless to resist his desire.

But after tonight, when he told her the truth at his cocktail party—hell, from the moment she saw his *house*, when she obviously believed he lived in some grim studio apartment—he'd have no choice but to do without her.

Just thinking about it, Leonidas barely restrained himself all afternoon from biting the heads off his vice presidents and other employees when they dared ask him a question. But there was no point in blaming anyone else. It was his own fault.

Sitting in his private office, with its floor-to-ceiling windows with all of Manhattan at his feet, Leonidas gazed sightlessly over the city.

Was there any chance he could keep her?

Daisy Cassidy was in love with him. He'd seen her love in her beautiful face, shining in those pale green eyes, though she'd made some hopeless attempts to hide it. And she believed him to be some salesclerk in a Manhattan boutique. She loved him. Not for his billions. Not for his power. For himself.

If she could love some poverty-stricken salesclerk, couldn't she love Leonidas, too, flaws and all?

Maybe if he revealed why he'd been so angry about the Picasso, and the horrible secret of his childhood…

He shuddered. No. He could never tell anyone that. Or about his true parentage.

So how else could he convince her to stay?

Leonidas barely paid attention to a long, contentious board meeting, or the presentations of his brand presidents, discussing sales trends in luxury watches and jewelry in Asia and champagne and spirits in North America. Instead, he kept fantasizing about how, instead of losing Daisy with his confession tonight, he could manage to win her.

She would arrive at his cocktail party, he thought, and hopefully be dazzled by his famous guests, along with his fifty-million-dollar mansion. He would wait for just the right moment, then pull her away privately and explain. There would be awkwardness when she realized he'd been the one who'd arranged for his lawyer to press charges against her father. But Leonidas would make her understand. He'd seduce her with his words. With his touch. And with the lifestyle he could offer.

Daisy was living in the borrowed apartment of some middle-aged artist, an old friend of her father's. But if she came to live with Leonidas, as the cosseted girlfriend of a billionaire, she'd never have to worry about money again. He'd give her a life of luxury. She could quit her job at the diner and spend her days shopping or taking her friends to lunch, and her nights being worshipped by Leonidas in bed. They could travel around the world together, to London and Paris, Sydney, Rio and Tokyo, to his beach house in the Maldives, his ski chalet in Switzerland. He'd take her dancing, to parties, to the art shows and clubs and polo matches attended by the international jet set. He would shower her with gifts, expensive baubles beyond her imagination.

Surely all that could be enough to make her forgive and forget his part in her father's imprisonment? Surely such a life would be worth a little bit of constructive amnesia about her father? Who had been guilty, anyway!

Daisy had to forgive him, he thought suddenly. Why wouldn't she? Whatever Leonidas desired, he always possessed. Daisy Cassidy would be no different. He would pull out all the stops to win her. And though he'd never offer love or marriage, he knew he could make her happy. He'd treat her like the precious treasure she was, filling her days with joy, and her nights with fire.

Leonidas had never failed to seduce any woman he wanted. Tonight would be no different. He would make her forgive him. And forget her foolish loyalty to her dead father.

Tonight, Leonidas thought with determination, a sensual smile curving his lips. He would convince her tonight.

CHAPTER TWO

Daisy looked up at the five-story brownstone mansion with big eyes. There had to be some mistake.

"You're sure?" she asked the driver, bewildered.

The uniformed chauffeur hid a smile, dipping his head as he held open the passenger door. "Yes, miss."

Nervously, Daisy got out of the Rolls-Royce. She'd been astonished when the limo had picked her up in Brooklyn. Her neighborhood was prosperous, filled with a mix of artists and intellectuals, plumbers and stockbrokers. But a Rolls-Royce with a uniformed driver had made people stare. She'd been dismayed. The fancy French restaurant had been bad enough. How much had Leo spent renting this limo out? He shouldn't spend money he didn't have, just to impress her! She already thought he was perfect!

Although it was true she didn't know everything about him…

Standing on the sidewalk, she looked back up at the five-story mansion. This tree-lined lane in the West Village of Manhattan was filled with elegant houses only billionaires could afford. She craned her head doubtfully. "Is there a basement apartment?"

The chauffeur motioned toward the front steps. "The main entrance, miss. I believe the party has already started."

There was indeed a stream of limousines and town cars letting people out at the curb. An elderly couple went by Daisy, the wife in an elegant silk coat and matching dress, the husband in a suit.

She looked down at her own cocktail dress, which she'd borrowed from a friend. It was green satin, a little too tight and *way* too low in the bosom. Her cheap high heels, which she'd worn only once on a humiliating gallery night where she hadn't sold a single painting, squeezed her feet painfully.

She glanced behind her, longing to flee. But the driver had already gotten back into the Rolls-Royce and was driving away, to be immediately replaced by arriving vehicles, Italian and German sports cars attended by three valets waiting at the curb.

Daisy glanced toward the subway entrance at the far end of the lane, which ended in a busier street. She could make a run for it. Her puppy, who still didn't have a name, had been left in the care of the same friend, Estie, who'd been her pal in art school. Daisy could still go back home, cuddle the dog and eat popcorn and watch movies.

Except she couldn't. With a deep breath, she faced the brownstone mansion. She had to talk to Leo and tell him she was pregnant. Because she needed answers to her questions.

Would he help her raise the baby?

Would he marry her?

Could he love her?

Or would she face her future all on her own?

Swallowing hard, Daisy followed the elderly couple up the steps to the open door, where they were welcomed by a butler. As he looked over Daisy's ill-fitting cocktail dress and cheap shoes, the butler's eyebrows rose. "Your name, miss?"

"Daisy Cassidy." She held her breath, half expecting that, whatever the chauffeur had said, she'd been dropped at the wrong house and would be tossed out immediately.

Instead, the butler gave her a warm smile.

"We've been expecting you, Miss Cassidy. Welcome. Mrs. Berry," he glanced at a plump, white-haired woman nearby, "will take you inside."

"I'm Mr. Niarxos's housekeeper, Miss Cassidy," the older woman said kindly. "Will you please come this way?"

Bewildered, wondering who Mr. Niarxos was—perhaps the butler?—Daisy followed the housekeeper through a lavish foyer. She gawked at the brief vision of a gold-painted ceiling above a crystal chandelier, high overhead, and a wide stone staircase that seemed straight out of *Downton Abbey*. They followed a steady crowd of glamorous guests through tall double doors into a ballroom.

Daisy's jaw dropped. A ballroom! In a house?

The ballroom was big enough to fit three hundred people, with a ceiling thirty feet high. The walls were gilded, and mirrors reflected the light of chandeliers that would have suited Versailles. Waiters wearing black tie walked through holding silver trays with champagne flutes on them. On the small stage, musicians played classical music.

Daisy felt like she'd just fallen through the floor to Wonderland. And there, across the ballroom—

Was that Leo in a tuxedo? Talking to the most famous movie star in the world?

"I'll tell him you're here, Miss Cassidy," Mrs. Berry said. "In the meantime, may I get you a drink?"

"What?" It took her a minute to understand the question. Yes. A stiff drink was an excellent idea. Then she remembered she was pregnant. "Uh...no. Thank you."

"Please wait here, Miss Cassidy." The white-haired woman departed with a respectful bow.

Across the crowds, she watched the housekeeper speak quietly to Leo on the other side of the ballroom. He turned, dark and powerful and devastatingly handsome. His eyes met Daisy's, and she felt a flash of fire.

Nervously, Daisy turned away to stare at a painting on the wall. It was a very nice framed print, a Jackson Pollock she didn't immediately recognize. Then her lips parted as she realized it probably wasn't a print. She was looking at a real Jackson Pollock. Just hanging in someone's home.

Although this didn't feel like a home. It felt like a royal palace. The castle of the king of New York...

"Daisy." Leo's voice was husky and low behind her. "I'm glad you came."

She whirled around. He was so close. Her knees trembled as her limbs went weak. "The puppy is fine," she blurted out. "If you were worried."

"Oh. Good." His expression didn't change. He towered over her, powerful and broad shouldered, the focus of all the glamorous guests sipping cocktails in the ballroom. And no wonder. Daisy's gaze traced unwillingly from his hard jawline, now smoothly shaved, to the sharp cheekbones and his cruel, sensual mouth. How could she tell him she'd fallen in love with him? How could she tell him she was pregnant?

"Thank you for inviting me." She bit her lip, looking around at the glittering ballroom. "Whose house is this really?"

His black eyes burned through her. "It's mine."

She laughed. Then saw he was serious. "But how can it be?" she stammered. Her forehead furrowed. "Are you a member of the staff here?"

"No. I work for Liontari."

"Is that a store?"

"It's a company. We own luxury brands around the world."

"Oh." She felt relieved. So he *did* work for a shop. "Your employer owns this mansion? They're the ones throwing the party?"

"I told you, Daisy. The house is mine."

"But how?" Did being a salesclerk pay better than she could possibly imagine? Was he the best salesman in the world?

Leo looked down at her, then sighed.

"I never told you my full name," he said slowly. "Leonidas Gianakos... Niarxos."

He stared down at her, waiting. A faint warning bell rang at the back of her head. She couldn't quite remember where she'd heard it before. From the butler at the front door? Or before that? She repeated, "Niarxos?"

"Yes." And still he waited, watching her. As if he expected some reaction.

"Oh." Feeling awkward, she said, "So who is this fundraiser for?"

Looking relieved, he named a politician she'd vaguely heard of. She looked around the gilded ballroom. This party was very fancy, that was for sure. She saw people she recognized. Actors. Entrepreneurs. And even—she sucked in her breath. A world-famous artist, which impressed her most of all.

What was Daisy even doing here, with all these chic, glamorous people, people she should properly only read about in magazines or social media, or see on the big screen?

"How—" she began, then her throat dried up.

Across the ballroom, she saw someone else she recognized. Someone she'd glared at every day for a month. Someone she'd never, ever forget. A gray-haired villain in a suit.

Edgar Ross.

The lawyer who'd called the police on her father. The last time she'd seen him, he'd been sitting behind the prosecutor in the courtroom. A ruthless lawyer who worked for an even more ruthless boss, some foreign-born billionaire.

"Daisy?" Leo looked down at her, his handsome face concerned. "What is it?"

"It's... It's... What is he—"

At that moment, Edgar Ross himself came over to them,

with a pretty middle-aged blonde on his arm. "Good evening, Mr. Niarxos."

Daisy's lips parted as Leo greeted the man with a warm handshake. "Good evening." He gave the blonde a polite peck on the cheek. "Mrs. Ross."

"It's a great party. Thanks for inviting us." Edgar Ross smiled vaguely at Daisy, as if he were trying to place her.

She stared back coldly, shaking with the effort it took not to slap him, wishing she'd taken a glass of champagne after all, so she could throw it in his face. Including the glass.

"Admiring your most recent acquisition?" Ross asked Leo. For a moment, Daisy thought he meant *her*. Then she realized he was referring to the painting on the wall.

He shrugged. "It's an investment."

"Of course," Ross said, smiling. "It will just have to hold you, until we can find that Picasso, eh?"

The Picasso.

It all clicked horrifyingly into place. Daisy suddenly couldn't breathe.

Edgar Ross.

The Picasso.

The wealthy billionaire reported to be behind it all. The Greek billionaire.

Leonidas Niarxos.

In the background, the orchestra continued to play, and throughout the ballroom, people continued to talk and laugh. As if the world hadn't just collapsed.

Daisy slowly turned with wide, stricken eyes.

"Leo," she choked out, feeling like she was about to faint. Feeling like she was about to die.

He looked down at her, then his expression changed. "No," he said in a low voice. "Daisy, wait."

But she was already backing away. Her knees were shaking. The high heel of her shoe twisted, and she barely caught herself from falling.

No. The truth was she hadn't caught herself. She'd fallen in love with Leo, her first and only lover. He'd taken her virginity. He was the father of her unborn baby.

But Leo didn't exist.

He was actually *Leonidas Niarxos*. Edgar Ross's boss. The Greek billionaire behind everything. The real reason the prosecutor and the judge had thrown the book at her father, penalizing him to the fullest extent of the law, when he should have just been fined in civil court—or better yet, found innocent. But no. With his money and power, Leonidas Niarxos had been determined to get his pound of flesh. The spoiled billionaire, who already owned million-dollar paintings and palaces, hadn't gotten the toy he wanted, so he'd destroyed her father's life.

A year ago, when her father had been convicted of forgery, Daisy had been heartbroken, because she'd known he was innocent. Her father was a good man. The best. He never would have broken the law. She'd been shocked and sickened that somehow, in a miscarriage of justice, he'd still been found guilty. Then, six months ago, Patrick had died of a stroke, alone and scared, in a prison surrounded by strangers.

Daisy had vowed that if she ever had the chance, she would take her revenge. She, who'd never wanted to hurt anyone, who always tried to see the best in everyone, wanted *vengeance*.

But she'd naively given Leo everything. Her smiles. Her kisses. Her body. Her love. She was even carrying his baby, deep inside her.

Daisy stared up at Leo's heartbreakingly handsome face. The face she'd loved. So much.

No. He wasn't Leo. She could never think of him as Leo again.

He was Leonidas Niarxos. The man who'd killed her father.

"Oh, my God." Edgar Ross stared at Daisy, his eyes wide. "You're Cassidy's daughter. I didn't recognize you in that dress. What are you doing here?"

Yes, what? The ballroom, with its gilded glitter, started to swim in front of her eyes.

Daisy's breaths came in short wheezing gasps, constricted as her chest was by the too-tight cocktail dress. With every breath, her breasts pushed higher against the low neckline. She felt like she was going to pass out.

She had to get out of there.

But as she turned away, Leonidas grabbed her wrist.

"No!" she yelled, and wrenched her arm away. Everyone turned to stare at them in shock, and the music stopped.

For a moment, he just looked down at her, his handsome face hard. He didn't try to touch her again.

"We need to talk," he said through gritted teeth.

"What could you possibly have to say to me?" she choked out, hatred rising through her, filling every inch of her hollow heart. She gave a low, brittle laugh. "Did you enjoy your little joke? Seducing me? Laughing at me?"

"Daisy..."

"You took *everything*!" Her voice was a rasp. She felt used. And so fragile that a single breeze might scatter her to the wind. "How could you have lied to me? Pretending to love me—"

"I didn't lie—"

"You lied," she said flatly.

"I never claimed to love you."

His dark eyes glittered as they stared at each other.

All around them, the glamorous people were frankly staring, tilting their heads slightly to hear. As if Daisy hadn't been humiliated enough last year by the New York press gleefully calling her beloved, innocent father names like *con artist* and *fraud*, and even worse, calling him too stupid to properly commit a crime.

But she was the one who was stupid. All along, she'd known Leo was hiding things from her. She'd ignored her fears and convinced herself he was perfect. She'd trusted her heart.

Her stupid, stupid heart.

Her shoulders sagged, and her eyes stung. She blinked fast, wiping her eyes savagely.

"Daisy." Leonidas's voice was a low growl. "Just give me a moment. Alone. Let me explain."

She was trembling, her teeth chattering almost loud enough to hear. There was nothing he could possibly say that would take away her sense of betrayal. She should slap his face and leave, and never look him in the face again.

But their baby.

Her joints hurt with heartbreak, pain rushing through her veins, pounding a toxic rhythm. Her heart shut down, and she went numb. Whatever he'd done, he was still her baby's father. She had to tell him.

"I'll give you one minute," she choked out.

Leonidas gestured toward the ballroom's double doors. She followed him out of the glittering, glamorous ball-room, away from the curious crowd, into the deserted foyer of the New York mansion. Wordlessly, she followed him up the wide stone staircase, to the dark quiet of the hall-way upstairs.

She felt like a ghost of the girl she'd been. As they climbed the staircase, she glanced up at his dark shadow, and felt sick inside.

Discovering she was pregnant earlier that day, she'd felt so alone, so scared. Her first thought had been that she couldn't raise a child without him. But now, Daisy sud-denly realized there was something even more terrifying than raising a baby alone.

Doing it with your worst enemy.

* * *

As Leonidas led Daisy past the security guards in the foyer, up the wide stone staircase of his New York mansion, his heart was beating oddly fast.

He glanced back at her.

Daisy looked so beautiful in the emerald green cocktail dress, with high heels showing off her slender legs. Her long honey-brown hair brushed against her shoulders, over the spaghetti straps, past the low-cut neckline which revealed full breasts, plumped up by the tight satin. Against his will, his eyes lingered there. Had her breasts always been so big? Just watching the sensuous way she moved her hand along the stone bannister, he imagined being the one she touched, and he stirred in spite of himself.

But her eyes were downcast, her dark lashes trembling angrily against her pale cheeks.

Leonidas wondered what she was thinking. It was strange. He'd never cared before about what his lovers might be thinking. And with Daisy, he'd always been able to read her feelings on her face.

Until now.

She glanced up at him, her lovely face carefully blank. She looked back down as they climbed the sweeping staircase.

This was not how Leonidas had hoped this evening would go.

Thinking about it at the office, he'd pictured Daisy being dazzled by his mansion, by the glitter and prestige of his guests, by his wealth and power. He'd convinced himself that she would be in a receptive frame of mind to learn the truth. That Daisy would be shocked, dismayed, even, to learn his identity, but she would swiftly forgive him. Because he was so obviously right.

Daisy loved her father. But she had to see that Patrick Cassidy had been a criminal, protecting his accomplice to the end, refusing to say who'd painted the fake Picasso. What else could Leonidas have done but have his lawyer press charges? Should he have paid millions for a painting he knew was fake, or allowed someone else to potentially be defrauded? He'd done the right thing.

Obviously Daisy didn't see it that way. He had to help her see it from his perspective. Setting his jaw, he led her down the dark, empty upstairs hallway and pushed open the second door, switching on the bedroom light.

She stopped in the doorway, glaring at him.

He felt irritated at her accusatory gaze. Did she really think he'd brought her into his bedroom to seduce her? That he intended to simply toss her on the bed and cover her with kisses until the past was forgiven and forgotten?

If only!

Leonidas forced himself to take a deep breath. He kept his voice calm and reassuring, just the way Daisy had spoken when she'd held that abandoned puppy in the alley.

"I'm just bringing you in here to talk," he said soothingly. "Where no one else can hear us."

She flashed him another glance he couldn't read, but came into the bedroom. He closed the door softly behind her.

His bedroom was Spartan, starkly decorated with a king-sized bed, walk-in closet and a lot of open space. Through a large window, he could see the orange and red leaves of the trees on the quiet lane outside, darkening in the twilight.

Standing near the closed door, Daisy wrapped her arms around herself as if for protection, and said in a low voice, "Did you know who I was? The day we met?"

He could not lie to her. "Yes."

She lifted pale green eyes, swimming with tears. "Why did you seduce me? For a laugh? For revenge?"

"No, Daisy, no—" He tried to move toward her, wanting to take her in his arms, to offer comfort. But she moved violently back before he could touch her. He froze, dropping his hands. "I saw a drawing of the trial, when your father's verdict was read. It made me feel sorry for you."

The emotion in her face changed to anger. "*Sorry* for me?"

That hadn't come out right. "I heard your father died in prison, and I came looking for you because…because I wanted to make sure you were all right. And perhaps give you some money."

"Money?" Her expression hardened. "Do you really think that could compensate me for my father's death? Some… some *payoff*?"

"That was never my intention, it—" Leonidas cut himself off, gritting his teeth. He forced his voice to remain calm. "You never deserved to suffer. *You* were innocent."

"So was my father!"

Against his best intentions, his own anger rose. "You cannot be so blind as to think that your father was innocent. Of course he wasn't. He tried to sell a forgery."

"Then he foolishly trusted the wrong person. Someone must have tricked him and convinced him the painting was real. He never would have tried to sell it otherwise! He was a good man! Perfect!"

"Are you kidding? Your father was selling forgeries for years."

"No one else ever accused him—"

"Because either they were too embarrassed, or they didn't realize the paintings were fakes. Your father knew he wasn't selling a real Picasso."

"How would he know that? No one has seen the painting for decades. How did that lawyer lackey of yours even know it wasn't real?"

Leonidas had a flash of memory from twenty years before. His misery as a boy at his parents' strange neglect and hatred. The shock of his mother's final abandonment.

His heartbroken fury, as a boy of fourteen. He could still feel the cold steel in his hand. The canvas ripping beneath his blade in the violent joy of destruction, of finally giving in to his rage—

Looking away, Leonidas said tightly, "I was the one who knew it was a fake. From the moment I saw it in Ross's office."

"You." Daisy glared at him in the cold silence of his bedroom, across the enormous bed, which he'd so recently dreamed of sharing with her. "Why couldn't you just let it go? What's one Picasso to you, more or less?"

Leonidas's shoulders tightened. He didn't want to think about what it meant to him. Or why he'd been looking for it so desperately for two decades.

"So I should have just let your father get away with his deceit?" he said coldly. "Allowed him to continue passing off fake paintings?"

"My father was innocent!" Her expression was fierce. "He looked into my eyes and *swore* it!"

"Because he couldn't bear for you to know the truth. He loved you too much."

Anguish shone in her beautiful face. Then her expression crumpled.

"And I loved him," she said brokenly. She wiped her eyes. "But you're wrong. He never would have lied to me. He had no reason—"

"You would have forgiven him?"

"Yes."

"Because you loved him." Leonidas took a deep breath and looked into her eyes. "So forgive me," he whispered.

She sucked in her breath. "What?"

"You're in love with me, Daisy. We both know that."

Her lush pink lips parted. She seemed to tremble. "What…how—"

"I've seen it on your face. Heard it in your voice. You're

in love—" He took a step toward her, but she put her hand up, warding him off.

"I loved a man who doesn't exist." She looked up, her green eyes glittering. "Not you. I could never love you."

Her words stabbed him like a physical attack. He heard echoes of his mother's harsh voice, long ago.

Stop bothering me. I'm sick of your whimpering. Leave me alone.

Leonidas had spent three decades distancing himself from that five-year-old boy, becoming rich and powerful and strong, to make sure he'd never feel like that again. And now this.

Senseless, overwhelming rage filled him.

"You could never love a man like me?" He lifted his chin. "But you're full of love for a liar like your father?"

"Don't you call him that. *You're* the liar! Don't you dare even *speak* of him—"

"He was a criminal, Daisy. And you're a fool," he said harshly.

"You're right. I am." Her lovely face was pale, her clenched hands shaking at her sides. "But you're a monster. You took everything. My father. My home. My self-respect. My virginity…"

"Your father made his own bed." He looked down at her coldly. "So did you."

Her lips parted in a gasp.

"I never took anything that wasn't willingly—*enthusiastically*—given to me," he continued ruthlessly.

"I hate myself for ever letting you touch me," she whispered. Her tearful eyes lifted to his. "I wish I could hurt you like you've hurt me."

Leonidas barked a humorless laugh. "You can't."

New rage filled her beautiful face. "Why? Because you think I'm so powerless? So meaningless?"

"No." He wasn't being rude. If Daisy knew about the

pain of his childhood, he suspected it would satisfy even her current vengeful mood.

But she couldn't know. Leonidas intended to keep those memories buried until the day he died, buried deep in the graveyard that existed beneath his ribs, in place of a heart.

"I hate you," she choked out. "You don't deserve—"

"What?" he said, when she didn't finish. "What don't I deserve?"

She turned her head away. "You don't deserve another moment of my time."

Her voice was low and certain, and it filled him with despair. How had he ever thought he could win her?

Leonidas saw now that he'd never make her see his side. She hated him, just as he'd always known she would, the moment she learned his name.

It was over.

"If you think I'm such a monster," he said hoarsely, "what are you still doing here? Why don't you go?"

She stared at him, her arms wrapped around her belly. For a moment, she seemed frozen in indecision. Then—

"You're right," she said finally. She crossed the bedroom and opened the door. He briefly smelled her perfume, the scent of sunshine and roses. As she passed him, he could almost feel the warmth from her skin, from her curves barely contained beneath the tight green dress. "I never should have come up here." She gave him one last look. "As far as I'm concerned, the man I loved is dead."

Daisy walked out of his bedroom without another glance, disappearing into the shadows of the hall. And she left Leonidas, alone in his mansion, feeling like a monster, surrounded by rich and powerful friends, in a world that was even more dark and bleak than it had been before he'd met her.

CHAPTER THREE

Five months later

IT WAS EARLY MARCH, but in New York, there was no whisper of warmth, not yet. It was gray and cold, and the sidewalks were edged with dirty snow from a storm a few days before. Even the trees had not yet started to bud. The weather still felt miserably like winter.

But for Daisy, spring had already begun.

She took a deep breath, hugging herself as she stepped out of the obstetrician's office. At six months' pregnant, her belly had grown so big she was barely able to zip up her long black puffy coat. She'd had to get new clothes from thrift shops and friends with discarded maternity outfits; aside from her swelling belly, she'd put on a good amount of pregnancy weight.

After a six-hour morning shift at the diner, Daisy had already been exhausted before she'd skipped lunch to go straight to a doctor's appointment. But the medical office had been running late, and she'd sat in the waiting room for an hour. Now, as she finally left, her stomach was growling, and she thought with pity of her dog at home, waiting for her meal, too.

She quickened her step, her breath a white cloud in cold air that was threatening rain. She couldn't stop smiling.

Her checkup had gone perfectly. Her baby was doing well, her pregnancy was on track, and after the morning sickness misery of her first trimester, and the uncertainty of her second, now she was in her final trimester. She finally felt like she knew what she was doing. She felt...*hope*.

It was funny, she thought, as she hurried down the crowded Brooklyn sidewalk, vibrant with colorful shops. Her past was filled with tragedy that she once would have thought she could not survive: her mother's illness and death when Daisy was seven, her own failure at becoming an artist, her father's accusation and trial followed by his sudden death, falling in love with Leo and accidentally getting pregnant then finding out he was actually Leonidas Niarxos.

She had decided to raise her baby alone, rather than with a man who didn't deserve to be her child's father, but it was strange now to remember how, five months ago, she'd been so sure she wasn't strong or brave enough to do it alone. But the fight with Leonidas at his cocktail party had made it clear she had no other choice.

And she'd made it through. She was stronger and wiser. She'd never again be so stupidly innocent, giving her heart to someone she barely knew. She'd never be that young again.

Becoming an adult—a *mother*—meant making responsible choices. She'd given up childish dreams of romance, and someday becoming an artist. Her baby was all that mattered. Daisy put a hand on her belly over her black puffy coat. She'd found out a few months earlier she was having a little girl.

Daisy's friends in Brooklyn had rallied around her. Claudia Vogler, her boss at the diner, had given her extra hours so Daisy could save money. She'd forgiven all of Daisy's missed shifts due to morning sickness, and, when Daisy started having trouble being on her feet all day, Claudia had even created a new job for her—to sit by the cash register at the diner and ring out customers. Since most customers just paid their server directly with a credit card, Daisy mostly just greeted them as they came, and said goodbye as they left.

And she was still living in Franck's apartment, rent free. The middle-aged artist had returned to New York a week after her breakup with Leonidas. He'd been shocked, walking into his apartment, expensive suitcase in hand, to discover a puppy living in his home, which was full of easily breakable sculptures and expensive modern art on the walls.

She'd named her puppy Sunny, to remind herself, even in the depths of her worry, to focus on the brightness all around her. But Sunny was an excitable puppy, and she'd already managed to pee on his rug and chew Franck's slippers.

"I'm so sorry," Daisy had choked out, confessing her puppy's sins. She'd half expected him to throw both her and the dog out.

But to her surprise, Franck had been kind. He'd allowed her to keep the dog and told her she could stay at his apartment as long as she liked, since he was leaving anyway, to snowbird at his house in Los Angeles. That had been in October.

She'd fallen to her lowest point in early January, shivering in the depths of a gray winter despair, she'd felt scared and alone.

Franck, returning to New York on a two-day business trip, had discovered Daisy sitting on the fireside rug, crying into Sunny's fur. When she'd looked up, the gray-haired man had seemed like a surrogate for the father she missed so much, and she'd tearfully told him about her unexpected pregnancy, and that the baby's father was no longer in the picture.

He'd been shocked. After vaguely comforting her, he'd left for his studio. He'd returned late, sleeping in his bedroom down the hall.

Then, the next morning at the breakfast table, right before his return flight to Los Angeles, Franck had abruptly offered to marry her.

Overwhelmed, Daisy had stammered, "You're so kind, Franck, but... I have no intention of marrying anyone."

It was true. In addition to the fact that he was so much older, and had obviously asked her out of pity, Daisy had no desire to marry anyone. Getting her heart broken once was enough for a lifetime.

Franck had seemed strangely disappointed at her refusal. "You're in shock. You'll change your mind," he'd said. And no amount of protesting on her part had made him think differently. "But whether you marry me or not, you're welcome to stay here," he'd added softly, looking down at her. "Stay as long as you want. Stay forever."

It had all been a little awkward. She'd been relieved when he'd left for Los Angeles.

But hearing Franck describe how lovely and warm it was in California had given her an idea. She'd had a sudden memory of her father, two years before.

Daisy had been crying after her first gallery show, heartbroken over her failure to sell a single painting, when her father had said, "We could start over. Move to Santa Barbara, where I was born. It's a beautiful place, warm and bright. We could buy a little cottage by the sea, with a garden full of flowers."

"Leave New York?" Wiping her eyes in surprise, Daisy had looked at him. "What about your gallery, Dad?"

"Maybe I'd like a change, too. Just one more deal to close, and then...we'll see."

Shortly after that, Patrick had been arrested, and there had been no more talk of fresh starts.

But the memory suddenly haunted Daisy. Pregnant and alone, she found herself yearning for her parents' love more than ever. For comfort, for sunshine and warmth, for flowers and the sea.

Her mother had once been a nurse, before she'd gotten sick. Daisy liked helping people, and she knew her income as a waitress would not be enough to support a child, at least not in Brooklyn. She needed grown-up things, like financial security and insurance benefits. Why not?

Holding her breath, Daisy had applied to a small nursing school in Santa Barbara.

Miraculously, she'd been accepted, and with a scholarship, too. She would start school in the fall, when her baby was three months old.

Soon after, her morning sickness had disappeared. She'd managed to save some money, and she had a plan for her future.

But now, Franck was due to return to New York next week for good. Daisy couldn't imagine sharing his apartment with him. She needed to move out.

Where else could she live? None of her friends had extra space, and she couldn't afford to rent her own apartment, not when she was saving every penny for baby expenses and moving expenses. It was a problem.

If she'd had enough money, she would have left for California immediately. In New York City, she was scared of accidentally running into Leonidas. If he ever learned she was pregnant, he might try to take custody of their baby. She was desperate to be free of him. Desperate for a clean break.

But she had a job here, friends here, and—as uncomfortable as it might make her—at least at Franck's, she had a roof over her head. She just had to hold on until summer. Her baby was due in early June. By the end of August, she'd have money to get a deposit on a new apartment, and the two of them could start a new life in California.

Until then, she just had to cross her fingers and pray Leonidas wouldn't come looking for her.

He won't. It will all work out, Daisy told herself, as she had so many times over the last few months. *I'll be fine.*

The difference was, she'd finally started to believe it.

In the distance, dark clouds were threatening rain, and she could see her breath in the cold air. Quickening her pace, Daisy started humming softly as she hurried home. She'd heard that a baby, even in the womb, could hear her mother's voice, so she'd started talking and singing to her at all hours. As she sang aloud, some tourists looked at her with alarm. Daisy giggled. Just another crazy New Yorker, walking down the street and singing to herself!

Reaching her co-op building, she greeted the doorman with a smile. "Hey, Walter."

"Good afternoon, Miss Cassidy. How's that baby?" he asked sweetly, as he always did.

"Wonderful," she replied, and took the elevator to the top floor.

As she came through the door, her dog, Sunny, still a puppy at heart in spite of having grown so big, bounded up with a happy bark, tail waving her body frantically. She acted as if Daisy had been gone for months, rather than hours. With a laugh, Daisy petted her lavishly, then went to the kitchen to put food in her dog dish.

She didn't bother to take off her coat. She knew how this would go. As expected, Sunny gulped down her food, then immediately leaped back to the door with a happy bark. Daisy sighed a little to herself. Sunny did love her walks. Even when it was cold and threatening rain.

Grabbing the leash, Daisy attached it to the dog's collar and left the apartment.

Once outside, she took a deep breath of the cold, damp air. It was late afternoon as she took the dog for their usual walk along the river path. By the time they returned forty minutes later, the drizzle was threatening to deepen into rain, and the sun was falling in the west, streaking the fiery sky red and orange, silhouetting the sharp Manhattan skyline across the East River. As busy as she'd been, she'd forgotten to eat that day, and she was starving. Seeing her co-op building ahead, Daisy hurried her pace, fantasizing about what she'd have for dinner.

Then she saw the black Rolls-Royce parked in front of the building. A chill went down her spine as a towering, dark-haired figure got out of the limo.

She stopped cold, causing a surprised yelp from Sunny. She wanted to turn and run—a ridiculous idea, when she knew Leonidas Niarxos could easily run her down, with his powerful body and long legs.

Their eyes met, and he came forward grimly.

She couldn't move, staring at his darkly powerful form, with the backdrop view of the majestic bridge and red sunset.

Please, she thought as he approached. Let her black puffy coat be enough to hide her pregnancy. Please, please.

But her hope was crushed with his very first words.

"So it's true?" Leonidas's voice was dangerously low, his black eyes gleaming like white-hot coal in the twilight. He looked down at her belly, bulging out beneath the long black puffy coat. "You're pregnant?"

Instinctively, she wrapped her hands over her baby bump. How had he heard? She trembled all over. "What are you doing here?"

"Are you, Daisy?"

She could hardly deny it. "Yes."

His burning gaze met hers. "Is the baby mine?"

She swallowed hard, wanting more than anything to lie.

But she couldn't. Even though Leonidas had lied to her about his identity, and lied about Daisy's father, she couldn't fall to his level. She couldn't lie to his face. Not even for her child.

What kind of mother would she be, if she practiced the same deceit as Leonidas Niarxos? She felt somehow, even in the womb, that her baby was listening. And she had to prove herself worthy. She, at least, was a good person. *Unlike him.*

"Am I the father, Daisy?" he pressed.

Stiffening, Daisy lifted her chin defiantly. "Only biologically."

"Only?" Leonidas's eyes went wide, then narrowed. Setting his jaw, he walked slowly around her, as if searching for weaknesses. He ignored her dog, who traitorously wagged her tail at him. "Why didn't you tell me?"

"Why would I?"

"Because it's the decent thing to do?"

She glared at him. "You don't deserve to be her father."

Leonidas stopped, as if he'd been punched in the gut. Then he said evenly, "You are legally entitled to child support."

She tossed her head. "I don't want it."

"You'd really let your pride override the best interests of the child?"

"Pride!" she breathed. "Is that what you think?"

"What else could it be? You want to hurt me. You don't care that it also injures our baby in the process."

It was strange, Daisy thought, that even after all this time, he could still find new ways to hurt her.

It didn't help that Leonidas was even more devastatingly handsome than she remembered, standing in the twilight dressed in black from head to toe, in his dark suit covered by a long dark coat. His clothing was sleek, but his black hair was rumpled, and his sharp jawline was edged with five o'clock shadow. Everything about him seemed dark in this moment.

"This isn't about you," she ground out. "It's about her. She doesn't need a father like you—a liar with no soul!"

For a moment, they glared at each other as they stood on the empty pathway along the East River, with the brilliant backdrop of Manhattan's skyline against the red sunset. Her harsh words hung between them like toxic mist.

"You only hate me because I told the truth about your father." His voice was low. "But I am not the one you should hate. I never lied to you."

"How can you say that?" She was outraged. "From the day we met, when you told me your name—"

"I didn't tell you my full name. But that was only because I liked talking to you and didn't want it to end." His deep voice was quiet. "I never lied. I never tried to sell a forgery. I am not the criminal."

She caught her breath, and for a moment she felt dizzy, wondering if he could be telling the truth. Could her father have been guilty? Had he known the Picasso was a forgery when he'd tried to sell it?

I didn't do it, baby. I swear it on my life. On my love for you.

Daisy remembered the tremble in her father's voice, the emotion gleaming in his eyes the night of his arrest. All throughout his trial and subsequent imprisonment, he'd maintained his innocence, saying he'd been duped just like his wealthy customers. But he'd refused to say who had duped him.

Who was she going to believe—the perfect father who'd raised her and loved her, caring for her as a single parent after her mother died, or the selfish billionaire who'd had him dragged into court, who'd taken Daisy's virginity and left her pregnant and alone?

"Don't you dare call my father a criminal!"

"He was convicted. He went to prison."

"Where he died—thanks to you!" Her voice was a rasp.

"You ruined his life out of spite, over a painting that meant nothing—"

"That painting means more than—"

"You ruined my life on a selfish whim." Daisy's voice rose. "Why would I want you near my baby, so you could wreck her life as well? Just go away, and leave us alone!"

Leonidas stared at her in shock. He'd never imagined that he'd become a father. And he'd never imagined that his baby's mother could hate him so much.

The soft drizzle had turned to sleet, falling from the darkening sky. Nearby, he could almost hear the rush of the East River, the muffled roar of traffic from the looming bridge.

Just go away, and leave us alone.

He heard the echo of his mother's voice when he was five years old.

Stop bothering me. I'm sick of your whimpering. Leave me alone.

Since their breakup last October, through a gray fall and grayer winter, Leonidas had tried to keep thoughts of Daisy at bay. Yes, she was beautiful. But so what? The world was full of beautiful women. Yes, she was clever. Diabolically so, since she'd lured him so easily into wanting her, into believing she was different from the rest. Into believing her love could somehow save his soul and make him a better man.

Ridiculous. It humiliated him to remember. He'd acted like a fool, believing their connection had been based on anything more than sexual desire.

He couldn't let down his guard. He couldn't let himself depend on anyone's love.

Daisy Cassidy had been the most exhilarating lover he'd ever had, but she was also the most dangerous. He'd needed to get her out of his life. Out from beneath his skin.

So the day after their argument, he'd left New York, vowing to forget her. And he had.

By day.

But night was a different matter. His body could not forget. Against his will, all these months later, he still dreamed of her, erotic dreams of a sensual virgin, luring him inexorably to his destruction. In the dream, he gave her everything—not just his body, not just his fortune, he gave her his heart. Then she always took it in her grasp and crushed it to dripping blood and burned ash.

Two days before, he'd woken after one particularly agonizing dream at his luxury apartment on the Boulevard Saint-Germain in Paris, gasping and filled with despair.

Ever since their affair had ended, his days had been gray. He barely cared about the billion-dollar conglomerate which had once been his passion. Even his formerly docile board was starting to whisper that perhaps he should step down as CEO.

Leonidas could hardly blame them. He'd lost his appetite for business. He'd lost his edge. The truth was, he just didn't give a damn anymore. How long would he be tormented by these dreams of her—dreams that could never again be real?

Then he'd suddenly gotten angry.

He realized he hadn't visited his company's headquarters back in New York once since that disastrous cocktail party. Daisy had driven him out of the city. He'd left his ex-girlfriend in victorious possession of the entire continent. But even on the other side of the world, she destroyed his peace.

No longer.

Grimly, he'd called his chief of security at the New York office. "Find out about Daisy Cassidy. I want to know what she's doing."

Then he'd called his pilot to arrange the flight back to New York. He was done running from her. He'd done nothing wrong. *Nothing.* Maybe, once he was back amid the hum and energy of his company's headquarters, he'd regain some of his old passion for the luxury business.

But he didn't relish the thought of Daisy ambushing him at some Manhattan event, or seeing her on another man's arm. He hoped his chief of security would tell him she'd moved to Miami—or better yet, Siberia. Either way, Leonidas wanted to be prepared.

But he'd had no defense against what his security chief had told him.

Daisy Cassidy was six months pregnant, according to her friends. And refusing to say who the father might be.

But Leonidas knew. Daisy had been a virgin their first night, and she'd been faithful for the month of their affair— he had no doubt of that.

The baby had to be his.

Leonidas had felt restless, jittery, on the flight back to New York yesterday, wondering if she'd already known she was pregnant the night she'd walked out on him. Back at his West Village mansion, he'd collapsed, and slept like the dead. But at least he hadn't been tormented by dreams.

Waking up late, he'd gone to the office, but had lasted only two hours before he'd called his driver to take him across the river. He'd waited outside the Brooklyn co-op where Daisy lived, tension building inside him as he tried to decide whether to go inside. Once he confirmed her pregnancy, there would be no going back.

Then he saw her, walking her dog on the street.

Leonidas hadn't been able to tear his eyes away. Daisy was more beautiful than ever, her green eyes shining, her face radiant, and her body lush with pregnancy. She'd gained some weight, and her fuller curves suited her, making her even more impossibly desirable.

Why hadn't she told him she was pregnant? Did she really hate him so much that she wouldn't even accept his financial support for their child? It seemed incredibly reckless and wrong. She could have been pampered in her pregnancy. Instead, by all accounts she was still working on her feet as a waitress, and living in another man's apartment. The same apartment where she and Leonidas had conceived this child. No wonder he felt so off-kilter and dizzy.

Then she'd said it.

Just go away, and leave us alone.

Leonidas stared at her, still shocked that the tender-hearted girl who'd once claimed to love him could say anything so cruel. His whole body felt tight, his heart rate increasing as his hands clenched at his sides.

His voice was hoarse as he said, "You really believe I'm such a monster that you need to hide your pregnancy from me? You won't even let me support my own child?"

Daisy's expression filled with shadow in the twilight, as if even she realized she'd gone too far.

"We don't need you," she said finally, and turning, she hurried away, almost running with her dog following behind, disappearing into the apartment building.

You little monster. His mother's enraged voice, when he was fourteen. *I wish you'd never been born!*

For a moment, the image of the bleak bridge and water swam before Leonidas's eyes, malevolent and dark against the red twilight. His heart hammered in his throat, his body tense.

Those had been his mother's final words, the last time Leonidas saw her. He'd been fourteen, and had just come from the funeral of the man he'd always believed was his father, when his mother had told him the truth, and that she never intended to see Leonidas again. Heartsick, he'd hacked into her precious masterpiece with a pair of scissors. Ripping the broken Picasso from his hands, his mother had left him with those final words.

She'd died in the Turkish earthquake a week later, and

the Picasso had disappeared. That day, Leonidas had lost his only blood relative in the world.

Until now.

Leonidas looked up at the co-op building, with its big windows overlooking the river. His eyes narrowed dangerously.

Daisy had kept her pregnancy a secret, because she didn't want him to be a father to their baby.

Why would I want you near my baby, so you could wreck her life as well?

Her life. Leonidas suddenly realized the import of Daisy's words. They were having a baby girl.

And whether Daisy liked it or not, Leonidas was going to be a father. He would soon have a daughter who'd need him to protect and provide for her. This baby was his family.

His only family.

Gripping his hands at his sides, Leonidas went toward the building. He gave a sharp shake of his head to his driver, waiting with the Rolls-Royce at the curb, and went forward alone into the apartment building. He opened the door, going into the contemporary glass-and-steel lobby, with modern, sparse furniture. He headed straight for the elevator, until he found his way blocked.

"Can I help you, sir?" the doorman demanded.

"Daisy Cassidy," he barked in reply. "I know the apartment number."

"You must wait," the man replied. Going to the reception desk, the man picked up his phone. "Your name, sir?"

"Leonidas Niarxos."

The doorman spoke quietly into the phone, then looked up. "I'm sorry, Miss Cassidy says she has nothing to say to you. She asks you to leave the building immediately."

A curse went through his mind. "Tell her she can talk to me now or talk to an army of lawyers in an hour."

The doorman raised his eyebrows, then again spoke quietly. With a sigh, he hung up the phone. "She says to go up, Mr. Niarxos."

"Yes," he bit out. He stalked to the elevator, feeling the doorman's silently accusing eyes on his back. But Leonidas didn't give a damn. His fury sustained him as he pushed the elevator button for the fifth floor.

He straightened, his jaw tight. He was no longer a helpless five-year-old. No longer a heartsick fourteen-year-old. He was a man now. A man with power and wealth. A man who could take what he wanted.

And he wasn't going to let Daisy steal his child away.

The elevator gave a cheerful ding as the door slid open. He grimly stalked down the hall to apartment 502. Lifting his hand, he gave a single hard knock.

The door opened, and he saw Daisy's furious, tear-stained face.

In spite of everything, his heart twisted at the sight. Her pale green eyes, fringed with thick black lashes, were luminous against her skin, with a few adorable freckles scattered across her nose. Her lips were pink and full, as she chewed on her lower lip, as if trying to bite back angry words.

Her body, in the fullness of pregnancy, was lush and feminine. She'd taken off her long puffy coat, and was dressed simply, in a long-sleeved white shirt over black leggings. But she was somehow even more alluring to him than the night of the cocktail party, when she'd been wearing that low-cut green dress, with her breasts overflowing. He'd thought the dress was simply tight, but now he realized her breasts had already been swollen by pregnancy. Pregnant. With his baby.

A baby she was trying to keep from Leonidas, who was here and ready to take responsibility. Who wanted to be a father!

Interesting. He blinked. He hadn't realized it until now.

He'd always thought he had no interest in fatherhood, no interest in settling down. What did he know about being a good parent?

But now he wanted it more than anything.

Daisy tossed her head with an angry, shuddering breath. "How dare you threaten me with lawyers?"

"How dare you try to steal my child?" he retorted, pushing into the apartment without touching her.

It was the first time he'd been back here since their days as lovers. The apartment looked just as he remembered, modern and new, with a gas fireplace and an extraordinary view of the bridge and Manhattan skyline. The only new changes were a slapdash Van Gogh pastiche now hanging in the foyer, and the large dog bed sitting near the fire, where a long-limbed, floppy yellow dog drowsed.

Leonidas took a deep breath, dizzy with the memory of how happy he'd been here, in those stolen hours when he'd been simply Leo, nothing more. This was enemy territory—Daisy's home—but it somehow still felt warm. Far more than his own multimillion-dollar homes around the world.

He felt suddenly insecure.

"You said this is Franck Bain's apartment," he said slowly.

"So?"

"Why has he let you stay so long? Are you lovers?"

Closing the door behind him, Daisy said coldly, "It's none of your business, but no. He was my father's friend, and he is trying to help me. That's all."

"Why would I believe that?"

"Why would you even care?" She looked at him challengingly. "I'm sure you've had lovers by the score since you tossed me out of your house."

But he hadn't. He hadn't had sex in five months—not since their last time together. But that was the last thing

Leonidas wanted to admit to Daisy. He lifted his chin. "I did not toss you out."

"You asked me what I was still doing at your house. And told me to go!"

"Funny, I mostly remember you insulting me, calling me a liar and saying how badly you wished you could hurt me." He gave a low, bitter laugh. "I guess you figured out a way, didn't you? By not telling me you were pregnant."

The two of them stared at each other in the fading red light, an electric current of hatred sizzling the air between them.

They were so close, he thought. Their bodies could touch with the slightest movement. His gaze fell unwillingly to her lips.

He saw a shiver pass over Daisy.

"You're a bastard," she whispered.

Those were truer words than she knew. He took a deep breath, struggling to hold back his insecurity, his pain. He met her gaze evenly.

"You didn't always think so." His gaze moved toward the hallway, toward the dark shadow of her bedroom door. "When we spent hours in bed. You wanted me then. Just as I wanted you."

Her lips parted. Then she swallowed, stepping back.

"You're charming when you want to be." Her jaw hardened. "But beneath your good looks, your money, your charm—you're nothing."

You little monster. I wish you'd never been born!

In spite of his best efforts, emotion flooded through him—emotion he'd spent his whole adult life trying to outrun and prove wrong, by the company he'd built, by his massively increasing fortune, by the beautiful women he'd bedded, by his worldwide acclaim.

But Leonidas suddenly realized he would never escape it. Even with all of his fame and fortune, he was still the same worthless, unwanted boy, without a real family or home. Without a father, with a mother who despised him— raised by the twin demons of shame and grief.

He said tightly, "How you feel about me, or I feel about you, is irrelevant now. What matters is taking care of our baby."

Daisy looked at him incredulously. "I know that. Don't you think I know that? Why else do you think I tried to hide my pregnancy?"

"Don't you think our daughter needs a father?"

"Not a father like you!"

Blood rushed through his ears. With her every accusation, the stunned rage he'd felt on the river pathway built higher, making it harder to stay calm. But he managed to say evenly, "You accuse me of being a monster. All I'm trying to do is take responsibility for my child."

"How?" she cried. "By threatening me with lawyers?"

"I never actually meant—" He ground his teeth. "You were refusing to even talk to me."

"For good reason!"

"Daisy," he said quietly, "What are you so afraid of?"

She stared at him for a long moment, then looked away. He waited out her silence, until she finally said in a small voice, "I'm scared you'll try and take her from me. I saw what your money and lawyers did in court, with my father. I'm scared you'll turn them against me and try to take her— not because you love her. Out of spite. Because you can."

She really did think the worst of him. Leonidas exhaled. "I would never try to take any baby away from a loving parent. Never."

Daisy slowly looked at him, and he saw a terrible hope rising in her green eyes. "You wouldn't?"

"No. But I'm her parent, too. Whether you like it or not, we're both responsible. I never imagined I'd ever become a father, but now that she exists, I can't let her go. She's my only family in the world, do you know that?"

Silently, Daisy shook her head.

"I can't abandon her," he said. "Or risk having her wonder about me, wonder why I didn't love her enough to be there for her every day, to help raise her, to love her. To truly be her father."

Looking down at the hardwood floor, she said in a small voice, "So what can we do?"

Yes—what? How could Leonidas make sure he was part of his child's life forever, without lawyers, without threats? Without always fearing that Daisy might at any moment choose to disappear, or marry another man—a man who might always secretly despise his stepdaughter for not being his own?

His lips suddenly parted.

A simple idea. Insane. Easy. With one stroke, everything could be secure. Everything could be his.

It was an idea so crazy, he'd never imagined he would consider it. But as soon as he thought of it, the vibrating tension left his body. Leonidas suddenly felt calmer than he'd felt in days—in months.

He gave her a small smile. "Our baby needs a father. She needs a name. And I intend to give her mine." He met her gaze. "And you, as well."

She stared at him, her lovely face horrified. "What are you saying?"

"The answer is simple, Daisy." He tilted his head, looking down at her. "You're going to marry me."

CHAPTER FOUR

MARRY LEONIDAS NIARXOS?

Standing in the deepening shadows of the apartment, Daisy stared at Leonidas, her mouth open.

"Are you crazy?" she exploded. "I'm not going to marry you!"

His darkly handsome face grew cold. "We both created this child. We should both raise her." His black eyes narrowed. "I never want her to question who she is. Or feel anything less than cherished by both her parents."

"As if you could ever love anyone!" She still felt sick remembering how he'd once said, *I never claimed to love you*.

"You're right. I'm not sure I know how to love anyone." As she gaped at his honesty, Leonidas shook his head. "But I know I can protect and provide. It is my job as a man. Not just for her. Also for you."

"Why?" she whispered.

Leonidas looked down at her.

"Because I can," he said simply. He took a deep breath. "I might not have the ability to love you, Daisy. But I can take care of you. Just as I can take care of our daughter. If you'll let me."

Daisy swallowed hard.

"But, marriage…" she whispered. "How could we promise each other forever, without love?"

"Love is not necessary between us—or even desirable. Romantic love can be destructive."

Destructive? Daisy looked at his clenched jaw, the tightness around his eyes. Had someone broken Leonidas's heart? She fought the impulse to reach out to him, to ask questions, to offer comfort. Sympathy was the last thing she wanted to feel right now.

"What about marrying someone you despise?" she pointed out. "That seems pretty destructive."

"Do you really hate me so much, Daisy? Just because I was afraid to tell you my last name when we met? Just because, when a man tried to sell me a forgery, I pressed charges? For that, you're determined to hate me for the rest of your life? No matter what that does to our child?"

She bit her lip. When he put it like that...

Her heart was pounding. She thought of how she'd felt last October, when she'd loved him, and he'd broken her heart. It would kill her if that ever happened again. "I can't love you again."

"Good." Leonidas looked down at her in the falling light. "I'm not asking you to. But give me a chance to win back your trust."

Her heart lifted to her throat. Trust?

It was a cruel reminder of how she'd once trusted Leo, blindly believing him to be perfect. How could she ever trust him again?

Daisy looked down at her short waterproof boots. "I don't know if I can."

"Why won't you try?" His face was in shadow. He tilted his head. "Are you in love with someone else? The artist who owns this apartment, Franck Bain?"

"I told you, he's a friend, nothing more!" Daisy kept Franck's marriage proposal to herself. No point in giving Leonidas ammunition. She shook her head fiercely. "I don't want to love anyone. Not anymore. I've given up on that fairy tale since—"

Her voice cut off, but it was too late.

Leonidas drew closer. The light from the hallway caressed the hard edges of his face. "Since you loved me?"

A shiver went through Daisy. Against her will, her gaze fell to his cruel, sensual lips. She still couldn't forget the memory of his kiss, his mouth so hot against her skin, making her whole body come alive.

No, she told herself angrily. No! She'd allowed her body to override her brain once before. And look what had happened!

But she still felt Leonidas's every movement. His every breath. Even though he didn't touch her, she could still feel him, blood and bone.

He looked down at her. "You don't need to worry, then," he said softly. "Because we agree. Neither of us is seeking love. Because romantic love is destructive."

She agreed with him, didn't she? So why did her heart twist a little as she said, "Yes, I guess you're right." She took a deep breath. "That doesn't mean I can just forgive or forget what you did."

"You loved your father."

"Yes."

"He meant everything to you."

"Yes!"

Leonidas looked at her. "Don't you think our daughter deserves the chance to have a father, too?"

She caught her breath.

Was she being selfish? Putting her own anger ahead of their baby's best interests—not just financially, but emotionally?

"How can I know you'll be a good father to our daughter?" she said in a small voice.

"I swear it to you. On my honor."

"Your *honor*," she said bitterly. Her hands went protectively over her baby bump, over her cotton shirt.

He gently put his larger hand over hers.

"Yes. My honor. Which means a great deal to me." He looked her straight in the eye. "I have no family, Daisy. No siblings or cousins. Both my parents are dead. I never intended to marry or have a child of my own. But now... This baby is all I have. All I care about is her happiness. I will do anything to protect her."

Daisy heard the words for the vow they were. Her heart lifted to her throat. He truly wanted to be a good father. She heard it in his voice. He cared about this child in a way she'd never expected.

Her heart suddenly ached. How she wished she could believe him! How lovely it would be to actually have a partner in her pregnancy, someone else looking out for her, rather than having to figure out everything herself!

But could she live with a man who'd done what Leonidas had done? Even if she never loved him—could she live with him? Accept him as her co-parent—trust him as a friend?

His hand tightened over hers. "There could be other benefits to our marriage, Daisy," he said huskily. "More than just being partners. Living together, we could have other...pleasures."

He was talking about sharing a bed. Images of their lovemaking flashed through her, and she felt a bead of sweat between her breasts.

"If you think I'm falling into bed with you, you're crazy," she said desperately. She stepped back, pulling away from his touch. Just to make sure she didn't do something she'd regret, like reach for his strong, powerful body, pull it against her own, and lift her lips to his...

She couldn't. She mustn't!

"I can't forget how it felt to make love to you," he said in a low voice. "I still dream about it. Do you?"

"No," she lied.

His dark eyes glinted. His lips curved wickedly as he

came forward, and without warning, he swept her up into his powerful arms.

"Shall I remind you what it was like?" he said softly, his gaze hot against her trembling lips.

For a moment, standing in this apartment where they'd made love so many times, in so many locations—on that sofa, against that wall—all she wanted was to kiss him, to feel his hands against her naked skin. It terrified her, how easily he made her body yearn to surrender!

But if she did, how long would it take before she gave him everything?

Trembling, she wrenched away. "No."

He looked at her, and she thought she saw a flash of vulnerability in his dark eyes. Then his handsome face hardened. "I'm not going away, Daisy. I'm not going to abandon her."

"I know." She prayed he didn't realize how close she was to spinning out of control. She needed to get him out of here, out of this apartment with all its painfully joyful memories. "I'm tired. Can we talk tomorrow?"

"No," he said, unyielding. "This needs to be settled."

Sunny rose from her dog bed to sniff curiously at Leonidas. The dog looked up at him with hopeful eyes, clearly waiting to be petted. He briefly scratched her ears. As he straightened, the dog licked his hand.

Traitor. Daisy glared at her pet. Just when she most wanted her canine protector to growl and bark, another female fell helplessly at the Greek tycoon's feet!

Leonidas stood before her, illuminated by the bright Manhattan skyline and the starry night, and a lump rose in her throat. Did he know how memories of their love affair haunted her?

If it had been Leo wanting to kiss her, she would have already fallen into his arms. If it had been Leo proposing, she would have married him in an instant.

But it wasn't. Instead, it was a handsome stranger, a coldhearted billionaire, the man who'd put her father in jail.

"I can see you're tired," Leonidas said gently, looking at her slumped shoulders and the way her hands cradled her belly. "Are you hungry? Perhaps I could take you to dinner?"

He sounded hesitant, as if he were expecting her to refuse. But after her early morning shift at the diner, followed by her checkup at the obstetrician's office and then walking her energetic dog, Daisy *was* tired and hungry.

"Another fancy restaurant?" she said.

"Whatever kind of restaurant you want. Homey. Casual." Leonidas smiled down at Sunny, who was by now licking his hand and flirtatiously holding up her paw. He added, "You can even bring your dog." He straightened, giving her a slow-rising, sensual smile. "What do you say?"

It was really not fair to use her dog against her. Or that smile, which burned right through her. Daisy hated how her body reacted to Leonidas's smile, causing electricity to course through her veins. She was no better than her pet, she thought in disgust.

But she *was* hungry. And more than anything, she wanted to get Leonidas out of this apartment, with all its sensual memories, before she did something she'd regret.

"Fine," she bit out. "Dinner. Just dinner, mind. Someplace homey and casual. Where dogs are allowed."

Leonidas's smile became a grin. "I know just the place."

Leonidas looked at Daisy, sitting next to him in the back seat of the Rolls-Royce. Daisy's floppy yellow dog was in her lap, sticking her head excitedly out the window. The animal's tongue lolled out of her mouth as they crossed over the East River, into Manhattan.

Sadly, the pet's mistress didn't seem nearly so pleased.

Daisy's lovely face was troubled as she stared fiercely out the window.

But it was enough. He'd convinced Daisy to come to dinner. He'd given quiet instructions to his chauffeur, Jenkins, and sent a text to his assistant. Everything was set.

Now he had Daisy, he never intended to let her go.

It was strange. Leonidas had never imagined wanting to get married, and certainly never imagined becoming a father. But now he was determined to do both and do them well. In spite of—or even perhaps because of—his own awful childhood.

For his whole life, he'd been driven to prove himself. His first memories involved desperately trying to please the man he thought was his father, who called him stupid and useless. Leonidas had tried to do better, to make his penmanship, his English conjugations, his skill with an épée all perfect. But no matter his efforts, Giannis had bullied him and sneered at him, while his mother ignored him completely—unless they were in company. Appearances were all that mattered, and as violently as his parents fought each other, they were united in wanting others to believe they had the perfect marriage, the perfect son, the perfect family.

But the truth was far from perfect. His parents had seemed to hate each other—but not as much as they hated Leonidas. From the age of five, when he'd first noticed that other children were hugged and loved and praised by their parents, Leonidas had known something was horribly wrong with him. There had to be, or why would his own parents despise him, no matter how hard he tried?

He'd never managed to impress them. When he was fourteen, they'd died, leaving him with no one but distant trustees, and boarding school in America.

At twenty-one, fresh out of Princeton, he'd seized the reins of Giannis's failing leather goods business, near bankruptcy after seven years of being run into the ground by trustees. He decided he didn't need a family. He didn't need love. Success would be the thing to prove his worth to the world.

And he'd done what no one expected of an heir: he'd rebuilt the company from the ground up. He'd renamed it Liontari, and over the next fifteen years, he'd made it a global empire through will and work and luck. He'd fought his way through business acquisitions, hostile takeovers, and created, through blood and sweat, the worldwide conglomerate now headquartered in New York.

But none of those battles, none of those hard-won multimillion-dollar deals, had ever made him feel as triumphant as Daisy agreeing to dinner tonight.

This was personal.

Leonidas had never been promiscuous with love affairs, having only a few short-term relationships each year, but the women in his life had often accused him of being cold, even soulless. "You have no feelings at all!" was an accusation that had been hurled at him more than once.

And it was probably true. He tended to intellectualize everything. He didn't *feel* things like everyone else seemed to. Even when he beat down business rivals, he didn't glory in the triumph. Losing a lover made him shrug, not weep.

But he told himself he was lucky. Without feelings, he could be rational, rather than pursuing emotional wild goose chases as others did. The only emotion he really knew was anger, and he kept even that in check when he could.

Except when he'd been Leo.

It was strange, looking back. For the month he'd been Daisy's lover, it had been exhilarating to let down his guard and not have to live up to the world's expectations of Leonidas Niarxos, billionaire playboy. In Daisy's eyes, he'd been an ordinary man, a nobody, really—but somehow she'd still thought him worthy.

And he'd loved it. He'd been free to be truly himself, instead of always being primed for battle, ready to attack or defend. He'd been able to show his silly side, like the time they'd nearly died laughing together while digging through vintage vinyl albums at a Brooklyn record shop, teasing each other about whose taste in music was worse. Or the time they'd brought weird flavors of ice cream home from an artisanal shop, and they'd ended up smearing each other with all the different flavors—chocolate cinnamon, whiskey banana and even one oddly tart sugar dill... He shivered, remembering how it had tasted to suckle that exotic flavor off Daisy's bare, taut nipple.

In the back of his mind, Leonidas had always known it could not last.

But this would.

He would marry Daisy. They'd raise their child together. Their daughter would have a different childhood than Leonidas had had. She would always feel wanted. Cherished. Encouraged. Whether she was making mud pies or learning calculus or kicking soccer balls, whether she was succeeding or failing, she would always know that her father adored her.

But marriage was the key to that stability. Otherwise, what would stop Daisy from someday becoming another man's wife? Leonidas wanted to be a full-time father, not a part-time one. He wanted a stable home, and for their daughter to always know exactly who her family was. And if Daisy married someone else, how could he guarantee that any other man could care for Leonidas's child as she needed—as she deserved?

He had to be there for his child. And Daisy.

He had to convince her that he was right.

But how?

Leonidas looked at Daisy, sitting next to him in the spacious back seat of the limo. Convincing her to join him for dinner was a good start. But as they crossed into Manhattan, she still stared fiercely out the window, stroking her dog as if it were an emotional support animal. Her lower lip wobbled, as if she were fighting back tears.

The smile slid away from Leonidas's face. A marriage where the husband and wife fought in white-knuckled warfare, or secretly despised each other in a cold war, was the last thing he wanted. He'd seen that in his own parents, though they'd supposedly once been passionately in love.

He wanted a partnership with Daisy. A friendship. That was the best way to create a home for a child. At least so he'd heard.

Leonidas took a deep breath. He had to woo Daisy. Win her. Convince her he was worthy of her trust and esteem, if not her love. Just as he'd done with Liontari—he had to take their bankrupt, desolate relationship, and make it the envy of the world.

But how?

As the Rolls-Royce crossed into the shadowy canyons between Manhattan's illuminated skyscrapers, the moonlight was pale above them. The limo finally pulled up in front of his five-story mansion in the West Village. Daisy looked up through her car window.

"You call that homey?" she said in a low voice.

He shrugged. "It's home. And very dog friendly."

"Since when?"

"Since now." Getting out of the car, Leonidas shook his head at his driver, and opened her door himself.

But as Daisy got out of the back seat, she wouldn't meet Leonidas's eyes, or take his offered hand. Cuddling her dog against her chest, she looked up at Leonidas's hundred-year-old brownstone, her lovely face anxious.

"I'm not sure this is a good idea."

"It's just dinner. A totally casual, very homey, dog-friendly dinner."

Her expression was dubious, but she got out of the car. Daisy and her dog followed him slowly up the steps to the door, where he punched in the code. They went into the foyer, beneath crystal chandeliers high overhead.

"Where's the butler?" she asked, the corners of her lips curving up slightly as he helped her take off her long black coat.

"He quit a few months ago."

"Quit?"

"I've been living in Paris. He went in search of less boring employment." He shrugged. "I still have Mrs. Berry and a few other staffers, but they've all gone home for the night."

Daisy drew back, her face troubled in the shadowy foyer. "So we're alone?"

He took off his coat, adding it to the nearby closet beside hers. "Is that a problem?"

Her gaze slid away. "Of course not. I'm not scared of you."

"Good. You're safe with me, Daisy. Don't you realize that? Don't you realize I would die to protect you—you and the baby?"

Her eyes met his. "You would?"

"I told you. Our baby is my only family. That means you're under my protection as well. I will always protect and provide for you. On my honor." Remembering how little she'd thought of his honor, he added quietly, "On my life."

As their eyes locked, the air between them electrified. Her gaze fell to his lips. His hand tightened on her shoulder as he moved closer—

The doorbell rang behind them, jarring him. Then he smiled. "That must be dinner."

She looked surprised. "You ordered takeout?"

"My housekeeper's gone home. How else could I serve

dinner? I swore to protect you, not poison you with burned meals."

The edges of her mouth lifted. "True."

For a moment, they smiled at each other, and he knew she was remembering the single disastrous night he'd tried to cook for her in the Brooklyn apartment. Somehow he'd turned boiled spaghetti noodles and canned marinara sauce into a full-scale culinary disaster that had required a fire extinguisher.

Then her smile fell, and he knew that she was thinking of everything that had happened since.

That was a battle he could not win. So he turned to answer the door. Speaking quietly to the delivery person, he took the bags, then turned to face Daisy. "Shall we?"

She looked at the bags. "What is it?"

"Chinese." He hesitated. "I know it used to be your favorite, but if you'd rather have something else…"

"Kung pao chicken?" she interrupted.

"Of course."

"It's exactly what I want." She looked almost dismayed about it.

Leonidas led her through the large, spacious house to a back hallway which led to an enormous kitchen, her dog's nails clicking against the marble floor as she followed behind. On the other side of the kitchen was a small, cozy breakfast room with wide windows and French doors overlooking a private courtyard.

Outside, in the moonlight, a few snowflakes were falling. As Leonidas put the bags of Chinese takeout on the breakfast table, Daisy looked out at the courtyard in surprise. "You have your own yard? In the middle of Manhattan?"

Leonidas shrugged. "It's why I bought this house. I always want fresh air and space."

Daisy's forehead furrowed. "*You* like fresh air?"

He barked a laugh. "Is that so shocking?"

"I just picture you only in boardrooms, or society ballrooms, or the back seat of a Rolls-Royce or..."

"Let me guess," he responded, amused. "Sitting in the basement of a bank, counting my piles of gold like Scrooge McDuck?"

Her green eyes widened at mention of the old cartoon character. "How do you know who that is?" she said accusingly. "Do you have a child?"

She really did believe the worst of him. His smile faded. "No, but I was one."

"In Greece?"

"I was sent to an American boarding school at nine."

Daisy blinked, her face horrified. "Your parents sent you away? At *nine*?"

"They did me a favor. Believe me." Turning away, he went back to the big gleaming kitchen and grabbed two plates and two bowls, china edged with twenty-four-carat gold. He placed the plates on the table, and the bowls on the marble floor.

Taking three bottles of water from the small refrigerator beneath the side table, he poured water into one of the bowls. Her dog came forward eagerly.

"Are you crazy?" Daisy looked incredulously at her dog lapping water from the gold-edged china bowl. "Don't you have any cheap dishes?"

"No. Sorry."

"We're going to need some, before—" She cut herself off.

"Before our baby needs a plate?" Tilting his head, he looked down at her. "I'm looking forward to it," he said softly. "All of it. I'd like this house to be your home, Daisy. Yours and the baby's. Make it your own. Whatever you want, your slightest desire, it will be yours."

She looked at him with wide stricken eyes, then changed

the subject, turning away to stare at a painting on the opposite wall. "You like modern art."

"Yes," he said cautiously.

"Do you own any of Franck's?"

Leonidas snorted. "He's overrated. I don't know anyone who owns his paintings."

"Well, lots of people must buy them, because he's very successful. He travels first class around the world." She tilted her head. "Everyone loves him."

"Everyone including you?" he said unwillingly.

Daisy looked at him in surprise. "Are you jealous?"

"Maybe."

"You were never jealous before."

He shrugged. "That was before."

"Before?"

"Before you stopped looking at me like you used to." He did miss it, the way Daisy used to look at him. As if he were the whole world to her, Christmas and her birthday all at once. It was a shock to realize that. He'd thought he didn't care if Daisy loved him. In fact, after what he'd seen his parents go through, he'd convinced himself that romantic love was a liability.

But he missed having her love him.

"That was a long time ago," Daisy mumbled, her cheeks red. She reached over to scratch Sunny's ears. "Before I found out the man I loved was just a dream."

Leonidas looked down, realizing that his hands were trembling. "We can find a new dream together."

"A new dream?"

"A partnership. Family. Respect."

"Maybe." Daisy tried to smile. "I don't know. But I've lost dreams before. Did I ever tell you how thoroughly I failed when I tried to become an artist?"

"No."

"I didn't sell a single painting. Not even a pity sale." Her cheeks colored. "I don't expect you to understand what it feels like. I'm sure you've never failed at anything."

"You feel empty. Helpless. Like there's nothing you can do, and nothing will ever change for you."

She looked at him in surprise. He gave her a small, tight smile, then started unpacking the takeout cartons from the bags. "I asked my housekeeper to get organic dog food. It's in the kitchen." He quirked a dark eyebrow. "Unless Sunny would prefer kung pao chicken, too?"

"You're hilarious." But Daisy's expression softened as she looked at him. "Sunny already ate. She's fine for now."

"As you wish." As he pulled out carton after carton from the bags, she looked incredulous.

"Will there be a crowd joining us?"

"I wasn't sure if you might be having pregnancy cravings, so I got a little of everything. As well as double of the kung pao." Leonidas handed her a plate, which she swiftly filled with food. He gave her a napkin and chopsticks from the bag, and a bottle of water. He made himself a plate, then sat beside her at the table.

But the truth was, he didn't care about food. He was more interested in watching her.

As they ate, they spoke of inconsequential things, about anything and everything but the obvious. He was mesmerized, watching her eat everything on her plate, then go back for more.

Everything about Daisy drew him—not just her body, her pregnancy-swollen breasts, or the curve of her belly. Everything. The way she drew the chopsticks back slowly from her lips. The flutter of her dark lashes against her cheeks. The graceful swoop of her neck before it disappeared beneath the white cotton collar of her shirt. Her thick brown hair falling in waves over her shoulders. Even her voice, as she teased him about the fundraiser he'd held last year, because his favored politician had lost.

He looked at her. "Will you stay with me?" he asked quietly. "At least until the baby is born?"

Her seafoam green eyes pulled him into the waves, like a siren luring him to drown.

"It's not that simple," she said.

"I know. For you, it is not. But it is for me." Folding his hands, he leaned forward. "Give me the chance to earn your trust. And show you that I can be the partner you need. That our baby needs."

Her cheeks burned red beneath his gaze. He felt out of his element. He knew he should probably play it cool. Act cold. Manipulate, seize control.

But for the first time in his adult life, he could not. Not now. Not with her.

All he could do was ask.

Daisy looked away. "I'm planning to move to California in September. For nursing school."

"Why? You don't need to work." The thought of her moving three thousand miles away chilled him. "I will always support you."

"What if you change your mind?" She snorted. "Do you expect me to just give myself up to your hands?"

An erotic image went through him of his hands stroking her naked body. He took a deep breath. "At least stay with me until September. Let me take care of you while you're pregnant. Give me a chance to bond with our daughter after she's born. Then you can see how you feel."

She bit her lip. "Stay here through the summer?"

He could feel her weakening. "As long as you like. Either way, you and the baby will never worry about money again."

"I'm not asking you to support me, Leonidas."

"You're the mother of my child. I will always provide for you. It's my job as a man." Looking down at her, he said quietly, "You would not try to deny me that."

She chewed her lip uncertainly, then sighed. "I guess I could stay until September. If you're sure you really want me here that long?"

"I'm sure," he said automatically.

"Three months living with a pregnant woman? A whole summer with a crying baby? That won't cramp your style?"

"It's what I want."

"Well." She gave a reluctant smile. "I've imposed on Franck's charity long enough. I might as well impose on you for a while."

"It's no imposition. I want to marry you."

She looked away. Her cheeks burned as she mumbled, "So does he."

Leonidas gaped. "What!"

Daisy rolled her eyes. "It was a pity proposal. He felt sorry for me."

Leonidas doubted pity had anything to do with it. "Did he try to kiss you?"

She looked shocked. "*Kiss* me? Of course not—Franck is old enough to be my father!" But Leonidas saw sudden uneasiness in her eyes, and he wondered exactly what Franck Bain had said to her. He made a mental note to keep the middle-aged artist on his radar.

He was furious that another man had made a move on her. How dared he? She was carrying Leonidas's baby!

But could he blame Bain for wanting her? Any man would want Daisy. It made Leonidas all the more determined to marry her, and claim her as his own.

She tilted her head, looking up at him through dark lashes. "At least you have good reason to want me here. You love our baby." She paused. "I never expected that."

Relief flooded through him. "So you'll stay?"

"With one condition." She lifted her chin. "You have to promise, when I want to leave, you'll let me go."

He saw there was no arguing with her on this point. He

hesitated. Once Daisy was here, living in his house, he believed he'd soon convince her they should marry. They both loved their baby. That was a good enough reason.

He hoped.

"If you'll promise," he said slowly, "you'll never try to keep me from my daughter. Or hide her from me, even if you leave New York."

Biting her lip, she gave a single nod.

Leonidas held out his hand. "Then I agree."

"Me too." Daisy shook his hand. He felt the slow burn of her palm against his, before she quickly drew it away.

"What changed your mind?" he asked quietly.

She looked up at him. "I loved my dad. That was what convinced me. Because you're right. How could I deny our daughter the same chance for a father?"

The father that Daisy had lost, because of him. Leonidas felt a lump in his throat. The ghost of Patrick Cassidy would always be between them. How would they ever get past it?

He said in a low voice, "Will you stay tonight?"

"Yes. So will Sunny. Where I go, my dog goes."

"She's very welcome. Like I said. We're dog friendly." Looking at the dog lazing nearby, he added, "Besides, I think she likes me."

"I noticed," she said wryly. She yawned. "Though I didn't pack any clothes."

"I can send someone back—"

"Wake up one of your employees to send them to Brooklyn and back? I'm not that evil. I'll just sleep naked."

Leonidas broke out in a hot sweat, remembering her bare body against his, the soft sweetness of her skin as she moved against him. He wondered what it would feel like to touch her now, what she looked like naked, so heavily pregnant with his child...

No! He forced the image from his mind. He couldn't seduce her. Not yet. She was still skittish, looking for an excuse to flee. He couldn't give her one. He had to take his time. He had to win her trust.

"Fine. We can pick up your things tomorrow," he said, breathing deeply.

"There's not much to collect." She gave a brief smile. "You don't have to help me. I can just take the subway over."

"Leave you to struggle with suitcases and boxes on the subway? Forget it. I'm helping you."

"Fine," she sighed. She yawned again. "I think I need to go to bed."

He tried not to think about her in bed. "Sure."

"I just need to let Sunny out first." She rose to her feet, opening the door for her dog, who quickly bounded out into the courtyard.

As she stood in the doorway, Leonidas couldn't stop his gaze from lingering over her belly and full, swollen breasts, imagining them beneath her white shirt and black leggings. Turning back, she caught his gaze. He blushed like a guilty teenager.

Clearing his throat, he gathered up the take-out bags and trash, leaving the plates in one of the kitchen sinks. A moment later, after Sunny returned from outside, Leonidas said in a low voice, "I'll show you to your room."

He led her through the kitchen, the dog following them down the hall and up the sweeping staircase to the second floor.

As they passed, Daisy glanced nervously at his master bedroom, where they'd had their blowout fight last autumn. But he didn't pause. He led her to the best guest room.

Reaching inside, he turned on the light, revealing a beautiful suite, elegantly decorated in cream and light pink. "There's an en suite bathroom. All stocked with toothbrushes and toiletries and anything else you might require."

"Do you often have guests?" she asked, smiling awkwardly as her dog went ahead to sniff, scouting out the bedroom.

"You're the first," he said honestly. "Mrs. Berry always seemed to think someone might come to visit. Even though I told her I have no family."

"Had," Daisy said. "Now you do."

His heart twisted strangely. "Right. Good night."

"Thank you," she said softly.

He turned back to face her, standing at the door. "Thanks for staying."

She licked her lips nervously. "Leonidas, you know that... even if someday I agree to marry you, far in the future...and I'm not saying I will...but..."

"But?"

"You know I'll never be yours again. Not like I was."

Never? Leonidas could still remember how she'd felt in his arms. Soft. Sensual. Making love to her had been like fire. And now she was pregnant with his child. Her body was even more lush, with a rounded belly beneath full breasts. He wanted to see her. To feel her. He was hard just thinking about it.

Reaching out, Leonidas cupped her cheek. Her skin felt warm and soft, so soft. "I will do everything I can to win you back," he said softly. "In every way. And soon..."

For a moment, he was lost in the maelstrom of her velvety black pupils. His gaze fell to her full pink lips. He forgot his earlier vow not to seduce her in his thundering need to kiss her, and claim what was his, after months of agonizing desire.

Slowly, he lowered his head—

Daisy jerked back violently. "No." Her eyes were luminous with sudden tears. "No!"

And she slammed the bedroom door in his face.

CHAPTER FIVE

LEONIDAS DID NOT sleep well.

He tossed and turned, picturing the woman he wanted sleeping in the next room down the hall. So close, and yet she might as well have been a million miles away.

Finally, he saw the early gray light of dawn through the window. Rising wearily from bed in his boxers, he stretched his tired, aching body, as the cool air of the room invigorated his muscles, from his shoulders to his chest and thighs. Going to the window, he pushed open heavy white curtains. Below, he saw the quiet West Village street was covered with a dusting of white. Snow had fallen during the night.

Leonidas's hand tightened on the white curtains. He was furious with himself. Why had he tried to kiss her? How had he ever thought that would be a good idea, in their relationship's current fragile state?

He hadn't been thinking. At all. That was the problem.

He'd let his desire for Daisy override everything else. The stakes were so high. He had to make her feel comfortable here, so she would remain. So they could become friends. Partners. *Married*. For their baby's sake.

Instead, he could still hear the echo of her door, slamming in his face.

How could he have been so stupid? Frustration pounded through him.

Pulling on exercise shorts and a T-shirt from his walk-in closet, Leonidas dug out his running shoes. He peeked down the darkened hallway and saw Daisy's door was closed. He didn't even hear her dog. He wondered how she'd slept.

After going downstairs, Leonidas went out into the gray dawn and went on a five-mile run to clear his head. With most of the city still asleep, he relished the quiet, the only sound his shoes crunching in the thin layer of snow.

Daisy had such a warm heart. He'd seen it in her devotion to her father, to her friends—and their devotion to her. Her kindness. Her loyalty.

He had to win her trust. Prove to her he could deserve it. Even if that meant he had to wait a long time to make love to her.

Even if that meant he had to wait forever.

He could do it. He was strong enough to fight his own desire. He *could*.

Returning home with a clear head and a determined will, he ran upstairs, taking the steps two at a time. He paused when he saw Daisy's door open. But her bedroom was empty. Had she already gone downstairs? Could she have left? Fled the city in the night—

No. He took a steadying breath. She'd promised she'd never try to keep his child from him. And he believed in her word.

But still. He wanted to find her. Going to his en suite bathroom, he quickly showered and dressed in a sleek black suit with a gray button-up shirt. The Liontari corporate office had recently loosened up the dress code, allowing men to skip ties and suits, though of course, the creatives and designers of the specific luxury clothing brands played by their own rules.

But Leonidas had his own strict rule, to always represent the best his company had to offer. And so, he always wore the same cut of suit from his favorite men's brand, Xerxes, altered to fit his unusually broad shoulders, biceps and thighs. He checked the clock. He always had breakfast around seven; he was expected at work in an hour. The thought gave him little pleasure.

Going downstairs, he couldn't find either Daisy or Sunny. Phyllis Berry, his longtime housekeeper, was cooking eggs and sizzling bacon in the kitchen, as she always was this time of the morning.

"Good morning, sir."

"Good morning, Mrs. Berry." Sitting at the breakfast table as usual, he hesitated. "I don't suppose you've seen—"

"Miss Cassidy?" The petite white-haired woman beamed at him as she dished up a plate. "Yes. And all I can say is— finally!"

"Finally?"

"Finally, you're settling down. Such a nice girl, too. And pregnant! You wasted no time!" With a chuckle, she brought the plate of bacon and eggs, along with a cup of black coffee, and put them down on the table in front of him with a wistful sigh. "I can hardly wait to have a baby about the place. The pitter-patter of little feet. And a dog! I must admit I'm surprised. But better late than never, Mr. Niarxos. After all these years, you finally took my advice!"

Raising his eyebrows, Leonidas sipped hot coffee, while he was pretending to skim the business news. "You met Daisy?"

"Yes, about a half hour ago, when she left to walk her dog. Such a lovely girl." Mrs. Berry sighed, then gave him a severe look before she turned away. "Why you still haven't asked her to marry you is something I don't understand. Young people today…"

Leonidas's lips curved upward. *Young person?* He was thirty-five. But then, Mrs. Berry, who'd worked for Leonidas for many years, regarded her employer with a proprietary eye. She seemed to regard him as the grandson she'd never had, and never hesitated to tell him the error of his ways.

He heard the slam of the front door, the dog's nails clacking against the marble floor, and the soft murmur of Daisy's voice, greeting some unseen member of his house staff down the hall. Trust Daisy to already have made friends.

Her dog, no longer a puppy in size but clearly very much in temperament, bounded into the kitchen first, her tongue lolling, her big paws tracking ice and snow from her walk. Mrs. Berry took one look and blanched. She moved at supersonic speed, picking the animal up off the floor. But her wrinkled face was indulgent as she looked down at the dog.

"Let's get you into the mudroom," she said affectionately. "And after we clean your paws, we'll get you properly fed." The dog gave her a slobbery kiss. Mrs. Berry smiled at Daisy, who'd followed her pet into the kitchen. "If that's all right with you, Miss Cassidy."

"Of course. Oh, dear. I'm so sorry!" Daisy glanced with dismay at the tracks her dog had made on the previously spotless floor. "I'm afraid it's a great deal of trouble—"

"No trouble at all," Mrs. Berry said, with a purposeful glance at Leonidas. The crafty old lady was leaving them alone. He wondered irritably if she expected, as soon as she left the room, for him to immediately go down on one knee in front of Daisy and pull a diamond ring out of his pocket? He would have done so gladly, if it would have done any good!

"Good morning, Leonidas." Daisy's voice was shy. She was, of course, wearing the same clothes from yesterday, her long black coat unzipped over her belly. "I saw you come back from my window. Were you running?"

"It helps me relax."

"Does it?" She snorted. "You should walk my dog sometime, then. She'd probably love running with you. She has more energy than I do these days, always tugging at the leash!"

He furrowed his brow. "Is walking her a problem? I could get one of my staff to handle the chore..."

"Chore?" She looked at him incredulously. "It's not a chore. She's my dog. I like walking her. I just thought *she* might like running with *you*."

"Oh." He cleared his throat. "Sure. I could take her running with me." He pictured Daisy walking around the streets of New York in the darkness of early morning, and suddenly didn't like it. "Or I could come walking with you, if you want. Either way."

She blinked. "Really? That wouldn't be too much of a...a chore for you?"

"Not at all. I like her." Leonidas looked up from the table. "And I like you."

She bit her lip. He saw dark circles under her eyes. Apparently she hadn't slept very well either.

"Sit down." Rising to his feet, he pulled out a chair at the table. "Can I get you some breakfast? Are you hungry?"

She shook her head. A smile played about her full pink lips. "Mrs. Berry already made me eat some toast and fruit before she'd let me take the dog out."

Score one for Mrs. Berry. "Good." He paused awkwardly, still standing across from her. "How are you feeling?"

Her lovely face looked unhappy. Her hands clasped together as she blurted out, "I think we've made a big mistake."

Danger clanged through him. "A mistake?"

She tucked a loose tendril of brown hair behind her ear. She said softly, "I don't think I can stay here."

Leonidas stared at her in consternation. Then he understood.

"Because I almost kissed you last night," he guessed grimly. She nodded, not meeting his eyes.

He had to soothe her—make her feel safe. He took a deep breath. Going against all his instincts, he didn't move. Instead, he said gently, "You have no reason to be afraid of me."

"I'm not afraid of you. I'm afraid of—"

She cut off her words.

"Afraid of what?"

Her pale green eyes lifted to his, and he knew, no matter how Daisy tried to pretend otherwise, that she felt the same electricity. Every time her gaze fell to his lips. Every time their eyes met, and she nervously looked away. Every time he touched her and felt her tremble.

She was afraid of herself. Of her own desire. Afraid, if she gave in, that she would be lost forever.

And she was poised to flee. If he didn't reassure her, he'd scare her straight back into Franck Bain's apartment—if not his arms.

Taking a deep breath, he said, "What if I promise I won't try to kiss you?"

Silence crackled as they faced each other in the breakfast nook. Outside in the courtyard, there was a soft thump as snow fell from the branches onto the white-covered earth.

"Would you really make that promise?" she said finally.

"Yes. I'll never try to kiss you, Daisy. Not unless you want me to."

"On your honor?"

He tried to comfort himself with the fact that at least she now believed he *had* honor. "Yes."

Daisy bit her lip, then said slowly, "All right. If I have your word, then…then I'll stay."

He exhaled. "Good." He tried not to think about how hard it would be not to kiss her. How hard it was not to kiss her even now.

He took a deep breath. "I need to go to work today."

"Work?"

"I'm CEO and principal shareholder of Liontari."

"That's a store?"

"An international consortium of brands. You've probably heard of them. Vertigris, for instance."

"What's that?"

"Champagne."

"No. But I don't really drink…"

He was surprised. Vertigris was as globally famous as Cristal or Dom Perignon. "Ridenbaugh Watches? Helios Diamonds? Cialov Handbags?"

Looking bemused, Daisy shook her head.

And all of Leonidas's plans to go into the office flew out the window. He set his jaw. "Okay. I'm taking you out."

"Out?"

"We'll collect your clothes from Bain's apartment, as I promised. Then I'm taking you to a few shops." When she frowned, still looking bewildered, he added, "We can buy a few things."

"What kind of things?"

"For your pregnancy. For the baby."

"You don't need to buy me stuff."

"Think of it as you helping *me*," he said lightly. "Market research. You're a totally virgin consumer. I'd like your take on my brands."

Her cheeks colored at the word *virgin*. "I don't see how my opinion would be useful to you."

"It would be. But more than that, I'd really like you to understand what I do." He gave her a brief smile. "Isn't that what you were asking me? To understand my world?"

"That was before…"

"There was so much I never was able to show you before. We spent our whole time together in Brooklyn." He paused. "Let me show you Manhattan."

Her light green gaze looked troubled, then she bit her lip. "I'm not sure I can leave Sunny alone here…"

"Mrs. Berry can watch her. She's good with dogs." At least, she'd seemed good with Sunny just now. He'd never really thought about it. He'd certainly never lived with a dog before. His parents had despised the idea of pets. "She's very trustworthy." That at least was true.

He could see Daisy weighing that, and wondered if she was setting such a high bar for who was allowed to watch her dog, would any potential babysitter for their daughter need two PhDs and a letter of reference from the Dalai Lama?

"I suppose," she said finally. "As long as we're not gone for too long."

Reaching out, he took her left hand in his own, running his thumb over her bare ring finger. "We could go to Helios," he said casually. "Look at engagement rings."

He felt her shiver and saw the flash of vulnerability in her eyes. Then she pulled her hand away.

"No," she said firmly. "No rings."

Couldn't blame a man for trying. "There must be something you need, you or the baby."

She tilted her head, then sighed, resting her hand on her swelling belly peeking out from the open black puffy coat. "I suppose it would be nice to get a new coat," she admitted. "This morning, I suddenly couldn't zip it up anymore."

As she rubbed her belly, he saw a flash of cleavage at the neckline of her white button-down shirt, and he wondered what touching those breasts would feel like. A very dangerous thing to wonder. He couldn't think about seducing her. Because he was the kind of man that if he let himself think about something, he would soon take action to achieve it.

"But you don't need to pay for it," she said quickly. Inwardly, he sighed. He'd never had so much trouble convincing a woman to let him buy her things. "While we're at Franck's," she continued, "I need to pick up my waitress uniform. I have a shift tomorrow."

Leonidas frowned. "You're not thinking of going back to work at the diner?"

"Of course." Daisy frowned. "Do you really think I'd just quit my job? And leave my boss in the lurch?"

"Why would you—" Gritting his teeth, he said, "You don't have to be a waitress anymore. Ever. I will take care of you!"

She put her hand on her hip. "Are you telling me not to work?"

Raising his eyebrow, he countered, "Are you telling *me* it's comfortable to stand on your feet all day, when you're this pregnant?"

Daisy's expression became uncertain, and her hand fell to her side. "I'll think about it," she said finally. "On the drive to Brooklyn." She paused. "Actually, could we…um… take the subway or something?"

"You don't like the Rolls-Royce?"

She rolled her eyes. "It's a *limo*. With a uniformed driver."

"So?"

"Well, the whole thing's a little bit much, isn't it?"

As much as he wanted to please her, Leonidas wasn't quite ready for the subway. They compromised by having his driver, Jenkins—wearing street clothes, not his uniform—take them in Leonidas's Range Rover.

When the two of them arrived at the Brooklyn co-op overlooking the river, the building's doorman greeted Daisy with a warm smile, then glared at Leonidas.

"You all right, Miss Cassidy?" the man asked her.

She gave him a sweet smile. "Yes. Thank you, Walter." She glanced at Leonidas, clearly enjoying his discomfiture.

"Thank you, Walter," he echoed. The man scowled back. Obviously their last meeting, when Leonidas had threatened Daisy with lawyers, had been neither forgiven nor forgotten.

But Leonidas was even more discomfited, ten minutes later, when, upstairs in Bain's apartment, Daisy announced she was entirely packed.

"That's it?" Leonidas looked with dismay at her two suitcases and a large cardboard box full of books and a single canvas painting. "That is everything you own?"

Daisy shrugged. "I sold most of our family's belongings last year, to pay for my father's legal defense." She hesitated as she said quietly, "The rest was sold to pay for the funeral."

Her eyes met his, and his cheeks burned. Though she didn't say more, he imagined her silently blaming him. When would she realize it wasn't his fault? Not his fault that her father had decided to sell forgeries and needed a lawyer. Not his fault that Patrick Cassidy had died of a stroke in prison!

But arguing wouldn't help anything. Choking back a sharp retort, he tried to imagine her feelings.

He took a deep breath.

"I'm sorry," he said slowly. "That must have been very hard."

Looking down, she whispered, "It was."

Leonidas glanced at the painted canvas resting in the cardboard box. It was a messy swirl of colors and shapes that seemed to have no unifying theme.

Following his glance, Daisy winced. "I know it's not very good."

Reaching down to the cardboard box, he picked up the painting. "I wouldn't say that…"

"Stop. I know it's terrible. I did it my final semester of art school. All I wanted was for it to be spectacular, amazing, so I kept redoing it, asking advice and redoing it based on everyone's advice. I wanted it to be as good as the masters."

"Maybe that's the problem. It looks like a mash-up of

every well-known contemporary artist. What about your own voice? What were you trying to say?"

"I don't know," she said in a low voice. "I don't think I have a voice."

"That's not true," he said softly, looking at her bowed head. He thought of her years of love and loyalty. "I think you do."

Looking up, she gave an awkward laugh. "It's okay. Really. I tried to be an artist and failed. I never sold a single painting, no matter how hard I tried. So I threw them all away, except this one. I keep thinking," she said wistfully, brushing that canvas with her fingertips, "maybe someday, I'll figure it out. Maybe someday, I'll be brave enough to try again." She gave him a small smile. "Stupid, huh?"

Before he could answer, their driver knocked on the door. He'd come upstairs to help carry the suitcases. Leonidas lifted the big cardboard box in his arms. But he noticed Daisy continued to grip the painting in her hands. She carefully tucked it on top of everything else, so it wouldn't get crushed in the back of the Range Rover.

"Do you mind if we stop at the diner before we go back?" she said into the silence. He turned to her.

"Sure."

Her lovely face looked a little sad. "I think I need to talk to my boss."

They arrived at the cheerful, crowded diner, with its big windows overlooking vintage booths with Naugahyde seats. Jenkins pulled the SUV into the loading zone directly in front of the diner.

"Do you want me to come with you?" Leonidas asked.

"No," Daisy said.

Leonidas watched as she disappeared into the busy, bright diner. He thought of the morning they'd first met. She'd taken one look at his expensive designer suit and laughed. "Nice suit. Headed to court? Unpaid parking tickets?" With a warm smile, she'd held up her coffee pot. "You poor guy. Coffee's on me."

They'd ended up spending the rest of the day together. If it had been one of his typical dates, he would have taken Daisy to the most exclusive restaurant in Manhattan, then perhaps out dancing at a club, then a nightcap at his mansion. But he'd known it couldn't be a date, not when he couldn't even tell her his real name.

So they'd simply spent the afternoon walking around her neighborhood in Brooklyn, visiting quirky little shops she liked, walking down the street lined with red brick buildings, ending with the view of the East River, and the massive bridge sticking out against the sky. Daisy greeted people by name on the street, warmly, and their eyes always lit up when they saw her.

It had been a wild ride, one that would put the roller coasters at Coney Island to shame. She'd made him come alive in a way he'd never imagined. Joy and color and light had burst into his life that day, from the moment he'd met her in this diner. It had been like a vibrant summer after a long, frozen winter.

But it could never be like that again. He would never be Leo again. Daisy would never look at him with love in her eyes again.

No. They would be partners. He wouldn't, couldn't, ask for more. Not when he had nothing more to give in return.

Waiting in the back seat of the Range Rover, he tried to distract himself with his phone. He had ten million messages from board members and designers and marketing heads, all of them anxious about various things; he found it difficult to care. He was relieved when he finally heard the SUV's door open.

"Everything all right?" he asked.

"I quit." Daisy gave a wistful smile. "Claudia—that's my boss—said she didn't need me to give notice. Turns out my job sitting at the cash register was not actually that useful, but she couldn't fire a pregnant single mother." She paused. "But now that I've got a billionaire baby daddy…"

Leonidas smiled. "You told her about me?"

She paused, then looked away. "Not everything."

Silence fell as his driver took them out of Brooklyn, crossing back over the bridge into Manhattan.

Leonidas watched her, feeling strangely sad. He fought to push the emotion away. Work, he thought. Work could save them.

"So you haven't heard of Vertigris or Helios," he said finally. "What about Bandia?"

Still looking out the window, Daisy shook her head.

"It's a small luxury brand that does only maternity clothing and baby clothing. We could go there to look for your coat."

"Okay." Her voice was flat.

"Or Astrara. Have you heard of that?"

Daisy finally looked at him, her face annoyed. "Of course I've heard of Astrara. I don't live under a rock."

Finally, she'd actually heard of one of his brands. He was slightly mollified. He maybe should have started with Astrara, as famous as Gucci or Chanel. "Which do you prefer to visit first? Bandia? Astrara? One of the others?"

"Does it matter?"

"Of course it matters," he said. He waited.

Daisy sat back against the seat. "Bandia," she sighed. "It sounds like it has the most reasonable prices."

Leonidas was careful not to disabuse her of that notion as they arrived at the grand Fifth Avenue boutique. After pulling in front, the driver turned off the engine. Tourists passing on the sidewalk gawked at them.

"Even in Manhattan," she grumbled. "Everyone stares at you."

Hiding a smile, Leonidas turned to help Daisy out. "They're looking at you."

Biting her lip, she took his hand, but to his disappointment, dropped it as soon as she was out of the SUV. As they walked into the boutique, Bandia's shop assistants audibly gasped.

"Mr. Niarxos!"

"You honor us!"

"Sir! We are so happy to…"

He cut them off with a gesture toward Daisy: "This is my—" *future wife…baby mama…lover…* "—dear friend, Miss Cassidy. She needs a new wardrobe. I trust you can help her find things to her taste."

"Wardrobe!" Daisy gasped. She immediately corrected, "I just need a coat."

The assistants turned huge, worshipful eyes to Daisy. "Welcome to Bandia!"

"Miss Cassidy, may I get you some sparkling water? Fruit?"

"This way, if you please, to the private dressing suite, madam."

Perfect, Leonidas thought in approval. Just as he'd expected. He'd send the CEO of Bandia a note and let her know he approved of staff training levels.

"Madam, what type of clothes do you prefer?" The store's manager hurried to pay her obeisance as well. "Our newest releases for the fall line? Or perhaps the latest for resort?"

Daisy stared at them like a deer in headlights. "I just… need a coat," she croaked.

"Bring everything and anything in her size," Leonidas answered. "So she can decide."

They were both led to the VIP dressing suite, which had its own private lounge, where Leonidas could sit on a white leather sofa and drink champagne, as salesgirls brought rack after rack of expensive, gorgeous clothing for Daisy to try on in the adjacent changing room behind a thick white velvet curtain.

"I don't need all these clothes," she grumbled to Leonidas. "Why should I try them on, when I don't need them?"

"Market research?"

"Fine," she sighed.

Reluctantly, she tried on outfit after expensive outfit. Each time she stepped in front of the mirrors in the lounge, the salesgirls joyfully exclaimed over her.

"You look good in everything!"

"Beautiful!" another sighed.

"I hope when I'm pregnant someday I'll look half as good as you!"

It was true, Leonidas thought. Daisy looked good in everything. As she stood in front of the mirrors in an elegant maternity pantsuit, he marveled at her chic beauty.

"Do you like it?" he called.

Glancing back at him, she shrugged. "It's all right."

"Just all right?"

"It's not very... comfortable."

He frowned. That wasn't something he ever worried about. *Comfortable?*

"I prefer my T-shirts and stretch pants," she said cheerfully.

"Keep looking."

Rolling her eyes a little, Daisy continued to try on clothes for the next hour, as Leonidas sat on the leather sofa, sipping complimentary Vertigris champagne—one of Liontari's other brands, from a two-hundred-year-old vineyard in France. His company was nothing if not vertically integrated.

Every time she stepped out of the changing room, to stand in front of the large mirrors in the lounge, Leonidas asked hopefully, "Do you like it?"

Always, the shrug. "It's fine."

"Fine?" A thousand-dollar maternity tunic was fine?

"Not as good as my usual T-shirts. Which, by the way, you can buy three for ten dollars." She tilted her head. "Is this the kind of market research you were looking for?"

Leonidas felt disgruntled. He'd hoped to impress her. Obviously it wasn't working. The only thing that had made Daisy's eyes sparkle was when the salesgirls brought over baby outfits that matched the postpartum clothes, cooing, "This will be perfect after your little one is born!"

Then Daisy looked at the price tag. "Three hundred dollars? For a baby dress that will be covered in spit-up, and probably only worn twice before she outgrows it?" She'd shaken her head. "And it's kind of scratchy. I want my baby to be comfortable and cozy, too!" Then Daisy looked around with a frown. "Don't you have any winter coats?"

The salesgirls looked at each other sheepishly. "I'm sorry, Miss Cassidy," one said. "It's March. We cleared out all the winter clothes for our new spring line."

"It's still snowing, and you're selling bikinis," Daisy said, her voice full of good-humored regret.

"There might be a few coats on the sales rack," one salesgirl said hesitantly.

Daisy seemed overjoyed when one puffy white coat fit her—if anything, it was a little too big. "And it's cozy, too!" Then she saw the price, and her smile disappeared. "Too much!"

"It's fifty percent off," Leonidas pointed out irritably.

"Still too much," Daisy said, but she continued hugging the coat around her tightly, as if she never wanted to take it off.

"We'll take it," he told the sales staff.

"I can't possibly let you pay—"

"You won't let me buy a cheap coat, from my own company? To warm the mother of my child? Are you really so unkind?"

Daisy hugged the coat around her, then said in a small voice, "All right, I guess. Thank you." She looked at Leonidas. "Are you ready to go?"

Finally. He'd convinced her to let him buy *something*. But he'd wanted to buy her so much more. "Not quite." He looked at the salesgirls. "She needs a ball gown."

As the staff left the lounge to gather the dresses, Daisy looked at him incredulously. "A ball gown? You can't be serious."

"I'm taking you to a party on Saturday."

She groaned. "A party?"

"It's for charity." He quirked an eyebrow. "A fundraiser for homeless children. Don't you want to come and make sure they get a healthy chunk of my ill-gotten fortune?"

"Fine," she sighed. A moment later, when the salesgirls rolled a large rack of maternity ball gowns into the lounge, she grabbed the closest one, which was a deep scarlet red. She went back into the private changing room to try it on.

Leonidas waited to see it, practically holding his breath.

But when Daisy pushed back the curtain a few moments later, she was dressed in her white shirt and black leggings. "I'm done."

"But the gown?"

"The gown is fine."

She wasn't going to let him see it, he realized. Disappointed, he said hastily, "You must need new lingerie for—"

Daisy snorted. "I'm *not* trying that on in front of you. Are you ready to go?"

"Aren't there any other things you want to try on? Anything at all?"

"Nope." She turned with a smile to the salesgirls, hugging them. "Thank you so much for your help, Davina, Laquelle, Mary. And Posey—good luck on law school!"

Trust Daisy to make friends, instead of picking out designer outfits. As they left Bandia, going outside to where the SUV waited, Leonidas helped Daisy—now wearing her new white coat—into the back seat, as Jenkins tucked the carefully wrapped red ball gown into the trunk.

Daisy's pink lips lifted mischievously. "I'm sorry I didn't love all the clothes."

"It's fine." But he felt irritated. If not Bandia, surely one of his other luxury brands would make her appreciate his multibillion-dollar global conglomerate! He turned to Jenkins. "Take us to Astrara."

But even the dazzling delights of the famous three-story boutique, as enormous as a luxury department store, seemed to leave her cold. Daisy made friends with the salesgirls, and marveled at the cost of the clothes, which she proclaimed were also "weird looking" and "scratchy."

After that, he took Daisy to a luxury beauty and skincare boutique, which seemed to bore her. "I like the stuff from the drugstore," she informed him.

Finally, in desperation, he took them to a famous perfumery on Fifth Avenue, Loyavault.

As she walked through the aisles of luxury perfume, she seemed dazzled by the lovely colors and bright boxes and lush scents. She bent her head to smell one perfume in a pink bottle, and her green eyes lit up with a bright smile.

"Wow," she whispered.

Leonidas felt the same, just looking at her.

He took the bottle from her hand. "Floral, roses and white jasmine, with an earthy note of amber." They stood close, so close, almost touching. "I'll have them wrap it up for you."

She bit her lip. "I shouldn't."

"I missed your birthday," he said quietly. "Won't you let me get you a present?"

She exhaled, then slowly nodded.

"But after this, we're done shopping."

Giving in to the inevitable, he sighed.

Daisy wasn't impressed by luxury. Or his company. Or him. It hurt his pride, a little. In each store, Daisy had been treated as if she were the queen of England, visiting from Buckingham Palace. Each time, she blushed with confusion, but was soon chatting with the staff on a first-name basis. And before long, the employees seemed to forget the powerful Liontari CEO was even there.

The salesgirls treasured Daisy for herself. He wasn't the only one to see Daisy's bright warmth. She shone like a star.

What a corporate wife she would make!

"Shall we go for lunch?" he asked as they left Loyavault. Outside, the March sun had come out, and the air was blue and bright, as the spring snow started to melt like it had never existed. She looked at him with a skeptical eye.

"Let me guess. Some elegant Midtown restaurant, French and fancy?"

He hastily rethought his restaurant choice.

"There's a place just a block away. It's French, but not fancy. Strictly speaking, it's not precisely French, but Breton. Crepes."

"You mean like pancakes? Yum."

Thus encouraged, he said, "Shall we walk? Or ride?"

"Walk."

They strolled the long city block to the small hole-in-the-wall establishment, tucked into a side street, where it had existed for fifty years. He led her into the wood-paneled restaurant, rustic as a Breton farmhouse, with a crackling wood-burning fire.

Unlike the more elegant restaurants, no one knew Leonidas here. He'd been here only once before, when he'd visited the city on a weekend from Princeton. They had to wait for a table.

But Daisy didn't seem to mind. She took his arm as

they waited together in the tight reception space, and all of Leonidas's ideas of trying to bribe someone for an earlier table flew out the window.

Soon, a wizened host with a white beard led them to a tiny table for two near the fire. He didn't give them menus.

"You want the full?" the elderly man asked in an accented, raspy voice.

Leonidas and Daisy looked at each other.

"Yes?" he said.

"Sure?" she said.

"Cider," the man demanded.

"Just water," Leonidas replied. "Thank you."

After the waiter departed, he looked at Daisy across the table. "You don't really seem to like luxury. Fancy restaurants, fancy cars, fancy clothes."

She suddenly looked guilty. "I'm sorry. I don't mean to be rude…"

"You're never rude," he said. "I'm just curious why?"

"More market research?"

"If you like."

She sighed. "It all just seems so expensive. So…*unnecessary*."

"Unnecessary?" He felt a little stung. "Would you call *art* necessary?"

Daisy looked at him with startled eyes. "Of course it's necessary! It's an expression of the soul. The exploration and explanation of what makes us human."

"The same could be said of clothing. Or makeup or perfume. Or food."

She started to argue, then paused, stroking her chin.

"You're right," she admitted.

Leonidas felt a surge of triumph way out of proportion for such a small victory.

"Here," the white-bearded man said abruptly, shoving plates at them with savory buckwheat galettes, filled with the traditional ham, cheese and a whole cooked egg in the middle.

"Thank you." Daisy's eyes were huge. Then she took a bite. The sound of her soft moan of pleasure shook Leonidas. "It's—so—good," she breathed, and holding her fork like a weapon, she gobbled down the large crepe faster than he'd ever seen anyone eat before. He looked at her, and could think of nothing else but wanting to hear her make that sound again.

"Would you like another?"

"Another?" She licked her lips, and he had to grip the table.

"Save room for—dessert—" He managed to croak out. If only the dessert could be in his bedroom, with her naked, like that time with the ice cream. That would be the perfect end to their meal. Or anytime. Forever—

"Are you going to eat that?" Daisy said, looking longingly at his untouched crepe.

He pushed it toward her. "Please take it."

"Thank you," she almost sang, as if he'd just done something worthy of the Nobel Prize. And she ate that one, too, in rapid time.

Leonidas couldn't tear his eyes away as she lifted the fork to her mouth, before sliding it out again. As she leaned forward, her collar gaped, and he saw the push of her soft breasts against the hard wood of the table—

With a gulp, he looked away. A moment later, the plates were cleared.

"Ready for dessert?" the elderly man barked.

"Yes, please," she said, smiling back at him warmly. "I've never tasted anything so delicious in my life."

The old man frowned, and then his wrinkled eyes suddenly beamed at her. "You have good sense, madame."

Another conquest fell at Daisy's feet. But then, who could resist her?

Not Leonidas.

But he was, stupidly, the only man on earth who'd given his word of honor never to kiss her.

How strange it was, he thought. To want a woman like this, but not be able to touch her, not be able to seduce her. He thought he might literally die if he never possessed her again.

He would win her, he told himself fiercely. He would. And not just for one night, but forever.

"This is so good," Daisy moaned softly over the sweet crepe, drizzled with butter and sugar. Automatically pushing his own dessert crepe toward her, he tried to distract himself from his unbearable desire.

"I'm sorry you didn't care much for the shopping today."

"I liked the *people*… They were very nice."

"Some other day I'll show you more of Liontari's brands. I want you to appreciate my company. It will all belong to our child one day."

Daisy's eyes almost popped out of her head. She actually put down her fork. "Our daughter will inherit your company?"

Hadn't she realized that? Incredible. With any other woman, he thought, his business empire would have been the first thing on her mind. "Of course. It will all be hers."

Her forehead furrowed. "But what if…she doesn't want it?"

Now Leonidas was the one to be shocked. "Not want Liontari? Why would she not want it?"

Daisy took another bite, slowly pulling her fork out of her mouth, leaving a bit of sugar on her lower lip. He was distracted, until she said thoughtfully, "Not every child wants to follow in the footsteps of her parents' professions."

He looked up, annoyed. "It's not just a *profession*. It's a multibillion-dollar conglomerate, with the biggest luxury brands in the world—" He steadied himself, took a deep breath. Daisy couldn't have meant her words as an insult. "Don't worry." He made his voice jovial, reassuring. "I will teach her everything she needs to know. When it's her time to lead, she'll have the board members eating out of the palm of her hand."

"Yes. Maybe. If she wants."

"If she wants?" Leonidas repeated incredulously. "Why would anyone not want an empire?" Especially one he'd created out of his own sweat, blood and bone!

Daisy shrugged. "She might find running a corporation boring. Maybe she'll want to be… I don't know…an accountant. An actress. A firefighter!"

He was offering everything he had, everything he'd spent his life pursuing—everything that proved to the world, proved to himself, that his parents had been wrong, and Leonidas Niarxos had value, had a right to be alive.

But Daisy, who had such warmth and concern for strangers, didn't think his empire was worth anything? He thought their daughter might not want it?

He stared at her. "Are you serious?"

"I just want her to find her true passion. Like you found yours."

"My passion?"

"Isn't it obvious?" She gave him a cheeky smile. "Business is your passion."

Her smile did crazy things to his insides. "Business is my passion?"

"The way you've done it—yes. What else would you call it? There's no guidebook for creating a world empire. No business degree could tell a person how to do it."

"What's your passion, then?" he countered.

Her face fell, and she looked down at her plate. "Art, I guess. Even though I'm not very good at it."

She looked sad. He thought again about how she'd treasured that old painting.

Leonidas wanted to reassure her, but he didn't know how. At work, his leadership style was based on giving criticism, not reassurance.

As they left the restaurant, he thought about her words. *Business is your passion.* If that were true, why was it that for the last six months, he'd just been going through the motions at Liontari? He hardly cared about it at all anymore. He had yet to drag himself into the New York office, and the last few months in Paris, he'd barely bothered to criticize his employees.

As they walked out to where their driver waited with the Range Rover, Daisy suddenly nestled against him, wrapping her arm around his.

"Thank you," she whispered, and he felt her lips brush against the flesh of his ear. "For the crepes. The coat. The perfume." Pulling back, she looked at him, her eyes sparkling in the spring sun. "Thank you for a wonderful day."

He looked down at her, his heart pounding at the intimacy of her simple touch.

And suddenly, Leonidas couldn't imagine any passion, any longing, any desire greater than the one he had for her.

CHAPTER SIX

DAISY STARED AT herself in the mirror of her pretty cream-and-pink guest suite in Leonidas's New York mansion.

A stranger looked back at her, a glamorous woman in a red gown straight out of *Pretty Woman*. The dress caressed her baby bump, showcasing her full breasts, with a slit up the side of the skirt that showed off her legs. Long honey-brown hair hung thickly over her bare shoulders. Her eyelashes were darkened with mascara, her lips as red as the dress, all bought from the drugstore a few months ago. But she was wearing the scent Leonidas had bought her on their shopping excursion three days earlier. Even the shoes on her feet were new. That morning, just as she'd realized she could not possibly wear her scuffed-up black pumps with this dress, new shoes had mysteriously appeared at her door—strappy sandals covered with crystals in her exact size.

"Who are you?" Daisy said to the woman in the mirror. Her voice echoed against the bedroom's high ceilings and white bed.

From the dog bed by the elegant fireplace, Sunny lifted her head in confusion. With a sigh, Daisy said to her, "It's all right, Sunny. I'm all right."

But was she?

She glanced back at her cell phone sitting on the vanity table, feeling dizzy. She didn't just look different now. She *was* different.

When she'd come out of the shower an hour before,

she'd anxiously checked her online bank account to see if her most recent payment, a deposit for nursing school, had cleared yet. Once that money disappeared from her account, she expected to have very little left, so she was nervous about checks bouncing if she'd forgotten anything.

But looking at her bank account, she'd lost her breath. She'd closed her eyes and counted to five. Then she'd looked at her account again.

Her bank account had the scant hundreds she'd expected—*plus an extra million dollars.*

Leonidas had just made her a rich woman.

Why? How could he? She'd never asked for his money! Daisy shivered in the red dress. But she knew it wasn't for her, not exactly. It was to protect their baby, so she'd never worry or be afraid.

I will always provide for you. It's my job as a man. You would not try to deny me that.

Especially since she'd denied him other things. Like kisses. When, her first night here, he'd almost kissed her outside her bedroom door, she'd been far too tempted. It had scared her. She'd known, if she ever let him kiss her, that she would surrender everything.

And her life had already become unrecognizable enough. She looked at herself in the ball gown. Could she really keep his money—even for her baby?

It was true she'd already quit her job. When she'd gone to the diner, her boss had been all too happy for Daisy to leave her job, no advance notice required.

"We don't actually need an employee sitting at the register," Claudia had confided. "But I knew it hurt your feet to wait tables, and I couldn't fire you." She'd glanced at the Range Rover through the window. "But look at you now! It's a fairy tale! You said this Greek billionaire even wants to marry you?"

Daisy had winced. "I haven't agreed."

"Are you crazy?" Claudia gazed reverently at the handsome dark-haired tycoon, typing on his phone in the back seat. Then she frowned. "Have you told Franck?"

"I don't know why Franck would care." Daisy had smiled weakly. "I'm sure he'll just be glad to get me out of his apartment,"

"You know he's in love with you."

Daisy rolled her eyes. "He was my father's best friend. He's not in love with me."

Claudia lifted an eyebrow. "Isn't he?"

She'd thought of his strange awkwardness when the middle-aged artist had proposed to her. *Stay as long as you want. Stay forever.*

And now, as Daisy looked in the mirror at the glamorous stranger in the red dress and red lipstick, she felt guilty that she hadn't told Franck she'd moved out and was now living with her baby's father. She didn't look forward to confessing Leonidas's name. Daisy hadn't even shared *that* with Claudia. Her bohemian friends had been her father's friends, too; they hated billionaires in general, but Leonidas Niarxos in particular, after he'd put her father in prison.

They would be horrified if they found out Daisy was having his baby. And if she ever became Leonidas's wife...

She took a deep breath. She didn't want to imagine it. Bad enough that tonight she'd be facing all of Leonidas's friends at a charity ball. They'd probably feel the same scorn for Daisy. They'd ask themselves what on earth the billionaire playboy saw in her. They'd think Leonidas was slumming with a waitress. Worse. Sleeping with the daughter of the convicted felon he'd put in prison.

Swallowing hard, Daisy looked at herself one last time in the mirror. Steadying herself on her high-heeled sandals, she lifted her chin, straightened her spine, and went downstairs.

Leonidas stood waiting at the bottom of the wide stone

staircase. Her heart twisted when she saw him, darkly powerful and wide shouldered in a sleek black tuxedo. Their eyes locked.

"You look beautiful," he said in a low voice as she reached the bottom of the stairs. He visibly swallowed. "And *that dress.*"

She gave him a shy smile. "You like it?"

Leaning forward, he whispered huskily, "You make me want to stay home tonight."

She shivered as he touched her, wrapping her faux fur stole around her bare shoulders. Taking his arm, she went out with him into the cold spring night, where Jenkins waited with the Rolls-Royce at the curb.

"Sorry," Leonidas said with a grin. "For tonight, a limo is required."

When they arrived at a grand hotel in Midtown Manhattan, Daisy was alarmed to see a red carpet set up at the entrance, where paparazzi waited, snapping pictures of the arriving glitterati. She turned accusingly on Leonidas. "You didn't say the charity ball was this big of a deal!"

"Didn't I?" His cruel, sensual lips curved upward. "Well. It's all for homeless kids."

Daisy looked with dismay at all the wealthy people walking the red carpet with photographers snapping. "I'll stick out like a sore thumb!"

"Yes." Leonidas looked at her in the back of limo, his black eyes gleaming as his gaze lingered on her red lips and red dress. "You're the most beautiful of them all."

As their driver opened the door, Leonidas stepped out, then reached back to her. "Shall we?"

Nervously, she took his hand. As they walked the red carpet, she clung to his muscled arm, trying to focus just on him, ignoring the shouts and pictures flashing.

"Leonidas Niarxos—is that your girlfriend?"

"Is she pregnant with your baby?"

He didn't answer, just kept looking down at Daisy with a soothing smile. For a moment she relaxed, lost in his dark eyes. Then she heard one of the paparazzi gasp.

"Oh, my God! That's the Cassidy kid! The daughter of the art forger who tried to swindle him!"

At that, there was a rush of questions. She quickened her step and didn't take a full breath until they were safely inside the hotel ballroom.

"How—how did they know who I was?" she choked out.

"They were bound to figure it out." Leonidas's dark eyes looked down at her calmly. "It's better this way."

"How can you say that?"

"There was always going to be some kind of scandal about us. Better for it to happen now, rather than later, after our daughter is born." He put his hand gently on her belly. "That way, it will only affect us. Not her."

It was the first time Leonidas had touched her belly. Even over the red fabric, she felt his gentle, powerful touch, felt his strength and how he wanted to protect them both.

It was strangely erotic.

"Are you ready?" he asked.

Holding her breath, she nodded. His dark eyes crinkled as he took her hand and led her through the double doors.

The hotel's grand ballroom was enormous, far larger than the one in his house, which now seemed quite modest by comparison. A full orchestra played big band hits from the nineteen forties as beautiful women in ball gowns danced with handsome men in tuxedos. On the edges of the dance floor, large round tables filled the space, each with an elaborate arrangement of white and red roses. Crystal chandeliers sparkled overhead.

Leonidas took two flutes of sparkling water from a waiter's silver tray. He handed her one of them, then nodded toward the far wall, his dark eyes gleaming. "Over there

are the items that will be up for bidding in the auction tonight. Would you like to go see them?"

"Sure." Anything to give her something to do. To make
her feel less out of place. People were staring at her, and
she had no idea whether that was because her dress looked
strange, or because they'd heard she was the art forger's
daughter, or just because she wasn't beautiful enough to be
on Leonidas's arm. She knew she wasn't, fancy ball gown
or no. He was a handsome Greek billionaire. Who was she?

An ex-waitress. The daughter of a felon. A failed artist.
Pregnant and unwed.

Nervously sipping the sparkling water, Daisy followed
Leonidas to the long table lining the far wall of the hotel
ballroom. Walking past all the items put forward in the
upcoming charity auction, she stared at them each incredulously.

There was a guitar that had apparently once belonged to
Johnny Cash. A signed first edition of a James Bond novel.
Two-carat vintage diamond earrings. A small sculpture by
a famous artist. And if the items weren't enough to whet
the appetite, there were experiences offered on small il-
lustrated posters: a week at someone's fully staffed vacation house in the Maldives. An invitation to attend Park
City Film Festival screenings as the guest of a well-known
actor. A dinner prepared at your home, for you and twelve
of your best friends by a world-famous chef, who would
fly in from his three-Michelin-star Copenhagen restaurant
expressly for the occasion.

Walking past all the items, each more insane and over-
the-top than the last, Daisy shook her head. Rich people
really did live a life she could not imagine.

But on the other hand, it was all for charity, and if it really helped homeless kids…

She nearly bumped into Leonidas, who'd stopped at the
end of the final table, in front of the very last item.

"Hey." She frowned up at him. "You nearly made me spill my—"

He glanced significantly toward that last item, his dark eyebrows raised. She followed his glance.

Then her hand clutched her drink. She felt like she was going to faint.

"That's—that's my—"

"Yes," he said. "It's your painting."

It was. Her final project from art school, in all its pathetic mess. Sitting next to all those amazing items that rich people might actually want.

Daisy looked around wildly. The noise and music and colors of the ballroom seemed to spin around her. She felt like she was in one of those awful dreams where you were in the hallway of your school and everyone was standing around you, laughing and pointing, and you suddenly realized you'd forgotten your homework—and your clothes.

She looked up at Leonidas with stricken eyes. "What have you *done*?"

He looked back at her. "Given you another chance."

"A chance at what!" she gasped. "Humiliation and pain?"

"A chance to believe in your dream," he said quietly. "I believe in you."

Shaking, Daisy wiped her eyes. She wanted to grab the painting and run, before any of these glamorous people could sneer at it.

But too late. She stiffened as two well-dressed guests came up behind them.

"What is this?" said the woman, who was very thin and draped in diamonds. "It's not signed."

Her escort peered doubtfully at the painting's description. "It says here that the artist wishes to be anonymous."

"How very strange." The woman turned to call to another friend, "Nan. Come tell me if you can guess who this artist is."

Daisy's cheeks felt like they were on fire, and her heart was beating fast, as if she'd just run two miles without stopping. Leonidas took her arm, and gently led her away from the auction table.

"It's to earn money for the charity. For the kids."

"It won't earn anything. No one will bid on it," she whispered. Why did he want to hurt her like this? She knew Leonidas didn't love her. But did he outright hate her? What other reason could he have to humiliate her, in front of all his ritzy friends?

She felt like she'd been ambushed, just when she'd started to trust him. Leonidas believed in her? How could he, when she didn't believe in herself?

Later, after they sat down at their table for an elegant dinner of salmon in sauce, roasted fingerling potatoes and fresh spring vegetables, Daisy could hardly eat. She barely said a word to the guests sitting around them, in spite of their obvious curiosity about her. She let Leonidas speak for them. Yes, she was his date. Her name was Daisy. They were good friends. He was proud to say they were expecting a child together in June.

And all the while, Daisy was wondering how he could have done this to her.

During the days she'd stayed at his house, he'd gone out of his way to be kind to her. Leonidas Niarxos, the supposedly ruthless tycoon, had spent almost no time at work, other than the day he'd taken her shopping at Liontari's luxury boutiques. Instead, he'd kept her company doing the activities she enjoyed, like walking the dog, watching movies on TV and playing board games. Leonidas had listened patiently for hours as she'd read aloud from her pregnancy book, especially the section titled "How To Be an Expectant Father." She'd started to think he cared. She'd started to think he actually…liked her.

So why was he trying to hurt her like this?

"Cheer up," Leonidas whispered, as dinner ended and they rose to go out on the dance floor. "The auction will be fun."

"Easy for you to say." Daisy tried not to feel anything as he pulled her into his arms. He was so powerful, so impossibly desirable in his sleek tuxedo. As he swayed her to the music, an old romantic ballad from the forties, he was the most handsome man in the world. Damn him.

He smiled down at her, his dark eyes twinkling. "Everything will be fine. I promise."

"Yes, it will," she retorted. "Because I'm leaving before the auction starts."

His smile dropped. "No. Please stay." Licking his lips, he added, "For the kids."

"For the kids," she grumbled. But it was strange. He didn't *seem* like a man bent on her destruction. Was it possible Leonidas wasn't actively trying to wreck her, but honestly believed someone might bid for her awful painting—against all those other amazing auction items?

If he did, he was deluding himself. Just like Daisy had, for years. In spite of getting mediocre marks in art school, she'd always hoped that somehow she might succeed and make a living from art, as her father had. That she'd find her voice, as Leonidas once said.

But she never had. Instead, she'd spent years suffering that terrible hope, getting gallery shows in Brooklyn, Queens and Staten Island through her father's connections, only to sell nothing. Friends *had* offered to come to the shows and buy her paintings, but of course Daisy couldn't allow that. Her friends didn't have money to waste, and anyway, she would have been glad to paint them something for free.

But none of her friends had asked for a free painting. Which could mean only one thing: even her friends didn't like her art, not really.

Even Daisy herself wasn't sure about it. But she'd still tried to force herself to be upbeat, desperately trying to promote her art to bored strangers.

A year of that. Of awful hope, and finally crushing despair. There had been only one good thing to come from her father's trial—a horrible silver lining that she'd never admitted, even to herself. He had needed her, and that had given her an excuse to surrender the horror of her dream.

But now, Daisy was being forced to relive it all. She would never forgive Leonidas for this.

"Are—you—ready?" The auctioneer chanted from the stage. There was an excited hubbub from guests at the cleared tables. Women in ball gowns and men in tuxedos sat on the edge of their seats, ready to bid vast fortunes for amusements and whims. *For the kids*, Daisy repeated to herself.

Leonidas put his arm around her. "Try to enjoy this," he whispered. Daisy stared at the oversize arrangement of white and red roses on the table and tried to breathe. Soon this would all be over.

"Let's get started," the auctioneer boomed into the microphone. "For our first item…"

Everything sold quickly—the guitar, the autographed book, the week in the Maldives. The audience was full of smiles and glee, happily getting into bidding wars with their friends, as if they were bidding with counterfeit money, and no amount was too high.

And finally…

"For our last item, we have an unsigned painting, by Anonymous. Do I have a bid?" Even the auctioneer sounded doubtful. "Uh, let's start the bidding at…two hundred dollars."

It was the lowest starting bid of the night, by far. And Daisy knew that no one would even want to give that much. She braced herself for a long, awkward silence, after which

Leonidas would be forced to make a pity bid, to try to save face. He would see he had no reason to believe in her. Even *he* would be forced to admit that Daisy was a talentless hack. She was near tears.

"Two hundred dollars," someone called from the back.

Who was it? Daisy blinked, craning her neck.

"Three hundred," called a woman from a nearby table. She was a stranger. Daisy didn't know anyone here, except Leonidas.

"Five hundred," someone else said.

"A thousand," cried an elderly man from the front.

The bidding accelerated, became hotly contested— even more than the guitar once owned by Johnny Cash. Daisy sat in shock as the number climbed.

Five thousand. *Ten.* Twenty. Fifty thousand. *A hundred thousand dollars.*

Daisy was hyperventilating. Through it all, Leonidas kept silent.

Until...

"One million dollars." His deep, booming voice spoke from beside her. Sucking in her breath, she looked up at him. He smiled back, his dark eyes warm.

"Sold! To the gentleman at table thirteen!"

As people at their table clustered around him, shaking his hand and congratulating him on the winning bid, Daisy trembled with emotion. She couldn't believe what had just happened.

I believe in you.

But it hadn't just been Leonidas who'd bid for her painting. He hadn't said a word, not until the end. Other people had bid for it. A bunch of strangers who had no idea Daisy was the artist. She hadn't had to beg them to buy it. They'd all just wanted it.

Was it possible she'd been wrong, and she did have some talent after all...?

Leonidas turned away from his friends. He looked down at her, his dark gaze glittering. "They'll deliver the painting later. Do you want to leave?"

Wordlessly, Daisy nodded.

Outside, the Manhattan street was dark and quiet, except for the patter of cold rain. As they hurried toward the limo waiting in a side lane near the hotel, the rain felt like ice against her skin. Leaning over her, Leonidas tried to protect Daisy from the weather with his arms, with only a small amount of success. They were both laughing as they slid damply into the back seat of the Rolls-Royce.

"Take us home," Leonidas told Jenkins, who nodded and turned the wheel.

"Home," Daisy echoed, and in that moment, the brownstone mansion almost did feel like home. For a moment, they smiled at each other.

Then the air between them electrified.

She abruptly turned away, toward the window, where the lights of the city reflected in the puddles of rain. She felt Leonidas's gaze on her, but she couldn't look at him. Emotions were pounding through her like waves.

Once they arrived at his mansion, she followed him up the steps to the entrance. He punched in the security code, and they entered, to find it dark and quiet.

"Everyone must have gone to bed." He gave a low laugh. "Even your dog must be asleep, since she's not rushing to greet us." He flicked on the foyer's light, causing the crystal chandelier to illuminate in a thousand fires overhead, reflecting on the stately stone staircase behind them.

Taking her fur stole, Leonidas hung it in the closet. He looked down at Daisy, who was still silent. His handsome face became troubled.

"Daisy, did I do wrong?" He set his jaw. "If I did, I'm sorry. I thought if—"

"You believed in me, when I didn't believe in myself," she whispered.

His dark eyes met hers. "Of course I believe," he said simply. "I always have. From that first day at the diner, I saw you were more than beautiful. You're the best and kindest woman I've ever met—"

Reaching up, Daisy put her hands on his broad shoulders, feeling the fabric of his tuxedo jacket, damp with rain. And lifting her lips to his, she kissed him passionately.

A moment before, entering the house, Leonidas had looked at Daisy's lovely, distant face as she'd stood half in shadow. For the first time, he'd questioned whether he'd done the right thing, offering her painting at the charity fundraiser without her knowledge or permission.

But the idea of Daisy giving up her dreams was unbearable to Leonidas. Whether her painting was actually worth a million dollars, or a hundred, he didn't care. He was accustomed to his own despair, but a world where a warm, loving woman like Daisy had no hope was a world he did not want to live in.

So he'd taken the painting from the guest room, and offered it to the charity's auction committee. He'd known if the painting was the last item up for auction, that at least a few people in the audience, after imbibing champagne all night, would assume the painting was an unknown masterpiece, and that others, seeing the bidding war heat up, would not want to be left out, and would swiftly follow suit.

Leonidas would never forget the look on Daisy's beautiful face when her student painting had sold for a million dollars. Not until the day he died.

As they'd left the grand hotel, he'd gloried in the successful outcome of his plan. But she'd been silent all the way home, refusing to meet his eyes. He'd started to have doubts. Perhaps he should have asked her permission. Perhaps—

And so he'd turned to her, as they stood alone at the base of the stone staircase. But even as he'd tried to ask, he'd been unable to look away from her.

Daisy was more beautiful than any art ever created.

Her long brown hair fell over her bare shoulders. Her full breasts thrust up against the low sweetheart neckline of her red column dress, the fabric falling gently over the swell of her pregnant belly. Her dark lashes fluttered against her cheek as her teeth worried against her lower lip, so plump and red.

In the shadows of the foyer, the sparkling light refracted in the hundred-year-old crystal chandelier, gleaming against her lips, her cheekbones, her luminous eyes.

And then she'd kissed him.

As her soft lips touched his, he felt a shock of electricity that coursed down his body, from his hair to his fingertips to his toes. His muscles went rigid. He burned, then melted.

He'd been forcing himself to abide by his promise not to touch her. But every day, every hour, he'd felt the agony of that. All he'd wanted to do was kiss her, seduce her, possess her.

But now she was kissing *him.*

With a rush, he cupped his hands along her jawline, moving back to tangle in her hair, drawing her close. He kissed her hungrily, twining his tongue with hers. He felt out of control, as if his hunger might devour them both. He wrenched away, looking down at her. His heart was pounding.

"Come to bed with me," he whispered, running his hand down her throat, along the bare edge of her collarbone. He felt her tremble. Lowering his head, he softly kissed her throat, running his hand through her hair. "Come to bed…"

Her green eyes were reckless and wild. Wordlessly, she nodded. But as he took her hand to lead her to the stairs, she swayed and seemed to stagger, as if her knees had gone weak.

With one swoop, Leonidas lifted her up into his arms. She weighed nothing at all, he thought in wonder. As he carried her up the carved stone staircase, he looked down at her, marveling that she had such power over him.

She'd bewitched him, utterly and completely. As he carried her up the stairs, all the darkness of his world receded. When he looked into her eyes, his heart felt warm and alive, instead of frozen in ice. Beneath the soft glow of her eyes, he could almost believe he wasn't the monster his parents had believed him to be. Maybe he was someone worthy. Someone good.

Leonidas carried her down the hall, into his shadowy bedroom, lit by dappled lights from the window. Outside, the city had fallen into deepening night. Across the street, he could see the illuminated tips of skyscrapers peeking over the rooftops, and beyond that, the twinkling stars, cold and distant.

He lowered her reverently to the king-sized bed. Her honey-brown hair swirled like a cirrus cloud across the pillows. She looked up at him with heavy-lidded eyes, and he caught his breath.

Leonidas dropped his tuxedo jacket and tie to the floor. Kicking off his shoes, he fell next to her on the bed. He slowly removed each of her high-heeled sandals, first one, then the other. Leaning forward, he cupped her face and kissed her tenderly. Her lips parted as he felt her sigh, and it took every ounce of his willpower to hold himself back, when all he wanted to do was possess her. *Now.*

But he held himself back. She was pregnant with his baby. He would not overwhelm her. He would be gentle. He'd take his time. Lure her. *Seduce her.*

And make her his own—forever.

Reaching out, he gently cupped her cheek. His hand stroked whisper soft down her neck, to her bare shoulder.

With an intake of breath, she met his gaze. Her eyes were full of tears as she tried to smile.

"Leo," she whispered.

His heart lifted to his throat.

Leo. She'd called him Leo. The name she'd used long ago, before she knew his true identity, back when she'd loved him…

Leonidas shuddered with emotion. Wrapping his arms around her, he pulled her tight. As he kissed her, memories from last fall, when he'd known such joy in her arms, filled him body and soul. The night he'd first kissed her in Brooklyn, the night he'd taken her virginity, all the nights after.

But this kiss was even better.

Because now, Daisy knew who he was. She'd kissed him first. She knew the worst of him, but still wanted him.

Except she *didn't* know the worst. He sucked in his breath. And she must never know…

No. He must not think of it. Not now. Not ever.

He deepened the kiss, until it became rough, almost savage in his need to obliterate all else. Daisy's embrace was passionate and pure, like the woman herself. Being in her arms was the only thing that made him forget…

All thought, all reason, fled his mind as her lips seared his. Part of him almost expected she'd stop him, pull back, tell him she was too good for him—and how could he deny the truth of that?

But she did not pull away. Instead, her lips strained against his, matching his fire. The whole world seemed to whirl around him as he held her, facing each other on the bed. He kissed slowly down her throat.

"Sweet," he groaned against her skin. "So sweet."

Her hands reached for the buttons of his white shirt. When they wouldn't easily open, she reached beneath the fabric in her impatience, and stroked his bare chest. Sitting up, he ripped the shirt off his body, causing the final buttons to scatter noisily across the marble floor, along with his platinum cufflinks.

Turning back to her, he unzipped the back of her red gown and gently pulled it down her body, revealing her white strapless bra, barely containing her overflowing breasts, and then her full, pregnant belly, her white lace panties clinging to her hips.

He tossed the ball gown to the floor. He almost could not bear to look at her, she was so beautiful, looking up at him in the tiny white lingerie that revealed her explosive curves, her brown hair glossy and coiled over the pillows, her green eyes dark with desire.

"Kiss me," she whispered.

A low groan escaped him, and he obeyed. He turned her to face him, kissing her for moments, or maybe for hours. Time seemed to stretch and compress as he was lost in her embrace. He kissed down her throat to the edge of the white satin bra. Reaching around her back, he loosened the clasp, and the fabric fell away. He looked at her breasts, so deliciously full, and holding his breath, he reached out to cup them with his hands.

Her lips parted and her eyes closed, her expression lost in pleasure. He stroked her full nipples, causing them to pebble beneath his touch. Lowering his head, he pulled one into his mouth, swirling it with his tongue, suckling her.

Her hands gripped the white duvet, as if she felt herself flying into the sky. He tenderly kissed around the curve of her full, pregnant belly. Moving back up, he kissed her lips long and lingeringly, before he finally drew back.

Cupping her cheek, he looked down at her with sudden

urgency in the darkness of the bedroom, with the twinkling lights of Manhattan slanted across the marble floor like trails of diamonds.

"Marry me," he whispered. "Marry me, Daisy."

CHAPTER SEVEN

MARRY HIM?

Daisy's eyes flew open. She was naked, melting beneath his touch. She wanted him; oh, how she wanted him.

But marry him?

"I…" She shivered as Leonidas slowly stroked his warm hand down her cheek to her throat and the crevice between her breasts. Every part of her ached for his touch. Not just her body. Her heart.

Looking at him in the shadowy bedroom, she'd suddenly seen the man she'd loved last fall. Leo. Her Leo. Her lover, with whom she'd spent so many days laughing, talking, kissing in the sunlight, holding hands beneath the autumn leaves. He hadn't taken her virginity. She'd given it to him. Her Leo.

But could she surrender everything? Could she ever forgive herself if she did? What kind of woman would she be?

"I can't marry you," she whispered.

"You know me." His hands stroked softly down her body. Closing his eyes, he rested his head in the valley between her breasts. Surprised, she looked down and placed her hands gently against his dark hair. "I want to be with you. Always."

That couldn't be tears in his eyes. No, impossible. Leonidas Niarxos was ruthless. He had no heart. He himself had said so.

And yet, somehow Leonidas had become her Leo again. His eyes were like pools of darkness glittering with stars, as deep and unfathomable as the night. His body was Leo's. His tanned, muscular chest was powerful, his skin like satin over steel. Daisy's fingers wonderingly stroked his rough dark hair, his small, hard nipples, then down over the flat muscles of his belly.

Leo, but not Leo. Not exactly. She knew too much now. *Leo* had been her equal. This man was more powerful than Daisy in every possible way. He was a famous, self-made billionaire who'd crushed the world beneath his Italian leather shoe, building a global fortune. He was the most eligible playboy in the world, handsome and rich, the man every woman wanted.

And yet—

And yet, in this moment, she saw a strange vulnerability in his black eyes. He watched her as if he expected, at any moment, she might break the spell, and break his heart.

It was an illusion, she told herself.

But as he lowered his mouth passionately to hers, she was lost in his embrace as he wrapped his powerful arms around her. His lips plundered hers, his tongue teasing and tempting. His hands stroked down her body, cupping her full breasts, moving down her full belly to the curve of her hip.

Then his kiss gentled. He held her against his muscular chest as if she were a precious treasure. His hand cupped her cheek tenderly.

"Marry me," he whispered. "And I'll hold nothing back. I will give you everything."

Everything? What did he mean? "You already gave me too much. That money in my bank account—"

"I'm not talking about money."

Then what? Her heart lifted to her throat. He couldn't mean—he might be able to truly love her?

Lowering his head, he kissed her. His sensual fingertips caressed her bare skin, from her shoulder, to the sensitive crook of her neck. He softly stroked the tender flesh of her earlobe, his fingers tangling in her long hair, as need sizzled through her.

He cupped her breast, rubbing his thumb against her nipple. Leaning forward, he drew her tight, aching nipple into the wet heat of his mouth. She gasped as she felt the hot swirl of his tongue suckling her, the roughness of his chin against her skin.

Pushing her legs apart, he knelt between her thighs on the bed. His broad-shouldered body was silhouetted by the city's dappled light outside. His black eyes gleamed as he slowly pulled her white lace panties down from her hips, like a whisper over her thighs, past her knees and calves, tossing them to the floor.

Shivering with desire, she closed her eyes, her head straining back against the pillows. He spread her thighs wide with his powerful hands, moving his head between her legs. He paused, and she felt the heat of his breath against her skin.

Then, finally, he lowered his head to taste her. His hot, sensual tongue swirled against her, lightly, delicately, then lapping with more force, pushing inside her as she gasped with pleasure. The delicious tension coiled inside her, building higher and higher, until, suddenly, she cried out with joy, rocked by ecstasy.

She was still gasping beneath waves of pleasure when he lifted himself up, holding himself over her belly with his powerful arms. Positioning himself between her legs, he pushed inside her with one deep thrust.

A hoarse groan escaped him as filled her, stretching her to the hilt. For a split second, it was too much.

Then, as he held himself still, allowing her body to adjust, incredibly, new pleasure began to build inside her. He thrust inside her again, slowly. But the muscles of his arms seemed to bulge and shake, and a bead of sweat formed on his forehead, from the effort of holding himself back.

Suddenly, he pulled back. Falling onto the bed beside her, he gently rolled her on top of him.

"Take me," he said huskily, his dark eyes like fire. "I'm yours, if you want me."

If she wanted him?

She wanted him—yes. But he'd never asked her to take control before. Feeling uncertain, she hesitated, her body suspended over his. He was so huge. Then, slowly, she positioned herself, lowering her body, pulling him inside her, inch by delicious inch. The pleasure was almost too much to bear.

Then she looked down at his face.

His expression was worshipful, almost holy, as if he held his breath, as if he were barely holding on to the shreds of self-control. Her confidence grew.

Slowly, she began to ride him. As she picked up rhythm, he gasped aloud, a single choked groan. He suddenly gripped her thighs with his large hands.

"Daisy—slow down—I can't—I can't—"

But she was merciless, driving forward. Pulling him inside her deeply, she increased her speed, going faster and faster. Her full breasts swayed as she rocked back and forward, sliding hot and wet against him, until, gripping her fingernails into his shoulders, she hit another sharp peak, even higher and more devastating than the one before, and she screamed.

He exploded, pouring himself into her with a guttural roar.

She collapsed forward against him, sweaty and spent. He cradled her gently into his arms, kissing her temple.

"Daisy—*agape mou*—"

It had been his old nickname for her, and at that, her heart finally could take no more.

How could she have ever thought she couldn't love him again? How could she have imagined she could ever protect her heart?

Daisy's eyes flew open in the darkness.

She was in love with him. She always had been, even in the depths of her hatred and hurt. She'd never stopped loving him.

Turning to face him on the bed, she looked at his handsome face beneath a beam of silvery moonlight pouring like rain through the window. She whispered, "Yes."

Leonidas grew very still. "Yes?"

Tears filled her eyes, tears Daisy didn't understand. Were they tears of grief—or joy?

Twining her fingers in his dark hair, she tried to believe it was joy.

"I'll marry you, Leo," she said.

They were wed four days later.

The ceremony was small and quiet, held in the ballroom of Leonidas's house—"Your house now," he'd told her with a shy smile. A home wedding was perfect. The last thing Daisy wanted was more attention.

After all the pictures paparazzi took of them together at the charity ball, the story that Leonidas Niarxos had impregnated the daughter of the man he'd put into prison had exploded across New York media. For a few days, photographers stalked their quiet West Village lane. Daisy felt almost like a prisoner, afraid to go outside.

Even after they'd decided to have the wedding ceremony at home, Daisy had nervously wondered how her friends would be able to get through the media barricades.

Then a miracle happened.

The day before their wedding, a scandal broke about a movie star having a secret family in New York, a longtime mistress and two children, while he also had a famous actress wife and four children at his mansion in Beverly Hills. The national scandal trumped a local one, and all the paparazzi and news crews and social media promoters left Leonidas and Daisy's street to stalk the movie star and his two beleaguered wives instead.

Daisy spent her last day before the ceremony finalizing the details with the wedding planner, who'd been provided by Liontari's PR department, and then going to a lawyer's office to sign a prenuptial agreement which, in her opinion, was far too generous. "I'm not looking to get more money," she'd protested to her fiancé. "You've already given me a million dollars."

"That money means nothing to me. I always want you and the baby to feel safe," Leonidas said.

"But the prenuptial agreement would give me millions more. It just doesn't seem fair."

"To who?"

"To you."

Smiling, he'd taken her in his arms. "I'm fine with it. Because I never intend for us to get divorced." Lowering his head to hers, he'd whispered, "You've made me so happy, Daisy…"

They spent the last night before their wedding in bed. Daisy never wanted him to let her go.

And now he never would.

On the morning of their wedding, as she got ready, Daisy was overjoyed to see the spring sun shining warmly, with almost no paparazzi left on the street to bother them.

She invited only about twenty friends to the ceremony. She'd been too cowardly to call Franck in California and tell him she was getting married. She'd decided to tell him after the honeymoon. She told herself she didn't want to have to refuse him, if he offered to walk her down the aisle in lieu of her father. No one could replace her father.

Daisy already felt disloyal enough, marrying the man who'd killed him.

No, she told herself. Leonidas didn't kill my father. He just accused him of forgery.

If only she could believe her father really had been guilty. Because if her father had knowingly tried to sell a forged painting, how could she blame Leonidas for refusing to be swindled?

But her father had sworn he was innocent. How could Daisy doubt his word, now that he was dead? Even now, she felt guilty, wondering if her father was spinning in his grave at her disloyalty.

She would walk down the aisle alone.

Coming down the stairs, Daisy paused in the quiet foyer before entering the ballroom. Giving a nervous smile to the hulking guards who stood by the mansion's front door, providing security for the event, she clutched her bouquet of lilies against her simple white silk shift dress. A diamond tiara glittered in her upswept hair, along with the huge diamond on her finger.

Everything for today's ceremony, including Leonidas's tuxedo, had been carefully chosen from Liontari's various luxury brands, ready to be pictured, packaged and posted by the official wedding photographer onto social media accounts, and released to newspapers around the world.

"You can't buy this kind of press," the PR woman had said, smacking her lips.

Daisy might have preferred something a little less fancy. But Leonidas had already given her so much. He'd barely gone to work all week. When he'd asked her if she minded if their wedding promoted Liontari brands, she'd wanted to help. She'd had only one prerequisite.

"As long as the dress is comfortable," she'd said. And it was, the white silk loose and light against her skin.

With a deep breath, Daisy opened the ballroom doors.

The bridal march played, and all the guests turned to look at her. As she came down the makeshift aisle between the chairs, her knees shook. She wished she'd taken Mrs. Berry's idea and let Sunny walk her down the aisle. But the dog was still so young, not fully trained, and liable to rush off and chase or sniff. She glanced at the dog, sitting in the front row, tucked carefully at the housekeeper's feet. Daisy gave a nervous smile, and the dog panted back happily, seeming to smile.

The emotions of the other guests were more complicated.

On one side of the aisle she saw her own friends, artists and artisans, in wacky, colorful clothes. On the other side sat Wall Street tycoons, Park Avenue socialites and international jet-setters in sleek couture.

The only thing which both sides seemed to agree on was that Daisy was a greedy sellout, a gold digger cashing in, marrying the man who'd killed her father.

She stopped to catch her breath. No. She was just imagining that. No one would think that. She forced herself forward.

But as Daisy walked past the bewildered eyes of her friends, and the envious, suspicious faces of the glitterati, she felt very alone.

Then her eyes met Leonidas's, where he stood beside the judge at the end of the aisle. And she remembered all the joys of the last week. The sensuality. The laughter. The trust. They were going to be a family.

Gripping her bouquet, she came forward. The judge took a deep breath.

"My friends," the man intoned, "we are gathered here today…"

There was a hubbub at the door. Someone was hoarsely yelling, trying to push in. Daisy whirled to look.

A gray-haired man was trying to push into the ballroom, struggling against the two beefy security guards.

Franck Bain.

Daisy's lips parted. Why was he here? How had he found out?

"You can't marry him!" the middle-aged artist cried, his shrill voice echoing across the ballroom. "Don't do it, Daisy! I can take care of you!"

Leonidas made a gesture to two other guards hovering nearby, and they quickly moved to assist. The four security guards grabbed the thin man, who was struggling and panting for breath.

"Don't marry him!" Franck gasped. "He's a liar who killed your father—an innocent man!"

As he was forcibly pulled from the ballroom, the double doors closed with a bang.

A very uncomfortable silence fell.

"Shall I continue?" the judge said.

The guests looked at each other, then at the bridal couple. The PR team, who were filming the event live for Liontari's social media feeds, seemed beside themselves with delight at the unscripted drama.

Daisy's heart thundered in her chest. She wanted to fling away her bouquet, to make a run for it—run from all the judgment and guilt, her own most of all.

But her gaze fell on her engagement ring, sparkling on her hand, resting on her pregnant belly. Run away? That would truly be the act of a coward. No matter how much anyone criticized her for it, she'd already made her decision. She was bound to Leonidas, not just by their child, but by her word, freely given four days before.

I'll marry you, Leo.

Daisy met Leonidas's burning gaze, and she tried to smile. She nodded at the judge, who swiftly resumed the ceremony.

Ten minutes later, they were signing the marriage certificate. And just like that, they were wed.

Leonidas kissed her as the judge pronounced them husband and wife, but his kiss was oddly polite and formal. As they accepted the congratulations of their guests, Daisy's friends also seemed uncomfortable, their eyes sliding away awkwardly even as they pretended to smile.

At the wedding reception, held on the other side of the elegant ballroom, the very best champagne and liquor was served, all from Liontari's brands. The PR crew gleefully filmed all the glamorous, exotic guests, the wealthy and the beautiful and brightly bohemian, laughing and dancing and eating lobster, pretending to have the time of their lives.

But underneath it, Daisy felt hollow.

Don't marry him. He's a liar who killed your father— an innocent man.

The reception seemed to last forever. Leonidas was strangely distant, even though he was right beside her, and after hours of forced smiling, Daisy's face ached. Finally, the last guest drank the last flute of champagne, left the last gift, and departed. Even Mrs. Berry left, with Sunny in tow, leaving only the bridal couple and the PR team in the ballroom.

"You can go," Leonidas told them. The PR woman looked back brightly.

"I was thinking, Mr. Niarxos, we could come on your honeymoon, if you like, and get shots of you two kissing and frolicking on the beach—"

Beach? What beach? Daisy frowned. They hadn't planned a honeymoon. Did the woman imagine them at Coney Island or the Jersey shore? Only if "frolicking" meant shivering to death in the cool March weather!

"That kind of access would be invaluable," the PR woman chirped. "It would almost certainly go viral—"

"No," Leonidas said firmly. "No more filming."

Daisy went almost weak with gratitude as the PR team departed, leaving them alone at last.

Leonidas turned to Daisy.

"Mrs. Niarxos," he said quietly.

She swallowed. Her heart pounded as her husband pulled her closer. She felt his warmth and strength. She felt so right in her husband's arms. This marriage was right. It had to be right.

He lifted a dark eyebrow. "Did you know Bain was going to come here?"

She shook her head a little shamefacedly. "I'm sorry." She bit her lip, her cheeks hot. "I don't know how he found out about the wedding. I didn't tell him—"

"It's all right. I don't blame the man for wanting you."

"You—you don't?"

"Any man would," Leonidas whispered. Lowering his head, he kissed her tenderly. Then he pulled back with a smile. "Our plane is waiting."

"Plane?"

Leonidas took a deep breath. "I told you, if you agreed to marry me, I would hold nothing back. I'm a man of my word."

Marry me. And I'll hold nothing back. I will give you everything. When he'd said the words to her, she'd hoped he meant his heart. "So that means a honeymoon?"

He mumbled something. Frowning, she peered up at him.

"What?"

He lifted his head. "I'm taking you to Greece. To the island where I was born." He gave her a crooked smile. "Mrs. Berry has already packed your suitcase."

"What about Sunny?"

Leonidas smiled. "Mrs. Berry has promised to give her the same love she gives her own Yorkies at home."

It was strange not to have Sunny with her, as they left ten minutes later for an overnight flight. After all the drama of the last few days leading up to their wedding, once they were settled on the private jet, Daisy felt her exhaustion. She promptly fell asleep in her husband's arms and did not wake again until an hour before they landed on the small Greek island in the Aegean.

As they came down the steps from their private jet to the tarmac, Daisy looked around, blinking in the bright Greek sun. A burst of heat hit her skin.

It was already summer on this island. She was glad she'd taken a shower on the plane and dressed for the weather, in a white sundress and sandals. Her hair was freshly brushed and long, flowing over her bare shoulders. Even Leonidas was dressed casually—at least, casually for him—in a white shirt with the sleeves rolled up, top buttons undone, over black trousers.

To her surprise, no driver came to the small airport to collect them; instead, a vintage convertible was parked near their hangar, left by one of his staff members.

"Get in," Leonidas said with a lazy smile, as he tossed their suitcases in the back. He drove them away from the tiny airport, along the cliffside road.

Daisy's hair flew in the warm breeze of the convertible, as she looked around a seaside Greek village. She'd never seen anything so lovely as the picturesque white buildings, many covered with pink flowers and blue rooftops, with the turquoise sea and white sand beach beneath the cliffs.

Turning off the slender road, Leonidas pulled up to a gate and typed in a code. The gate swung open, and he drove through.

Daisy gasped when she saw a lavish white villa, spread out across the edge of the beach, overlooking the sea.

"This was your childhood home?" she breathed, turning to him. "You were the luckiest kid alive."

His eyes seemed guarded as he gave a tight smile. "It is very beautiful. Yes."

Parking in the separate ten-car garage, which was almost empty of cars, he turned off the engine. After taking their luggage from the trunk, he led Daisy inside the villa.

They were greeted by a tiny white-haired woman who exclaimed over Leonidas in Greek and cried and hugged him. After a few moments of this, he turned to Daisy.

"This is Maria, my old nanny. She's housekeeper here now."

"Hello," Daisy said warmly, holding out her hand. Maria looked confused, looking from Daisy's face to her belly. Then Leonidas spoke a few words in Greek that made the white-haired woman gasp. Ignoring Daisy's outstretched hand, the housekeeper hugged her, speaking rapidly in the same language.

"She's thrilled to meet my wife. She says it's about time I was wed," he said, smiling.

"Maria helped raise you?"

His expression sobered. "I don't know how I would have survived without her."

"Your parents weren't around?"

"That's one way to put it." He turned to Maria and said something in Greek.

The white-haired woman nodded, then called out, bringing two men into the room. They spoke to Leo and then took their suitcases down the hall.

Leonidas turned to Daisy. "You must be hungry."

"Well—yes," she admitted, rubbing her belly. "Always, these days." She bit her lip. "And I didn't eat much at the reception last night…"

"We can have lunch on the terrace. The best part of the house."

He led her through the spacious villa, which was elegant and well maintained, but oddly old-fashioned, almost desolate, like a museum. She asked, "How long has it been since you've visited?"

He glanced around the music room, with its high ceilings

and grand piano, its wide windows and French doors overlooking the sea. He scratched his head. "A few years. Five?"

"You haven't been home for *five years*?"

"I was born here. I never said it was home." He looked away. "I don't have many good memories of the place. I was away at school from when I was nine, remember. I've hardly come back since my parents died."

She knew he was an orphan. "I'm so sorry…how old were you?"

"Fourteen." His voice was flat. No wonder. It was heartbreaking to lose your parents. Daisy knew all about it.

Her voice was gentle as she said, "Why did you choose this place for our honeymoon?"

"Because…" He took a deep breath. "Because it was time. Besides." He gave a smile that didn't meet his eyes. "Doesn't every bride dream of a honeymoon on a Greek island?"

"It's more than I ever dreamed of." She nestled her hand in his. "I'm sorry about your parents. My own mom died when I was just seven. Cancer. And then my…"

She stopped herself, but too late. Their eyes locked. Would the memory of her father always stand between them?

He pulled his hand away. "This way."

Leonidas led her outside through the French doors. Daisy stopped, gasping at the beauty.

The wide terrace clung to the edge of the bright blue sea, with a white balustrade hovering between sea and sky. On the walls of the villa behind them, bougainvillea climbed, gloriously pink, between the white and blue.

"It's beautiful," she whispered, choking up. "I never imagined anything could be so beautiful."

"I can," Leonidas said huskily, looking down at her. He roughly pulled her into his arms.

As he kissed her, Daisy felt the sun on her bare shoulders, the warm wind blowing against her dress and hair, and she breathed in the sweet scent of flowers and the salt of the sea. She felt her husband's strength and power and heat. He wanted her. He adored her.

Could he ever love her?

He'd told her once that he couldn't. But then, hadn't Daisy said the same after learning his true identity—telling him she could never, ever love him again?

And she'd been wrong. Because in this moment, as Leonidas held her passionately in this paradise, she felt her love for him more strongly than ever.

A voice chirped words in Greek behind them, and they both fell guiltily apart. Maria, the housekeeper, was smiling, holding a lunch tray. With an answering smile, Leonidas went to take the tray from her.

"We'll have lunch at the table," he murmured to Daisy.

The two of them spent a pleasurable hour, eating fish and Greek salad and freshly baked flatbreads, along with briny olives and cheeses. It was all so impossibly delicious that when Daisy finally could eat no more, she leaned back in her chair, looking out at the sea, feeling impossibly happy.

She looked at her husband. As he gazed out at the blue water, his darkly handsome face looked relaxed. Younger. He seemed...different.

"Do you have any drawing paper?" Daisy asked suddenly. He turned to her with a laugh.

"Why?"

"I want to draw you."

"Right now?"

"Yes, now."

He went inside the villa, and a moment later, came back with a small pad of paper and a regular pencil. "It's the best I could find. It's not exactly an art studio in there."

"It's perfect," she said absentmindedly, taking it in hand.

She looked at him as he sat back at the small table on the terrace. "Don't move."

He shifted uneasily. "Why are you drawing me?"

How could she explain this strange glow of happiness, this need to understand, to hold on to the moment—and to him? "Because…just because."

With a sigh, he nodded, and sat back at the table. As Daisy drew, she focused completely on line and shadow and light and form. Silence fell. He sat very still, lost in his own thoughts. As Leonidas stared at the villa, his relaxed expression became wooden, even haunted. To draw him back out, she prodded gently, "So you grew up here?"

"Yes." If anything, he looked more closed off. She tried again.

"You must have at least a few good memories of this place."

"I have good memories of Maria. And the hours I spent on this terrace. As a boy, I used to look out at the water and dream about jumping in the sea and swimming far, far away. Not stopping until I reached North America." The light slowly came back into his eyes. "The village is nice. The food. The people. I was free to walk around the island, to disappear for hours."

"Hours?" She lifted her eyebrows, even as she focused on the page. "Your parents didn't worry?"

"They were happy I was gone."

Moving the pencil across the white page, Daisy gave a snort. "I'm sure that's not true…" Finishing the sketch, she held it up to him with quiet pride. "Here."

Reaching out, Leonidas looked at the drawing. Daisy smiled. It was the best thing she'd done in ages, she thought. Maybe ever. He looked younger in the drawing, happy.

He touched the page gently, then whispered, "That's how you see me?"

"Yes." She'd drawn him the way she saw him. With her heart.

Silence fell, a silence so long that it became heavy, like a dark cloud covering the sun. Then Leo roughly pushed the drawing back to her.

"You've got me all wrong," he said in a low voice. "It's time you knew." He lifted his black eyes. "Who I really am."

CHAPTER EIGHT

THIS WAS A MISTAKE. A huge mistake.

Behind him, Leonidas could hear the roar of the sea—or maybe it was his heart. He looked at Daisy, sitting across from him at the table.

His wife's eyes were big and green, fringed with dark lashes, and her full pink lips were parted. Her honey-brown hair fell in waves against her bare shoulders, over the thin straps of her white sundress. Behind her the magnificent white villa reached up into the blue sky, with brilliant pink flowers and green leaves along the white wall.

For the last few days, he'd tried to convince himself he was going to tell her everything, as he'd promised. She was his wife now. She was having his baby. If he couldn't finally let down his guard with her, then who?

Then he remembered how he'd felt when that gray-haired artist—Franck Bain—had burst in on their wedding and tried to take Daisy from him.

Don't marry him. He's a liar who killed your father— an innocent man.

If the security guards hadn't rushed the man out, Leonidas might have throttled Bain himself. Since the wedding yesterday, the man had been politely warned to leave New York. *Politely* might be an exaggeration. But he had left for Los Angeles and with any luck, they'd never see him again.

But Bain had been right about one thing. Leonidas was a liar. Not about Daisy's father, who hadn't been innocent in the forgery scheme.

But about himself.

For Leonidas's whole life, he'd lied about who he was.

He was tired of pretending. He wanted one person on earth to know him, really know him. And who could be more trustworthy than Daisy?

He wanted to tell his wife the truth. But the idea was terrifying. Even as he'd held his new bride, snuggled up against him, on the overnight flight from New York, tension had built inside him.

So he'd promised himself that he'd tell her at the *end* of their honeymoon, after a week of lovemaking, eating fresh seafood and watching the sun set over the Aegean.

Appearance is what matters. How many times had his parents drilled that into him as a child—not just by words, but by example? At twenty-one, he'd thrown himself into the luxury business, determined to do even better than Giannis and Eleni Niarxos had in projecting an aura of perfection. Leonidas had become his brand—global, wealthy, sophisticated, cold.

Except there was this quiet voice inside him, growing steadily harder to repress, that he was more than his brand, so much more. He wasn't the monster his parents had called him; he could be warm and alive. *Like her.*

Daisy licked her delicious pink lips. "What do you mean?" she said haltingly, her voice like music. "I don't know who you are?"

In her arms, pressed against her breasts and belly, she cradled her sketch of him.

It was the sketch which had made him blurt out the words. The man in her drawing looked strong and warm and kind and sure, with humor gleaming from his eyes. Nothing like Leonidas had ever been. Not even as a boy.

But perhaps he could still become that man if—

"Leo?"

"I was never meant to be born," he said. "My very existence is a lie." He gave a grim smile. "You might say I'm a forgery."

"What are you talking about?"

Leonidas took a deep breath. "You think I'm Leonidas Gianakos Niarxos, the son of Giannis Niarxos."

Her lovely face looked bewildered. "Aren't you?"

This was harder than he'd thought. He could not force the words from his lips. His whole body was screaming *Danger!* and telling him to be quiet before it was too late, before he risked everything.

Rising from the chair, he paced the wide terrace. He felt her eyes follow him. He probably looked crazy. Because he was. Keeping this story buried inside him for so long had made him crazy.

Turning, Leonidas gripped the railing of the balustrade, looking out at the sea beneath the hot Greek sun. "My parents married for love." He paused. "That was unusual for wealthy Greek families at the time. And they were young. My father was heir to the Niarxos company, which made luxury leather goods. My mother was the heiress to a shipping fortune. She brought money as her dowry— and a Picasso."

"Love with Birds," Daisy whispered, then cut herself off.

"Yes." He glanced back at her. "From everything I've heard, my parents were crazy about each other." His hands tightened. "But years passed, and they could not have a baby. Society's golden couple was not perfect after all. All of their friends, who'd been secretly jealous of their flaunted passion, taunted them with their smug pity. And when it turned out to be my father's fault that they could not conceive, my mother started complaining about him to her friends. Their love evaporated into rage and blame." He glanced back at her. "I only heard of this years later, you understand."

Daisy's face was pale. "Then you were born…"

"Right." Leonidas gave a crooked smile. "Nine months later, I was born. Their marriage was saved. And that was the end of it."

Setting down her sketchbook carefully on the table, she rose to her feet. Going to him on the edge of the terrace, she said quietly, "What really happened?"

His heart was pounding painfully beneath his ribs. "I'm the only one alive," he whispered, "who knows the full story."

Leonidas looked down at the pounding surf on the white sand beach below.

"From the time I was born, everything I did or said seemed to set my father on edge, making him yell that I was useless and stupid. My mother just avoided me. It was only at fourteen, after my father's funeral, that I learned the reason why."

Standing beside him, Daisy didn't say a word.

"I always had the best clothes, the best education money could buy. *Appearance* was what mattered to them. No one must criticize how they treated their only child." He paused. "If not for Maria, I'm not sure I would have survived."

Reaching out, she put her hand over his on the railing. "Leo…"

Leonidas pulled his hand away. He couldn't bear to be touched. Not now. Not even by her. "I knew something was wrong with me. I could not please them, no matter how I tried. Something about me was so awful that my own father and mother despised me. And though everyone in Greece seemed to think my parents still had this great love affair, at home, they ignored each other—or threw dishes and screamed. Because of me."

"Why would you blame yourself for their marriage problems?"

For a moment, he fell silent. "I heard them sometimes, arguing at night, when I was home during school holidays." He glanced back at the villa. "This is a big house. But sometimes they were loud. One of them always seemed to be threatening divorce. But neither was willing to give up the Picasso. That was the sticking point. Custody of the painting. Not me."

Her stricken eyes met his.

Leonidas paused, then said in a low voice, "When I asked if I could stay at my boarding school year-round, they agreed. Because they could tell other people they'd only done it to make me happy. Appearance was all that mattered to them. My parents stayed together in their glamorous, beautiful lives, pretending to be happy."

"How could they live like that?"

"My father quietly drank himself to death." His lips twisted upward. "When I came home to attend his funeral, I was shocked when my mother hugged me, crying into my arms. I was fourteen, still young enough to be desperate for a mother's love." Leonidas still hated to remember that rainy afternoon, as he'd stared at his father's grave, and his mother, dressed all in black, had embraced him. "I thought maybe she needed me at last. That she…loved me." He gave a bitter smile. "But after the service was over, and her society friends were gone, my mother stopped pretending to be grief stricken. She calmly told me that she was leaving me in the care of trustees until I inherited my father's estate. She was moving to Turkey to be with her lover. She said there was no reason for us to ever see each other again."

"What?" Daisy cried. "She said that? At your father's funeral? How could she?"

He gave a low laugh. "I asked her. *Why, Mamá? Why have you always hated me? What's wrong with me?*" His jaw tightened. "And she finally told me."

Silence fell on the villa's terrace. Leonidas heard the wind through nearby trees, ruffling the pages of his wife's sketchbook on the table.

"My father had been enraged at my mother telling their friends that it was his fault they couldn't conceive, that he wasn't *a real man*. He wanted to shut her up—and go back to being the golden couple of society." He narrowed his eyes. "He had a brother, Dimitris, his identical twin, a few minutes younger. My grandfather had cut off Dimitris without a dime for his scandals, leaving him nothing to buy drugs with. Until my father came to him with an offer—asking him to make love to my mother in the dark and cause her to conceive a child without realizing that the man impregnating her wasn't my father." He paused. "My uncle agreed. And he succeeded."

"What are you saying?"

"My uncle was my real father." Leonidas took a deep breath. "I never knew him. Before I was born, he burned himself out in a blaze of drugs. My father had believed that after I was born, he'd be able to forget he wasn't my real father. After all, biologically I would be, or close enough. But he couldn't forget that his brother had made love to his wife. And he couldn't forgive her for not noticing the difference. Shortly after I was born, when my mother lashed out at him for ignoring their new baby, he exploded, and called her a whore."

Daisy's face was stricken. "Oh, Leo…"

"She forced him to explain. After that, she couldn't forgive what he'd done to her, that she'd made love to her drug-addicted brother-in-law without knowing it. Her own husband had tricked her. Every time she looked at her newborn baby—*me*—she felt dirty and betrayed."

Tears welled in her eyes. "But it wasn't your fault—none of it!"

He took a deep breath, looking up bleakly as plaintive seagulls flew across the stark blue sky. "And yet, it all was."

"No," Daisy whispered.

"Appearance is what matters," he said flatly. "Giannis

wasn't really my father, and my parents despised each other. But to the outside world, they pretended they were in love. They pretended they were happy." He paused. "They pretended to be my parents."

Tears were streaking Daisy's cheeks.

"When my mother said there was no need for us ever to see each other again, right after she'd just been hugging me and crying in my arms, something snapped. And... And..."

"And?"

Leonidas took a deep breath. "I saw her Picasso, sitting nearby, waiting to be wrapped and placed in a crate. Something in my head exploded." He looked away. "I grabbed some scissors from a nearby table. I heard my mother screaming. When I came out of my haze, I'd slashed the entire side of *Love with Birds*, right across its ugly gray heart."

He exhaled. "My mother wrenched the scissors out of my hands, and told me I was a monster, and that I never should have been born." He looked back at Daisy. "Those were her last words to me. A few weeks later, she died in the Turkish earthquake. Her *yali* was smashed into rubble and rock. Her body was found but the painting was lost."

"So that's how you knew the Picasso was a fake," Daisy whispered, then shook her head. "And no wonder you wanted it so badly. No wonder you were so angry when..." She swallowed, looking away.

Looking down, he said thickly, "After I became a man, I thought if I could own the painting, maybe I would understand."

"Understand what?"

"How they could love it so much, and not—"

His throat closed.

"Not you," she whispered.

His knees felt like rubber. He couldn't look at her. Would he see scorn in her eyes? Or worse—pity?

He'd grown up swallowing so much of both. Scorn from

his family. Pity from the servants. He'd spent his whole life making sure he'd never choke down another serving of either one.

But he was about to become a father. His eyes fell to Daisy's belly, and he felt a strange new current of fear.

What did he know about being a parent, with the example he'd had? What about Leonidas—either as a desperate, unloved boy, or an arrogant, coldhearted man—had made him worthy to raise a child?

"Leo," Daisy said in a low voice. With a deep breath, he met her gaze. His wife's eyes were shining with tears. "I can't even imagine what you went through as a kid." She shook her head. "But that's all over. You have a real family now. A baby who will need you. And a wife who…who…" Reaching up, she cupped her hands around his rough jawline and whispered, "A wife who loves you."

Leonidas sucked in his breath, his eyes searching hers. Daisy loved him? After everything he'd just told her?

"You…what?"

"I love you, Leo," she said simply.

His heart looped and twisted, and he couldn't tell if it was the thrill of joy or the nausea of sick terror.

"But—how can you?" he blurted out.

Her lovely face lifted into a warm smile, her green eyes shimmering with tears. "I've always loved you, from the moment we met. Even when I tried not to. Even when I was angry… But I love you. You're wonderful. Wonderful and perfect."

She loved him.

Incredulous happiness filled his heart. On the villa's white terrace, covered with pink flowers and overlooking the blue sea, Leonidas pulled her roughly into his arms, and kissed her passionately beneath the hot Greek sun.

Hours later, or maybe just seconds, he took her hand and

led her inside the villa, to the vast master bedroom, with its wide open windows overlooking the Aegean.

Taking her to the enormous bed, he made love to her, as warm sea breezes blew against gauzy white curtains. He kissed her skin, made her gasp, made her cry out her pleasure, again and again.

Much later, when they were both exhausted from love-making, they had dinner, seafood fresh from the sea, along with slow-baked lamb marinated in garlic and lemon, artichokes in olive oil, goat's milk cheese, salad with cucumber and tomatoes, and freshly baked bread.

Full and glowing, they changed into swimsuits and walked along the white sand beach at twilight, as the water rolled sensuously against their legs. They stopped to kiss each other, then chased the waves, laughing as they splashed together like children in the turquoise-blue sea, the sunset sky aflame.

Leonidas watched her, the way she smiled up at him, her eyes so warm and bright. Daisy glowed like a star, her wet hair slicked back, the white bathing suit clinging to her pregnant body. His heart was beating fast.

I love you, Leo.

The setting sun was still warm on his skin as he came closer in the water. She looked at his intent face, and her smile disappeared. Taking her hand, he led her back to the villa, neither of them speaking.

Once they reached the bedroom's en suite bathroom, he peeled off her swimsuit, then his own. He led her into the shower, wide enough for two, and slowly washed the salt and sand off their bodies.

Drawing her back to the enormous bed, he made love to his wife in the fading twilight, with the dying sun falling to the west, as the soft wind blew off the pounding surf. In that moment, Leonidas thought he might die of happiness.

I love you.

For the first time in his life, he felt like he was home, safe, wanted, desired. He and Daisy were connected in a way he'd never known, in a way he'd never imagined possible. Their souls were intertwined, as well as their bodies. *She loved him.* As he held her in the dark bedroom, he knew he'd never be alone again. He could finally let down his guard—

His eyes flew open.

But what if Daisy ever *stopped* loving him?

He felt a sudden vertigo, a sickening whirl as the earth dropped beneath him. He didn't think he could survive.

But how could he make sure her love for him endured, when he had no idea why, or *how*, she could love him? Even his own mother had said Leonidas should never have been born. Whatever Daisy might say, he knew he wasn't good enough for her.

And as for being good enough for their child…

Stop it, Leonidas told himself desperately, trying to get back to the perfect happiness of just a moment before. Squeezing his eyes shut, he held Daisy close. He kissed his wife's sweaty temple, cradling her body with his own.

It was a perfect honeymoon. When they returned to New York a few days later, Leonidas vowed that Daisy would never regret marrying him. If he could not feel love for his wife in his cold, ashy heart, he would at least show her love every day through his actions.

And for the first three months of their marriage, she did seem very happy, as they planned the nursery, went to the theater and even took cooking and baby prep classes together. Leonidas felt like a fool as he burned every type of food from Thai to Tuscan, no matter how hard he tried.

In order to spend his days—and nights—with her, he ignored work, and did not regret it. Even when Leonidas did go in to the office, instead of focusing on sales throughout his global empire, he found himself asking his employees random questions about their lives, as Daisy did. For the first time, he was curious about their families, their goals and what had brought them to work at Liontari.

His vice presidents and board members obviously thought Leonidas was lost in some postnuptial sensual haze. But they forgave him, because the explosive global reaction to his wedding to the daughter of the man he'd sent to prison had caused brand recognition to increase thirty percent. Leonidas and Daisy had had calls for interviews on morning shows, and even four calls from Hollywood, offering to turn their story into a "based on a true story" movie. Daisy had been horrified.

Leonidas had been happy to refuse. He'd discovered to his shock that he was happy working fewer hours. His heavily pregnant wife wanted him at home. She *needed* him at home. How could profit and loss reports compare with that?

But everything changed the day their baby was born.

On that early day in June, when the flowers were blooming outside the modern hospital in New York and the sky was the deepest blue he'd ever seen, Leonidas finally held his sweet tiny sleeping baby in his arms.

The newborn fluttered open her eyes, dark as his own. Her forehead furrowed.

And then, abruptly, she started to scream, as if in physical pain.

"She's just hungry," the nurse said soothingly.

But Leonidas was clammy with sweat. "Here. Take her. Just take her—"

He pushed the shrieking bundle into his wife's welcoming arms. Holding their daughter in the bed, Daisy murmured soft words and let the rooting baby nurse. Within seconds, the hospital suite was filled with blessed silence. Daisy smiled down at her baby, touching her tiny fingers wonderingly. Then she looked up at Leonidas.

"Don't take it personally," she said uncertainly.

"Don't worry," he ground out. But Leonidas knew it was personal. His own daughter couldn't stand to be touched by him. Somehow, the newborn had just known, as his parents had, that Leonidas was not worthy of love. Though Daisy's kind heart had momentarily blinded her to his flaws, her love for him would not last. And it would not save him.

He was on a ticking clock. Any day now, she would realize what their baby already knew.

And by the end of the summer, his prophecy came true. As weeks passed and Leonidas refused to hold the baby again—for her own sake—he watched with despair as his wife's expression changed from bewilderment to heartbreak, and finally cold accusation.

It was the happiest day of Daisy's life when their baby was born in the first week of June.

At least, it should have been.

Labor was hard, but when it was over, she held her little girl for the first time. She looked up at her husband, wanting to share her joy.

But for some reason, his handsome face was pale, as if he'd just seen a ghost.

Their baby was perfect. Little hands, little feet, a scrunched-up beautiful face. They named her Olivia—Livvy—after Daisy's mother, Olivia Bianchi Cassidy. Daisy was nervous, but thrilled to bring her back to the brownstone that had somehow become home to her, to the sweet pink nursery she and Leonidas had lovingly prepared.

It was hard to believe that was two months ago. Now, as Daisy nestled her baby close, nursing her in the rocking chair, she couldn't get over how soft Livvy's skin was, or how plump her cheeks had become in nine weeks. The baby's dark eyelashes fluttered as she slept. Her hair was darker than Daisy's, reflecting her namesake's Italian roots, as well as Leonidas's Greek heritage.

"Come and look at your daughter," she'd said to him more than once. "Doesn't she look like you?"

And every time, Leonidas would give their newborn daughter only the slightest sideways glance. "Yes."

"Won't you hold her?" she would ask.

And with that same furtive glance at his daughter, her husband would always refuse. Even if Daisy asked for help, saying she needed to have her hands free to do something else, like start the baby's bath, even *then* he would refuse, and would loudly call for Mrs. Berry to assist, as he backed away.

Leonidas disappeared from the house, claiming he was urgently needed at work. He started spending sixteen-hour days at the office and sleeping in the guest room when he came home late.

He claimed he did not want to disturb Daisy and the baby, but the end result was that Daisy had barely seen her husband all summer. He'd simply evaporated from their lives, leaving only the slight scent of his exotic masculine cologne.

For weeks, Daisy had felt heartsick about it. Obviously, their daughter wasn't to blame. Livvy was perfect. So it must be something else.

Back in March, during their honeymoon, when he'd told her about his tragic, awful childhood, it had broken Daisy's heart. But it had also given her hope. Some part of Leonidas must love her, for him to be so vulnerable with her.

And so she'd been vulnerable, too. She'd told him she loved him.

For months after that, Leonidas had held her close, made love to her, made her feel cherished and adored. He'd let her draw his portrait in six different sketches, all of them in different light.

Now she felt like those sketches were all she had of him.

Had there been a shadow beneath his gaze, even then? Had he already been starting to pull away?

In the two months since Livvy's birth, Daisy hadn't had the opportunity to do another drawing of Leonidas. But she'd done dozens of sketches of their baby. Looking through them yesterday, she'd been astonished at how much the infant had changed in such a short time.

Mrs. Berry, seeing the sketches, had shyly asked if she could hire Daisy to do her portrait, too, as a gift for her husband's birthday. Daisy had done it gladly one afternoon when the baby was sleeping, without charge. She'd done the drawing with her yellow dog stretched out over her feet, on the floor. Sunny had grown huge, and was always nearby, as if guarding Daisy and the baby from unknown enemies. She was particularly suspicious of squirrels.

Sunny always made her laugh.

Mrs. Berry had loved the drawing. Word of mouth began to spread, from the house's staff, to their families. Friends who came from Brooklyn to see the baby saw the drawings of Livvy, and requested portraits of their own grandchildren, of their spouses, of their pets. Just yesterday, Daisy had gotten five separate requests for portraits. She didn't know what to think.

"Why weren't you doing drawings like this all along?" Her old boss at the diner, Claudia, had demanded earlier that week. "Why were you doing those awful modern scribbles—when all along you could do pictures like this?"

Remembering, Daisy gave a low laugh. Trust her old boss not to be diplomatic.

But still, it made her think.

When she'd done her painting at art school, long ago, she'd been desperate to succeed. Art had always felt stressful, as she'd tried to guess what others would most admire. Each effort had been less authentic than the last, a pastiche of great masterpieces, as Leonidas had said. The painting her husband had bought at the auction for a million dollars was still buried in a closet. In spite of its success that night, she hadn't felt joy creating it. In spite of all her effort, the painting had never connected with her heart.

But these sketches were different. They were of *people*.

It felt easy to simply draw her friends—even new friends she'd just met—and see what was best in them.

Was it possible that Daisy did have some talent? Not for painting—but for *people*?

With a rueful snort, she shook her head. Talent for people? She couldn't even get her own husband to talk to her! Or hold their baby daughter!

Two days ago, heartsick, she'd been thinking of how, as an agonized fourteen-year-old, Leonidas had struck out at the Picasso with scissors. And she'd had a sudden crazy idea.

What if she found the painting for him?

It was a long shot. He'd been looking for it for decades. But maybe he hadn't been doing it the right way. Daisy had a few connections in the art world. If she could give him his heart's desire, would it bring Leonidas back to them?

It was her best chance. A grand gesture Leonidas would never forget. She pictured his joyful face when she presented him with the Picasso. Then he would take her in his arms and tell her he loved her.

Her heart yearned for that moment!

So she called a young art blogger she knew in Brooklyn. Aria Johnson had a huge social media following and a ruthless reputation. The woman was like a bloodhound, searching out stories about priceless art and scandals of the rich and famous. Even Daisy's father had been a little afraid of her.

Picking up the phone, she called her and told Aria haltingly about her husband's history with the lost Picasso.

Daisy didn't explain *everything*, of course. She didn't say a word about the way he'd been conceived. *That* was a secret she'd take to the grave. She just told her that *Love with Birds* had been lost when Leonidas's mother had died in a big Turkish earthquake, some two decades before.

"Yeah. I know the story." The blogger popped her gum impatiently. "People have looked for that Picasso for twenty years. Wild-goose chase. Why else would your father have thought he could forge it?"

"He didn't—"

Aria cut her off. "They only found the woman's body. No painting." Daisy had flinched. *The woman* had been Leonidas's mother. "Other bodies were found, though. Her household staff. A young man who no one came forward to claim."

"Could you look into it?" Daisy said.

"A widow. With money. Hmm… Was she beautiful?"

"I guess so," Daisy replied. What difference did Eleni Niarxos's beauty make?

"Anything else you can tell me?"

She swallowed hard. It felt like breaking a confidence— but how else could she be sure it was the right painting? She said reluctantly, "There's a cut in the canvas. Someone sliced the painting with a pair of scissors."

"Someone?"

"Yes. Someone." Quickly changing the subject, Daisy said, "If you could find it, I'd be so grateful. And I'll pay you—"

"You can pay my expenses, that's it. I don't need a finder's fee. I just need to own the *story*. Deal?"

Daisy took a deep breath. It felt like a devil's bargain, but she was desperate. "Deal."

The art blogger paused. "If I find the painting, it might not have provenance."

Meaning, the painting might have been stolen. Which

would make sense. How else could it have simply disappeared during the earthquake?

"I don't care," Daisy said. "As long as the Picasso is genuine. And I want the story of where the person found it."

Aria popped her gum. "Don't worry. I'll get the story."

That had been a few days ago. Now, holding her sleeping baby, Daisy was rocking in the chair in the nursery. It was late August, hot and sweaty summer in New York, but cool and calm inside their West Village mansion. She looked down at Livvy, softly snoring in her arms, in rhythm with the much louder snoring of the large dog snoozing at Daisy's feet.

"Soon," she whispered to her baby. "Aria will find it. And then your father will be home, and he'll realize at last that he's really, truly loved—"

The nursery door was suddenly flung open, hitting the wall with a bang. The dog jumped at her feet. Livvy woke and started wailing, then Sunny started barking.

Looking up at the doorway in shock, Daisy saw her husband, dark as a shadow. He was dressed in a suit, but his handsome face held a savage glower.

For a moment, in spite of her baby's wails, Daisy's heart lifted. Her husband had come home to her at last. Her body yearned for his embrace, for connection, for reassurance. A smile lifted to her lips.

"Leonidas," she breathed. "I'm so glad to see you—"

"Do you really hate me this much, Daisy?" His voice was low and cold. "How could you do it?"

"What?" she cried, bewildered.

"As if you didn't know." Leonidas gave a low, bitter laugh. "I should have known you would betray me. Just like everyone else."

CHAPTER NINE

THE WELCOMING SMILE on his wife's face fled.

She'd made such a lovely picture, snuggled in the rocking chair beside the nursery's window, holding their sleeping baby, with the floppy golden dog at her feet.

Now Daisy's beautiful face was anguished, the baby was wailing and Sunny was dancing desperately around Leonidas, wagging her tail, trying to get his attention.

He ignored the dog, looking only at his wife.

Turning away, she calmed the baby down, pulling out a breast and tucking her nipple into Livvy's tiny mouth as comfort.

It shouldn't have been erotic, but it was. Probably because he hadn't made love to her in months. Leonidas tried not to look. He couldn't let himself want her. He couldn't.

He forced himself to look away.

She'd hurt him. In a way he'd never thought he'd hurt again.

He never should have told her about his past. Never...

As the baby fell quiet, falling asleep with her tiny hand pressed against his wife's breast, Daisy finally looked up at him. Her green eyes narrowed.

"What do you mean, I betrayed you?"

Ignoring the dog still pressing against his knees, Leonidas glared back, but lowered his voice so as not to wake their child. "You spoke with Aria Johnson."

"Oh, that." She relaxed, then gave a soft smile. "I was

trying to help. I know what the Picasso means to you, and I asked her to find it. I didn't think—"

"No, you *didn't* think, or else you wouldn't have told a muckraking *blogger* that I cut into the painting with a pair of scissors!"

"What?" she gasped. "I never told her it was *you*!"

"Well, she knows. She just called me at the office. And if that weren't enough she's been looking into my mother's past," he said grimly.

Daisy went pale. She whispered, "What did she find?"

"My mother apparently had many lovers, both in Greece and Turkey. She tracked them all down, except for her last one, who apparently died with her in the earthquake." He glared at Daisy. "One of the lovers knew how I was born. My mother must have confessed. So now that blogger knows I'm not really my father's son, but the son of my drug-addicted uncle. She asked me to confirm or deny!"

"What did you say?" Daisy cried.

"I hung up the phone!" Clawing back his hair, Leonidas paced the nursery. Every muscle felt tense. "How could you have told her to look into my past?"

"I didn't! I just told her to find the Picasso!"

He looked down at her, his heart in his throat. "Aria Johnson has a reputation. She can't be bought off. All she cares about is entertaining her army of followers with the most shocking scandal she can find. And she always finds them. This is going to be all over the internet within hours."

Daisy looked up at him miserably, her eyes glistening with unshed tears. "I'm so sorry. I was trying to help."

"Help? Now the whole world is going to learn my deepest, darkest secret, which I've spent a lifetime trying to hide." He clenched his hands at his sides. "I never should have trusted you."

"I'm sorry." She blinked fast, her face anguished. "I didn't mean to hurt you. I was trying to bring you back!"

"What are you talking about?"

"The day Livvy was born, you disappeared!" The baby flinched a little in her arms at the rise in her voice. With a deep breath, Daisy carefully got to her feet, then lifted Livvy into her crib. Gently setting down the sleeping infant, she quietly backed away, motioning for Leonidas to follow, Sunny at his feet. Closing the nursery door silently behind them, Daisy turned to face him in the hallway.

The window at the end of the hallway slanted warm light into the hundred-year-old brownstone, gleaming against the marble floors. The big golden dog stood between them, her tongue lagging, looking hopefully first at one, then the other.

"I need you, Leonidas," Daisy whispered. "Our baby needs you. Why won't you even hold her?"

A tumble of feelings wrenched though him. He couldn't let them burst through his heart, he couldn't. He said stiffly, "I held her."

"Just once, in the hospital. Since then, you've avoided her." Her eyes lifted to his. "You've avoided me."

His wife's stricken expression burned through him like acid. He turned away.

"Work has been busy. You cannot be angry at me for trying to secure our daughter's empire..." Then he remembered that Daisy didn't care about his business empire. It wasn't enough for her. And if that wasn't, how could Leonidas ever be? "I haven't been avoiding you."

The lie was poison in his mouth.

"Please," she said in a low voice. "I need you."

"You don't. You're doing fine. And Livvy is better off with you than with me."

"What is that supposed to mean?"

How could he explain that his baby daughter already knew he was no good? And from the pain and hurt in his wife's eyes, Daisy was rapidly learning the same thing, too. "It doesn't matter."

Reaching out, she put her hand on his arm. "You helped me love art again, after all my hope was lost. Drawing you on our honeymoon, I realized that people are my passion. Not random smudges or colors. *People*." Blinking fast, she tried a smile. "You helped me find my voice."

Daisy had never looked more beautiful to him than she did right now, her green eyes so luminous, her heart fully in her face.

And her love. He saw her love for him shining from her eyes. He didn't deserve it. He couldn't bear it. Because it wouldn't last.

His fate was in her hands, as he waited for Daisy to finally realize he wasn't worthy of her love. *You're wonderful*, she'd told him. *Wonderful and perfect*.

He wasn't. He knew his flaws; he could be cold and arrogant and selfish. But from the moment she'd decided to love him, she had become willfully blind. She had rose-colored glasses and was determined to see only the best of him.

But sooner or later she'd see the real him. Then her love would crumble to dust. To *disgust*.

Just the thought of that ripped him up.

And soon, the whole world would learn about his scandalous birth and not even his wealth or power would protect him. He'd done everything he set out to do. He'd built an empire. He was rich and powerful beyond imagination. But it had changed nothing.

All his worst fears were about to come true. The world would learn that his very birth had been a deceit. His parents had despised him and wished he'd never been born.

Leonidas was unlovable. Unworthy. Empty.

And now he was dragging Daisy into it as well.

"I'm sorry, Leonidas," she said quietly. "I never meant to hurt you. Can you ever forgive me?"

Shaking his head, he looked toward the window at the end of the hallway. If he had any decency, he would let both her and the baby go.

But just the thought of that made his soul howl with grief...

Daisy bit her lip. "Even if Aria publishes everything, why would anyone care? What does the way you were conceived have to do with you?"

He looked at her incredulously. "Everything."

She shook her head. "You had an awful childhood and triumphed in spite of it all. That's the *real* story, whoever your father was."

Leonidas didn't answer.

"Besides. You never know," she tried, "maybe the Picasso will be found..."

"It will never be found." He gave a low, bitter laugh. "It was buried beneath ten tons of rock and fire."

"But you said they never found it—"

"It must have been destroyed." Like so much else.

A long, empty silence fell between them in the hallway.

"Leonidas," she said quietly. "Look at me."

It took him a moment to gather the courage. Then he did. His heart broke just looking at her, so beautiful and brave, as she faced him, her shoulders tight.

"I'm sorry if I've caused you pain," she said quietly. "My desperation made me reckless." Her lovely face was bewildered. "You asked me to marry you. You *insisted* on marriage. You said there was nothing you wanted more than to be Livvy's father. What happened?"

"I don't know."

"If you're never going to hold her, never going to look at me—why are we married? Why am I even here?"

It was clear. He had to let them go. If he didn't, he'd only ending up hurting them so much more.

But how could he let them go, when they were every-thing?

Hurt them—or hurt himself. There was only one choice to make. But it hurt so much that Leonidas thought he might die. He looked around the hallway wildly, then gasped, "I need some fresh air—"

Turning, he rushed down the stone staircase and stumbled outside, desperate to breathe.

Outside the brownstone mansion, the tree-lined street was strangely quiet. The orange sun, setting to the west, left long shadows in the hot, humid August twilight. He stopped, leaning over, gasping for breath, trying to stop the frantic pounding of his heart.

Daisy came out of the house behind him, to stand in the fading light.

"I love you, Leonidas," she said quietly.

His hands clenched. Finally, he turned to face her.

"You can't."

"The truth is, I've always loved you, from the moment we met at the diner, and I thought you were just Leo, a salesclerk in a shop." Reaching up, she cupped his unshaven cheek. "I fell in love with you. And who you could be. And I only have one question for you." She tilted her head. "Can you ever love me back?"

Trembling beneath the shady trees of summer twilight, Leonidas closed his stinging eyes. He felt like he was spinning out of control, coming undone. But his heart was empty. He'd learned long ago that begging for love only brought scorn. The only way to be safe was to pull back. To not care.

The only way to keep Daisy and Livvy safe from him, to make sure he never hurt or disappointed them, was to let them go.

He had to. No matter how much it killed him. He had to find the strength, for their sakes.

Closing his eyes, he took a deep breath.

Then he opened them.

"No. I'm sorry." He covered her hand gently with his own. "I thought I could do this but I can't."

"Do what?"

He looked down at her.

"Marriage," he said quietly.

Her eyes widened, her face pale. He pushed her hand away.

"No," she choked out. "We can go to counseling. We can—"

"You're in love with some imaginary man, not me. I'm not *wonderful*. I'm not *perfect*. I'm a selfish, cold bastard."

"No, you're not, you're *not*!"

"I am. Why can't you admit it?" he said incredulously. "Whatever you say, I know you've never forgiven me for killing your father."

"I have… I've *tried*." Tears were streaming down her face. "Dad was innocent, but I know now you never meant to cause his death."

"Stop." He looked at her, feeling exhausted. "It's time to face reality."

"The reality is that I love you!"

"You're forcing yourself to overlook my flaws. But I've known from the moment Livvy was born that you'd soon see the truth, as she did from the first time I held her."

"Because she cried? That's crazy! She's a baby!"

"It's not crazy. You both deserve better than me. And I'm tired of feeling it every day, tired of knowing I'm not good enough. I'm not this perfect man you want me to be. Seeing the cold accusation in your eyes—"

"What are you *talking* about?"

"Better to end it now, rather than…" Turning away, he said in a low voice, "You and the baby should go."

"Go?" She gave a wild, humorless laugh. "Go where?"

"Anywhere you want. Your old dream of California."

"You're my dream! You!"

Every part of Leonidas's body hurt. He felt like he was two hundred years old. Why was she fighting him so hard? Why—when everything he said was true? "Or if you want, you can keep this house." He looked up at the place where they'd been so happy, the house with the ballroom where they'd quarreled and the garden where they'd played with the dog in the spring sunshine, where wild things grew in the middle of Manhattan. "I'll go to a hotel." He paused. "Forget what the prenup said. You can have half my fortune—half of everything. Whatever you want."

She looked up at him, tears in her eyes.

"But I want you."

"Someday, you'll thank me," he said hoarsely. It was true. It had to be true. He looked one last time at her beautiful, heartbroken face. "Goodbye, Daisy."

Squaring his shoulders, he turned away, walking fast down the quiet residential lane, filled with the soft rustle of leaves in the warm wind.

But even as he walked away, he felt her tears, her anguished grief, reverberating through his body, down to blood and bone.

It's better this way, Leonidas repeated to himself fiercely, wiping his eyes. *Better for everyone.*

So why did he feel like he'd just died?

Daisy watched in shock as her husband disappeared down the quiet lane in the twilight. At the end of the street, she saw him hail a yellow cab.

Then he was gone.

Once, long ago, she'd made Leonidas promise that if she ever wanted to leave, he had to let her go.

She'd never imagined he would be the one to leave.

All her love hadn't been enough to make him stay. He'd turned on her.

Yes, she'd blamed Leonidas once, for her father's unjust imprisonment and death. But she'd forgiven that, even if she hadn't forgotten it. Right?

Well. It didn't matter now.

Tears streamed down her face. Turning unsteadily, she stumbled back up the stoop to enter the house he'd just told her was hers. He'd given up the fifty-million-dollar brownstone easily, as if it meant nothing. Just like Daisy and their daughter.

If he'd cared at all, he never would have abandoned them. He would have tried to make their marriage work. Tried to love her.

But he hadn't.

Daisy closed the door behind her and leaned back against it. Above her, the crystal chandelier chimed discordantly in the puff of air.

The luxury of this mansion mocked her in her grief. This place was a palace. It was heaven. But it felt like an empty hell.

She stared blankly at the sweeping stone staircase where her husband had once carried her up to the bedroom, lost in reckless passion.

Her knees gave out beneath her and she slid back against the wall with a sob, crumpling onto the floor.

Her dog, coming downstairs to investigate, gave a worried whine and pushed her soft furry body against Daisy, offering comfort. She wrapped her arm around the animal and stared dimly at the opposite wall, where she'd framed sketches of her husband and baby.

"Mrs. Niarxos."

She looked up to see Mrs. Berry looking down at her with worried eyes. Swallowing, she whispered, "He left me."

"Oh, my dear." The white-haired housekeeper put her

hand on Daisy's shoulder. Her voice was gentler than she'd ever heard before. "I'm so sorry."

The ache in Daisy's throat sharpened to a razor blade. "I thought, if I loved him enough…" Her image shimmered through a haze of tears. "I thought I could love him enough for both of us."

Mrs. Berry's hand tightened, and she said quietly, "I've known the boy for a long time. He never learned to love anyone. Least of all himself."

"But why wouldn't he? He's amazing. He's wonderful. He…" She heard the echo of his words. *I'm not wonderful. I'm not perfect. I'm a selfish, cold bastard.*

"What can I do, my dear?"

"I…" Shaking, Daisy closed her eyes. Still sitting on the marble floor, she gripped her knees against her broken heart. She couldn't imagine any future. All she saw ahead of her was a bleak wasteland of pain.

Then Sunny put her chin against Daisy's leg, her black eyes looking up mournfully, and Daisy remembered that she couldn't fall apart. She had a baby relying on her.

Five months ago, she'd thought she was ready to raise their baby alone. She'd made plans to go to nursing school, to move to California. She'd been strong in herself. She hadn't needed him.

Where had that strong woman gone?

She'd long since canceled her college registration. Daisy blinked fast, trying to see clearly. She stroked her dog's soft golden fur. She took a deep breath. Strong. She had to be strong.

She looked up at Mrs. Berry. "I need to go."

"Go?"

Daisy slowly got up. She looked around the elegant foyer. "I can't stay here. It reminds me too much of him. And how happy we were…"

The housekeeper gave her a strange look. "Were you really?"

Staring at her, Daisy held in her breath. Had they been happy?

"I thought we were," she choked out. "At least at first. But something happened when our baby was born…"

Across the foyer, Daisy's eyes fell again on the framed sketch she'd done of her husband on their honeymoon. They'd been happy then. Next to that, there was a framed sketch of their baby's smiling face and innocent dark eyes. Just like Leonidas's—and yet nothing at all like them.

With a deep breath, Daisy lifted her chin.

So be it.

Ahead of her, the empty future stretched as wide as a vast ocean.

She could fill that terrifying void with flowers and sea breezes.

"I need to pack," she said aloud, hardly recognizing the sound of her own voice.

By the next morning, Daisy, her baby and her dog were en route to California, in search of a new life, or at least a new place, where she could build new memories. And, she prayed, where she could heal and raise her daughter with love.

"We've found it, Mr. Niarxos."

Leonidas stared at his lawyer.

"No," he said faintly. "Impossible."

Edgar Ross shook his head. "I waited to be sure. We were contacted two weeks ago. It's been authenticated. There can be no doubt."

The two men were standing in his chief lawyer's well-appointed office, with its floor-to-ceiling windows and view of the Empire State Building.

When his lawyer had called him that morning, Leonidas

had assumed that the man must have heard that he'd separated from Daisy. After all, for the last three weeks, Leonidas had been living in a Midtown hotel suite. It wouldn't exactly take a detective to figure out the Niarxos marriage was over.

Even though he'd told his wife to go, part of him still couldn't believe that Daisy and their baby had left New York. He'd returned to the mansion only once since she'd gone, and it had felt unbearably empty.

After that, he'd returned to the hotel suite, where he'd been riding out the scandal ever since the sordid truth about his past had been revealed on Aria Johnson's website, in all its ugly glory. This visit to his lawyer's office, on the thirty-fourth floor of a Midtown skyrise, was his first public outing in days. At least the scandal was starting to abate. Only two paparazzi had followed him here, which he took as a victory.

Misinterpreting his silence, his lawyer gave Leonidas a broad smile. "I don't blame you for being skeptical. But we really have found the Picasso."

"How can you be sure?" Leonidas's voice was low. "I don't want my hopes raised, only to have them crushed. I'd prefer to have no hope at all."

Just like his marriage.

He could still see Daisy's beautiful face in the warm Greek sun, surrounded by flowers on the terrace of his villa. *I love you,* she'd said dreamily. *You're wonderful. Wonderful and perfect.*

So different from her agonized, heartbroken face when, on the street outside their New York home, he'd told her he was leaving her.

Leonidas couldn't get those two images out of his mind. For the last three weeks, he'd been haunted by memories, day and night, even when he was pretending to work. Even when he was pretending to sleep.

"Would you like to see your Picasso, Mr. Niarxos?"

Leonidas focused on the lawyer. He took a deep breath, forcibly relaxing his shoulders as they stood in the sleek private office with its view of the steel-and-glass city, reflecting the merciless noonday sun. "Why not."

With a big smile, the lawyer turned. Crossing the private office, he reached up and, with an obvious sense of drama, drew back a curtain.

There, on the wall, lit by unflattering overhead light, was the Picasso. There could be no doubt. *Love with Birds.*

Coming forward, Leonidas's eyes traced the blocky swirls of beige and gray paint. His fingers reached out toward a jagged line in the upper left corner, where the image was slightly off kilter, clumsily stitched back together. In the same place where he'd stabbed it with scissors, as a heartsick, abandoned fourteen-year-old.

"How did you find it?" he whispered.

"That art blogger found it. Aria Johnson. She found a relative of your mother's…er…last lover." He coughed discreetly. "A twenty-two-year-old college student in Ankara. He'd taken the painting to his aunt's house the day before he disappeared in the earthquake."

"Took it? Stole it, you mean."

"Apparently not. The young man told his aunt the painting was a gift from some rich new girlfriend. She never learned who the girlfriend was, and she had no idea the painting was worth anything. She only kept it because she loved her nephew."

Leonidas stared at him, barely comprehending.

After years of fighting tooth and claw to keep her husband from taking the painting from her, Eleni had simply *given it away*? To a young lover she barely knew? How? Why?

And then he knew.

His mother had been broken, too. Betrayed, heartsick, desperate for love.

The thought was overwhelming to him. So it wasn't just Leonidas who felt that way. His mother had taken young lovers and given away her biggest treasure. His father had quietly drunk himself to death. Did everyone in the world feel broken? Feel like they were desperate for love they feared they'd never find?

He looked at the jagged tear across the priceless masterpiece. Ross followed his gaze.

"Er…yes. The aunt tried to repair the cut with a needle and thread, out of respect for her nephew's memory." His lawyer flinched. "You see the result."

It took Leonidas a moment to even find his voice. "Yes."

"She nearly had a heart attack when Aria Johnson told her she'd been keeping a Picasso in her gardening shed for the last twenty years."

"How much does she want for it?"

"The art blogger told her she'd be a fool to take less than ten million. That seemed a reasonable price to me, since she could potentially have gotten even more at auction. So as soon as it was authenticated, I paid her."

"You're saying the painting's mine?"

"Yes, Mr. Niarxos."

Leonidas took another step toward the painting. With his parents now dead, there was no longer anyone to scream at him for trying to touch it. Reaching up, he gently stroked the roughly stitched edge where he'd once hacked into it.

"We will of course send it to be properly restored—"

"No. I'll keep it as it is." Drawing back his hand, Leonidas looked at the treasure he'd chased all his life. *Love with Birds.* Looking at the gray and beige boxy swirls, he waited for joy and love to fill his heart.

Nothing happened.

"I thought you might wish to arrange something with

Liontari's PR department," the lawyer said behind him. "Let them do outreach on social media. This will make a nice end to the soap opera story currently making the rounds about your, *er*, origins. If there's one thing the public likes more than a scandal, it's a happy ending."

Barely listening, Leonidas narrowed his eyes, tilting his head right and left to get a better angle as he looked at the painting, waiting for happiness and triumph to fill his heart.

All his life, he'd chased fame and fortune, luxury and beauty. He'd chased this masterpiece most of all.

Why didn't he feel like he'd thought he would feel? This was the possession that was supposed to make him feel *whole*. This painting was supposed to be love itself.

But Leonidas felt nothing.

Looking at it, he saw neither love nor birds. He saw meaningless swirls and boxes of gray and beige paint.

He felt cheated. Betrayed. His hands tightened at his sides. This painting meant *nothing*.

"Sir?" His lawyer sounded concerned. "Is there a problem?"

Leonidas looked away. "Thank you for arranging the acquisition." The sharp light from the skyscrapers of the merciless city burned his eyelids. His throat was tight. "You will, of course, receive your finder's fee and commission."

"Thank you, sir," Ross said happily. When Leonidas didn't move, he said in a different tone, "Uh...is there something else you wish to discuss, Mr. Niarxos?"

This was the moment to ask for his divorce to be set in motion. Leonidas had already been dragging his feet for too long. Just last week, when he'd stopped by his old house, hoping for a glimpse of his family, Mrs. Berry had told him Daisy had rented a cottage in California, three thousand miles away.

"Rented…a cottage?" he'd asked, bewildered. "I gave her this house!"

"She didn't want it without you," his housekeeper said quietly. "I'm sorry, sir. I'm so sorry."

He'd felt oddly vulnerable. "I'm the one who ended it."

"I know." The white-haired woman had given him a sad smile. "You hated for her to love you. How could she, when you can't love yourself?"

Hearing those awful, true words, Leonidas had fled.

He could never go back to that house or see Mrs. Berry again. Never, ever. He'd pay her off, put the house on the market—

"Ah. I was afraid of this," the lawyer said with a sudden sigh. Turning, he sat down behind his huge desk, and indicated the opposite chair. "Don't worry, Mr. Niarxos. We can soon get you free."

Still standing, Leonidas frowned at him. "Free?"

Edgar Ross said gently, "It's all over town you've been living in a suite at the Four Seasons. But don't worry." He shook his head. "We have your prenup. Divorce won't be hard, as long as Mrs. Niarxos doesn't intend to fight it."

No, he thought dully. Daisy had already fought as hard as she could for their marriage. She would not fight anymore. Not now he'd made it clear there was no hope.

He'd lost her. Lost? He'd pushed her out of his life. Forever.

He looked up dully. In place of a loving, beautiful, kind-hearted wife, he had a painting. *Love with Birds.*

"Sir?" Ross again indicated the leather chair.

Leonidas stared at it. All he had to do was sit, and he'd soon get his divorce. His marriage would be declared officially dead. He'd lose Daisy forever, and their child, too. Just as he'd wanted.

He could take the painting to join the rest of his expensive possessions, back at his empty house in the West Village, or any of his other empty houses around the world. Instead of love and legacy, instead of a family, he'd have the painting.

You hated for her to love you. How could she, when you can't love yourself?

Leonidas had never been worthy of Daisy's love. She'd called him wonderful. She'd called him perfect. He was neither of those things. No wonder he was scared to love her. Because the moment he did—

The moment he did, she'd see the truth, and he would lose her.

But he'd lost her anyway.

The thought made his eyes go wide. He'd sent her away because he was terrified of ever feeling that hollowness again in his heart, of wanting someone's love and not getting it.

But he loved Daisy anyway.

With a gasp, Leonidas stared out the window. A reflected beam from another skyscraper's windows blinded him with sharp light.

He loved her.

He was totally and completely in love with his wife. And he had been, from the moment he'd married her. No, before. From the moment he'd kissed her. From the moment she'd first smiled at him in the diner, her face so warm and kind, so beautiful and real in her waitress uniform—

Nice suit. Headed to court? Unpaid parking tickets? You poor guy. Coffee's on me.

Daisy always saw the best in everyone. Including him.

Leonidas looked again at the Picasso. The painting was not love. It could never fill his heart.

Only he could do that.

All these years, he'd blamed his parents for his inability to love anyone, including himself. And maybe it was true.

But sooner or later, a man had to choose. Would he bury himself in grief and blame, and die choking on the dirt? Or would he reach up his hands, struggle to pull himself up and out of the early grave, to breathe sunlight and fresh air?

Leonidas chose life.

He chose her.

"I have to go," he said suddenly.

"What?" His lawyer looked bewildered, holding a stack of official-looking papers on his desk. "Where?"

"California." Leonidas turned away. He had to see Daisy. He had to tell her everything, to fall at her feet and beg her to forgive him. To take him back. Before he'd even reached the door, he broke into a run.

Because what if he was already too late?

CHAPTER TEN

THE BOUGAINVILLEA WAS in bloom, the flowers pink and bright, climbing against the snug white cottage overlooking the sea.

After three weeks of living there, Daisy still couldn't get over the beauty of the quiet neighborhood near Santa Barbara. From the small garden behind her cottage, filled with roses and orange trees, she could see the wide blue vista of the Pacific. Looking straight down from the edge of the bluff, she could see the coastal highway far below, but the noise of the traffic was lost against the sea breezes waving the branches of cypress trees.

Looking out at the blue ocean and pink flowers, Daisy couldn't stop herself from remembering her honeymoon, when Leonidas had kissed her passionately, on the terrace of a Greek villa covered with flowers, overlooking the Aegean. Even now, the backs of her eyelids burned at the memory.

When would she get over him? How long would it take for her to feel whole again?

"So? Did you decide?"

Hearing Franck Bain's voice behind her, she turned with a polite smile. "No, not yet. I'm not even sure how long I'm going to stay in California, much less whether I'll open my portrait business here."

"Of course." The middle-aged artist's words were friendly, but his gaze roamed over her, from her white peasant blouse and denim capri pants to her flat sandals. The echo of her old boss's words floated back to her. *You know he's in love with you.*

No, Daisy thought with dismay. Franck was her father's old friend. He couldn't actually be in love with her.

Could he?

Franck had called her from his home in Los Angeles that morning, saying he'd heard she'd moved to Santa Barbara, just an hour to the north. He'd offered to drive up for a visit. Remembering how he'd burst in at her wedding, she'd been a little uneasy. But he'd explained smoothly, "My dear, I was just trying to keep you from making a big mistake. If you'd listened to me, you wouldn't be going through a divorce now."

Which was true.

Daisy *did* want to get to know Santa Barbara, and look at possible locations for a portrait studio. Living in New York, she'd never learned to drive. When Franck offered to drive her wherever she wanted, even putting a baby seat in the back of his car, how could she refuse? Didn't a person going through a divorce need all the friends she could get?

Divorce. Such an ugly word. Every day for the last three weeks, since she'd rented the snug cottage, she'd waited in dread for the legal papers to arrive.

But there was no point putting it off. Leonidas didn't want her. He didn't want Livvy. He was done with them. He didn't care how much he'd hurt them.

Maybe Franck had been right when he'd shouted out at her wedding that Leonidas was a liar who'd killed her father.

Because there was no mercy in her husband's soul. He'd had her father sent to prison for an innocent mistake. For Daisy's own innocent mistake of trying to help him find the Picasso, Leonidas had cut her and their baby out of his life—forever.

With a lump in her throat, Daisy looked at their sweet,

plump-cheeked baby in the sunlight of the California garden. Three-month-old Livvy had fallen asleep in the car and was still tucked snugly into her baby carrier outside.

"Thanks for showing me some of your drawings," Franck said, smiling at her. He considered her thoughtfully. "You're very good at portraits."

"Thanks." She hoped he wasn't about to suggest that she do a drawing of *him*. She felt weary of his company, and a little uncomfortable, too.

The way Franck had looked at her all afternoon was definitely more than *friendly*. Ten minutes before, on their way back to her cottage, he'd invited her to dinner, "to discuss your business options." Yeah, right. She'd been relieved to say no. Thank goodness she had a dog waiting at the cottage who needed to be let out into the garden!

Now Sunny bounded around them happily, sniffing everything from the vibrant rose bushes to the cluster of orange trees, checking on baby Livvy like a mother hen, then running a circle around the perimeter of white picket fence.

The only thing the large golden dog didn't seem to like was Franck.

The dog had growled at him at first sight, when he'd arrived to pick them up in his car. Daisy had chastised her pet, and so Sunny had grudgingly flopped by the stone fireplace to mope. But even now, the normally happy dog kept her distance, giving him the suspicious glare she normally reserved for squirrels.

"Yes," Franck said, stroking his chin as he looked at Daisy. "You have talent. More than I realized. I wonder if…"

Oh, heavens, was he about to proposition her? "If what?"

"I've moved my business to California." His thin face darkened. "Your husband ran me out of New York."

That was news to her. "Leonidas? Why?"

He shook his head. "It doesn't matter. He'll soon be

your ex." Franck smacked his lips—she could swear he did. "Your divorce will make you very wealthy."

The last thing Daisy wanted to do was discuss the financial details of her divorce with Franck Bain. She looked at his sedan parked on the other side of the picket fence, wishing he would leave already. "Um…"

"So obviously you won't need an income. But I wonder," his gaze swept over her, "if you might be interested in doing something with me. For pleasure."

Ugh. The way he said *pleasure* made her cringe. She responded coldly, "What are you talking about?"

He lifted a sparse eyebrow. "You could be part of something big."

"I'm sure you are involved in many big things. Don't let me keep you from them."

"There's a good market in lost masterpieces." He tilted his head slyly. "Especially old portraits."

Daisy stared at him. Unease trickled down her spine. Could he possibly mean…? "What market?"

"Don't pretend you don't understand." He grinned. "How do you think I got so rich? I help clients find the paintings they most desire."

Time seemed to stop beneath the warm California sunshine. "You mean…by creating them?"

Franck shrugged.

"It was you," she whispered. "All this time you said my father was innocent. But you knew he was guilty. You were his accomplice."

Franck shook his head scornfully. "How else do you think Patrick was able to stay home and take care of you after your mother died? *She* brought in the income. His gallery barely made a penny."

She said hoarsely, "I can't believe it…"

"Patrick refused my offer for years. Then he suddenly had to take care of a little kid by himself. He came to me, desperate. We agreed that I would paint, and he'd use his connections to sell the art. We did very well. For years." Franck's reptilian eyes narrowed. "Until he wanted to go for the big score, selling a Picasso. We never should have tried it."

"Why did you, then?" she said in a small voice.

He shrugged. "Your father was worried about you. You'd just flamed out as an artist. And he was sick of selling forgeries to the nouveaux riches. He wanted to leave New York. Move somewhere and start over."

Memory flashed through her, of the night she'd been crying over her failure to sell a single painting.

We could start over, her father had told her suddenly. *Move to Santa Barbara.*

What about your gallery, Dad?

Maybe I'd like a change, too. Just one more deal to close, and then...

Could he have possibly taken such a risk—done something so criminal—just because he couldn't bear to see his daughter cry? Guilt flashed through her.

She glared at Franck. "You sat through his trial every day and never admitted you were his accomplice. You let him go to prison alone!"

He rolled his eyes. "The Picasso was your father's idea. I was happy selling cheap masterpieces to suckers. Selling a Picasso to a billionaire? I never liked the risk." He scowled. "And then your husband ruined everything. I'd done a perfect copy of the Picasso. But I heard last week that Niarxos had chopped it up with a pair of scissors as a kid?" He glowered. "How was I supposed to know? Who *does* that?"

"Someone who's hurting," Daisy whispered over the lump in her throat. Her heart was pounding. The foundation of what she'd thought was true in her life was dissolving beneath her feet.

I didn't do it, baby, her father had pleaded. *I swear it on my life. On my love for you.*

Her father had lied. He'd told her what she wanted to hear. What he'd desperately wanted her to believe.

But why had Daisy let herself believe it?

When her mother got so sick, her father had stopped spending time at the gallery, spending it instead at home with his beloved wife, and their young daughter. Yet somehow, his gallery had done better than ever. He'd hired more people. Instead of their family having less money, they'd had *more*.

Why hadn't Daisy ever let herself see the truth?

Because she hadn't wanted to see. Because she'd wanted to believe the best of her father. Because she'd loved him.

And she still loved him. She would have forgiven everything, if he'd just given her the chance...

"Why didn't Dad tell me?" she said brokenly.

Franck shook his head. "He said you had to believe the best of him, or he was afraid that you wouldn't survive."

"That *I* wouldn't survive?" she said slowly. She frowned. "That doesn't make sense. It..."

She had a sudden memory of her father trying to talk to her, the day he'd been questioned by the police.

Daisy, I've been arrested... He'd paused. *You should know I'm not perfect—*

Of course you are, Dad, she'd rushed to say. *You're perfect. The best man in the world. Don't try to tell me anything different.*

Would he have told her then? If she hadn't made it clear she didn't want to know about his mistakes?

And Leonidas. It was true that she'd never totally forgiven him for what he'd done to her father. She'd tried to forget. She'd told him he was perfect. Because she loved him.

The men she loved had to be perfect.

I'm not wonderful. I'm not perfect. I'm a selfish, cold bastard, he'd told her. And she'd insisted he was wrong.

But he wasn't. Leonidas could be selfish. He could be cold. Why couldn't she admit that, and say she loved him anyway?

Rose-colored glasses were a double-edged sword. She'd believed in her father, believed in her husband. She'd boxed them in, pressuring them to live up to that image of perfection, an image no one could live up to for long.

No wonder Leonidas had fled.

She'd insisted on his perfection, as if he were a shining knight on a white charger. And when he'd finally shown his weaknesses, she'd betrayed him, by telling his secrets to some reporter.

The fact that the lost Picasso had been finally found, as she'd heard that morning in the news, did not absolve her. Her cheeks went hot with shame.

Leonidas had been right. She'd betrayed him.

"We could be partners, you and I." Speaking softly in the sunlit garden, Franck moved closer to her. "My hands aren't what they used to be, but I have connections now. Even if you don't need the money after your divorce, you could do the paintings just for fun." He cackled. "Old masters for suckers. Much more satisfying than sketching fat babies and dogs!"

Daisy jerked back, glaring at him. "I *like* fat babies and dogs!"

His forehead furrowed. Seeing rejection in her set jaw, he stiffened, scowling. "Fine." Then his pale blue eyes gleamed. "But you owe me. For all those months I took care of you." He gave an oily smile. "If you won't paint for me, I'll take payment in other ways—"

He grabbed her roughly. She tried to pull away. "What are you doing—don't!"

"Don't you think I deserve a little kindness," he panted,

his long fingers digging into her shoulders, "for all those months I took care of you—"

She struggled desperately as he lowered his head. Before he could force a kiss on her, she screamed—

Then everything happened at once.

Her baby woke and started wailing in the baby carrier...

Her dog rushed toward Franck, showing her teeth with a growl...

Daisy lifted her knee up, hard and sharp, against Franck's groin, causing him to give a choked grunt, and release her...

And—

"Get the hell away from her!"

Leonidas's enraged, deep voice boomed behind her. As Franck was stumbling back from her blow, her husband was suddenly there, vengeful in his black shirt and trousers, his powerful body stepping in front of her. Daisy's mouth parted in shock as Leonidas punched the other man hard in the jaw, knocking him to the ground.

"Don't you dare touch her!"

"Leo," she whispered, wondering if she was dreaming.

His tall, muscular form turned anxiously. "Are you all right, *agape mou*? He did not hurt you?"

Rubbing her shoulders a little, she shook her head, her eyes wide. "I'm all right."

Leonidas exhaled with relief. He scooped up their crying baby, who immediately quieted, comforted in her father's arms. Then he drew Daisy close, searching her gaze intently with his own.

"I'm so sorry," he said in a low voice. "Can you ever forgive me?"

Daisy stared up at Leonidas's handsome face. His jaw was dark with five o'clock shadow, as if he hadn't had time to shave. His usually immaculate clothes were rumpled, as if he'd rushed straight from the airport. His black eyes were vulnerable, stricken.

"Can *I* forgive *you*?" she repeated, bewildered.

"Very touching," Franck snarled at them from the grass.

"Shut up," Daisy told him, at the same moment Leonidas said pleasantly, without looking at the man, "Another word, and I'll set the dog on you."

Their normally goofy, people-loving dog was, indeed, growling at the man threateningly.

As Sunny approached, Franck Bain scrambled back, flinging himself over the white picket fence into a tangle of rose bushes. Daisy heard his sharp yelp followed by swift footsteps. His car engine started with a roar, then he peeled off down the road.

"Sunny!" Daisy's blood was still up as she called her pet back into the middle of the garden. Kneeling into the soft grass, she petted her dog again and again, crooning, "Good girl!" as the dog's tail wagged happily.

"I couldn't understand why you got involved." Behind her, Leonidas's voice was low. "The first time you heard crying in an alley, I didn't know why you insisted on going to see what it was. It seemed better to ignore it."

Still kneeling beside her dog, Daisy turned her head. Her husband stood behind her, tall and broad shouldered. His handsome face was full of emotion.

"You insisted on taking care of the puppy, when you barely had enough money to take care of yourself. It was foolish." He took a deep breath, his dark hair gleaming in the sun. "Why try to save something abandoned? Something so unloved and broken?"

She saw sudden tears in his black eyes.

"Now I understand," he whispered. "Because you did the same with me."

Daisy's lips parted. Rising to her feet, she reached for him. He pulled her into his powerful arms.

"Oh, my darling," Leonidas breathed into her hair, holding her close against his hard-muscled chest. "How can you ever forgive me for leaving you? I thought I could never be the man you needed me to be, and I couldn't bear to let you down. But I never should have run away like a coward..."

"Stop." Daisy put her hand on his rough cheek. "I was wrong about so much. All that time I blamed you for putting an innocent man in prison... Franck admitted that my father was guilty, all along. And I refused to see it. Because I needed my dad to be perfect." She lifted her gaze to his. "Just like I needed my husband to be perfect. I'm so sorry."

"I would give anything to be perfect for you." Holding their precious baby in the crook of one arm, he looked intently into her eyes. "You deserve it, Daisy. But I knew I could never be. I could never be good enough to deserve your love."

She clung to him in her cottage's flower-filled garden, overlooking the wide blue Pacific. "But you can—you *are*—"

"I convinced myself that you and Livvy would be better off without me. But after you left, my soul was empty. Nothing mattered. Even when I finally acquired the Picasso—thanks to you—"

"I heard about that. Was it everything you dreamed of?"

Leonidas looked down at her. "I finally had it, this thing I'd been searching for half my life, and I felt *nothing*. It was just swirls of paint. And I realized that everything I'd ever feared had come true. I'd lost the love of my life, by being too proud and stupid when you tried to save me, by not being brave enough to risk my heart. Now the only thing I fear," he said quietly, "is that I've lost you forever."

Her lips parted. "What did you say? The love of your life?"

"I love you, Daisy." Leonidas looked from her to the small, drowsy baby still cuddled against his hard-muscled arm. "You and Livvy are my life." He took a deep breath. "And I'll spend the rest of that life trying to be perfect for you, trying to be whatever you need me to be—"

"No," she cut him off. His handsome face looked stricken. Reaching her hand up to his rough, unshaven cheek, Daisy said, "You don't need to be perfect, Leo. You don't need to do anything or change anything. I love you. Just as you are."

His dark eyes shone with unshed tears. Taking her hand in his own, he lifted it to his lips and kissed it passionately. *"Agape mou—"*

Sooner or later, we all learn the truth, Daisy thought later. The truth about others, the truth about ourselves. If you could be brave enough to face it. Brave enough to understand, and forgive, and love in spite of everything.

As her husband pulled her against his chest, into the circle of his arms, with their tiny baby tucked tenderly between them, and their dog leaping joyfully around their feet, he lowered his head and kissed her with lips like fire.

And Daisy really knew, at last, what love was.

It wasn't about rose-colored glasses or knights on white horses. It wasn't about being perfect. It was about seeing each other, flaws and all. Loving everything, the sunshine and shadow inside every soul. And not being afraid.

As Leo kissed her beneath the orange trees, with their feet in the grass and dirt, it was better than perfect.

It was real.

Leonidas looked out of the back window of their West Village mansion with dismay. Amid a snowy January in New York City, another foot of snow had fallen the night before.

In their yard, Sunny was leaping back and forth through the blanket of white, chasing a terrified-looking squirrel. Snow clung to their dog's golden fur, including her ears and eyelashes.

"This is a disaster," Leonidas groaned to his wife, who was watching from the breakfast nook.

She looked up at him tranquilly, turning a page of her book. "How so?"

"If we let her inside again, Mrs. Berry will kill us." He sighed. "Sunny will just have to live in the yard from now on. I'll build her a dog house."

"*You* will?"

"I'll hire someone," he conceded. "Because Sunny can never come back inside. She'd track snow and dirt all over the floors and make the whole house smell of dog."

"No, she won't," his wife said serenely, turning another page. "You're going to give her a bath."

He looked back with alarm. "Me?"

Daisy smiled. "Who better?"

Leonidas's eyes lingered on her. Even after a full night of lovemaking, his wife looked more desirable than ever, sitting at their breakfast table in a lush silk nightgown and robe, sipping black tea and reading a book, as baby Livvy, now seven months old, batted toys in a baby play gym on the floor.

Leonidas said with mock severity, "Do you really think you can give me orders and I'll just obey? Like a pet?"

She looked up from her book, her pale green eyes limpid and wide, fringed with dark lashes. Tilting her head, she bit her pink lower lip. Her shoulders moved slightly, causing the neckline of her robe to gape, hinting at the cleavage of her full breasts beneath the silk. His heartbeat quickened.

"Fine," he said. "I'll give the dog a bath. Not because you asked me. Because I want to."

Her smile widened, and she turned back to her book, calmly taking another sip of tea. He watched her lips press enticingly against the edge of the china cup, edged with twenty-four-carat gold.

"Maybe we can have a little quality time later," he suggested.

Daisy looked at him sideways beneath her lashes. "Maybe."

Glancing at their innocent baby, who seemed to be staring at them with big brown eyes, drool coming from her mouth as she'd just gotten her first tooth, Leonidas sat down next to his wife at the table. "Maybe we can have a *lot* of quality time later."

Smiling, she put her hand on his cheek. "Maybe."

They'd been married for nearly a year, but for Leonidas, it felt like they'd just met. Every day, he felt a greater rush, a greater thrill, at the joy of being with her.

But at the same time, he felt safe. He felt adored. He felt…home.

In the four months since they'd returned to New York, many things had changed. Daisy had become the most in-demand portrait artist in the city, all the more celebrated because she took so few clients. "I'm already so busy with our baby, and you," she'd said. "I simply don't have time for more right now."

Who was Leonidas to argue? Whenever she was ready to become a full-time artist, he suspected Daisy would take over the world. He felt so proud to be her man. Especially since, as she often told him, he was the one who'd given her the courage, and inspiration, to draw again.

He was home more now, too. His company was in the process of hiring a new CEO, as Leonidas had decided to step back and merely be the largest shareholder. "I don't have time for more," he'd told his wife tenderly. "I'm already so busy with the baby. And you."

He was glad to be leaving the company in good shape. The shocking scandal of his birth, building on the soap-opera-like quality of his wedding and fatherhood—which had already gone viral on social media— had created so much outrageous publicity that Liontari's brands had all gone up an average of six percent, causing a huge leap in shareholder value. Even the story that, as a rebellious, heartsick teenager, Leonidas had chopped up his mother's Picasso with scissors when she abandoned him, somehow had added a darker, sexier edge to some of his more traditional brands. Even the most elite, art-loving clientele had forgiven Leonidas for it, after he'd donated the Picasso to a museum last month.

He'd once believed that if people ever learned the truth about him, they would destroy him with pitchforks and scorn. Instead, he'd become some sort of folk hero. He'd heard rumors of a telenovela in development, based on his life.

People were complicated, he thought. Success could be fleeting. All you had to do was look at Franck Bain, once so successful, to see that. A week after the man had fled Daisy's rented cottage in California, he'd been arrested in Japan for trying to pass off a supposedly lost Van Gogh.

Leonidas shook his head. He couldn't pretend he regretted the man's imprisonment. He deserved it. Though Leonidas liked to believe he was a changed man, an understanding, loving person who would never think of taking vengeance on others, he was glad he didn't have to prove it with Bain.

And it left Leonidas free to move on with his life, to more important things, like spending time with his wife, his child and his friends. They were all that mattered. The people who loved him. He loved them, too. Daisy and Livvy most of all.

He looked down at his wife now as she sat at the kitchen table. She gave him a mysterious smile. He was intrigued.

"Are you hiding something from me?"

"Wouldn't you like to know."

"Yes," he whispered, leaning forward. Drawing his hand

down her long dark hair, he moved his lips against her ear, soft as breath. "And you're going to tell me."

He felt her shiver beneath his touch. He ran his hands over the blush-colored silk, softly over her shoulders, to her back, to her full breasts...

Her *very* full breasts.

He blinked, then pulled back, his eyes wide as he searched his wife's gaze. "Are you... You're not..."

"Not pregnant? I'm not."

He exhaled, shocked by his own disappointment. He hadn't even been thinking about trying for another baby, not yet. After all, Livvy was only seven months old. Was he really ready for another baby in the house?

More mayhem. More chaos. More love.

Yes, Leonidas realized. Yes, he was. He wanted another baby. Or six. A large family, big enough for a football team—that sounded perfect.

But there was no rush. He'd just keep putting in the practice, intensely and passionately, every night in bed. A smile traced the edges of his lips. It was a tough job, but someone had to do it.

"It's all right," he said huskily, lowering his head toward hers. "We'll keep trying..."

Daisy put her hand on his chest, stopping him before he could kiss her.

"I'm not," her green eyes twinkled, "*not* pregnant."

His forehead furrowed as he searched her gaze. Then he sucked in his breath. "Not *not* pregnant?"

Daisy ducked her head, her smile suddenly shy. "It must have happened at Christmas. Maybe Christmas Eve. That time under the tree..."

"Agape mou," he said, dazzled with joy. Taking her in his arms, he kissed his wife passionately at the kitchen table. As he held her, he wondered what he'd done to deserve such happiness.

Then the dog door thudded loudly, and suddenly there was a large wet hairy dog between them, shaking water and snow all over the room, and their baby girl gurgled with laughter. As Daisy pulled back from her husband's embrace, her eyes danced as she laughed, too.

And Leonidas knew their joy would last forever. Their lives wouldn't be all laughter, for sure. But they'd build their future together, day by day, through snow and sun, rain and roses.

It would never be perfect. But it would be happy.

Just like him. Once, he'd been lost. He'd been broken. But Daisy had loved him anyway. He'd learned the meaning of love from the woman who, in spite of his flaws, had given him her precious heart.

* * * * *

STEALING
THE PROMISED
PRINCESS

MILLIE ADAMS

For all the Mills & Boon Modern Romance
that came before this one.
It is the other books, and the other authors,
that brought me my love of romance.
And it is why I'm writing them now.

CHAPTER ONE

"I HAVE A debt to collect, Violet King."

Violet stared out the windows of her office, glass all around, providing a wonderful view of the Pacific Ocean directly across her desk, with a view of her staff behind her. There were no private walls in her office space. She preferred for the team to work collaboratively. Creatively.

Her forward-thinking approach to business, makeup and fashion was part of why she had become one of the youngest self-made billionaires in the world.

Though, self-made might be a bit of a stretch considering that her father, Robert King, had given her the initial injection of cash that she needed to get her business off the ground. Everyone worked with investors, she supposed. That hers was genetically related to her was not unheard-of nor, she supposed, did it fully exclude her from that self-made title. But she was conscious of it. Still, she had made that money back and then some.

And she did *not* have debt.

Which meant this man had nothing to say to her.

"You must have the wrong number," she said.

"No. I don't."

The voice on the other end of the phone was rich and dark, faintly accented, though she couldn't quite nail down what accent it was. Different to her family friend, now her sister's husband, Dante, who was from Italy and had spent many years in the States since then. Spanish, perhaps, but with a hint of Brit that seemed to elongate his vowels.

"Very confident," she said. "But I am in debt to no man."

"Oh, perhaps I misspoke then. You are not in debt. You are the payment."

Ice settled in her stomach. "How did you get this number?"

In this social media age where she was seemingly accessible at all hours, she guarded her private line with all the ferocity of a small mammal guarding its burrow. She—or her assistants—might be available twenty-four hours a day on the internet, but she could only be reached at this line by business associates, family or personal friends. This man was none of those, and yet somehow he was calling her. And saying the most outlandish things.

"How I got this number is not important to the conversation."

She huffed. "To the contrary, it is extremely important."

Suddenly, she felt the hairs on the back of her neck stand on end and she turned around. The office building was empty, just as she thought it was. It was late in the day and everyone had gone home. Her employees often worked from home, or at the beach, wherever creativity struck them.

Her team wanted to be there, and she didn't need to enforce long office hours for them to do their work. The glass walls of the building made it possible for her to see who was in residence at all times, again, not so she could check up on them, but so there was a sense of collaboration.

It also made it easy to see now that she was alone here.

Of course she was. A person couldn't simply walk into this building. Security was tight, and anyone wanting entrance would have to be buzzed in.

But then suddenly she saw a ripple of movement through the outermost layer of glass, motion as a door opened. A dark shape moved through each clear barrier, from room to room, like a shark gliding beneath the surface of clear water. As each door opened, the shape moved closer, revealing itself to be the figure of a man.

Her chest began to get tight. Fear gripped her, her heart beating faster, her palms damp.

"Are you here?" she whispered.

But the line went dead, and she was left standing frozen in her office, her eyes glued to the man steadily making his way deeper and deeper into the office building. The glass, however transparent, was bulletproof, so there was that.

There were so many weirdos in the world that an abundance of caution never went amiss. She had learned about that at a fairly early age. Her father being one of the wealthiest businessmen in California had put her in the public eye very young. The media had always been fascinated with their family; with her brother, who was incredibly successful in his own right; her mother, who was a great beauty. And then, with her for the same reason.

It had always felt so…unearned to her. This great and intense attention for doing nothing at all. It had never sat well with her.

Her father had told her to simply enjoy it. That she was under no obligation to do anything, considering he'd done all the work already.

He'd always been bemused by her desire to get into business, but he'd helped her get started. He'd been humoring her, that much had been clear. But she'd been determined to prove to him that she was smart. That she could make it on her own.

Even now she had the feeling he regarded her billion-dollar empire as a hobby.

The only one of them who had seemingly escaped without massive amounts of attention was her younger sister, Minerva, who Violet had always thought might have been the smartest of them all. Minerva had made herself into the shape of something unremarkable so that she could live life on her own terms.

Violet had taken a different approach, and there were times when the lack of privacy grated and she regretted living the life that she had.

Sometimes she felt an ache for what might have been. She wondered why she had this life. Why she was blessed with money and a certain amount of success instead of being anonymous or impoverished.

Some of that was eased by the charity she ran with her sister, which made it feel like all of it did mean something. That she had been granted this for a reason. And it made the invasions of privacy bearable.

Though not so much now. She felt vulnerable, and far too visible, trapped in a glass bowl of her own making, only able to watch as a predator approached her, and she was unable to do anything but wait.

She tried to call the police, her fingers fumbling on the old-fashioned landline buttons. It wasn't working. She had that landline for security. For privacy. And it was failing her on every level.

Of course she had her cell phone, but it was…

Sitting on the table just outside the office door.

And then suddenly he was *there*. Standing right on the other side of her office door. Tall, broad, clad all in black, wearing a suit that molded to his exquisitely hard-looking body, following every cut line from the breadth of his shoulders to his tapered waist, on down his long muscular legs. He turned around, and how he saw she was thinking of him in those terms she didn't know. Only that he was a force. Like looking at a sheer rock face with no footholds.

Hard and imposing, looming before her.

His face was...

Like a fallen Angel. Beautiful, and a sharp, strange contrast to the rest of him.

There was one imperfection on that face. A slashed scar that ran from the top of his high cheekbone down to the corner of his mouth. A warning.

This man was dangerous.

Lethal.

"Shall we have a chat?"

The barrier of the glass between them made that deep, rich voice echo across the surface of it, and she could feel it reverberating inside of her.

She hated it.

"How did you get in here?"

"My darling, I have a key."

She shrank back. "I'm not your darling."

"True," he said. "You are not. But you are my quarry. And I have found you."

"I'm not very hard to find," she said. She lifted her chin, trying to appear confident. "I'm one of the most famous women in the world."

"So you are. And that has me questioning my brother's sanity. But I am not here to do anything but follow orders."

"If you're here to follow orders, then perhaps you should follow one of mine. Leave."

"I answer to only one man. To only one person. And it is not you."

"A true regret," she said tightly.

"Not for me."

"What do you want?"

"I told you. I am here to collect payment. And that payment is you."

She was beautiful. But he had been prepared for that. When his brother had told him that it was finally time for him to make good on a promise given to him by Robert King ten years ago, Prince Javier de la Cruz had held back a litany of questions for his lord and master. He wondered why his brother wished to collect the debt now. And why he wished to collect it at all, at least in the form of this woman.

She was conspicuous. And she was everything his brother was not. Modern. Painfully so in contrast with the near medieval landscape of Monte Blanco. Yes, the kingdom had come a long way under his brother's rule during the last two years, but there was still a long way to go to bring it out of the Dark Ages their father had preferred. If a woman such as Violet King would be something so foreign to their people, then imagining her his queen was impossible.

But then, on some level, Javier imagined that was his brother's aim. Still, it was not Javier's position to question. Javier was as he had ever been. The greatest weapon Monte Blanco possessed. For years, he had undermined his father, kept the nation from going to war, kept his people safe. Had freed prisoners when they were wrongfully withheld. Had done all that he could to ensure that his father's impact on their people was as minimal as possible. And he had done so all under the oversight of his older brother, who—when he had taken control—had immediately begun to revive the country, using the money that he had earned with his business acumen. The Tycoon King, he was called.

And this—this deal with Robert King—had been one of those bargains he'd struck in secret. Apparently this deal had been made long ago, over drinks in a casino in Monte Carlo. A bet the other man had lost.

Javier was surprised his brother would hold a man to a drunken bargain.

And yet, here he was.

But Matteo was not a thoroughly modern man, whatever moves he was making to reform the country, and this sort of medieval bargain was just the type he knew his brother might favor.

Still…

Looking at her now, Javier could not imagine it.

She was wearing a white suit. A crisp jacket and loose-fitting pants. Her makeup was like a mask in his estimation. Eyelashes that seemed impossibly long, full lips played up by the gloss that she wore on her mouth. A severe sort of contour created in her cheeks by whatever color she had brushed onto them.

Her dark hair was in a low ponytail, sleek and held back away from her face.

She was stunningly beautiful. And very young. The direct opposite of their poor mother, who had been so pale and defeated by the end of her life. And perhaps that was the point.

Still, forcing a woman into marriage was possibly not the best way to go about proving your modernity.

But again. He was not in a position to argue.

What mattered most was his brother's vision for the country, and he would see it done.

He was a blunt instrument. Not a strategist.

Something he was comfortable with. There was an honesty to it. His brother had to feign diplomacy. Had to hide his agenda to make the world comfortable.

Javier had to do no such thing.

"I don't know who you are. And I don't know what you're talking about," she said.

He made his way over to the door, entered in the code and it unlocked.

Her father had given him all that information. Because he knew that there was no other choice.

She backed against her desk, her eyes wide with fear.

"What are you doing?"

"This is growing tiresome. I'm Prince Javier de la Cruz, of Monte Blanco. And you, Violet King, are my brother's chosen bride."

"What?" She did something he did not expect at all. She guffawed. It was the most unladylike sound he had ever heard. "I am *nobody's* chosen bride."

"You are. Your father owes my brother a debt. Apparently, he ran out of capital at a gambling table and was quite…in his cups, so to speak. He offered you. And I have come to collect you."

"My father would not do such a thing. He would not… gamble me away. My brother, on the other hand, might play a prank on me that was this ridiculous. Are there cameras somewhere? Am I on camera?"

"You are not on camera," he said.

She laughed again. "I must be. If this is your attempt to get a viral video or something, you better try again. My father is one of the most modern men that I have ever known. He would never, ever sell one of his daughters into marriage. You know my sister came home from studying abroad with a baby, and he didn't even ask where the baby came from. He just kind of let her bring it into his house. He does not treat his daughters like commodities, and he does not act like he can sell us to the highest bidder."

"Well, then perhaps you need to speak to him."

"I don't need to speak to him, because this is ridiculous."

"If you say so."

And so he closed the distance between them, lifted her up off the ground and threw her over his shoulder. He was running low on time and patience, and he didn't have time to stand around being laughed at by some silly girl. That earned him a yelp and a sharp kick to his chest. Followed by another one, and then another.

Pain was only pain. It did not bother him.

He ignored her.

He ignored her until he had successfully transported her out of the building, which was conveniently empty, and down to the parking lot where his limo was waiting. Only then, when he had her inside with the doors closed and locked, did she actually stare at him with fear. Did she actually look like she might believe him?

"Violet King, I am taking you back to my country. Where you are to be Queen."

CHAPTER TWO

SHE DIDN'T HAVE her phone. She might as well have had her right hand amputated. She had no way to reach anybody. She was an undisputed queen of social media. And here she was, sentenced to silence, told she was going to be Queen of a nation, which was something else entirely.

But this guy was clearly sick in the head, so whatever was happening…

She looked around the limousine. He might be sick in the head, but he also had someone bankrolling his crazy fantasy.

"Is this your limousine?"

He looked around and rolled his shoulders back, settling into the soft leather. "No."

"Who are you working for?"

"I told you. My brother. The King of Monte Blanco."

"I don't even know where that is."

She searched her brain, trying to think if she had ever heard of the place. Geography wasn't her strong suit, but she was fairly well traveled, considering her job required it. Also, she loved it. Loved seeing new places and meeting new people. But Monte Blanco was not on her radar.

"It's not exactly a hot tourist destination," he said.

"Well."

"It's not my brother's limousine either, if you are curious. Neither of us would own something so..." His lip curled. "Ostentatious."

Old money. She was familiar enough with old money and the disdain that came with it. She was new money. And often, the disdain spilled over onto her. She was flashy. And she was obvious. But her fortune was made by selling beauty. By selling flash. Asking women to draw attention to themselves, telling them that it was all right. To dress for themselves. To put makeup on to please themselves, not necessarily to please men.

So yes, of course Violet herself was flashy. And if he had an issue with it, he could go... Well, jump out of the limo and onto the busy San Diego Freeway. She would not mourn him.

"Right. So you're a snob. A snob who's somehow involved in a kidnapping plot?" She supposed, again, he could be an actor. Not someone wealthy at all. Somebody hired to play a prank on her.

Somebody hired to hurt her.

That thought sent a sliver of dread through her body. She wouldn't show it. After all, what good were layers of makeup if you couldn't use them to hide your true face?

"I'm not a snob. I'm a prince."

"Right. Of a country I've never heard of."

"Your American centric viewpoint is hardly my problem, is it, Ms. King? It seems to me that your lack of education does not speak to my authenticity."

"Yes. Well. That is something you would say." The car was still moving, farther and farther away from where they had originated. And she supposed that she had to face the fact that this might not be a joke. That this man really thought she was going to go back to his country with him. If that country existed. Really, she had nothing but his word for it, and considering that he seemed to think that she was going to marry his brother, he might be delusional on multiple levels.

"I want to call my dad."

"You're welcome to," he said, handing her the phone.

She snatched it from him and dialed her father's personal number as quickly as possible. Robert King picked up on the second ring.

"Dad," she said, launching into her proclamation without preamble. "A madman has bundled me up and put me in his limousine, and he's claiming that you made a deal with him some decade ago, and I'm supposed to marry his brother?"

"I didn't make a deal with your dad," Javier said. "My brother did."

"It doesn't matter," she hissed. And then she sat there, waiting for her father to respond. With shock, she assumed. Yes, she assumed that he would respond with shock. Because of course this was insane. And of course it was the first time her father was hearing such a thing. Because there was no way he had anything to do with this. "So anyway, if you could just tell him that he's crazy…"

She realized how stupid it was the minute she said that. Because of course her father telling Javier he was crazy wouldn't likely reinforce it if the act of flinging her into his limousine hadn't done it.

"Violet…" Her father's voice was suddenly rough, completely uncharacteristic of the smooth, confident man that she had always looked up to.

Her father was imperfect. She wasn't blind to that. The fact that he was completely uninvested in her success was obvious to her. When it came to her brother, he was always happy to talk business. But because her business centered around female things, and she herself was a woman, she could never escape the feeling that her father thought it was some kind of hobby. Something insubstantial and less somehow.

But surely he wouldn't… Surely that didn't mean he saw her as currency.

"He's crazy, right?"

"I never thought that he would follow up on this," her father said. "And when you reached your twenties and he didn't… I assumed that there would be no recourse."

"You promised me to a king?"

"It could've been worse. I could have promised you to the used car salesman."

"You can't just promise *someone else* to *someone else*. I'm a person, not a… A cow."

"I'm sorry," he said. "Violet, I honestly didn't think that…"

"I won't stand for it. I will not do it. What's to stop me from jumping out of the car right now—" she looked out the window and saw the scenery flying by at an alarming clip, and she knew that that would keep her from jumping out of the car, but her father didn't need to know that "—and running for freedom?"

"The businesses. They will go to him."

"The businesses?"

"Yours and mine. Remember we sheltered yours under mine for taxes and…"

"Maximus's too?"

Because if he had sheltered her business, surely he had sheltered her brothers as well…

"No," her father said slowly.

"What's the real reason you kept mine underneath your corporation? Was it for this?"

"No. Just that I worried about you. And I thought that perhaps…"

"Because you don't think anything of me. You don't

think that I'm equal to Maximus. If you did, then you wouldn't have done this to me. I can't believe... I can't believe you."

She could keep on arguing with her father, or she could accept the fact that he had sold her as chattel to a stranger. And with that realization, she knew that she needed to simply get off the phone. There was no redeeming this. Nothing at all that would fix it.

She had come face-to-face with how little she meant to her father, how little he thought of her.

She had taken his reaction to Minerva coming home with the baby to mean that he was enlightened, but that wasn't it at all. Minerva was being traditional, even if she hadn't had a husband initially when she had brought the baby home.

Still, he would rather have seen Minerva, in all her quirky glory, with a baby, than see Violet as a serious businesswoman.

There was no talking to him. She stared across the limo at the man who had taken her captive, and she realized...

That he was a saner option than arguing with her father.

She hung up the phone.

"So you are telling the truth."

"I have no investment in lying to you," Javier said. "I also have no investment in this deal as a whole. My brother has asked that I retrieve you, and so I have done it."

"So, you're a Saint Bernard, then?"

A flash of icy amusement shot through his dark eyes, the corner of his mouth curving up in a humorless smile. "You will find that I am not so easily brought to heel, I think."

"And yet here you are," she said. "Doing the bidding of someone else."

"Of my king. For my country. My brother and I have

been the stronghold standing between Monte Blanco and total destruction for over a decade. My father was always a dictator, but his behavior spiraled out of control toward the end of his life. We were the only thing that kept his iron fist from crushing our people. And now we seek to rebuild. Who my brother wants as his choice of bride is his business. And if you'll excuse me… I don't care one bit for your American sensibilities. For your money. For your achievements. I care only that he has asked for you, and so I will bring you to him."

"Good boy," she said.

His movements were like liquid fury. One minute he was sitting across from her in the limousine, and the other he was beside her. He gripped her chin and held her fast, forcing her to look into his eyes. But there was no anger there. It was black, and it was cold. And it was the absence of all feeling that truly terrified her.

She did not think he would hurt her.

There was too much control in his hold. He was not causing her any pain. She could feel the leashed strength at the point where his thumb and forefinger met her chin.

"I am loyal," he said. "But I am not good. The cost of keeping my country going, the cost of my subterfuge has been great. Do not ever make the mistake of thinking that I'm good."

And then he withdrew from her. It was like she had imagined it. Except she shivered with the cold from those eyes, so she knew she hadn't.

"How are you going to make me get on the plane?"

"I will carry you," he said. "Or you could get on with your own two feet. Your father won't harbor you. I assume that he told you as much. So there's no use you running back home, is there?"

She was faced then with a very difficult decision.

Because he was right—she could try to run away. But he would overpower her. And she had a feeling that no one would pay much attention to what would look like a screaming match between two rich people, culminating with her being carried onto a private plane. They were far too adjacent to Hollywood for anybody to consider that out of the ordinary.

And even if she did escape… Her father had verified what he'd said. Her father saw nothing wrong with using her to get out of a bad situation. He had sacrificed not only her, but her livelihood.

"You're not going to hurt me," she said. And she searched those eyes for something. All right, he'd said that he wasn't good. But she had a feeling that he was honest. Otherwise, there would have been no reason for him to tell her he wasn't good, except to hit back at her, and she had a feeling that wasn't it. That wasn't why.

There was more to it than that.

Somehow she knew that if she asked this question, he would answer. Even if the answer was yes, he was going to hurt her. He had no reason to lie to her, that was the thing. She was at his mercy and he knew it.

"No," he said. "I swear to you that no harm will come to you. My brother intends to make you his bride, not his slave. And as far as I go… I'm your protector, Violet, not your enemy. I have been charged with transporting you back to Monte Blanco and if I were to allow any harm to come to you, you can rest assured that my brother would see me rotting in my father's favorite dungeon."

"Your father had a favorite dungeon?"

"More than one, actually."

"Wow."

She didn't know why she felt mollified by his assurance that he wouldn't hurt her. Especially not considering he had just said his father had a favorite dungeon. But he made it clear that he and his brother weren't like their father. So if she could believe that...

It was insane that she believed him. But the thing was, he hadn't lied to her. Not once. Her father had tricked her. Had made her believe that the life she was living was different than the one she actually had. That their relationship was different.

But this man had never lied.

Her world felt turned upside down, and suddenly, her kidnapper seemed about the most trustworthy person.

A sad state of affairs.

The car halted on the tarmac, and there was a plane. It didn't look like a private charter, because it was the size of a commercial jet.

But the royal crest on the side seemed to indicate that it was in fact his jet.

Or his brother's. However that worked.

"This way," he said, getting out of the limousine and holding the door for her.

The driver had gotten out and stood there feebly. "I think he was going to hold the door," she said, looking up at Javier.

Her heart scampered up into her throat as her eyes connected with his again. Looking at him was like getting hit with a force. She had never experienced anything quite like it.

It wasn't simply that he was beautiful—though he was—it was the hardness to him. The overwhelming feeling of rampant masculinity coming at her like a testosterone-fueled train.

Admittedly, she was not exposed to men like him all that often. Not in her line of work.

She actually hadn't been certain that men like him existed.

Well, there was her brother-in-law, Dante, who was a hard man indeed, but still, he looked approachable in comparison to Javier.

This man was like a throwback from a medieval era. The circumstances of her meeting him—the ones where she was being sold into marriage pit debt—certainly contributing to this feeling.

"Too bad for him," Javier shot back. "I don't wait."

And that, she concluded, was her signal to get out of the limo. She decided to take her time. Because he might not wait, but she did not take orders.

And if she was going to retain any kind of power in the situation, she had better do it now. Hoard little pieces of it as best she could, because he wasn't going to give her any. No. So she would not surrender what she might be able to claim.

"Good to know." She made small micromovements, sliding across the seat and then flexing her ankles before her feet made contact with the ground. Then she scooted forward a bit more, put her hands on her knees.

And he stood there, not saying anything.

She stood, and as she did so, he bent down, and her face came within scant inches of his. She forgot to breathe. But she did not forget to move. She pitched herself forward and nearly came into contact with the asphalt. He wrapped his arm around her waist and pulled her back against him. Her shoulder blades came into stark contact with his hard chest. It all lasted only a moment, because he released her and allowed her to stand on her own feet as soon as she was steady. But she could still feel him. The impression of him. Burning her.

"If I walk on my own two feet to the airplane, it is not a kidnapping, is it?"

"I'm certainly not married to the narrative of it being a kidnapping. Call it whatever you need to."

She straightened her shoulders and began to walk toward the plane.

Toward her doom.

Violet didn't know which it was.

But she did know that she was going to have to find her control in this, one way or another.

Even if it were only in the simple act of carrying *herself* aboard the plane.

CHAPTER THREE

JAVIER STUDIED THE woman sitting across from him. Her rage had shrunk slightly and was now emanating off her in small waves rather than whole tsunamis.

She had not accepted a drink, and he had made a show of drinking in front of her, to prove that no one was attempting to poison her, or whatever she seemed to imagine.

He was going to have to have words with Matteo once he arrived in Monte Blanco. "You might want to lower your shields," he said.

"Sure," she said. "Allow me to relax. In front of the man who is holding me against my will."

"Remember, you walked on your own two feet to the airplane, which you felt was the difference between a kidnapping and an impromptu vacation."

"It's a kidnapping," she said. "And I'll have some champagne."

"Now that you've watched me drink a glass and a half and are satisfied that I'm not going to fall down dead?"

"Something like that."

"Why are you in a temper now when you were fine before?"

"This is absurd. I haven't been able to check my social media for hours."

"Is that a problem for you?"

"It's my entire business," she said. "It's built off that. Off connectivity. And viral posts. If I can't make posts, I can't go viral."

"That sounds like something you would want to avoid."

"You're being obtuse. Surely you know what *going viral* means."

"I've heard it," he said. "I can't say that I cared to look too deeply into it. The internet is the least of our concerns in Monte Blanco."

"Well, it's one of my primary concerns, considering it's how I make my living. All fine for you to be able to ignore it, but I can't."

"Also not going to allow you to post from the plane. Anyway. We don't have Wi-Fi up here."

"How do you not have Wi-Fi? Every airplane has that."

"My father didn't have it installed. And my brother has not seen the use for it."

"I find that hard to believe. He's running a country."

"Again. That is not a primary concern in my country. You may find that we have different priorities than you."

"Do you have electricity?" she asked, in what he assumed was mock horror.

"We have electricity."

"Do you live in a moldering castle?"

"It's quite a bit less moldering than when my brother took the throne. But it is a bit medieval, I'm not going to lie."

"Well. All of this is a bit medieval, isn't it?"

"I felt it was quite modern, given you weren't traded for a pair of sheep."

"No. Just my father's gambling debt, extracted from him when he was drunk. What kind of man is your brother that he would do that?"

"I would say honorable. But his primary concern is the

country, and while I don't know what his ultimate plans are for you, or why he wants you specifically, I do know there is a reason. One thing I know about him is that he has his reasons."

"Woof," she said.

In spite of himself, amusement tightened his stomach. And that was the last thing he expected to feel at her insolence. She had no idea who he was. He was a weapon. A human blade.

And she... She taunted him.

He was used to women reacting to him with awe. Sometimes they trembled with fear, but in a way that they seemed to enjoy. He was not blind to the effect he had on women. No indeed. He was a powerful man. A man with a title. A man with wealth.

He commanded a military.

Violet King did not tremble with fear when she looked at him.

He took a champagne glass from the table next to him and poured her a measure of liquid, reaching across the space and handing it to her. She didn't move.

"You'll have to come and get it. Contrary to what you may have heard, I don't fetch or deliver."

She scowled and leaned forward, grabbing hold of the glass and clutching it to her chest as she settled back in her chair.

She looked around the expansive airplane. "Do you think this thing is a little bit big?"

"I've never had any complaints."

Color mounted in her cheeks. "Well. Indeed." She downed half the glass of champagne without taking a breath. "I really do wish there was an internet connection."

"But there isn't. Anyway, we left your phone back in your office."

She looked truly panicked at that. "What if somebody else gets a hold of it? I can't have anybody posting on my social media who wasn't approved."

"Such strange concerns you have. Websites. You know, I've been fighting for the life and health of my people for the last several years. I can't imagine being concerned that somebody might post something on a website in my name."

"Optics," she snapped.

"Optics are no concern of mine. I'm concerned with reality. That which you can touch and see. Smell. Feel. That is my concern. Reality."

"It's no less real. It changes people's lives. It affects them profoundly. I built an entire business off of influence."

"You make a product. I did a cursory amount of research on you, Violet. You don't simply post air."

"No. But for want of that air my products wouldn't sell. It's what exposes me to all those people. It's what makes me relevant."

"I should hope that more than a piece of code floating out in cyberspace would make you relevant."

Her lips twitched and she took another sip of champagne. "I'm not going to argue about this with a man who thinks it's perfectly reasonable to bundle me up and take me back to his country."

"I didn't say it was reasonable," he said. "Only that it was going to be done."

After that, they didn't speak.

Upon arrival in Monte Blanco, Javier parted with Violet and made a straight path for his brother's office.

"I've returned," he said.

"Good," Matteo said, barely looking up from his desk. "I assume you have brought the woman with you?"

"Yes. As promised."

"I knew I could count on you. Did she come quietly?"

He thought of the constant barbs that he had been subjected to on the trip.

"No. She is *never* quiet."

Matteo grimaced. "That could be a problem."

"Your Highness."

Javier turned around at the sound of the breathy voice. Matteo's assistant, Livia, had come into the room. She was a small, drab creature, and he had no idea why his brother kept her on. But Matteo was ridiculously attached to her.

"Yes," Matteo said, his voice gentling slightly.

"It's only that the United Council chief called, and he is requesting the presence of Monte Blanco at a meeting. It's about your inclusion."

This was something his brother had been waiting for. His father had stayed out of international affairs, but it was important to both Matteo and Javier that Monte Blanco have a voice in worldwide matters.

"Then I shall call him."

"I don't know that that will be necessary. He only wishes to know if you will accept his invitation to come to the summit this week."

"Well, I'm a bit busy," Matteo said, gesturing toward Javier.

"Oh?" she asked.

"Yes," he responded. "Javier has brought my bride to me."

Livia's eyes widened, but only for a moment. "Of course." That slight widening was the only emotional reaction given by the assistant. But Javier knew how to read people, and he could see that she was disturbed.

He could also see that his brother did not notice. "It is of no consequence," he said. "We must attend. Javier, you will make sure that Violet acclimates while I'm gone."

"Of course," he said. What he did not say was that he was not a trained babysitter for spoiled socialites, but a soldier. Still, he thought it.

"See that my things are collected immediately," Matteo said, addressing Livia. "All the details handled."

He spoke in such incomplete sentences to the woman, and yet she scurried to do his bidding, asking for no clarification at all.

"Don't you think this is a bit outlandish, even for you?"

"My mouse will have no trouble taking care of things," he said, using his nickname for Livia.

"Yes. I forgot. She is your mouse, living only to do as you ask. Though your appalling treatment of your assistant was not actually what I was referring to. That you had me drag this woman across the world, and you will not be in residence."

"It's perfect," he said. "A more traditional sort of relationship, yes? Hearkening back to the days of old. We won't meet until the wedding."

"You forget, she's an American. A thoroughly modern one."

"*You* forget: she has no choice."

"Why exactly do you want Violet King? That's something that I don't understand."

"Because we need to modernize. Because we need to change the way that the world perceives Monte Blanco."

"I was told by your fiancée that the world does not perceive it at all."

"A blessing," Matteo said. "Because if the world did have a perception of us before now, it would not be a good one."

"And you want to change that." He thought of everything Violet had said to him regarding the internet. "Why don't you have Wi-Fi on your plane?"

Matteo blinked. "What does that have to do with anything?"

"Violet seemed to find it odd that you didn't. I told her you weren't concerned with such things. But it appears that you are."

"Well, I've never needed it in the air."

"Your future bride would want it. Otherwise I think she will find traveling with you onerous."

"I didn't realize you would be so concerned for her comfort."

"Well, you put her comfort in my charge."

"And I leave it to you now." Matteo stood from behind the desk. "I understand that it's not ideal, but I know that you'll also trust me when I tell you this is necessary."

"I know," Javier said. "You never do anything that isn't."

"I'm not our father," Matteo said, and not for the first time Javier wondered if he was telling him or telling himself.

He was well familiar with that internal refrain. He knew his brother walked a hard road, but a different one than Javier did.

Javier had been part of his father's army.

Under Javier's oversight, missions had been carried out that had caused harm. He had believed, fully and completely, that he was in the right.

Until one day he'd seen the truth. Seen what love and loyalty had blinded him to.

And he had learned.

That a man could be a villain and not even know.

That with the right lie, a man could commit endless atrocities and call it justice.

"I know," Javier repeated. "You have spent all these past years defying him. I hardly thought that a little bit of power was going to corrupt you entirely."

"But I must be on guard against it. I understand that you may think it medieval for me to force the girl into marriage..."

Javier shrugged. "I have no thoughts on it one way or the other." And it was true. He knew that Violet was unhappy with the situation, but her happiness was not his concern.

Swaths of unhappiness had been cut through his country for decades, and he and his brother were working as hard as they could to undo it. If Matteo thought that making Violet his queen would help with the situation, then it was collateral damage Javier was willing to accept.

"You say that," Matteo said. "But I have a feeling that you always have thoughts."

"Are they relevant, My King?"

"I told you, I am not our father. But for the fact that I'm a few years older than you, you would be King. Or, if I were dead."

"Stay alive," Javier said. "I have no desire to bear the burden of the crown."

"And yet, the burden is heavy enough that I daresay you can feel the weight of it. It is not like you are immune to the responsibilities we face."

"What is the point of sharing blood with our father if we don't do everything, to the point of spilling it, to correct his wrongs?"

"No point at all," Matteo said, nodding. "I must go check on my mouse's progress."

"You call her that to her face?"

"Yes. She finds it endearing."

He thought back to the stricken look on Livia's face when Matteo had mentioned his fiancée. But Javier also thought of the slight note of warmth in his brother's voice when he said it. *Mouse.* He didn't say it as if she were small or gray, though in Javier's opinion she was both. No, he said it as if she were fragile. His to care for.

"She may."

"No. It is because of how I found her. Shivering and gray, and far too small. Like a mouse."

Javier was not certain that Livia liked to be reminded of her origins. However much Matteo might find his name for her affectionate. He meant what he had said to Violet. Javier was not a good man. Matteo might be, but for the two of them it was more honor than it was anything quite so human as goodness.

In fact, the only real evidence Javier had ever seen of softness in his brother was the presence of Livia in the palace. He didn't know the full story of how he had come into... Possession of her, only that he had found her in quite an unfortunate situation and for some reason had decided it was his responsibility to fix that situation.

"You will keep things running while I'm gone," Matteo said, a command and not a question.

"Of course I will."

"And I will endeavor to make sure these meetings go well. You remember what I told you."

"Of course. If ever you were to exhibit characteristics of our father, it would be better that you were dead."

"I meant that."

"And I would kill you myself."

His brother smiled and walked forward clasping his forearm, and Javier clasped his in return. "And that is why I trust you. Because I believe you would."

They were blood brothers. Bonded by blood they hated. The blood of their father. But their bond was unshakable and had always been. Because they had known early on that if they were ever going to overcome the evil of their line, they would have to transcend it.

And they could only do that together.

Their relationship was the most important thing in Javier's life. Because it was the moral ballast for them both. Because Javier knew how easy it was to upset morality. How emotion could cloud it.

How it could cause pain.

Whether he understood Matteo's being so intent to marry Violet or not, he would support it. All that mattered was Monte Blanco. Violet's feelings were a nonissue.

All that mattered was the kingdom.

CHAPTER FOUR

VIOLET HAD BEEN essentially born into money. So she was used to grandeur. She was used to the glittering opulence of sparkling shows of wealth. But the palace and Monte Blanco were something else entirely.

It wasn't that the walls were gilded—they were entirely made of gold. The floor, obsidian inlaid with precious metals, rubies and emeralds. The doorframes were gold, shot through with panels of diamond.

Given what Javier had said about the limo, she was somewhat surprised to see such a glaring display of wealth, but then she imagined the palace had been standing for centuries. She could feel it. As if it were built down into the mountain.

And it was indeed on a mountain. Made of white granite, likely the namesake of the country.

It reminded her of Javier himself. Imposing, commanding, and entirely made of rock. The view down below was... Spectacular.

A carpet of deep, dense pines swooping down before climbing back upward to yet more mountains. She could barely make out what she thought might be a city buried somewhere in there, but if it was, it was very small. The mountains loomed large, fading to blue and purple the farther away they were. Until they nearly turned to mist against the sky. A completely different color than she had ever seen before. As if it were more ice than sky.

She had not thought it would be cold, given that she didn't think of cold when she thought of this region, but nestled as it was between France and Spain at such a high elevation, it was shockingly frigid and much more rugged than she had thought.

Queen of the wilderness. He had brought her out here to be Queen of the wilderness.

The thought made her shiver.

Then she turned away from the view and back toward the bedroom she had been installed in by a helpful member of staff, and she couldn't think of wilderness at all. It was ornate to the point of ridiculousness.

The bed was made of gold. The canopy was comprised of layers of fabric, a glittering and a gauzy layer, with heavy brocade beneath. The covers were velvet, rich purple and gold.

It made the clean, modern lines of her all-white apartment stark in her memory.

She wasn't going to waste time pondering the room, though. What she needed to do was figure out how to talk the King out of this ridiculous idea that they needed to get married. First, she needed to figure out what his motives were. Obviously if he were crazed by lust where she was concerned, there wasn't much she could offer him. At least, nothing much that she was willing to offer.

Violet knew that no one would believe it if she told them, but she had no physical experience with men. She had never been carried away on a tide of passion, and she fully intended to be carried away on a tide of passion when she allowed a man to... Do any of that.

The problem was, she had met so many kinds of men in her life. Hazard of being well connected and well traveled. She had met rich men. Talented men. Actors, chefs, rock stars. CEOs.

Javier is the first prince you ever met...

Well. That didn't matter. The point was, she'd been exposed to a variety of powerful men early on, and inevitably she found them to be... Disappointments.

They either revealed themselves to be arrogant jerks with overinflated opinions of themselves, secret perverts who had only been pretending to listen to her while they contemplated making a move on her, or aggressive nightmares with more hands than a centipede and less sense.

And she had just always thought there could be more than that. More than shrugging and giving in to a wet kiss that she hadn't wanted anyway.

The richer she had become, the more men had seemed to find her a challenge. Whether she was actually issuing one or not.

And that had made her even more disenchanted with them.

And she hadn't held out for passion for all this time to just...

To just be taken by some king that she didn't even know.

She could Google him if she had any devices. But there was no damned internet in this place.

The first active business would be to find out what he wanted. Because she had a lot. She was a billionaire, after all. And, she was well connected. He could break off a chunk of this castle, and it would probably equal her net worth, so there was that. But there had to be something. There had to be. Otherwise, it wouldn't matter if it was her.

Which brought her back to sexually obsessed. Which really creeped her out.

There was a knock on the chamber door, and she jumped. "Come in."

She expected it to be the same woman who had led her to her room, but it wasn't. It was Javier. And when he came in he brought with him all of the tension that she'd felt in her chest the entire time they were together on the plane ride over.

"I wasn't expecting you," she said.

"What were you expecting exactly?"

She realized there was no point in being difficult. Because Javier might be the key to this. "Where is your brother?"

"Eager to see him?"

"No," she said, and she found that was honest. Better the devil she knew, after all. Even if said devil was as unyielding as a rock face. "Did he tell you why he wants to marry me?"

She needed to know. Because she needed to formulate a plan. She needed to get some power back. Or, rather than getting it back, needed to get some of it in the first place.

"Yes," Javier said.

He just stood there. Broad, tall and imposing.

"Would you care to share with the class?"

"I don't think it matters."

"You don't get that it matters to me why this stranger wants to marry me? I would like to know if it has to do with him harboring some sort of obsession for my body."

That made him laugh. And it offended her. "No. My brother has no designs on your body. He thinks that you will be useful in improving the world's view of Monte Blanco. It is in fact his sole focus. Which is what I came to tell you. He is not here."

"He's not here?"

"No. He has gone to the United Council summit. It is very important to him that Monte Blanco be granted inclusion into the Council. For too long, we have been without the benefit of allies. For too long, we have not had a say in how the world works. And it is something my brother feels is key to bringing us into the twenty-first century."

"So he wants my... Influencer reach?"

That was ridiculous. But she could work with that. "He wants me to make the country look better."

"Yes," Javier said.

"Well. That's easy. I can do that without marrying him."

"I'm not sure that's on his agenda."

"Well, then I'll just have to convince him that it's a better agenda. I'm very convincing. I entered a very crowded market, and I managed to essentially dominate it. You know that I'm the youngest self-made billionaire in the world?"

"Yes," Javier said. "We did in fact look at the basic headlines about you."

"Then he should know that I'll be of much more use to him as a business consultant."

"You sell makeup," he said.

She bristled. "Yes. And I sell it well. Enough that he seems to have taken notice of the impact that I've made on the world. So don't belittle it." She huffed a breath. "Anyway. All I need is a chance to get to know the country."

"Excellent. I'm glad that you think so. Because I believe that my brother's mouse is making an agenda for while they are away."

"His what?"

"His assistant. We have assignments for while he is away. And I am to oversee."

"Are you *babysitting* me?"

"In a sense."

"You know," she said, keeping her voice carefully deadpan. "I seem to recall a Saint Bernard that acted as Nana in a classic cartoon..."

"Don't push it. I can always tell him you met with an unfortunate accident."

"You said you wouldn't hurt me," she said, meeting his gaze, keeping her eyes as stern as possible.

He inclined his head. "So I did."

"Are you a man of your word, Javier?"

"I am."

The simple confidence in those words made her stomach tighten. "Somehow I knew that."

His eyes narrowed. "How?"

She shrugged. "I don't know. I'm a good judge of character, I think. I was born into wealth, and I will tell you that it's an easier life than most. But I had access to… Anything. Any excess that I wanted. Any sort of mischief that I might want to get into. Drugs and older men and parties. People were always after me to do favors for them. And I had to learn very quickly who my real friends might be. Because let me tell you… What people say and what they do are two very different things. Words don't mean anything if they're not backed up by actions."

"Well, I've kidnapped you. What does that action tell you?"

"I didn't think we were going with *kidnap*?"

"That was your call, not mine."

"Well, you're loyal to your brother. I also think you're loyal to… Your own sense of honor. You might say that you aren't good. But you have a moral code. And even if it does extend to allowing you to kidnap me if your brother says it's the right thing to do, I do not think it would ever extend to hurting someone who couldn't defend themselves against you."

He inclined his head. "Fair enough. My father enjoyed inflicting pain upon the weak. He enjoyed exploiting his power. I have no desire to ever involve myself in such a thing. It is an act of cowardice."

"And you're not a coward," she said confidently. "And I think that you might even want to help me prove to your brother that I don't need to marry him so that I can get back to my real life."

"That's where you're wrong. I genuinely don't care about your plan. Not one way or the other. Happiness, in that fleeting immediate sense, is quite immaterial to me. What matters is the greater good. If my brother feels the greater good is served by marrying you, then that is the goal I will help him accomplish. Not what will make you... Happier. As you said, you had a happier life than most. Drugs, parties and rich men, from the sounds of things."

"But I had none of those things," she said, not sure where she had lost the conversation. "It's just that I had access to them. I haven't experienced them. I have too much to live for. Too much experience to explore."

"It seems to me that you had ample opportunity to do so prior to your engagement to my brother."

"I am not engaged. I am *kidnapped*, as you just stated."

"Walked onto the plane with your own two feet, I think you mean."

"You were the one that introduced *kidnap* again."

"You're the one who seems hung up on the terminology."

"I'll prove it. I'll prove that we don't need marriage."

"Fantastic. Feel free. In the meantime, I will set about to fulfill the items on my brother's list. Because that is all I care about."

He turned and began to walk away from her. "Do you have any feelings about anything?"

When he turned back to face her, his eyes were blank. "No."

"You must be a great time in bed," she shot back, not

sure where that came from. Except she knew it made men angry when you called their prowess into question, and if she couldn't elicit sympathy from him, then she would be happy to elicit some rage.

"Thankfully for you," he said, his tone hard, "my bedroom skills will never be a concern of yours. You are not meant for me."

And then he was gone. Leaving her in the oppressive silence created by those thick, wealth-laden walls.

And she had a feeling that for the first time in her life she might have bitten off more than she could chew.

Except, it wasn't even her bite. It was her father's. And she was the one left dealing with it.

CHAPTER FIVE

HER WORDS ECHOED in his head all through the next day, and when he finally received the memo from his brother's assistant, his irritation was at an all-time high. Because what Violet King thought about him in bed was none of his concern. She had an acerbic tongue, and she was irritating. Beautiful, certainly, but annoying.

Had he been the sort of man given to marriage, she would not be the woman that he would choose. But then, marriage would never have to be for him. He didn't have to produce heirs.

He charged down the hall, making his way to her room, where he knocked sharply.

"Don't come in!"

"Why not?"

"I'm not decent."

"Are you undressed?" The image of Violet in some state of undress caused his stomach to tighten, and he cursed himself for acting like an untried boy. She was just a woman.

"No," she said.

He opened the door without waiting for further explanation. And there she sat, at the center of the massive bed looking...

Scrubbed clean.

She looked younger than when he had first seen her yesterday, than she did in any picture he had ever seen.

Her lashes were not so noticeable now, shorter, he thought. Her face looked rounder, her skin softer. Her lips were no longer shiny, but plump and soft looking. Her dark hair fell around her shoulders in riotous waves.

"I don't have my makeup," she said.

He couldn't help it. He laughed. He couldn't remember the last time he had felt actual humor. Until now. The woman was concerned because she did not have her makeup.

"And that concerns me why?"

"It's my… It's my trade. I don't go out without it. It would be a bad advertisement."

"Surely you don't think you need all of that layered onto your face to make you presentable?"

"That's not the point. It's not about being presentable, or whatever. It's just… It's not who I am."

"Your makeup is who you are?"

"I built my empire on it. On my look."

"Well. No one is here to see your look. And we have assignments."

"Assignments?"

"Yes. First, time to give you a tour of the palace. Then we are to discuss your… Appearance."

She waved a hand in front of her face. "I have been discussing my appearance this entire time."

"Well. I don't mean that, precisely. Your role as Queen will require a different sort of… A different sort of approach."

"I'm sorry. I've made it very clear that I'm not on board with this whole Queen thing, and you're talking about how you're going to change my appearance?"

"I'm only telling you what's on the list. We also need to go over customs, expectations. Ballroom etiquette."

"Don't tell me that I'm going to have to take dancing lessons."

"Precisely that."

"This is… *Medieval*."

"Tell me what it is you need from home, and I will accommodate you." Looking at the stubborn set of her face, he realized that he could drag her kicking and screaming into completing these tasks, or he could try to meet her in the middle. Compromise was not exactly second nature to him, but sometimes different tactics were required for dealing with different enemies.

He and his brother had been covert by necessity when dealing with their father. He could certainly manage a bit of finesse with one small makeup mogul.

"I… Well, I need all my beauty supplies. I might be able to come up with a queen-level look using my makeup, but nobody's doing it but me."

"We'll see."

"I can't wear someone else's products." She was verging on melodrama and he would not indulge it in the least if it weren't for his brother.

That was all.

"My concern is not centered on your business. And anyway, yours shouldn't be at this point either."

"Untrue. My primary concern is my business, because I think it's what I have to offer here."

"Why don't we discuss this over breakfast."

"I told you. I can't go out looking like this."

He pushed a button on the intercom by the door. Moments later the door opened, and in came breakfast for two.

"Oh," Violet said.

"You keep introducing issues that are not issues for me."

She looked deflated. "Fine. I don't actually care about my makeup."

"Then why exactly are you protesting?"

"Because. I want to win. And I figured if you thought I was this ridiculous and unable to function without a full face of makeup, you might send me back."

"Again. Whether or not you become the next Queen of Monte Blanco is not my decision. So you can go ahead and try to make me believe that you are the silliest creature on planet Earth, but it still won't change what's happening."

He moved the cart closer to her bed. She peered down at the contents. "Is that avocado toast?"

"It is," he said. "Of course, I'm told that it's quite trendy the world over. It has always been eaten here."

"Fascinating," she said. "I didn't realize that you were trendsetters."

He picked up his own plate of breakfast and sat in the chair next to her bed. Then he poured two cups of coffee. Her interest became yet more keen.

"I'm not going to poison you," he said. "You keep staring at me as if I might."

She scrabbled to the edge of the bed and reached down, grabbing hold of the plate of avocado toast, bringing it onto the comforter.

Her eyes met his and held. A shift started, somewhere deep in his gut. She didn't move. Or maybe it only felt like she didn't. Like the moment hung suspended.

Then her fingers brushed his as she took the cup, color mounting in her face as she settled back in the bed, away from him.

The distance, he found, helped with the tightening in his stomach.

She took a sip and smiled. "Perfect," she said. "Strong."

"Did you sleep well?"

"I slept about as well as a prisoner in a foreign land can expect to sleep."

"Good to know."

"The pea under the mattress was a bit uncomfortable." A smile tugged the edge of her lips.

She was a strange sort of being, this woman. She had spirit, because God knew in this situation, many other people would have fallen apart completely. But she hadn't. She was attempting to needle him. To manipulate him. From calling him a Saint Bernard to pretending she was devastated by her bare face.

And now she was drinking coffee like a perfectly contented cat.

"Why don't you go ahead and say what's on your mind. I can tell you're dying to."

"I will complete your list," she said. "Down to the dancing lessons. But I want you to show me around the country. Not just the palace."

"To what end?"

"I've been thinking. Your brother wants to bring this country into the modern era. Well. I am the poster child for success in the modern era. And I believe that I can bring some of that to you. I can do it without marrying your brother."

"As far as I'm concerned it's not up for negotiation."

"Fine. We'll table that. But I want you to give me the tools to make it a negotiation with him."

"Perhaps," he said, taking a long drag of his own coffee.

"Look. Even if I do marry your brother, you're going to want me to do this."

"He didn't leave orders to do it. I have no personal feelings on the matter."

"If you get your way, I'm going to live here for the rest of my life," she said, her voice finally overtaken by emotion. "You don't even want me to see the place? Don't you think that I should be able to... Envision what my life will be?"

This was not a business negotiation. Finally. She wasn't playing at being sharp and witty, or shallow and vapid. Not holding a board meeting curled up in her canopy bed. This, finally, was something real.

And he was not immune to it, he found.

"I'll see what I can accomplish."

She picked up her toast and took a bite of it with ferocity. "Well. At least I approve of your food." She set the toast back down on the plate and brushed some crumbs away from her lips.

She managed to look imperious and ridiculous all at once.

He could not imagine his brother wrangling this creature. She was as mercurial as she was mystifying, and Javier had never been in a position where he had to deal with a woman on this level.

When it came to his personal relationships with women, they weren't all that personal. They were physical. Suddenly, he was in an entanglement with a beautiful woman that was all... All too much to do with her feelings.

"Finish your toast," he said briskly. "I will send a member of staff to escort you downstairs in roughly an hour. And then, it is time we begin your training."

Violet muttered to herself as she made her way down the vast corridor and toward the ballroom. "Begin your training... Wax on. Wax off."

This was ludicrous. And she was beginning to get severely anxious. She had been in Monte Blanco for more than twelve hours. She had not seen the mysterious King—who had vanished off on some errand, if Javier was to be believed—and she didn't seem to be making any headway when it came to talking herself out of her engagement.

But she was the one who had decided she was better off trying to take the bull by the horns, rather than running and hiding in California. She supposed she had to own the consequences of that rash decision, made in anger.

The castle was vast, and even though she had received rather explicit instructions on how to get to the ballroom, she was a bit concerned that she might just end up lost forever in these winding, glittering halls. Like being at the center of a troll's mountain horde. All gems and glitter and danger.

And as she walked into the vast ballroom and saw Javier standing there at the center, she felt certain she was staring at the Mountain King. She knew he wasn't the King. Javier was acting on his brother's behest; he had said so many times. Except it was impossible for her to imagine that this man took orders from anyone.

It took her a moment to realize there was someone else in the room. A small round woman with an asymmetrical blond haircut and a dress comprised of layers of chiffon draped over her body like petals.

"The future Queen is here," she said excitedly. "We can begin. My name is Sophie. I will be instructing you in basic Monte Blancan ballroom dance techniques."

"They could be anyone's ballroom dance techniques," Violet said. "They would still be completely new to me."

"You say that like it should frighten me," Sophie said. "It doesn't. Especially not with the Prince acting as your partner."

Violet froze. "He dances?" She pointed at him.

"I have been part of the royal family all of my life," he said. "That necessitated learning various customs. Including, of course, ballroom dancing. There is nothing that you will be subjected to over the course of this training that I was not. And a great many things you will be spared."

There was a darkness to that statement that made a tremor resonate inside of her. But before she could respond to it, he had reached his hand out and taken hold of hers, drawing her up against the hardness of his chest.

He was hot.

And her heart stuttered.

And she felt…

She felt the beginnings of something she had read about. Heard about… But never, ever experienced before.

When he looked down at her, for a moment at least, it wasn't nice what she saw there in his dark eyes. No. It was something else entirely.

She looked down at the floor.

"I will start the music. Javier is a very good dancer, and he will make it easy by providing a solid lead."

He was solid all right. And hot. Like a human furnace.

His hand down low on her back was firm, and the one that grasped hers was surprisingly rough. She would have thought that a prince wouldn't have calluses. But he did.

She wondered what sort of physical work he did. Or if it was from grueling workouts. He certainly had the body of somebody who liked to exact punishment on himself in the gym.

Music began to play in the room, an exacting instrumental piece with clear timing. And then she was moving.

Sophie gave instructions, but Violet felt as if her feet were flying, as if she had no control over the movements herself at all. It felt like magic. And she would have said she had no desire to dance like this, in an empty ballroom in a palace that she was being held in, by the man who was essentially her captor, but it was exhilarating.

She hadn't lied to him when she said she had been given

the opportunity to indulge in a great many things in life. She had turned away from most of them. They just hadn't appealed.

But this…

Was this the evidence of being so spoiled that it took some sort of bizarre, singular experience to make her feel? No. She didn't think that was it.

She looked up slightly and could see his mouth. There was something so enticing about the curve of it. Something fascinating about it. She spent a lot of time looking at people's features. Using the natural planes and angles, dips and curves on people's faces to think about ways that makeup might enhance them.

But she had never been entranced by a mouth in quite the way she was now.

She licked her own lips in response to the feeling created inside her when she looked up at him. And she felt him tense. The lines in his body going taut. And when she found the courage inside of herself to look all the way up to his eyes, the ice was completely burned away. And only fire remained.

But she didn't feel threatened. And it wasn't fear that tightened her insides. Wasn't fear that made her feel like she might be burned, scorched from the inside out.

She took a breath and hoped that somehow the quick, decisive movement might cover up the intensity of her reaction to him. But the breath got hung up on a catch in her throat, and her chest locked, as she leaned forward. Her breasts brushed against the hardness of his chest and she felt like she was melting.

She swayed, and he seemed to think she was unsteady, because he locked his arm around her waist and braced her against his body. She felt weightless.

And she had the strangest sense of security. Of protection. She shouldn't. This man was her enemy. After the way he had dismissed her suggestions for finding ways of not being forced into marriage, he was her sworn enemy.

But in his arms she was certain that he would never hurt her. And when she looked up into those eyes, she could easily see an image of him in her mind, holding a sword aloft and pressing her against his body, threatening anyone who might try to claim her. Anyone who might try to take her from him.

She was insane.

She had lost her mind.

She never reacted to men like this. Much less men who were just holding her in captivity until they could marry her off to their brothers.

But looking up into his eyes now, looking at that sculpted, handsome face, made it impossible for her to think of that. It made it impossible for her to think of anything. How isolated she was here. How her friends weren't here, her family wasn't here. She didn't even have her phone. She hadn't thought about her phone from the moment she had woken up this morning.

She had gotten up, scrubbed the makeup off her face, discarded her fake eyelashes and seized on the idea to play a ridiculous damsel in distress. Over eyeliner. And see where that got her. She hadn't been able to stomach it. Because it was too ridiculous.

He might have believed it, but she found that her pride had to come into play somewhere.

So that had been her first waking thought. And then he had appeared.

There had been toast.

He had been handsome.

Now he was touching her.

And somewhere in there logic was turned upside down, twisted, then torn in half.

Because somehow she felt more connected, more present with this man, here in isolation, than she could remember feeling at home for a very long time.

But he's not why you're here.

The thought sent such a cold sliver of dread through her, and it acted like a bucket of icy water dropped over her head.

She was being ridiculous however you sliced it. But feeling... Physical responses to him were ludicrous. Not just because he had brought her here against her will, but because he wasn't even the reason she had been brought here.

It was his brother. His brother who she hadn't even met. She hadn't even googled anything about him, because she didn't have the means to do it.

She extricated herself from Javier's hold, her heart thundering rapidly. "I think I got the hang of it," she said.

"You are doing okay," Sophie said. "I wouldn't call it masterful."

"Well, I'm jet-lagged," Violet said. "Or did you not hear that I was forced onto a plane yesterday afternoon and flown from San Diego."

Sophie looked from Violet to Javier. "I admit I didn't know the whole story."

"Forced," Violet said. "I am being forced to marry King Whatever-his-name-is."

"King Matteo," Javier said.

"Are you?" Sophie's face turned sharp.

"She's fine," Javier said. "Cold feet."

"Oh yes, prewedding jitters are a real issue for kidnapped brides."

"You're clearly terrified for your life," Javier said dryly.

"You definitely treat me like I might kill you via lack of Wi-Fi at any moment."

"I'm in withdrawal."

"Leave us," Javier said to Sophie.

"Should I?" Sophie asked Violet.

"I'm not afraid of him," Violet said, tilting her chin upward.

Sophie inclined her head and left the room, doing what Javier told her. "You have my employees questioning me."

"Good. Maybe we'll start a revolution."

"I would advise against that."

"If you hear the people sing, you might want to make a run for it. And make sure you don't have any guillotines lying around."

"If revolution were that simple, I would have engaged in one a long time ago."

"The history books make it look simple enough."

"And full of casualties. My brother and I did our best to work behind the scenes to keep this country from falling apart. We prevented civil war."

"Good for you," Violet said, but she felt somewhat shamefaced now for making light of something that was apparently a very real issue here. And she shouldn't feel guilty, because she was being held here against her will. There was no place for her to be feeling guilty. He should feel guilty. But of course he wouldn't.

"I have work to do," he said.

"I thought you were going to take me into the city," she called after him.

"I have no desire to spend any more time with a spoiled brat."

"Oh, how awful of me. Do I have a bad attitude about being your prisoner?"

"This is bigger than you. Can't you understand that?"

He really thought that she should be able to take that on board. That she should just be willing to throw her life away because he was convinced that his brother thought she would be the best Queen for the country.

The longer she stood there staring at him, the longer she felt the burn of his conviction going through her skin, the more she realized they might as well be from different planets.

It wasn't a language barrier. It was... An *everything* barrier.

He had sacrificed all his life for the greater good. He could not understand why it didn't make sense to her. Why it wasn't the easiest thing in the world to abandon her expectations about her life and simply throw herself on the pyre of the good of many.

"Javier," she said.

His expression became haughty. "You know people don't simply address me by my first name."

"What do they call you?"

"His Royal Highness, Prince Javier of Monte Blanco."

"That's a mouthful. I'm going to stick with Javier."

"Did I give you permission?"

Tension rolled between them, but it was an irritation. She had a terrible feeling she knew what it was. That maybe he had felt the same thing she had when they had been close earlier.

She chose to ignore it.

She chose to poke at him.

"No. But then, did you ask me if I cared to get it?"

"What is it you want, Violet?"

Her throat went dry, and she almost lost her nerve to ask him what she had intended to.

"Do you do anything for yourself?" She decided that since she was already acting against what would be most people's better judgment, she might as well go ahead and keep doing it.

"No," he said. Then a smile curved the edges of his lips. "One thing. But I keep it separate. In general, no. Because that kind of selfishness leads to the sort of disaster my brother and I just saved our nation from."

"But you know that's not the way the rest of the world works."

"The rest of the world is not responsible for the fates of millions of people. I am. My brother is."

"We just don't expect that, growing up in Southern California."

"That isn't true. Because you're here."

"Because of my business," she said.

"And your father," he said. "Because whatever you think, you feel an obligation toward something other than yourself. Toward your father. Your family. You know what it is to live for those that you love more than you love your own self. Magnify that. That is having a country to protect."

Then he turned and left her standing there, and she found that she had been holding her breath. She hadn't even been aware of that.

She looked around the room. She was now left to her own devices. And that meant... That she would be able to find a computer. She was sure of that. And once she had the internet at her disposal, she would be able to figure out some things that she needed to know.

It occurred to her that she could contact home. If her brother had any idea what had happened to her...

She could also contact the media.

But something had her pushing that thought out of her mind. If she needed to. If she needed to, she could make an international incident. But for some reason she believed everything that Javier told her. And since she did, she truly believed that things in their country had been dire, and that he and his brother were working to make them better.

She didn't want to undo that.

So she supposed he was right. She did have some sense of broader responsibility.

But that was why she needed a better idea of what she was dealing with. Of who she was dealing with. And that meant she was going exploring.

CHAPTER SIX

JAVIER IMMEDIATELY WENT to the gym. He needed to punish his body. Needed to destroy the fire that had ignited in his veins when he had touched Violet King. It was an aberration. He knew he had to turn his desires on and off like a switch.

In his life, it had been a necessity. Sometimes he had to go months without the touch of a woman, when he and Matteo were deep in trying to redirect one of his father's plans from behind the scenes, or when they were actively harboring refugees, helping wrongly convicted citizens escape from prison... Well, sometimes there was no time for sex. When he wanted a woman, he went and found one.

Weekends in Monaco. Paris. Women who had appetites that matched his own. Voracious. Experience to match the darkness that lived inside of him.

And never, ever a woman who was meant for his brother.

He had far too much self-control for this.

Perhaps the issue was he had been too long without a woman.

It had been several months while he and Matteo worked to right the balance of Monte Blanco. And though he did not think they had been entirely celibate—either of them—since his brother had taken the throne, it had left little time for them to pursue personal pleasure.

Javier was feeling it now.

He growled and did another pull-up before dropping down to the floor, his breath coming hard and fast.

And he could still feel the impression of her softness in his arms. He had been in the gym for hours now, and it had not dissipated.

He would find a woman. He would have one flown in.

At this point, he felt deeply uncomfortable finding his pleasure with women in his own country. The power imbalance was too great.

And he was wary of being like his father.

So you're more comfortable lusting after the woman you're holding captive?

No, he was not comfortable with it. It was why he was here.

Because she was in his care, if one could say that of a captive. And he could so easily... Crush her.

He had harmed people before in the service of his father. A blot on his soul he would never scrub out.

"Oh."

He whirled around and he saw the object of his torment standing there, her mouth dropped open, her eyes wide.

"What the hell are you doing in here?"

"I asked around. They said that you might be in the gym. And I had found a computer, so I found an internal schematic for the palace and... Anyway. I found my way down here."

"A computer?"

"Yes," she said. "You see, conveniently, your staff doesn't know that I'm a prisoner. They all think that I'm here of my own accord. So of course there is nothing wrong setting me up with a computer that has internet. Really. You need to watch me more closely."

He crossed his arms over his bare chest. "I hear no helicopters. So I assume you did not call in the cavalry?"

"No. I figured I would wait for that."

Her eyes skittered down from his face, landed on his chest and held. Color mounted in her face.

He gritted his teeth. It was a dangerous game she was playing. Whether she knew it or not.

"If you have something to say," he said, his temper coming to an end point, "say it. I'm busy."

"I can see that," she said. "Do you suppose you could find a… You don't have a shirt on hand, do you?"

He didn't particularly care if she was uncomfortable. Not given the state of his own physical comfort over the last several hours. "No. And I'm in the middle of a workout. So I won't be needing a shirt after you leave. It would be wasted effort. Continue."

It was only then that he noticed she was clutching a portfolio in her hand.

She was still wearing the simple outfit that had been provided for her by the staff earlier in the day. Her hair was still loose, her face still free of makeup.

It was unconscionable, how attractive he found that.

He was a busy man. And consequently, his needs were simple. When he pursued a woman for a physical relationship, he liked her to be clearly sophisticated.

A very specific, sleek sort of look with glossy makeup, tight dresses and high-heeled shoes.

Obvious.

Because when you were short on time, *obvious* was the easiest thing.

Violet was anything but, particularly now, and yet she still made his blood boil.

Perhaps this was it. The taint of his father's blood coming to the fore. Bubbling up the moment there was a woman in proximity who was forbidden. Who was forbidden to him? No one and nothing. And so what had he done?

What had he done? He had made the forbidden the most attractive thing.

And that was it. It had to be his body creating this situation. Because there was nothing truly special about her.

Except that tongue of hers.

Razor-sharp and quick.

Her bravery in the face of an uncertain future.

He gritted his teeth again. None of those things mattered to him. A woman's personality meant nothing. She would serve his brother well when it came to a choice of bride, provided Matteo could handle the sharper edges of her, that was. But those things, Javier presumed, would make her a good queen.

When it came to a bedmate… No. It wasn't desirable at all. A construct. A fabrication.

Brought to him by the less desirable parts of him.

He and his brother had always known those things lurked inside of them.

How could they be of their father and consider themselves immune to such things? They didn't. They couldn't.

And so, Javier had to be realistic about it now.

"I have put together a portfolio. Everything I learned about your country. And the ways in which I think I could help by bringing my business here."

"What do you mean?"

"You used to have manufacturing here. You don't anymore. I do most of my manufacturing in the United States, but with products coming to Europe… I don't see why I couldn't have some of it manufactured here. In fact, I think it would be a good thing. It would allow me to keep costs down. And it would bring a substantial amount of employment to your country."

"We are not impoverished."

"No. But particularly the women here are underemployed. Child marriages are still happening in the more rural villages. I know your father looked the other way…"

"Yes," he said, his teeth gritted. "We fought to stop that. We did not look the other way."

"I know. And I know you're still fighting for it. Again. I did a lot of reading today. I feel like I understand… More of what you're trying to do here. Well. I believe in it. And you're right. It doesn't do us any good to live a life to serve only ourselves. And that has never been my goal. Don't you know I have a charity with my sister, for women who are abused?"

He shook his head. "I regret that I do not."

"My sister… She ended up raising her best friend's baby after her friend's ex-lover murdered her. My sister has always been so regretful that she couldn't do more. And so the two of us established a foundation in her honor. I've been looking for more ways to help vulnerable women. Minerva inspired me." She blinked. "I did work only for myself for a while. To try and make my father…" She shook her head. "It doesn't matter. Working on this charity has made me feel better about myself than anything else ever has. Making Monte Blanco my European base will bring an entirely new light to the country."

"You think very highly of yourself."

She shook her head. "No. But I do know a lot about public perception. And I'm very good with it. Gauging it, manipulating it, I suppose. If you want to call it that. I can help."

"Well. I don't think Matteo would be opposed to that."

"I know he wouldn't. And what does he think, anyway? That he could just put me on ice here until he gets back?"

Javier laughed. "I guarantee you he thinks exactly that."

"I'm to believe that he is the softest, most compassionate ruler this country has ever known?"

Javier nodded. "He is. You may find that hard to believe, but it's true."

"I have a question for you."

"Why bother to let me know? You don't seem to have any issue saying exactly what you think or asking for exactly what you want to know."

"All right. So tell me this. How did you know that what your father was doing was wrong? And what inspired you to try to fix it? How did you see outside of the way you were raised? Because a few hours ago when you were facing me down, I realized something. We were not speaking the same language. We expect different things. Because of our realities. For you… Caring about this entire nation of people is part of you the same as breathing. But it wasn't for your father. You weren't taught this… How did you know it?"

It was something he would have wondered, had the memory not been so emblazoned in his mind.

"The answer is the same as it always is. The moment you see the world outside of the little bubble you're raised in, is the moment you stop believing that your perspective is infallible. It is the moment that you begin to question whether or not your reality is in fact the true reality of the world. It was a child marriage. I was newly in the military. Sixteen years old. I happened upon a village. A six-year-old girl was being married off, and she was terrified."

Even now the memory made his teeth set on edge. Made him burn for blood.

"I put a stop to it. Rallied the military, ordered them to hold her father and the groom captive. I remember picking the child up. She was terrified. When I went to my father and told him I was appalled to see that these things were still happening in our country... He scolded me. He said it was not up to me to impose my beliefs on our citizens. My father was no great believer in liberty, Violet. His motivations were related to money. Peace, border protection. Not freedom." He stared hard against the back wall of the gym. "The minute I knew that was the minute that I stopped believing what I saw. It didn't take me long to realize my brother was in a similar crisis of faith. And that was when the two of us began to work to affect change."

"It's amazing," she said. And somehow, he truly believed her. He had never felt particularly amazing. Only like a grim soldier carrying out marching orders that he had never received. But the ones that should have existed. If their leader had had any integrity.

"Most people look away, you know," she said.

"Not me," he said.

"No. Will you please take me out into town?"

"Yes," he agreed.

Because he saw her purpose now. Saw her intent. And because she was correct. It wasn't reasonable for Matteo to keep her here on ice, so to speak.

Anyway, he did not have to check with his brother on every last thing. They had to trust each other. With the way things had been for the past decade and a half, they had no choice. And so, Matteo would have to trust him in this as well.

"Perfect. But I need... I need a phone."

"Your phone, along with your makeup, is making its way here. You will have it tomorrow. And then I promise you, we will go on your field trip."

"Thank you," she said.

It occurred to him then, the ludicrousness of it all. Of her thanking him when she hated him. Of him standing there, desire coursing through his veins when she was off-limits.

But it didn't matter. Nothing mattered more than Monte Blanco. Nothing mattered more than the good of the nation.

Certainly not his own errant lust.

But tomorrow everything would be as it should be.

He was a man of control. A man of honor.

And he would not forget.

CHAPTER SEVEN

IT HAD TAKEN her several hours to regain her breath after seeing him without his shirt. There it was. She was that basic.

She had known that he was spectacular. Had known that he was muscular and well-built. Because she wasn't blind, and it didn't take a physique detective to know that he was in very good shape underneath those clothes.

But then she had seen it.

His body. All that golden, perfect skin, the dark hair that covered his chest—she would have said that she didn't like chest hair, but apparently she did—and created an enticing line that ran through the center of his abdominal muscles.

He was hot.

Her captor was hot.

She did not have time to ponder that. She had a mission.

She steeled herself and took one last look in the mirror before leaving her room. She had told him they could meet in the antechamber. She was pretty sure she knew which room the antechamber was. She had made it her business to figure out the layout of the palace. It was difficult. But she had done it.

And she had her phone back.

She had been feeling gleeful about that since the moment it had been deposited into her hand this morning.

And yet... And yet.

She hadn't been able to think of a single thing to update her account with.

If she still didn't want to call home.

Because she was mad.

Because she didn't even know what to say.

She tucked her phone in her purse and made her way to the appointed meeting place. He was already there. She tried to force her eyes to skim over him, not to cling to the hard lines and angles of his body. To the terrifying symmetry of his face.

Terrifying and beautiful.

Saved only by that scar along his cheekbone.

She wanted to know how he got it.

She shouldn't want to know how he got it. She shouldn't want to know anything about him.

"Good morning. As you can see," she said, waving her hand over her face, "I'm restored to my former glory."

His eyes moved over her dispassionately. And she felt thoroughly dismissed. Insulted.

She shouldn't care.

"All right. Where are we going to first?"

"The capital city. I thought that would be the perfect place to start. It's about thirty minutes away. Down the mountain."

"Excellent."

Her stomach tightened, her hand shaking. And she didn't know if it was because of the idea of being in close proximity with him in a car for that long or if it was stepping outside of this palace for the first time in several days.

The lack of reality in the situation was underlined here. By her containment. In this glittering palace of jewels it was easy to believe it was all a dream. Some kind of childhood fantasy hallucination with the very adult inclusion of a massive, muscular male.

But once they left the palace, the world would expand. And the fantasy that it was a dream would dissolve. Completely.

There was no limousine waiting for them. Instead, there was a sleek black car that was somehow both intensely expensive looking and understated. She didn't know how it accomplished both of those things. But it did.

And it seemed right, somehow, because the car's owner was not understated and could not be if he tried.

Looking at him now in his exquisitely cut dark suit, she had a feeling that he was trying.

That this was the most inconspicuous he could possibly be. But he was six and a half feet tall, arrestingly beautiful and looked like he could kill a hundred people using only his thumb. So. Blending wasn't exactly an option for him.

He opened the door for her, and she got inside.

When he went to the driver's seat, her tension wound up a notch.

It was even smaller than she had imagined. She had thought they might have a driver. Someone to help defuse this thing between them.

Between them. He probably felt nothing.

Why would he?

He was carved out of rock.

Well. One thing.

She thought of his response to her question yesterday. The way that his lips had curved up into a smile.

One thing.

The idea of this rock as a sexual being just about made her combust. She did not need those thoughts. No, she did not.

He was not the kind of man for her. Even in fantasy.

She needed a sexual fantasy with training wheels. An accountant, maybe. Soft. One who wore pleated-front khakis and emanated concern. A nice man named Stephen.

The kind of man that would bring her cinnamon rolls in bed.

After… Making tender love to her.

Nothing about that appealed.

She had no idea why her sexuality was being so specific. She had never intended to make it to twenty-six a virgin.

And she had certainly never intended for this man to awaken her desire.

No. It was just exacerbated by the fact that this felt like a dream. That was all. She wasn't connected to reality. And she was… Stockholm syndrome. That was it. She was suffering from sexual Stockholm syndrome.

When the car started moving, she unrolled the window and stuck her head out of it. Breathed in the crystal mountain air and hoped that it would inject her with some sense.

It didn't.

It did nothing to alleviate the bigness of his presence in the tiny vehicle.

"Are you going to roll the window up? Because you know I don't make a habit of driving to public spaces with women hanging out my car."

She shot him a look and rolled the window up. It really did her no good to oppose him now. She was on a mission. Trying to prove something. "I was enjoying the air."

"Now which one of us is a Saint Bernard?"

"Did you just make a joke?" She looked at his stern profile and saw the corner of his lip tip upward. "You did. You made a joke. That's incredible."

"Don't get used to it."

It felt like a deeper warning of something else. But she

went ahead and ignored it. Along with the shiver of sensation that went through her body.

They were silent after that. And she watched as the trees thinned, gave way to civilization. The dirt becoming loose rocks, and then cobblestone.

The town itself was not modern. And she would have been disappointed if it was. The streets were made of interlocking stones, the sidewalks the same, only in a different pattern. Tight spirals and sunbursts, some of them bleeding up the sides of the buildings that seemed somehow rooted to the earth.

The streets were narrow, the businesses packed tightly together. There were little cafés and a surprising number of appealing-looking designer shops that Violet suddenly felt eager to explore.

"This is beautiful," she said. "If people knew... Well, if people knew, this would be a huge tourist spot."

"It was not encouraged under the rule of my father. And in these past years businesses have rebounded. But still..."

"There is ground to gain. Understood. Pull over."

"What?"

"Pull over."

She saw a bright yellow bicycle leaned against a wall. And right next to it was a window planter with bright red geraniums bursting over the top of it.

All backed by that charming gray stone.

"We need to take a photo."

He obeyed her, but was clearly skeptical about her intent.

She got out of the car quickly and raced over to the bike. Then she looked over into the courtyard of the neighboring café. People were sitting outside drinking coffee. "Excuse me? Is this your bike?" She asked the young woman sitting there working on her computer.

The woman looked at her warily and then saw Javier, standing behind her. Her eyes widened.

"It's fine," Violet said. "He's harmless. I just want to take a picture with your bike."

"Of course," the woman said.

She still looked completely frazzled, but Violet scampered to where it was, positioning herself right next to it and putting her hand over the handlebars. "A picture," she said. She reached into her purse and pulled her phone out, handing it to him.

"That's what all this is about? Also. I am not harmless."

"Yes. Very ferocious. Take my picture."

She looked straight ahead, offering him her profile, and tousled her hair lightly before positioning her hand delicately at her hip.

"There," he said. "Satisfied?"

"Let me verify." She snatched the phone from his hand and looked at the photo.

It had done exactly what she wanted to do, and with some tweaking, the colors would look beautiful against the simple gray stone.

"Yes," she confirmed. "I am."

She pulled up her account, touched the picture up quickly and typed:

Exploring new places is one of my favorite things. Stay tuned for more information on your next favorite vacation spot.

"There," she said. "That's bound to create speculation. Excitement."

He looked down at the picture with great skepticism. "That?"

"Yes."

"I do not understand people."

"Maybe they don't understand you," she said.

He looked completely unamused by that.

"Sorry. Joke. I thought you were getting to where you understood those sometimes."

The look he gave her was inscrutable.

"Show me the rest of this place," she said. "I'm curious."

He looked at her as if she had grown a second head. "You realize that I'm slightly conspicuous?"

"Usually I am too," she said. "I guess… I just figure you ignore it."

"You're not conspicuous here."

"No," she said. "But that won't last long, will it? I mean, if I'm going to be the Queen…"

"You're not going to be inconspicuous as long as you're walking around with me. That's a pretty decent indicator that you might be important."

"Wow. No points for humility."

"Do you have false humility about the degree to which you're recognized? Or what your status means? You've been throwing all sorts of statistics at me about your wealth and importance ever since we first met."

"All right," she said. "Fair enough."

They walked on in silence for a moment. She paid attention to the way her feet connected to the cobblestones. It was therapeutic in a way. There was something so quaint about this. It was more village than city, but it contained a lot more places of interest than she would normally think you would find in a village.

"What is the chief export here?"

"There isn't any. We are quite self-contained. What we make tends to stay here, tends to fuel the citizens."

"That's very unusual."

"Yes. It also feels precarious."

"So… If we were to manufacture my products here, I would be your chief export."

"In point of fact, yes."

"Though, if your other products became desirable because of tourism…"

"Yes. I understand it would mean a great deal of cash injection for the country. Though, thanks to my brother's personal fortune, the coffers of the country have been boosted as it is."

"Yes, I did some research on him. He's quite a successful businessman."

"You would like him. Other than the fact that he's a bit of a tyrant."

"More than you?"

"Different than me." He relented. "Perhaps not more."

"A family of softies."

The sound he made was somewhere between a huff of indignation and a growl. "I have never been called soft."

She looked at him. The wall of muscle that was his chest. The granite set of his jaw. She meant her response to be light. Funny. But looking at him took her breath. "No. I don't suppose you have."

There was a small ice-cream parlor up the way, and she was more than grateful for the distraction. "I want ice cream," she said.

"*Ice cream?* Are you a child?"

"Ice cream is not just for children," she said gravely. "Surely you know that, Javier."

"I don't eat ice cream."

"Nonsense. Everyone needs ice cream. Well, unless they're lactose intolerant. In which case, they just need to find a good nondairy replacement. And let me tell you, in Southern California they're plentiful."

"I'm not intolerant of anything."

She tried, and failed, to hold back a laugh. "Well, that just isn't true. I've only spent a few days in your company, but I can tell you that you're clearly intolerant of a whole host of things. But, it's good to know that dairy isn't among them."

"You are incredibly irritating."

"*Not* the first time I've heard that."

"And who told you that?"

"My older brother, for a start. Also, my surrogate older brother, Dante. He's now my brother-in-law, incidentally."

"That seems convoluted."

"It's not really. Not at all. Just the way things ended up. My father quite literally found him on a business trip and brought him home. Took care of him. I think my sister was in love with him for most of her life."

"But you weren't."

She laughed. "I remember very clearly telling Minerva that I didn't like men who were quite as hard as Dante."

A tense silence settled between the two of them. She hadn't meant to say that. Because of course that implied that perhaps it had changed. And perhaps there was a hard man that she might find appealing after all.

She gritted her teeth.

"And I still don't," she said. "So. Just so we're both clear."

"Very clear," he said.

"Now. Ice cream." She increased her pace and breezed straight into the shop. And she did not miss the look of absolute shock on the faces of the proprietors inside. It wasn't to do with her. It was to do with Javier.

"I saw that there was ice cream," she said cheerily. She approached the counter and looked at all the flavors.

"We make them all here," the woman behind the counter said, her voice somewhat timid. "The milk comes from our own cows."

"Well, that's wonderful," Violet said. "And makes me even more excited to try it." There was one called Spanish chocolate, and she elected to get a cone with two scoops of that. She kept her eyes on Javier the entire time.

"You don't want anything?"

"No," he said, his voice uncompromising.

"You're missing out," she said.

She went to pay for the treat, and he stepped in, taking his wallet from his pocket.

"Of course we cannot ask Your Royal Highness to pay," the woman said.

"On the contrary," Javier said, his voice decisive. "You should be asking me to pay double. Consider it repayment."

The woman did not charge Javier double, but she did allow him to pay.

"I didn't need you to buy my ice cream," she said when they were out on the street.

"It's not about need. It is about… What feels right."

"You're that kind of man, huh? The kind that holds open doors and pays for dinner?"

He laughed, a dark, short sound. "You make me sound quite a bit more conventional than I am."

"A regular gentleman."

"I would not say that."

"Well, what would you say, then? You're single-hand-edly setting out to save the country, and you saved a little girl from child marriage. You worked for years to undo the rule of your father." She took a short lick of her ice cream. It was amazing. "I would say that runs toward gentlemanly behavior, don't you?"

"I think that's overstating human decency. I would like to think that any man with a spine would do what I did in my position. Inaction in my position would be complicity. And I refused to be complicit in my father's actions."

"Well. Many people would be, for their comfort."

She looked down the alleyway and saw a lovely hand-painted mural. She darted there, and he followed. It was secluded, ivy growing over the walls, creeping between the brick.

"I just need a picture of this."

She held out her hand, extending her ice-cream cone to him. "Can you hold this?"

He took it gingerly from her grasp, looking at it like it might bite him. She lifted her brows, then turned away from him, snapping a quick picture and then another for good measure.

He was still holding the ice-cream cone and looking aggrieved, so when she returned, she leaned in, licking the ice-cream cone while he held it still.

His posture went stiff.

He was reacting to her, she realized. The same way that she reacted to him. And she didn't like how it made her feel. Giddy and jittery and excited in a way she couldn't remember feeling before.

And she should pull away. She should.

But instead, she wrapped her hand around his, and sent electric sensation shooting through her body.

"You should taste it," she said.

"I told you, I didn't want any."

"But I think you do," she insisted. "You should have some."

She pushed his hand, moving the cone in his direction, and she could see the moment that he realized it was better to take the path of least resistance. He licked the ice cream slowly, his dark eyes connecting with hers.

She realized she had miscalculated.

Because he had his mouth where hers had been.

Because she was touching him and he was looking at her.

Because something in his dark eyes told her that he would be just as happy licking her as he was this ice cream.

And all of it was wrong.

Why couldn't she hate him? She should.

Why couldn't she get it into her head that this was real? That it was insane. That she should want to kick him in the shins and run as far and fast as she could. Call for help at the nearest business, rather than lingering here in an alley with him.

"It's good," she said, her throat dry.

"Yes," he agreed, his voice rough.

Then he thrust it back into her hand. "I think I've had enough."

"Right."

Her heart clenched, sank. And she didn't know what was happening inside of her. Didn't know why her body was reacting this way, now, to him. Didn't know why she felt like crying, and not for any of the reasons that she should.

"I'm not done exploring the city, though. And I wouldn't want to take my ice cream back in your car. I might make a mess."

But the rest of the outing was completely muted. Not at all what it had been before.

And that it disappointed her confused her even more than anything else.

When she was back at the palace, back in her room, she lay down and covered her head. And only then did she allow herself to think the truth.

She was attracted to the man who was holding her captive.

She was attracted to the brother of the man she was being forced to marry.

But more important, he was attracted to her. She had seen it.

She had very nearly tasted it.

Thankfully, they had come to their senses.

She spent the rest of the night trying fitfully to be thankful when all she felt was frustrated.

And she knew that she had come up with a plan, no matter how it made her stomach churn to think of putting it into action.

She had no choice.

CHAPTER EIGHT

HIS BROTHER STILL hadn't returned.

Javier was tired of being tested. He had been avoiding Violet since they had come back from the city the other day. The temptation that she had presented to him was unacceptable.

That he had the capacity to be tempted was not something that he had first seen. But Violet King had tested him at every turn, and the true issue was that he feared he might fail a test if she continued.

He curled his fingers into fists. No. He was not a weak man.

Even before he had turned on his father, he had not had an easy life. He had faithfully served in his father's army. And that had required work guarding the borders in the forests, camping out for long periods of time. His father's paranoia meant that he was certain that enemies were lurking behind every tree.

And Javier had found that to be so. His father had had many enemies. And Javier had done his job in arresting them.

He wasn't sure what he wished to avoid thinking about more. That period of time in his life, or his current attraction to Violet.

"Of course, the architecture is nothing compared to the

natural beauty. You got a little peek outside the window, but more to come later on this beautiful vacation spot."

He heard Violet's voice drifting down the corridor, coming from the expansive dining room where his brother often held dinner parties.

It was a massive room with a view that stretched on for miles, a large balcony connecting it and the ballroom and making the most of those views.

Violet was standing right next to the window, her cell phone in her hand. She waved—not at him, but at her screen—then put the phone down at her side. "I was filming a live video. Doing more to tease my location."

"Of course you were," he said.

She gave him a bland look. "Just because you don't understand it doesn't mean it's not valid."

"Oh, I would never think that."

"Liar. If you don't understand it, you think it's beneath you."

"I didn't say I didn't understand it."

"But you do think it's beneath you."

"That was implied in my statement, I think."

"You're impossible."

She walked nearer to him, and he tried to keep his focus on the view outside. But he found himself looking at her. She had most definitely regained her precious makeup. She looked much as she did that first day he had seen her, which he assumed was a signature look for her.

"So you must go to all this trouble," he said, indicating her makeup, "to talk to people who aren't even in the room with you."

She winked. "That's how you know I like you. If I talk to you in the same room, and I don't bother to put my eyelashes on."

"Your eyelashes are fake?"

"A lot of people have fake eyelashes," she said sagely. "I used to have them individually glued on every week or so, but I prefer the flexibility of the strips so I can just take them off myself at the end of the day."

"I have to say I vastly don't care about your eyelashes."

He looked down at her, at the dramatic sweep of those coal black lashes they were discussing. And he found that he did care, more than he would like. Not about the application, but that he wished he could see them naturally as they had been the other morning. Dark close to her eyes, lighter at the tips. He appreciated now the intimacy of that sight.

And he should not want more.

"You know what I do care about?" she asked. "Outside. I would like to go outside."

"Well, the garden is fenced in, feel free to wander around. Just don't dig underneath it."

"Very cute. Another joke. We could write that in your baby book. However, I would like a tour."

"A tour of the grounds?"

"Yes."

"Of the garden, or of the entire grounds? Because I warn you, they are quite wild."

"I find I'm in the mood for wild."

She smiled slightly and enigmatically. He could not tell whether she intended for the statement to be a double entendre.

But the moment passed, and he found himself agreeing to take her out of the palace.

One path led to the carefully manicured gardens that had been tamed and kept for generations. A testament to the might of the royal family, he had always thought. And as a result, he had never liked them.

"This way," he said. "This is where Matteo and I used to play when we were boys."

The rocky path led down to a grove of trees. Heavily shaded, and next to a deep, fathomless swimming hole.

A waterfall poured down black, craggy rocks into the depths.

The water was a crystalline blue, utterly and completely clear. The bottom of the river was visible, making it seem like it might not be as deep as it was. But he knew that you could sink and sink and not find the end of it.

He and Matteo had always loved it here. It had seemed like another world. Somewhere separate from the strictures of the palace. Though, at that point he had not yet come to hate it.

Still. He had appreciated the time spent outdoors with his brother. His brother had been most serious at that age.

Perhaps because he had always known that the burden of the crown would be his.

"This is beautiful," she said. He expected her to reach for her phone immediately, but she didn't. Instead, she simply turned in a circle, looking at the unspoiled splendor around them.

"Yes. You know something? I know that my father never set foot down here." He stared at the pool. "And now he's dead."

"That's a tragedy," Violet said. "To live right next to something so beautiful and to never see it."

"There were a great many things my father didn't see. Or care about. He cared about his own power. He cared about his own comfort. This is just one of the many things he never truly looked at. Including the pain that he caused his own people."

"But you did. You do," she said.

"For better or worse."

"You used to swim down here?"

"Yes."

"Did you laugh and have fun?"

"Of course I did."

"I can't imagine you having fun."

"I can assure you I did."

"It's safe?" she asked.

"Yes."

She took her phone out of her pocket and set it on the shore. Then she looked back at him and kicked her shoes off, putting her toe in the water. "It's freezing," she said.

"I said it was safe. I didn't say it wasn't frigid water coming down from an ice melt."

She stared at him, a strange sort of challenge lighting her eyes.

"What?"

"Let's swim."

"No," he said.

He realized right then that the outright denial was a mistake. Because her chin tilted upward in total, stubborn defiance. And the next thing he knew she had gone and done it. Gone in, clothes and all, her dark head disappearing beneath the clear surface. And she swam.

Her hair streaming around her like silken ribbon, her limbs elegant, her dress billowing around her. And he was sure that he could see white cotton panties there beneath the surface. He felt punched in the gut by that. Hard.

"Swim with me," she said.

"No."

She swam up to the edge, giving him an impish grin. "Please."

He remembered her words from the other day. *Don't you do anything for yourself?*

He didn't. He didn't, because there was no point.

But swimming wasn't a betrayal.

He could feel his body's response to that in his teeth.

A twist in his gut. Because he knew what he was doing. Knew that he was pushing at that which was acceptable.

But the water would be cold.

And he would not touch her. Tension rolled from his shoulders, and he unbuttoned his shirt, leaving it on the banks of the river. His shoes, his pants. And leaving himself in only the dark shorts that he wore beneath his clothes.

Then he dived, clearing her completely, sliding beneath the surface of the water at the center of the pool, letting the icy water numb his skin like pinpricks over the surface of it. Maybe it would knock the desire that he felt for her out of his body.

Maybe.

He swam toward her, and he saw something flash in the depths of her eyes. Surprise. Maybe even fear.

He stopped just short of her.

"Is this what you had in mind?"

"I didn't expect the strip show."

The characterization of what had occurred made his stomach tighten. Or the cold water had no effect on his desire.

He couldn't understand why. Why this woman, at this moment, tested him so.

Any retort she might have made, any continuation of the conversation seemed to die on her lips.

And he knew. He knew that he had just gone straight into temptation. Had literally dived right in. Whatever he had told himself in that moment on the shore was a lie. All he had wanted to do was to be closer to her.

He had never experienced anything like this. Had never experienced this kind of draw to a woman before. To anyone.

She had nothing in common with him. A spoiled, sheltered girl from the United States. But when she looked at him, he felt something. And he had not felt anything for a long time.

She began to draw closer to him.

"Don't," he said.

"I just…" A droplet of water slid down her face, and her tongue darted out. She licked it off. She reached out and dragged her thumb over the scar on his cheek. "How did you get this?"

Her touch sent a lightning bolt of desire straight down to his groin. "It's not a good story."

"I don't care."

"You think you don't care, but you haven't heard it."

Her hand was still on him.

"Tell me," she insisted.

"You know you should be afraid of me," he said. "And here you are, pushing me."

"You said you wouldn't hurt me."

"And I wouldn't. Intentionally. But you are here touching me as if I cannot be tempted into anything that we would both regret."

"Who says I would regret it?"

He gritted his teeth. "You would."

"Javier…"

"I was helping a man escape from prison. Wrongfully arrested by my father. One of his guards attempted to put a stop to it. It was war, Violet, and I did what had to be done."

She said nothing. She only looked at him, her eyes wide.

"Yes. It is what you think."

"You did what you had to," she said softly.

"But that's what I am. A man who does what he has to. A man who is barely a man anymore."

She slid her thumb across his skin, and he shuddered beneath her touch. "You feel like a man to me," she whispered.

"You are not for me."

He pushed away from her and swam back to the shore. She watched him dress, the attention that she paid him disconcerting. Then she got out of the water, the thin fabric of her dress molded to her curves. He could see her nipples, clearly visible, and his arousal roared.

"You are not for me."

Then he turned, leaving her there. She would find her way back. Follow the path.

But he had to do them both a favor and remove himself from her. Because if he did not, he would do something that they would both come to bitterly regret.

He was familiar with the sting of failure. The process of deprogramming himself from his father's rule had been a difficult one when he had been sixteen years old and he had wanted to believe with intensity that his father was a benevolent ruler. And he had seen otherwise. The way that it had hurt his soul, torn him in two, to begin to look differently at the world, at his life and at himself, had been the last time he had truly felt pain. Because after that it was over. After that, the numbness had sunk in, had pervaded all that he was.

It was Matteo who had seen him through it. Matteo, who had been struggling with the exact same thing, who made Javier feel like he wasn't losing his mind.

His brother had been his anchor in the most difficult moment of his life.

And now there was another wrenching happening in his soul. It was all because of the luminous, dark eyes of Violet King.

In that alleyway, when she had put her hand over his, when she had tempted him with a bite of ice cream like she was Eve in the garden offering him an apple, he had not been able to think of anything but casting the frozen treat aside and claiming her mouth with his own.

In the water he had longed to drag her to the shore, cover her body with his own. Claim her.

And that was a violation of all that he had become.

He was a man of honor because he had chosen it.

None of it was bred into him. None of it was part of his blood.

He and Matteo knew that, so they were always on guard.

And this woman... This woman enticed him to betray that.

To betray his brother.

The one man to whom he owed his absolute loyalty.

The man he had promised to destroy should that man ever abuse his power. Such was their bond.

Such was his dedication.

But now... Lusting after his brother's fiancée made him compromised.

It compromised that promise. Compromised what he was. What he claimed to be.

His phone rang.

It was Matteo. As if his brother could feel his betrayal from across the continent.

"Yes?"

"We have been successful," Matteo said. "Monte Blanco will now be included in the United Council. My mouse has proven herself indispensable yet again."

"Is she in the room with you?"

"Of course she is."

Javier didn't even have the right to scold his brother for that. Not at this point. He had lost his right to a moral high ground of any kind.

"When do you return?" he said, his voice heavy.

"Two days. We have to make a stop in Paris for a diplomatic meeting."

"I suppose, then, that it is good you spent all those years studying business."

"Yes. Not the way our father did it, but there are similarities to diplomacy in business and when it comes to running a country. Of course, the bottom line is not filling your own pockets in the situation."

"No indeed."

The bottom line was not about satisfying themselves at all.

It stung particularly now. As he thought of Violet. As he thought of the deep, gut-wrenching longing to touch her.

And the anger that crept in beneath his skin. Anger that was not at himself, though it should have been. Anger at the cruelty of fate. That he should want this woman above all others when she was perhaps the only woman in the world who was truly off-limits to him.

He was a prince. He could snap his fingers and demand that which he wished.

Except her.

The insidious doubt inside of him asked the question. Was that why he wanted her? Was that why she presented a particular appeal? Because she was forbidden.

Because she was forbidden to him and no matter how hard he tried to pretend otherwise, he was born a man with a massive ego who didn't feel that a single thing on the earth should be barred from him should he take to it.

No. He would not allow it.

He would not allow that to be true.

"I look forward to your return."

"How is my fiancée?"

"Not exactly amenable to the idea of being your fiancée," he said.

It was the truth. Everything else could be ignored. For now.

"I must say, the connection between myself and her is one of the things that made our meetings the most interesting. She is well liked, world-renowned for her business mind. Such a fantastic asset to me she will be."

"You don't know her."

"And I suppose you do now. I will look forward to hearing how you think I might best manage her."

His brother hung up then. And left Javier standing there with his hand curled so tightly around the phone he thought he might break. Either his bones or the device, he didn't know. Neither did he care.

He gritted his teeth and walked out of his office. Something compelled him down to the ballroom where he had the dance lesson with Violet. Where he held her in his arms and first began to question all that he was. It was unconscionable. That this woman he had known for a scant number of days could undo twenty years' worth of restraint.

And when he flung open the doors to the ballroom... There she was.

Curled up in one of the tufted chairs that sat in the corner of the room, next to the floor-to-ceiling windows, sunlight bathing her beauty in gold.

Her legs were tucked up underneath her, and he could see the edges of her bare toes peeking out from beneath her shapely rear. She was wearing simple, soft-looking clothes, nothing fancy. Neither did she have on any of her makeup. She was reading.

Not on her phone.

And it made him want to dig deeper. To question all that she presented of herself to the world, all that she tried to tell him about who she was and who she actually might be.

She looked up when she heard his footsteps. "Oh," she said. "I didn't expect you to be lurking around the ballroom."

"I didn't expect you to be lurking around at all. Much less away from the computer."

"I found this book in the library," she said. "And the library's beautiful, but it doesn't have the natural lighting of this room."

"Protecting the books," he said.

"Makes sense."

"What is it you're reading?"

"It's a book of fairy tales. Monte Blancan fairy tales. It's very interesting. We all have our versions of these same stories. I guess because they speak to something human inside of us. I think my favorite one that I've read so far is about the Princess who was taken captive by a beast."

"Is that what you think me? A beast?"

She closed the book slowly and set it down on the table beside the chair. "Possibly. Are you under some kind of enchantment?"

"No."

"That's something I found interesting in your version of the story. The Prince was not a beast because of his own sins. He was transformed into one as punishment for something his father had done. And then, much like the story I'm familiar with, the woman is taken captive because of the sins of her father. It feels shockingly close to home, doesn't it?"

"Except I believe in the story my brother would be that enchanted Prince."

Her gaze was too frank. Too direct. "If you say so."

"You were shocked by your father's deal?"

She nodded slowly. "I was. Because I thought that we…

I knew he wasn't perfect. I did. But it's not like he was a raving villain like your father."

"You know, I didn't realize my father was a raving villain until I started to see, really see the things that he had done to our country. And I don't know that your father is a villain so much as he was made a desperate man in a desperate moment. And my brother took advantage of that. My brother does his best to act with honor. But like me, he is not afraid to be ruthless when he must be. I do not envy the man who had to go up against his will."

"He should have protected me. He should never have used me as currency. I can't get over that. I won't."

"Is that why you came? To teach him a lesson?"

Her lips twitched. "Maybe. And I won't lie, I did think that perhaps my notoriety would keep me safe. You know, because people will miss me if I'm not around. But I sort of like not being around. It's been an interesting vacation."

"Except you're going to marry my brother."

"Yes. I know you think so."

"You can take it up with him when he returns. He tells me he'll be back in two days."

Shock flared in the depths of her eyes. "Two days?"

"Yes. Don't look so dismayed."

"I can't help it. I am dismayed."

"Why exactly?"

"I just thought there was more time."

There was something wild in the depths of her eyes then, and he wanted to move closer to it. But he knew that would be a mistake. Still, when she stood, it was to draw closer to him.

"I know that you feel it," she said. "It's crazy, isn't it? I shouldn't feel anything for you. But you… I mean, look, I know it's chemistry, or whatever, I know it's not feelings. But…" She bit her full lower lip and looked up at him from beneath her lashes, the expression both innocent and co-quettish. "Don't you think that maybe we should have a chance to taste it before I'm sold into marriage?"

"I thought you were intent on resisting that," he said, his voice rough.

"With everything I have in me."

"I cannot. I owe my brother my undying loyalty. And I will not compromise that over something as basic as sex. You mistake me, *querida*, if you think that I can be so easily shaken."

"I know that you're a man of honor. A man of loyalty. But I feel no such loyalty to your brother. And it is nothing to me to violate it."

She planted her hand on his chest. And he knew that she could feel it then. Feel his heart raging against the muscle and blood and bone there. Feel it raging against everything that was good and right and real, that which he had placed his faith in all these years.

She let out a shaking breath, and he could feel the heat of it brush his mouth, so close was she. So close was his destruction.

He was iron. He was rock. He had been forced to become so. A man of no emotion. A man of nothing more than allegiance to an ideal. Knowing with absolute certainty that if he should ever turn away from that, he might become lost. That corruption might take hold of him in the way that it had done his father. Because he considered himself immune to nothing.

And so, he had made himself immune to everything.

Except for this. Except for her.

So small and fragile, delicate.

Powerful.

Not because of her success or her money. But because

of the light contained in her beauty. A storm wrapped in soft, exquisite skin that he ached to put his hands on.

And when she stretched up on her toes and pressed her mouth to his, no finesse or skill present in the motion at all, he broke.

He wrapped his arms around her, cupping her head in one of his hands, shifting things, taking control. And he consumed her.

What she had intended to be a tasting, a test, he turned into a feast. If he was going to be destroyed, then he would bring the palace down with him. Then he would crack the very foundations of where they stood. Of all that he had built his life upon. Of all that he was. If he would be a ruined man, then the world would be ruined as a result. As would she.

He nipped her lower lip, slid his tongue against hers, kissed her deep and hard and long until she whimpered with it. Until she had arched against him, going soft and pliant. Until there was no question now who was in charge. Until there was no question now who was driving them to the brink of calamity. It was him.

He had made his choice. He had not fallen into temptation; he had wrapped his arms around it. He had not slid into sin; he had gathered it against his body and made it his air. His oxygen.

And she surrendered to it. Surrendered to him.

The white flag of her desire was present in the way her body molded against his, in the way that she opened for him, the small, sweet sounds of pleasure that she made as he allowed his hands to move, skimming over her curves, then going still, holding her against him so that she could feel the insistence of his desire pressing against her stomach.

He was a man of extremes.

And if she wanted a storm, he would give her a hurricane.

If he could not be a man of honor, then he would be a man of the basest betrayal.

It was the sight of that book sitting on the side table that brought him back to himself. Just a flash of normality. A familiarity. A reminder of who he was supposed to be, that caused him to release his hold on her and set her back on her feet.

She looked dazed. Her lips were swollen. Utterly wrecked.

Just like he was.

"Never," he said. "It will never happen between us."

"But… It already did."

He chuckled, dark and without humor just like the very center of his soul. "If you think that was an example of what could be between us, then you are much more inexperienced than I would have given you credit for."

"I…"

"The things I could do to you. The things I could do to us both. I could ruin you not just for other men, but for sleep. Wearing clothes. Walking down the street. Everything would remind you of me. The slide of fabric against your skin. The warmth of the sun on your body. All of it would make you think of my hands on you. My mouth. And you would try… You would try to use your own hand to bring yourself the kind of satisfaction that I could show you, but you would fail."

"And what about your brother? Would he fail?"

"It is why I won't do it. Because yes. After me. After this… Even he would fail to satisfy you."

And he turned and walked out of the room, leaving her behind. Leaving his broken honor behind, held in her delicate hands. And he knew it. He only hoped that she did not.

The sooner Matteo returned, the sooner Javier could leave this place. Could leave her. Matteo needed to do what he thought was best for the country.

But Javier would not stand by and see it done.

CHAPTER NINE

SHE HAD FAILED. It kept her awake that night. The sting of that failure. She was supposed to seduce him. It had been her one job. Granted, it had all gotten taken out of her hands, and she had a feeling that her own inexperience had been played against her.

Her heart hadn't stopped thundering like it might gallop out of her chest since.

She hadn't expected him to find her in the ballroom. That was the real reason she had been in there. Who hung out in an empty ballroom? But then he had appeared. And she had realized it was her chance.

She hadn't actually been sitting there scheming. She had been avoiding her scheme.

After her failure at the waterfall, and after...

The problem was, he had shared something of his past with her there, and she felt like she knew him better. Felt guilty for her seduction plan even though it felt like the perfect solution to her problem.

Because she knew on some level that if Javier were to sleep with her, Matteo would not want her anymore.

And she had been... She had been excited about it, perversely, because for the first time in her life she was attracted to a man, so why not take advantage of it? She didn't want to marry him. He was... He was an unyielding rock face, and she had no desire to be stuck with a man like that for any length of time.

But then she had been sitting there reading that fairy tale. And not only had she—through those stories—come into a greater understanding of his culture, there was something about the particular story of the beast she'd been reading that had made her understand him.

Transformed into something due to the sins of his father and so convinced that the transformation was a necessity.

That he had to sit in the sins, in the consequence, to avoid becoming a monster on the inside as well as a monster on the outside.

She had been so caught up in that line of thinking that when he had appeared, she had clumsily made an effort at seduction, and she had been carried away in it.

That was the problem with all of this.

She was a reasonable girl. A practical one. A businesswoman. Thoroughly modern and independent in so many ways, but she had been swept up in a fairy tale, and nothing that she knew, nothing that she had ever achieved, had prepared her for the effect that it was having on her.

For the effect that he was having on her.

She had been kissed before.

Every single time it had been easy to turn away. Every single time she had been relieved that it was over. When she could extricate herself from the man's hold and go on with her day, untouched below the neck and very happy about it thank you.

But she wanted Javier to touch her. And she feared very much that the vow he had made to her before he had stormed out of the ballroom was true.

That if it were to become more, she would never, ever be able to forget. That she would be ruined. That she would be altered for all time.

"That's ridiculous," she scolded herself. *It's the kind of ridiculous thing that men think about themselves, but it's never true. You know that. It can't be.*

The idea that she might fail in her objective to avoid marrying Matteo terrified her. But somehow, even more, the idea that she might leave here without... Without knowing what it was like to be with Javier was even more terrifying. And she despised herself for that. For that weakness. Because it was a weakness. It had to be.

Without thinking, she slipped out of bed. She knew where his room was. She had studied the plans to the palace, and she was familiar with it now. Had it committed to memory. She had a great memory; it was one of the things that made her good at business. And, it was going to help her out now.

With shaking hands, she opened up the door to her bedroom and slipped down the corridor. It wasn't close, his chamber.

But suddenly she realized. That wasn't where he would be. She didn't know how she knew it, she just knew.

Where would he be?

His gym. That made sense. She had found him there that day, and the way that he was committed to the physical activity he was doing was like a punishment, and she had a feeling he would be punishing himself after today.

No. She stopped.

He wouldn't be there.

The library.

He would be in the library. Somehow she knew it. He would be looking at the same book that she had been earlier. She could feel it.

It defied reason that she could. And if she was wrong... If she was wrong, she would go straight back to her room. She would abandon this as folly. All of it.

She would leave it behind, and she would find another solution to her predicament. She would use her brain. Her business acumen.

Right. And you're still pretending that this is all about avoiding the marriage?

She pushed that to the side. And she went to the library.

She pushed the door open, and the first thing she saw was the fire in the hearth.

But she didn't see him.

Disappointment rose up to strangle her, warring with relief that filled her lungs.

But then she saw him, standing in the corner next to the bookshelf, a book held open in his palm. The orange glow of the flames illuminated him. The hollows of his face, his sharp cheekbones.

But his eyes remained black. Unreadable.

"What are you doing here?"

"I was looking for you," she said. "And somehow I knew I would find you here."

"How?"

"Because you wanted to read the story. You wanted to see how it ended."

"Happy endings are not real."

"They must be. People have them every day."

"Happy endings are not for beasts who spirit young maidens away to their castle. How about that?"

"I don't know. We all have that story. Every culture. Some version of it. We must want to believe it. That no matter how much of a beast you feel you might be, you can always find a happy ending."

"Simplistic."

"What's wrong with being simplistic? What is the benefit of cynicism? And anyway, what makes cynicism more complex?"

"It's not cynicism. It is a life lived seeing very difficult things. Seeing tragedy unfold all around you. Knowing there is no happy ending possible for some people. Understanding for the first time that when you have power, you must find ways to keep it from corrupting you or you will destroy the world around you. Great power gives life or takes it, it's not neutral."

"All right. But in here… In the library, it's just us, isn't it? What does anyone have to know outside this room? It doesn't have to touch anything. It never has to go beyond here."

That wasn't the point of what she was doing. She should want Matteo to know. She should want there to be consequences.

But she wasn't lying to Javier.

Because suddenly, she just wanted to take that heaviness from his shoulders. For just one moment. She wanted to soften those hard lines on his face. Wanted to ease the suffering she knew he carried around in his soul.

Because he truly thought that he was a monster.

And he believed that he had to be above reproach in order to keep that monster from gaining hold.

She had intended to taunt him. To ask why he was so loyal to a brother who left him behind to be a babysitter.

But she didn't want to. Not now.

She didn't want this moment to have anything to do with the world beyond the two of them.

Beyond these walls.

Beyond this ring of warmth provided by the fire.

The heat created by the desire between them.

She had never wanted a man before.

And whatever the circumstances behind her coming to be in this country, in this castle, she wanted this man.

She had waited for desire, and she had found it here.

But it was somehow more, something deeper than she had imagined attraction might be. But maybe that was just her ignorance. Maybe this was always what desire was supposed to be. Something that went beyond the mere physical need to be touched.

A bone-deep desire to be seen. To be touched deeper than hands ever could.

There was something inside of her that responded to that bleakness in him, and she didn't even know what it was.

Her life had been a whirlwind. Her loud, wonderful family, who she loved, including her father, even though he had wounded her as he had done. Parties. Vacations. Things.

The triumph in her business. The constant roar of social media.

But now all of it had faded away, and for the first time in her life…

For the first time in her life Violet King was truly self-made.

Was truly standing on her own feet.

Was making decisions for herself, and for no other reason at all.

This moment wasn't about proving herself to anyone.

It wasn't a reaction to anyone or anything but the need inside of her.

And she suddenly felt more powerful than she had ever felt before.

As a prisoner in a palace in a faraway land. Standing across from a man who should terrify her, but who filled her with desire instead.

And whatever this resulted in, it would be her choice. This, at least, was her choice.

She didn't have to close the distance between them. Not

this time. He was the one who did it. He wrapped his arm around her waist and brought her against him.

She shivered with anticipation. Because the pleasure that she had found in his kiss surpassed anything else she had ever experienced, and just thinking about it opened up a wide cavern of longing inside of her.

When his mouth connected with hers, she whimpered. With relief. To be touched by him again, consumed by him again…

Only days ago she had never met him. She had been living a life she had worked for. A life that she loved. And she had been missing this one elemental thing without realizing it. Had been completely blind to what desire could feel like. To what it could mean.

And she would have said that obviously if she could wake up tomorrow and just be back at home, back in her bed, if she could never have found out that her father did such a thing to her, then she would have gone back.

Until now. Until this. Until him. And she didn't think it was simplistic. Because as she'd said to him, why was happiness simplistic? Why was desire treated like it was simplistic or base? Desire like this was not cheap, and she knew it. It was not something that came to just everyone, that could occur between any two people. It was a unique kind of magic and she reveled in it.

In him.

His mouth was firm and taut, his tongue certain as it slid between her lips, sliding against her own.

That sweet friction drove her crazy. Made her breasts feel heavy. Made her ache between her thighs. Desperate to be touched.

She felt slick and ready, for what she didn't quite know. Oh, she knew. In a physical sense. But what she was learning was that there was a spiritual component to this sort of attraction that could not be defined. Could not be easily explained in a textbook.

Something that went beyond human biology and went into the realm of human spirituality.

It wasn't basic. It wasn't base.

But it was elemental. Like something ancient and deep that had been dug up from the center of the earth. An old kind of magic, presented as a gift, one she had never even known she needed. But she did know now. Oh, she knew now.

His hands were sure and certain as they roamed over her curves. As if he knew exactly where she needed him most. He slipped his hands upward, cupping her breasts, teasing her nipples with his thumbs. And she gasped. He took advantage of the gasp, tasting her deeper, making it more intense. Impossibly so.

In fact, it was so intense now, she wasn't sure she would survive it. He was not a rock. He was a man. And suddenly, the differences between the two of them felt stark and clear.

And, like everything else that had passed between them, just a little bit magical. That he was strength and hardness and heat and muscle. And he made her feel like her softness might just be strength in and of itself. A match for his.

Her world was suddenly reduced to senses. The texture of his whiskers against her face, the firmness of his mouth. Those rough, calloused hands tugging at her shirt, at her pants. She pushed her hands beneath his shirt, gasped when her palms made contact with his hot, hard muscles.

She lived in Southern California. She saw a lot of beach bodies. She had already seen him shirtless in the gym, and she already knew that visually, he was the most stunning man she had ever beheld. But touching him... Well, maybe it had to do with that chemistry between them. That spiritual element. But there was something that transcended mere aesthetic beauty. It was as if he had been created for her. Carved from stone and had breath infused into him, as if he had been created for this moment, for her to admire.

For her to revel in.

She moved her fingertips over the hard ridges of his abs, and when he sucked in a breath, all those gorgeous muscles bunched and shifted beneath her touch, and the very act of being able to affect him like she did was an intoxicant that transcended anything made by men.

She moved her hands up over his shoulders, across his back. Admired the sheer breadth of him. The strength inherent there.

The whole world rested on his shoulders. So much.

And she kissed him. Not just with all the desire inside of her, but with the formless, indefinable feeling that was expanding in her chest. The deep resonant understanding that was echoing inside of her. Because of him.

Because she saw herself clearly for the first time because of this moment. And whatever happened afterward, that could never be taken from her. This could never be taken from her.

He crushed her body against his, her now bare breasts feeling tender against his chest. Her nipples scraping against his chest hair. And she loved it. The intensity of it. That was another thing. She hadn't realized it would be like this. In her mind, making love was something gauzy and sweet. But this felt raw. A feast for her every sense. The smell of his skin, the touch of his hands. The rough and the soft. Pain and pleasure. Desire that took root so deep it was uncomfortable.

A desperation for satisfaction and a need for the torment to be drawn out, so she could exist like this forever.

Balancing on a wire, precarious and brave, suspended over a glittering and breathless night sky.

If she fell, she was sure she would fall forever.

But if she didn't fall…

Well, then she would never know.

Both were terrifying.

Both were exhilarating.

And when he laid her down on the plush carpet by the fire and pushed his hand beneath the waistband of her panties, she felt her control, along with that wire, begin to fray.

His fingers were deft, finding the center of her need, stoking the fire inside of her and raising the flame of her need to unbearable levels.

Dimly, she thought she should maybe be embarrassed about all of this. It was the first time a man had ever touched her like this. The first time a man had ever seen her naked. But she felt no shame. None at all. Because it was him. And that made no sense, because he was a virtual stranger.

But not in the ways that counted. Not in those places that no one else could see, or reach.

He was a beast, transformed by the sins of his father. And she was a captive because of the sins of hers.

They both had big houses. Wealth. Certain amounts of power.

They were both alone in many ways. But not here. Not now.

So there was nothing to be embarrassed about. Nothing to be ashamed of. When his mouth abandoned hers and began to move downward, her breath hitched, her body growing tense. He moved to her breast first, sucking one tightened bud between his lips, extracting a gasp from her, making her writhe with pleasure. He pressed his hand firmly between her breasts, his touch quieting her before he moved those knowing fingers back down between her legs. Teased her slick folds, pressed a finger inside of her.

She squirmed, trying to wiggle away from the invasion. Until he began to stroke the center of her need with his thumb, the strangeness of the penetration easing as desire began to build.

He kissed a path down her stomach, down farther still, and replaced his thumb with his wicked lips and tongue, stroking her inside in time with those movements.

She shivered, her desire building to unbearable levels.

"My name," he growled against her tender flesh. "Say my name. So that I know."

How could he doubt it? Of course it was only his name. She didn't care at all. Not for anyone else.

"Javier."

He searched upward, claiming her mouth with his, and she could taste her own desire on his lips. She wanted more. Wanted to taste him. Wanted to torment him the way that he had tormented her.

But he was easing himself between her thighs, the blunt head of him right there, causing a tremor of fear to rush through her. But that was stolen when he captured her lips again, kissed her to the point of mindlessness before easing deeper inside of her. Before thrusting all the way home.

The stretching, burning sensation took her breath away, but she didn't want it to stop. Because this was what she had been waiting for. This felt significant. It felt altering. This was the new, this was the different that she had known lay on the other side of this. The transformation.

And when he was fully seated inside of her, she lowered her head against his shoulder, shuddering against the pain, but embracing it all the same.

He froze for a moment, but then he began to move.

She was blinded by the intensity of it. That sense of

him, so large and hard filling her like this. It made it so she couldn't breathe. Couldn't think. Couldn't speak. Couldn't do anything but surrender to this thing that was overtaking them like a storm.

She clung to his shoulders, clung to him to keep herself rooted to the earth. Rooted to the floor. To keep it so that it was still the two of them in this library. So that no other thoughts could invade. No other people. No other expectations.

It was just them.

She didn't have to be the best. She didn't have to be better than her brother. She didn't have to make herself important.

She simply had to be.

All feeling. No calculation. No striving. Just bright, brilliant pleasure, crackling through her like fireworks.

And she was back again, poised on that wire, with the endless sea of nothing and brilliance shining beneath her. She was afraid. Because she didn't know what might happen next. But he was holding her, moving inside of her, over her, in her. And all she could do was cling to him. All she could do was trust in him, in a way that she had never trusted in another person.

But that's what this was. That's what it really was.

The giving of trust, sharing it. Because as vulnerable as she was in this moment, he was too. Because as much as she had to trust him to hold her in his arms, she was holding him as well.

And even as she felt so feminine, vulnerable and small, she had also never felt quite so equal. Quite so happy in those differences.

But then, she couldn't hold on, not any longer. He thrust inside of her one last time, and she was cast into the deep. And what she found there was an endless world of pleasure that she hadn't known existed. So deep and real and intense.

He followed her there. His roar of pleasure reverberating inside of her.

And all the stars around her were made of brilliance and fire. And when she opened her eyes, she realized that the flames were right there. In the fireplace. And she was still in the library.

And Javier was still with her.

She could feel his heart beating just like hers. A little bit too fast. A little bit too hard.

She wanted to cling to him. But he was already moving away.

"This cannot be endured," he growled.

He pushed his fingers through his dark hair, curving his muscular shoulders forward. And even as she realized that the bliss, the connection they had just shared was over, she couldn't help but admire his golden physique, illuminated in the firelight.

"I didn't mind it," she said quietly.

"Why didn't you tell me?"

"Tell you what?"

"You were a virgin."

"Oh. That. Well, if it helps, I didn't really plan to be."

"You realize that makes this worse."

"How?"

"Because I have... I have spoiled you."

"I thought you said that was a promise," she said quietly. "A vow, if I didn't mistake you. That you would ruin me for other men."

"That is not what I mean now," he said, his tone feral. He stood up, and she went dry mouthed at the sight of his naked body.

"No. What do you mean? Perhaps I need clarification?"

"If you were a virgin, then it was meant for him."

"It was meant for who I gave it to."

"Did you give it to me? Or did you fling it away knowing what you were doing."

"No." She winced internally, not because she'd been thinking of her virginity, but she had considered the fact that this would make the marriage to Matteo difficult. But in the end, it wasn't why she had done it. "We don't all live in the Dark Ages, Javier, and you know that. I don't come from this world. Who I decide to sleep with is my choice and my business, and it is not a medieval bargaining tool, however my father treated me and my body. I do not owe you an explanation."

"But I owed my brother my loyalty."

"Then the failure is yours," she spat, feeling defensive and angry, all the beautiful feelings that she had felt only moments before melting away. "It was my first time, and you're ruining it. It was really quite nice before you started talking."

"But it is a reality we must deal with," he said. "You are to marry my brother."

"You can't possibly think that I will go through with it after this."

He stared at her, his eyes dark, bleak.

"You do. You honestly think that whatever this greater good is that your brother plans… You honestly think that it's more important than what I want. Than what passed between us here. You know that I don't want to marry him. Putting aside the fact that we just made love… You know that I want to go home."

Fury filled her. Impotent and fiery. She just wanted to rage. Wanted to turn things over. Because she felt utterly and completely altered, and he remained stone.

"How can nothing have changed for you?"

"Because the world around me did not change. My obligations did not change."

"This was a mistake," she said. "It was a huge mistake."

She began to collect her clothes, and she dressed as quickly as possible. Then she ran out of the library without looking back. Pain lashed at her chest. Her heart felt raw and bloodied.

How could he have devastated her like this? It had been her plan. Her seduction plan to try to gain a bid for freedom, and it had ended...

She felt heartbroken.

Because this thing between them had felt singular and new, and so had she. Because it had felt like maybe it was something worth fighting for.

But not for him.

When she closed the bedroom door behind her, for the first time she truly did feel like a prisoner.

But not a prisoner of this palace, a prisoner of the demons that lurked inside of Javier.

And she didn't know if there would be any escaping them.

When Matteo returned two days later, Javier had only one goal in mind.

He knew that what he was doing was an utter violation of his position. But he had already done that.

But things had become clearer and clearer to him over the past couple of days. And while he knew that his actions had been unforgivable, there was only one course of action to take.

"You need to set her free," he said when he walked into his brother's office.

"Would you excuse us, Livia?"

Like the mouse he often called her, Livia scurried from the room.

"You must be very happy with her performance on the business trip to address her by her first name."

"I am. Now, who exactly do I have to set free?"

"Violet King. You cannot hold her. You cannot possibly be enforcing her father's medieval bargaining."

"I instigated the medieval bargain. So obviously I'm interested in preserving it."

"She will be willing to offer her business services. But she does not wish to marry you."

"Why exactly do you care?" Matteo asked, his brother always too insightful.

"I slept with her," Javier said. "Obviously you can see why it would be problematic for her to remain here."

Matteo appraised him with eyes that were impossible to read. "You know I don't actually care if you've slept with her. As long as you don't sleep with her after I marry her."

"You aren't angry about it?" The idea of Matteo touching Violet filled him with fury. That his brother could feel nothing...

Well, he didn't know her. He didn't deserve her.

Matteo waved a hand. "I have no stronger feelings about her than I do for my assistant. She's a useful potential tool. Nothing more. What she does with her body is her business."

"I betrayed you," Javier said.

"How? She has made no vows to me. And I don't love her."

For the first time, Javier found his brother's complete lack of emotion infuriating. Because he had wasted time having far too many emotions about the entire thing, and apparently it didn't matter after all.

"Let her go."

"Now see, that does bother me, Javier. Because my word is law."

"And you wanted to know when you were overstepping. And it is now. She doesn't wish to marry you. She wishes to leave."

"And her wishes override mine?"

"You would force a woman down the aisle?"

"I told you what I wanted."

"And I'm here to tell you it isn't going to happen. She is mine."

"Then you marry her."

He jerked backward. "What?"

"You marry her."

"Why the hell does anyone have to marry her?"

"Because I made a bargain with her father. And I don't like to go back on a bargain. It was what he promised me in exchange for his freedom. I didn't ask, if you were wondering."

"He simply… Offered her?"

"Yes. I think he liked the idea of a connection with royalty."

"She doesn't want it."

"But you see, I made a business deal with Robert King. He gave me some very tactical business advice that was needed at the time. In exchange I promised that I would make his daughter royalty. Make him a real king, so to speak."

"In exchange for?"

"Manufacturing rights."

"Violet is prepared to offer those for her makeup line."

"Great. I'm glad to hear it. I would like both. Either I marry her or you do it, younger brother, but someone has to."

Javier stared at his brother, more a brick wall than even

Javier was. And for the first time he truly resented that his brother was the leader of the nation and he owed him loyalty. Because he would like to tell him exactly where he could shove his edict. Because they were two alpha males with an equal amount of physical strength and a definite lack of a desire to be ruled by anyone.

But his brother was the oldest. So he was the only one that actually got to give that free rein.

But Javier thought of Violet. Violet.

And he could send her away, or he could keep her.

The beast in the castle.

He could have her. Always. Could keep her for his own and not have to apologize for it.

"Why did you make it sound like her father didn't have any power? Like he'd lost a bet?"

"That's what he told me. He didn't want her to know that he had traded her for a business deal. He instructed me that when the time was right… I should embellish a little bit."

"That bastard."

"Honestly. He's decent enough compared to our father."

"Our father should not be a metric for good parenting in comparison to anyone."

"Perhaps not. So, what's it to be?"

"Even if I marry her, you will still have to marry."

"I'm aware," Matteo said. "I'm sure my mouse can help with that."

"I'm sure she shall be delighted to."

"She is ever delighted to serve my every whim. After all, I am her Savior, am I not?"

"I cannot imagine a worse possible man to serve as Savior. To owe you a debt must be a truly miserable thing. I will marry Violet."

"Interesting," Matteo said. "I did not expect you to accept."

"If you touch her," Javier said, "I will make good on my promise and find an excuse to kill you."

"So you have feelings for her?"

He had, for many years, looked into his soul and seen only darkness. But she had somehow traversed into that darkness and left the tiniest shard of hope in him. A small sliver of light. But it wasn't his. It was hers. He feared that the laughter she'd placed in him, the smile she'd put on his lips…he feared in the end his darkness would consume it.

But like any starving creature, hungry for warmth, he could not turn away either.

Though he knew he should.

Though it went against all he knew he should do, all he knew he should be. "She's mine. I'm not sure why it took this long for me to accept it. I'm the one who went and claimed her. You've kept your hands clean of it the entire time. If I'm going to go to all the trouble of kidnapping a woman, she ought to belong in my bed, don't you think?"

"As you wish."

"I do."

"Congratulations, then. On your upcoming marriage."

CHAPTER TEN

VIOLET'S ANXIETY WAS steadily mounting. Everything had come crashing down on her that moment in the library. The reality of it all. And then in the crushing silence Javier had delivered in the days since, it had all become more and more frightening.

She knew that Matteo was back.

But she still hadn't seen him. Everything was beginning to feel...

Well, it was all beginning to feel far too real.

When she had gone back to her room after they'd made love, her body had ached. Been sore and tender in places she had never been overly conscious of.

And her heart had burned. The sting of his rejection, of pain that she hadn't anticipated.

And she couldn't decide exactly what manner of pain it was.

That he had still been willing to give her to his brother, that he didn't seem to care what she wanted.

That he didn't seem to want her in the way that she wanted him, because if he did then the idea of her being with another man would...

Well, it was unthinkable to her, and on some level she wished it were unthinkable to him.

That he didn't care that she wanted her freedom, because didn't the beast always let the beauty go?

But maybe this was the real lesson.

Because how many times had her female friends been distraught over one-night stands that had ended with silence? How often had they been certain that there was some sort of connection only to discover it was all inside of them? Violet had been certain that what was passing between herself and Javier had been magical. That it had been real, and that it had been real for both of them.

But that had been a virgin's folly. She was certain of that now.

And she was trapped here. Trapped.

For the first time, she knew that she needed to call home.

But not her father. Not her mother.

Instead, she took her phone out and dialed her sister, Minerva.

"Violet," Minerva said as soon as she answered. "Where are you?"

"Monte Blanco," she said, looking out her bedroom window at the mountains below.

Even the view had lost some of its magic. But then it was difficult to enjoy the view when you were finally coming to accept that you were in fact in prison.

"Why?"

It wasn't any surprise to her that her bookish younger sister had heard of the country.

"Well. It's a long story. But it involves Dad making a marriage bargain for me. With a king that I still haven't met."

"I'm sorry, what?"

"I'm serious. I got kidnapped by a prince."

"I... What is your life like?" she asked incredulously.

"Currently or in general?"

"I just don't know very many people who can say they've been kidnapped by a prince. At least not with such flat affect."

"Well, I have been. And it isn't a joke. Anyway. You lied and told the world that you had our brother's billionaire best friend's baby."

"Sure," Minerva said. "But Dante never kidnapped me."

"He did take you off to his private island."

"To protect me. That's different."

"Sure," Violet said. "Look. I don't know if I'm going to be able to get out of this. I'm trying… But I'm here now. I'm in the palace. Then… The worst part is… I… He's not the one that I want."

The door to her bedroom opened, and she turned around, the phone still clutched in her hand, and there Javier was, standing there looking like a forbidding Angel.

"I'm going to have to call you back."

"No. You can't say something cryptic like that and then go away."

"I have to. Sorry."

"Should I call the police?"

"I'm the captive of a king, Minerva. As in an actual king, not our last name. The police can't help me."

She hung the phone up then and stared at Javier. "Have you come to deliver me to my bridegroom?"

They hadn't been face-to-face since that night. The last time she'd seen him he had been naked. And so had she. Her skin burned with the memory.

"Who are you talking to?"

"My sister. Oddly, I have a lot on my mind."

"I spoke to Matteo."

She took a deep breath and braced herself. "And?"

"You are not marrying him."

A roar of relief filled her ears, and suddenly she felt like she might faint.

"You mean I'm free to go?"

"No," he said gravely.

"But you just said that I don't have to marry him."

"No. But you do have to marry me."

"I'm sorry, what?"

"It turns out that neither my brother nor your father were honest about the particulars of the situation. You may want to call him and speak to him. But my brother made a commandment. He said one of us had to marry you. But that sending you home was not an option."

"Except, what's to stop you from letting me go?"

"I refuse," Javier said. "He has turned your charge over to me completely. And that means you're staying here. With me."

"But I have a life, and you know that. We... We know each other."

"And you wanted me to be something other than what I am. You want to believe that I am a man made into a beast. But you never gave space to the idea that I might simply be a beast. Given free rein to keep you, I think that I will. We are very compatible, are we not?"

"You..."

And she realized that the strange, leaping, twisting in her heart was because she was as terrified about this new development as she was exhilarated.

This man, this beautiful man, was demanding she become his wife.

And he was the man that she wanted.

If his words had been filled with happiness. If there had been any indication that he felt emotion for her, then she would have been... She would have only been happy. But there wasn't. Not at all. He was hard and stoic as ever, presenting this as nothing more than another edict as impersonal as the one that came before it, as if they had not been skin to skin. As if he had not rearranged unseen places inside of her. As if he had not been the scene of her greatest act of liberation, and her greatest downfall.

"Just like that. You expect me to marry you."

"Yes," he said.

"I don't understand."

"There is nothing to understand. You will simply do as you're commanded. As you are in Monte Blanco now. And the law here is the law you are beholden to."

"But you don't care at all what I want."

"To be free. To go back to your life. To pretend as if none of this had ever happened. But it has. And you're mine now."

"Why? Why are you marrying me instead of him? I don't seem to matter to you. Not one bit."

That was when he closed the distance between them. He wrapped his arm around her waist and pulled her up against his body. "Because you are mine. No other man will ever touch you. I am the first. I will be the last."

She was angry then that she hadn't had the presence of mind to lie to him when they'd made love. Because it would have been much more satisfying in the end. To take that from him, when it clearly mattered.

"I will be the only one. Didn't I promise you? That no other man would ever satisfy you as I did?"

"Yes," she said, her throat dry.

"I know no man will ever have the chance to try."

"That's all you want. To own me?"

"It's all I can do."

There was a bleakness to that statement that touched something inside of her. This, for him, was as close to emotion as he could come. It was also bound up in his control.

In that deep belief that he was a monster of some kind. He had told her he was not good, but that he had honor.

And she could see now that he was willing to leave her behind, embrace greed.

And on some level she had no one to blame but herself. Because hadn't she appealed to that part of him when she had seduced him in the library? Hadn't it been on the tip of her tongue to ask him why he was so content to let his brother have what he so clearly wanted?

But he didn't need her goading him to embrace those things now. He emanated with them. With raw, masculine intent. With a deep, dark claim that she could see he was intent to stamp upon her body.

Unknowing he had already put one on her soul.

It wasn't that he didn't feel it, she realized. It was that he didn't understand it.

Perhaps she had not felt the depth of those emotions alone. It was only that he did not know how to name them. Only that he did not understand them.

"And what will it mean for me? To be your wife?"

He stared at her, his dark eyes unreadable. "You did not ask me that. About my brother."

"Because I wasn't going to marry him."

She let the implied truth in those words sit there between them. Expand. Let him bring his own meaning to them.

"There will be less responsibility as my wife. I do not have the public face that he does."

"And if I should wish to?"

"Whatever you wish," he said. "It can be accommodated."

"What about charities?"

"You know that we would actively seek to establish

them. We must improve the view of our country with the rest of the world."

"My charity in particular," she said.

"Supported. However much you would like."

"The control of my money?"

He shrugged. "Remains with you."

"And if I refuse..."

"Everything you have will belong to my brother. And you will be bound to us either way."

"Then I suppose there is no choice."

There was. They both knew it. It was just a choice with a consequence she wasn't willing to take on.

And there was a still, small voice inside of her that asked if she still thought she was lost in the fairy tale.

If she was still convinced that she was the maiden sent to tame a beast.

Whatever the reason, she found herself nodding in agreement. Whatever the reason, she knew what her course would be.

"All right. I'll marry you. I will be a princess."

The announcement happened the very next day. Media splashed it all over the world. And she was compelled to put up a post with a photograph of the view outside of her bedchamber and an assortment of vague gushing comments.

"Will I be expected to give up all forms of social media?"

"No," Javier said. "Your visibility is appreciated. An asset."

"Indeed," she mused, looking at the glorious meal spread out before her.

"I will need a ring," she said. "It will have to be spectacular. Don't mistake me. It's not because I have any great need of a massive diamond. Simply that you want me to make some kind of a spectacle. Getting engaged to a prince will require that I have a very strong jewelry game."

"I will bring the Crown Jewels out of the vault for your examination, My Princess."

"Are you teasing me or not?"

"I am not."

The problem was, she couldn't really tell. And the other problem was, in the days since the engagement announcement, there had been no further intimacy between them.

The sense that she had known him had dissipated with their thwarted afterglow, and now she simply felt… Numb.

"Well. I guess… I guess that would be acceptable."

It was more than acceptable to him, apparently, because as soon as they were finished with the meal, he ushered her into the library, which felt pointed, and told her that the jewels would appear.

And appear they did. Members of his staff came in with box after box and laid them all out on the various pieces of furniture throughout the room. On the settee, the different end tables, a coffee table.

She blushed furiously when her eyes fell on the place by the fire, where she had given herself to Javier and cemented her fate.

"This is maybe a little bit much…"

"You said you wanted spectacular. And so I have determined that I won't disappoint you." His dark eyes seemed to glow with black fire. She wondered how she had ever thought them cold. Now she felt the heat in them like a living flame inside her chest.

He moved to one of the end tables and opened the first box. Inside was a ring, ornate, laden with jewels that glittered in the firelight. And she would never be able to see firelight without thinking of his skin. Without thinking of his strong body searching inside of her. It was impossible.

She blushed, focusing on the jewel. Then, those large, capable hands moved to the next box. He opened it, revealing a ring filled with emeralds. The next, champagne diamonds. Citrine, rubies, every gem in every cut and color was revealed.

"There are the rings," he said.

"I…"

"Would you like me to choose for you?"

At first, she bucked against the idea. But what did it matter? Their marriage wasn't going to be a real one anyway. So what did it matter what she wore.

The idea made her eyes feel dry, made her throat feel raw. Because something about this felt real to her. More real than the diamonds that were laid before her. More real than the stones around them. This entire palace was made of gems; why she should be surprised and awed at the splendor laid before her she didn't know. But they were not real. Not in the way that the conviction and need that burned in her heart was.

This man was.

A man. Not a mountain. Not a beast. No matter how much he might want to believe that he was either of the latter.

The ring didn't matter, on that level. But it would matter what he chose for her. In the same way that it mattered the first night they had been together that she had known that he would be in the library. Known that he would be holding that book. Known that whatever he said, he was seeking a connection between the two of them. To deepen it. Because it was real. It was there.

She had spent her life seeking connections. Using connections. She had spent her life trying to show her father that she was worthy. That she was just as good as her brother, Maximus. Just as charming and delightful as her sister, Minerva.

But with Javier it was just there.

Whether they wanted it to be or not. And she had to cling to the fact that something in that was real.

"You can choose," she said.

"Very well."

It was the ruby that he picked up between his thumb and forefinger. He didn't even have to pause to think. With his dark eyes glowing with a black flame, he took her hand in his and he slipped that ring onto her finger.

"Mine," he said.

"Mine," she returned, curling her fingers around his. "If I am yours, then you must be mine."

There was something stark and shocked on his face as she said those words. "I'm a modern woman," she returned. "I believe in equality. If you expect that you will own my body, then I will own yours."

He inclined his head slowly. "As you wish."

"I like it," she said, looking down at the gem.

"Good. Because there is more."

He went to the coffee table, where wider, flatter jewelry boxes were set. He opened first one, then another. Necklaces. Spectacular and glittering with an intensity that mocked the fire.

There was one made of rubies, one that matched the ring. He pulled it out, held it aloft. All of her words were stolen from her. Lost completely in the moment.

And for her, it wasn't about the value of the gems, but about the care of the selection. About the fact that he knew what he wanted to see her wear. That he had chosen them for her. The necklace settled heavily across her breastbone, and he clasped it gently behind her neck.

The metal was cold against her skin and felt erotic somehow. She shivered. Of course, agreeing to be his wife meant more of this. This touching. This need.

This need satisfied and sated when they needed it.

He looked up at her, slid his thumb along her lower lip. And she shivered.

"Last time I had you here you belonged to him."

She shook her head. "No. I never did."

The corner of his mouth curved upward, and she recognized it for what it was: triumph.

"The tradition of what royal marriage means has been lost in my family," he said, his voice rough. "Have you read any of the other books on these shelves?"

She nodded. "A few."

"Did you happen to read about marriage customs?"

"No."

"Then I will explain. Because service is to be given, first to the country. Those who are royal do not belong to themselves. They belong to Monte Blanco. The woman who marries into the family surrenders in the same way."

"What about a man who marries into the family?" she asked.

"Women cannot sit on the throne here."

"That seems...unfair."

"I have seen how heavy the weight of the position is for my brother. I would call it a blessing."

"But it's gender bias either way."

"You may lobby for a change when we are wed."

He didn't even sound all that irritated with her.

It made her want to smile.

"A marriage into the royal family is a surrender of self," he said. "Except...except between the husband and wife there is a bond considered sacred. Nearly supernatural."

He moved his hand behind her back, and on an indrawing of her breath he undid the zipper on her dress with one fluid motion. It fell down her body, pooling onto the floor. Leaving her in her shoes, her underwear, the necklace and that ring.

Her nipples went tight in the cold air, her lack of a bra not a consideration before this moment, but now, with his hungry eyes on her…

She shivered.

"They have surrendered themselves to the greater good. To the nation. But in the walls of their bedchamber they surrender to each other. They belong only to each other. And it is ownership, *querida*. Not a partnership the way you think of it in your modern world."

"But they own each other," she pressed.

He nodded slowly, then he moved to the couch, and picked up another box. He opened it up and revealed two thick, heavy-looking bracelets. Gold and ruby, matching the rest of the jewels.

He moved close to her body and she responded. Being bare as she was with him so near made it impossible for her to breathe. To think.

He took the first bracelet out and clasped it tightly on her wrist. Then he took the second and put it around the other.

She felt the weight of them, heavy in a way that went beyond the materials they were forged from.

He moved again. "Surely there isn't more," she said breathlessly.

"Surely there is," he murmured.

The next box contained cuffs that looked much like the ones on her wrists.

"Do you know what these are?"

"No," she said, the word a whisper.

"These are very ancient. They have been in my family for hundreds of years."

"Oh."

"Out of use for generations. They are deeply symbolic. And they are never worn in public."

"Where are they worn?"

He looked at her with meaning.

"Oh."

"They speak of this ownership that I feel. The ownership I told you about, in these royal marriages."

"Oh," she said again, her throat dry, her heart fluttering in her chest like a trapped bird.

"Permit me."

And she didn't even consider refusing.

He knelt before her. With great care, he removed her shoes and set them aside. Then he lifted his hands, hooked his fingers in the waistband of her underwear and drew them slowly down her legs. A pulse beat hard at the apex of her thighs, and she closed her eyes tight for a moment, trying to find her balance.

She was embarrassed, to be naked with him kneeling down before her like this. And she didn't want to look. But also… She couldn't bear to not watch what he might do next.

So she opened her eyes, looked at him, his dark head bent, his position one of seeming submission.

But she knew better.

He clasped the first cuff to her ankle. Then the second.

Then, nestled in those jewelry boxes she spotted something she hadn't seen before. Gold chains. Without taking his eyes from her, he clasped one end of the first chain to her ring on the left ankle cuff, then attached it to the one on the right.

After that, he rose up, taking the other gold chain in his hand, sliding it between his fingers and looking at her with intent. Then he repeated the same motion he had completed on her ankles with her wrists.

She blinked several times, trying to gather herself. She took a fortifying breath. "I don't understand," she whispered. "Surely these wouldn't actually keep anyone captive. They're far too fine."

"They're not intended to keep anyone captive. Not really. This captivity is a choice," he said, curling his forefinger around the chain that connected her hands. He tugged gently, and she responded to the pressure, taking two steps toward him. "It is a choice," he said again.

Understanding filled her.

Because he was giving her a moment now. To make the choice. Or to run.

It fully hit her now that it was a choice she had made. To stay here. To say yes to him.

She stood, and she didn't move.

She tilted her face upward, the motion her clear and obvious consent. He wrapped his hand more tightly around the chain, bringing her yet closer, and he claimed her mouth with his.

The gold was fine, delicate and such a soft metal. She could break free if she chose. But she didn't. Instead, she let him hold her as a captive, kissing her deep and hard. His one hand remained around the chain, and his other came up to cup her face, guiding her as he took the kiss deep, his tongue sliding against hers, slick and wonderful.

Hot.

Possessive.

He released his hold on her, taking a step back and beginning to unbutton his shirt, revealing hard-cut muscles that never failed to make her feel weak. To make her feel strong. Because wasn't the woman who enticed such a man to pleasure, to a betrayal of all that he was, even more powerful than he in many ways?

Maybe, maybe not. But she felt it.

This, this thing between them, was something that was hers and hers alone.

His.

Theirs.

Two people who belonged to a nation. But belonged to each other first.

She understood it.

He shrugged his shirt off his powerful shoulders and cast it onto the ground. Then, he wrapped his hand around the chain again and began to tug downward. "Kneel before royalty," he said, his voice rough.

And she did. Going down to her knees, the cuffs pressing against her ankles, the chain from her wrists pooling in her lap.

She looked up at him and watched, her mouth going dry as he undid his belt, slid it through the loops on his pants. She was captivated as the leather slid over his palm before he unclasped his pants, lowered the zipper.

And revealed himself, hot and hard and masculine. Hard for her.

A choice.

This was her choice. No matter the position of submission.

Just as when he had knelt before her, fastening the cuffs, it had appeared that he was the one submitting, but he had been in power. It was the same for her.

She reached up and circled her fingers around his length, stroked him up and down.

It was amazing to her that she had never been overcome by desire for a man in her life before, but everything about him filled her with need. He was beautiful. Every masculine inch of him. She stretched up, still on her knees, and took him into her mouth. He growled, the beast coming forward, and she reveled in that.

Because here was the power. Here was the mutual submission. That belonging that he had spoken of. She in chains, on her knees, but with the most vulnerable part of him to do with as she pleased. His pleasure at her command. His body at her mercy.

She was lost in this. In the magic created between the two of them. Even more powerful than it had been the first time.

Because she had all these physical markers of who she belonged to. And everything about his surrender proved that he belonged to her.

She kept on pleasuring him until he shook. Until his muscles, the very foundation of all that he was began to tremble. Until his hands went to her hair and tugged tightly, moving her away from his body.

"That is not how we will finish," he growled.

He lifted her up from the ground, setting her on the edge of the settee. Then he kissed her, claiming her mouth with ferocity. He moved his hand to her thigh and lifted it to his shoulders, looping the chain so that it was around the back of his neck. Then he did the same with the other, so that he was between her legs, secured there.

Holding her tightly, he lowered his head, placing his mouth between her legs and lapping at her with the flat of his tongue. Giving her everything she had given to him, and then some. He feasted on her until she was shivering. Until she was screaming with her desire for release. Begging.

Until she no longer felt strong, but she didn't need to. Because she felt safe. Because she felt like his, and that was every bit as good.

When she found her release, she was undone by it. The walls inside of her crumbling, every resistance destroyed. Defeated. And then, the blunt head of his arousal was pressing against the entrance to her body, and she received him willingly.

He thrust hard inside of her, her legs still draped over his shoulders, the angle making it impossibly deep. Taking her breath away.

Their coming together was a storm. And she didn't seek shelter from it. Instead, she flung her arms wide and let the rain pour down on her. Let it all overtake her. Consume her.

She held on to his shoulders, dug her fingernails into his skin as her pleasure built inside of her again. Impossibly so.

And when they broke, they broke together. But when they came back to earth, they were together as well.

And she realized that he was circled by the chains as well. As bound to her as she was to him.

And they lay there in the library, neither of them moving.

Neither of them seeking escape.

And whatever he had said about his brother mandating the marriage, whatever she had said about not being able to surrender to his country, she looked into his eyes then, and she saw it. Clearly for them both.

It was a choice.

She was choosing him. The same as he was choosing her.

And the only sharp part of the moment was wishing that he might have chosen her for the same reason that she was choosing him.

She had fallen in love.

As she looked into those fathomless black eyes, she knew that it was not the same for him.

CHAPTER ELEVEN

HE DIDN'T SHARE her bed that night.

It wounded her more than a little. She had hoped that… that she tested his control a little more than that. Especially considering he had reshaped her into a person she didn't recognize.

One who had agreed to stay here.

Who had agreed to marry a man she barely knew.

Except…

Didn't she know him? On a soul-deep level? It was terrifying how real it all felt. She loved him. He had taken such a large piece of who she was in such a small amount of time.

And with the same certainty that she loved him, she knew he didn't feel the same.

She wasn't even sure he could.

It didn't change her heart, though.

Maybe she could change his. She hoped.

First, though, she had to take care of her life.

She took a deep breath and fortified herself. Then looked down at her phone.

Violet knew that it was time to speak to her father. She had been avoiding it for weeks now.

And it wasn't that she hadn't received calls from her family in the time since her engagement to Javier had been announced. She had. The only calls she had been at home to were from her brother and from her sister.

Maximus had been stern, and she had waved off his concerns. Minerva had been… Well, Minerva. Thoughtful, practical and a bit overly romantic. But then, Violet herself was being a bit romantic.

And anyway, she had talked Minerva through her situation with Dante, when the two of them had been having issues, and so of course Minerva had been supportive of whatever Violet wanted.

But her parents… She had avoided them. Completely. Not today. Today she was ready to have the discussion.

Today she was ready to hear whatever the answers might be.

That was the real issue.

If she was going to ask her father for an explanation, she had to be prepared to hear the explanation.

But something had shifted in her last night. That decisiveness.

She was no longer hiding from the fact that she had chosen this. That Javier was her choice.

That being in Monte Blanco was her choice.

She took a fortifying breath, and she selected her father's number.

"Violet," he said, his tone rough.

"Hi," she said, not exactly sure what to feel. A sense of relief at hearing his voice, because she had missed him even while she had been angry at him.

At least, missed the way that she had felt about him before.

"Are you all right?"

"It's a little bit late for you to be concerned about that."

"Why? I didn't expect that you would be cut off from communication with me."

"I haven't been. I've been perfectly able to call and communicate with whoever I wished."

"You haven't come back to California. You haven't been at work. From what I've heard you've only given minimal instruction to your team. It's not like you."

"Well. You'll have to forgive me. I've never been kidnapped before. Neither have I been engaged to be married to two different men in the space of a few weeks. Strangers, at that."

"I meant to speak to you about this," he said.

"You meant to speak to me about it?"

"It was never intended to be a surprise. But I lost my nerve when it came to speaking to you after I struck the deal."

"I can't imagine why. Were you afraid that I would be angry that you sold me like I was a prized heifer?"

"I figured that if I could position it the right way, you would see why it was a good thing. Being a businesswoman is one thing, Violet, but a princess? A queen?"

"Well, I'm not going to be Queen now. I got knocked down to the spare, rather than the heir."

"What happened?"

Her father sounded genuinely distressed by that. "Do you really care?"

"It would've been better for you to marry Matteo. He is the King."

"No," she said, "it wouldn't be better for me to marry Matteo, because I don't have any feelings for him."

"Are you telling me you have feelings for... The other one?"

"Why do you care? You let him take me. You let me be kidnapped and held for reasons of marriage without explaining to me why. Without... Dad, I thought that I was worth more to you than just another card to be dealt from your businessman hand. You would never have done this to Maximus."

"Well, quite apart from the fact that neither of them would have wanted to marry Maximus…"

"Why not Minerva?"

"It was clear to me from the beginning that Minerva would not have made a good princess. But you…"

"I went on to build my own business. To build my own fortune. You didn't know that I would do that when you promised me to him at sixteen. And in the last decade you didn't have the courage to speak to me even one time about it."

"It won't impact your ability to run your business. I mean, certainly you'll have to farm out some of the day-to-day, but you're mostly a figurehead anyway."

"I'm not," she said. "I brainstorm most of the new products. I'm in charge of implementation. I'm not just a figurehead." Her stomach sank. "But that's what you think, isn't it? You think that I've only accomplished any of this because of my connection with you."

It hit her then that her father genuinely thought he had been giving her a gift on some level. That there was nothing of substance that she had accomplished on her own, and nothing that she could.

And he couldn't even see that. It didn't even feel like a lack of love to him. And maybe it wasn't.

It was a deeply rooted way that he seemed to see his girls versus the way he saw his son. Perhaps the way he saw women versus the way he saw men.

"It was a good thing that you did," she said, "when you took Dante in from the streets of Rome. You thought he was smart. You sent him to school. If he had been a woman, would you have just tried to make a marriage for him?"

"I know what you're thinking," her father said. "That I don't think you're smart. I do. I think you're brilliant, Violet. And I think you're wonderful with people. Women have a different sort of power in this world. I don't see the harm in acknowledging that. I don't see the harm in allowing you to use that in a way that is easier. You can try to compete with men in the business world, but you'll always be at a disadvantage."

"I want to be very clear," Violet said. "I am choosing this. Not for you. Your views are not only antiquated, they're morally wrong. That you see me as secondary to you, as incapable, is one of the most hurtful things I've ever had to face."

"I'm protecting you. No matter what happens with commerce, you'll always be a princess once you marry…"

"Javier. I want you to know that I'm choosing to marry him. Because I care about him. I'm not afraid of losing everything, Dad. Not the way that you are."

"That's because you don't know what it's like to have nothing," her father said. "I do. I didn't have anything when I started out. And I built my empire from nothing. You built yours off mine. Easy enough for you to say that you're not afraid to lose it."

"Maybe so," she said. "And I've always felt that, you know. That I built this off something that you started. And I suppose you could say that my marriage here is built off something that you started. But I'm the one that's choosing this. I'm the one that's choosing to make all that I can from it."

"Violet, I know that you're not happy with me about this, but clearly it worked out for the best."

She thought of last night. Of the passion that had erupted between her and Javier. Of the way that she felt for him.

It didn't feel like the best. It felt necessary. It felt real and raw and closer to who she was than anything else ever had. But it wasn't easy. And it wouldn't be. Ever. Because Javier wasn't easy. And she wouldn't want him to be, not really.

She wished that he might love her.

The strength of their connection was so powerful she had to believe… He was wounded. She knew that. He was scarred by his past.

He would fight against his feelings.

But he had accepted the marriage. He wanted them to choose each other, own each other.

She was certain of nothing, but she trusted that commitment.

She had to hope that someday it could become more.

"It didn't work out for the best because of you," Violet said. "You can't take credit for what I felt. And believe me, the relationship I have with Javier I built."

She hung up the phone then.

She didn't know what she was going to do about her relationship with her father going forward. Though living half a world away was certainly helpful.

The kind of distance required for her to get her head on straight. That was for sure.

And now she had to clear her mind. Because tonight there was going to be a dinner with foreign dignitaries. And Javier had told her that in light of the fact he had no people skills, she was going to have to do the heavy lifting for him.

Conviction burned in her chest.

He needed her to be his other half.

And so she would be.

She would choose to be.

Perhaps if she went first, if she forged that path with love, he would be able to find his way into loving her back.

* * *

An impromptu dinner with foreign dignitaries was not Javier's idea of fun. But then, few things were his idea of fun. And if he had his way, he would simply walk out of the dining room and take Violet straight back to bed. But tonight was not about having his way. Unfortunately.

She looked radiant. She had sent one of the members of the palace staff to town and instructed them to return with a golden gown from a local shop. And they had delivered. She was wearing something filmy and gauzy that clung to her curves while still looking sedate.

Her hair was slick, captured in a low bun, and her makeup was similar to how it had been the first day they'd met. More elaborate than anything she had done during their time together here at the palace.

He found he liked something about that as well.

That this was her public face. And that the soft, scrubbed-fresh woman with edible pink lips and wild dark hair was his and his alone.

She was standing there, talking to a woman from Nigeria, both of their hand gestures becoming animated, and he could only guess about what.

But Violet was passionate about her charities. About businesses that centered around women, and he imagined it had something to do with that.

"She is quite something," his brother said, moving to stand beside him.

"Yes," Javier agreed. "She is."

Not for the first time he thought that she would be better suited to the position of Queen than being married to him.

"Come," Matteo said. "Let us speak for a moment."

"Are you going to have me arrested and executed?" Javier asked as they walked out of the dining room and onto the balcony that overlooked the back garden.

"No," Matteo said. "Had I done that, I would have made a much larger spectacle."

"Good to know."

"I wanted to thank you for following through with the marriage."

"You don't have to thank me."

"I can tell that you have feelings for her."

Javier gritted his teeth. "She's beautiful."

"Yes," Matteo agreed. "She is. But many women are beautiful."

Not like Violet. "Certainly."

"Without you, I never could have done this," Matteo said. "All the years of it. Making sure that the damage that our father was intent on inflicting on the country was not as severe as it might have been. You have been loyal to me. Even in this."

Loyalty? Was that what he called this? He had been a fox curled around a hen. Waiting, just waiting for her to be left alone. Vulnerable and beautiful and his to devour.

It had taken nothing for him to abandon his promise. His honor.

To prove that he was morally corrupt in his soul. Incapable of doing right if he led with his heart.

"You consider it loyalty?" Javier chuckled. "I slept with your fiancée."

"It does not matter which of us marries her. Only that it's done. I told you that. And I meant it."

"I didn't know it at the time."

"I brought you out here to say that you must not think our bond is damaged by this. And it must not become damaged by this. I don't want your woman."

"I didn't think you did."

"I would ensure that you do not labor under the impression that I might. Which I feel could drive a wedge between us. As I can see that you are... Distracted by her."

"Now we come down to the real truth of it," Javier said. "Do you have concerns about what you consider to be my state of distraction?"

"Not too many. But you must remember that we have a mission here. A goal."

"I am very conscious of it. In service of that goal, she might have been a better queen than anyone else you could choose."

"She will do well in her position as your wife. As for me... I will keep looking."

"You will never be him," Javier said, looking at his brother's profile. "Don't ever doubt that."

"I doubt it often," Matteo said. "But isn't that what we must do? Question ourselves at every turn. I often wonder how I can ever be truly confident in anything I believe in. Because once I believed in him wholeheartedly. Once I thought that he had the nation's best interests at heart. Once I thought our father was the hero. And it turned out that he was only the villain."

Matteo gave voice to every demon that had ever lurked inside of Javier. When you had believed so wrongly, how could you ever trust that what you believed now was correct?

"We have to remember. An allegiance to honor before all else. Because if you can memorize a code, then you can know with your head what is right. Hearts lie."

Javier nodded slowly. "Yes. You know I believe that as well as you do."

"Good."

He turned around and looked through the window, saw Violet now standing in the center of a group talking and laughing.

"It's made easier by the fact that I have no feelings." He shot his brother a forced grin.

"Good."

Matteo turned and walked back into the party, leaving Javier standing there looking inside. Whether he had meant to or not, his brother had reminded him of what truly mattered. Not the heat that existed between himself and Violet. But progressing their country. Righting the wrongs of their father.

Javier had his own debt to pay his country. He had, under the orders of his father, used the military against its people. Had arrested innocent men who had spent time in prison, away from their families.

Who he knew his father had tortured.

He had been a weapon in the hands of the wrong man, with the wrong view on the world.

He was dangerous, and he couldn't afford to forget it.

Nor could he afford to do any more than atone for all that he'd been.

Nothing, nothing at all, must distract him from that mission.

Not even his fiancée.

"Someone else can go with me."

Violet was becoming irritated by the stormy countenance of her fiancé. He was driving the car carrying them down to town, wearing a white shirt and dark pants, the sleeves pushed up past his forearms. His black hair was disheveled. Possibly because earlier today they had begun kissing in his office, and she had ended up on his lap, riding the ridge of his arousal, gasping with pleasure until she realized that she was going to be late for her appointment at the bridal store in town.

"No," he said.

"You're not allowed to see the wedding dress that I choose anyway."

"It doesn't matter. I will wait outside."

"You're ridiculous," she said. "If you're going to go wedding dress shopping with me, you have to at least look a little bit like you don't want to die."

A mischievous thought entered her brain, and she set her fingers on his thigh, then let them drift over to an even harder part of him. "Are you frustrated because we didn't get to finish?"

"Obviously I would rather continue with that."

His tone was so exasperated and dry that she couldn't help but laugh.

"If it doesn't impact your driving…" She brushed her fingertips over him.

"It does," he said.

She felt even more gratified by the admission that she affected him than she could have anticipated. She let that carry her the rest of the way down the mountain and into town. It was important to her that she get a dress from a local designer. It was part of an initiative that she was working on with King Matteo's assistant.

Livia was a lovely young woman, with large, serious eyes and a surprisingly dry sense of humor. She was extremely organized and efficient, and Violet could see that Matteo took her for granted in the extreme.

But between the two of them they had begun to figure out ways to naturally raise the profile of the country, coinciding with her marriage to Javier.

Acquiring everything from Monte Blanco that they would need for the wedding was part of that.

When Violet and Javier pulled up to the shop, he parked and got out, leaning against the car.

She made her way toward the shop and looked back

at him. He was a dashing figure. And she wanted to take his picture.

"I'm putting you on the internet."

His expression went hard, but he didn't say anything. And she snapped the shot, him with his arms crossed over his broad chest, a sharp contrast against the sleek black car and the quaint cobbled streets and stone buildings behind him.

And he was beautiful.

"Thank you." She smiled and then went into the shop.

Immediately she was swept into a current of movement. She was given champagne and several beautiful dresses. It would be difficult to choose. But the dress that she decided on was simple, with floating sheer cape sleeves and a skirt that floated around her legs as she walked.

She took a photo of a detail of the dress on a hanger and took all the information for the bridal store.

Because when all this was over, anyone with a big wedding coming up this year would want a gown from this shop, from this designer.

When she reappeared, Javier was still standing where she had left him. Looking like a particularly sexy statue.

"All right. Now you have to come with me for the rest of this."

They went through the rest of the city finding items for the wedding. They created a crowd wherever they went. People were in awe to see Javier walking around with the citizens like a regular person. Not that anything about him could be called regular.

"They love you," she said as they walked into a flower shop.

He looked improbable standing next to displays of baby's breath, hyacinth and other similarly soft and pastel-colored things.

"They shouldn't," he said.

"Why not?"

"Nobody should love a person in a position of power. They should demand respect of him."

"You have some very hard opinions," she said, reaching out and brushing her fingertips over the baby's breath.

"I have to have hard opinions."

He touched the edge of one of the hyacinth blossoms and she snapped a quick picture. She enjoyed the sight of his masculine hand against that femininity. It made her think of a hot evening spent with him. It made her think of sex. Of the way he touched her between her legs.

As if he were thinking the exact same thing, he looked at her, their eyes clashing. And she felt the impact of it low in her stomach.

"I'm definitely feeling a bit of frustration over having not gotten to finish what we started earlier," he murmured.

"Me too," she whispered. "But we are out doing our duty. And isn't that the entire point of this marriage?"

The question felt like it was balanced on the edge of a knife. And her right along with it.

"It is," he said, taking his hand away from the flower.

"Right. Well. I think I found the flowers that I want."

She spoke to the shop owner, placing her order. And then the two of them carried on.

"I think we ought to have ice cream for the wedding," she said, standing outside the store. She was searching for something. For that connection with him that they'd had earlier. That they'd had back when it was forbidden.

"I don't want any," he said.

"I... Well. I mean, we can order some for the wedding."

"I think you can handle that on your own," he said.

Her heart faltered for a beat. It felt too close to a metaphor for all that they were right now. She could also love him alone. She was doing it. But it hurt, and she didn't know if she was ever going to be able to close this gap between them.

"Of course," she responded. "I... I'll go and order it."

She did. Then she ordered an ice-cream cone for herself and ignored the pain in her chest. She ignored it all the way through the rest of the shopping, and when they arrived back at the palace and he did not continue where they had left off in his office.

And she tried not to wonder if she had chosen wrong.

She had to cling to the story.

Because eventually the beast would be transformed by love.

The problem was that her beast seemed particularly resistant to it.

And she wasn't entirely sure she understood why.

CHAPTER TWELVE

THE DAY OF the wedding dawned bright and clear. Violet was determined to be optimistic.

It has been a difficult few days. Javier's moods had been unpredictable. Some days he had been attentive, and others, she hadn't seen him at all.

He hadn't made love to her since the day he had given her the jewels.

They hadn't even come close since the day in his office, where they had been thwarted by her schedule. Something she bitterly resented now.

This distance made her feel brittle. Made her feelings hard and spiky, cutting her like glass each time her heart beat.

What would it mean to be with him like this, if it were this way forever?

When she'd imagined marriage to him, she'd imagined more nights like the ones they'd shared in bed together. With passion ruling, not duty.

But if their marriage would be like this…

She didn't know if she'd survive it.

She had bought a beautiful dress, a beautiful dress to be the most suitable bride she could be. What else could she do?

She knew that she couldn't wear the cuffs the way that

she had done the day he had given them to her. But she did put two of them on one wrist and attached the gold chain, wrapping it artfully between the cuffs to make it look like an edgy piece of jewelry, rather than an intentional statement of bondage.

The day was made better and easier by the fact that her family was present. Minerva would be Violet's only bridesmaid.

Minerva looked radiant and beautiful in a green dress that skimmed over the baby bump she was currently sporting. She and Dante had taken to parenthood with zeal. They had been instant parents, given that it was a vulnerable baby that had brought the two of them together. They had adopted her shortly after they'd married, and then had their second child quickly after.

This third one had only waited a year.

"You look beautiful," Minerva said, smiling broadly.

"So do you," Violet said.

Falling in love with Dante looked good on her younger sister. Violet would have never matched her sister with her brother's brooding friend. She would have thought that somebody with such an intense personality would crush her sister's more sunny nature. But that wasn't true at all. If anything, Minerva was even sunnier, and Dante had lost some of the darkness that had always hung over him.

He had maintained his intensity; that was for sure.

Of course, when he held their children protectively, when he looked at Minerva like he would kill an entire army to protect her, Violet could certainly see the appeal.

Really, what could she say? She had fallen in love with a beast of a man who was as unknowable as he was feral. She could no longer say that the appeal of an intense partner was lost on her.

"You really are happy to marry him?" Minerva asked gently.

"Yes. It's complicated, but I think you understand how that can be."

Minerva laughed. "Definitely."

"How did you manage it? Loving him, knowing he might never love you back?"

The corners of Minerva's mouth tipped down. "Well. Mostly I managed it by asking myself if I would be any happier without him. The answer was no. I really wouldn't have been any happier without him. And the time I did spend without Dante was so… It was so difficult. I loved him so much, and I had to wait for him to realize that what he felt for me was love. He couldn't recognize it right away because… He didn't know what it felt like. More than that, he was terrified of it. And after everything he had been through, I could hardly blame him."

"Javier is like that," Violet said softly. "He's so fierce. A warrior at heart. And he believes that he isn't good. But that he has honor, and that's enough. He doesn't seem to realize that the reason honor matters to him is that he is good. And I think he's afraid to feel anything for me."

"Have you said that to him?"

Violet shook her head. "No. I don't want him to… I don't want him to reject me." It was one thing to be uncertain. In uncertainty, hope still blossomed inside her, fragile and small though it was.

But if she did say the words… If he rejected her definitively… Well, then she would not even have hope left.

"I understand that. But you know, it might be something he needs to hear. Because until he hears it, he's not going to know. Because he won't recognize it."

"I'm thankful for you," Violet said, wrapping her arm

around her sister's shoulder. "I don't know very many other people who would understand this."

"My love was definitely a hard one," she said. "But I don't think it was wrong to fight for it. I feel like sometimes people think… If it doesn't just come together it isn't worth it. But the kind of love I have with Dante… There's nothing else like it. There's no one else for me. He was wounded. He needed time to heal. And it was worth it."

Minerva put her hand on her rounded stomach and smiled. "It was so worth it."

Violet smiled, determination filling her. This would be worth it too.

The love that she felt for him was so intense, it had to be.

It had to be enough.

Javier waited at the head of the aisle. The church was filled with people. Some who were from Violet's world, and many from his. Though he realized he didn't actually know any of the people in attendance.

He was disconnected from this. From the social part of his job. A figurehead.

It had been interesting going out into town with her. She drew people to them like a bright, warm flame drawing in moths. He had never experienced such a thing, because he was the sort of man who typically kept people at a distance simply by standing there.

But not Violet.

Everyone seemed to want to be around her. To be near her. He could understand why she had managed to build an empire over the internet. With people who wanted to look like her, be like her. People who wanted to experience a slice of what she was.

She was compelling.

And after today she would be his.

He gritted his teeth, curling his hands into fists and waiting.

She would come.

And the momentary hitch of doubt that he had was assuaged by the appearance of her sister, who walked down the aisle with a small bouquet of flowers.

He had met her sister for the first time this morning. The other woman had seemed cautious around him, and a bit wary. Her husband had been more menacing. As had her brother.

Her father had seemed shamefaced, and Javier felt that was deserved. Her mother had simply seemed excited to be in a palace.

Javier had no concept of a family like this. Large and together, even though they disagreed on things, and it was clear that they did.

Though, he imagined that most families that appeared dysfunctional disagreed on small things, and not whether it was appropriate that one of them sold another into marriage. But at this point, what was done was done.

And she would be here.

She wanted him.

And she seemed committed to serving her role for the country.

That was her primary motivation. She had made that clear in the flower shop.

And it was a good thing. Because he could not afford distractions. He could not afford to start thinking in terms of emotion.

The music changed and he turned his focus again to the doorway. Watching with great attention.

And then, there she was.

The sight of her stole his breath.

She was…

She looked like she did for him. Only for him. Her dark hair was long and loose, the veil that she had soft and flowing down her back. She looked almost as if she didn't have makeup on at all. Rather, she glowed. Her lips looked shiny and soft, her cheeks catching the light. It was magic. And so was she.

He had held himself back these weeks, because it had felt like something he should do until it was done. But now, here she was. Now she was his.

There would be no turning back.

When she reached the head of the aisle, she took his hand. And he pulled her to him. It was all he could do not to claim her mouth then and there. Not to make a spectacle of them both in front of the congregation.

And that was when he noticed the bracelets.

She had them both on one wrist. But the chain was there as well.

And when she looked into his eyes, he felt the impact of it all the way down to his gut.

She nodded slowly.

An affirmation.

She was choosing to give herself to him. And she was saying that she understood. The bond, the loyalty that traditionally existed here in this country between a royal husband and wife.

But he did not know where ownership fit into that. He did not know where duty and responsibility fit in.

He had told her about it. Mostly because he had wanted to see her wear those for him. Those rubies and nothing more. But also he had… He hadn't understood. But suddenly, here, with those bracelets on her wrist, in a church, where they were about to make vows… Where she had brought the carnal into the sacred and blended them together, made them one, he could not understand how this bond could remain just another promise he decided to keep.

Because as she spoke her vows, low and grave in a voice that only he could hear, he felt them imprint beneath his skin. Down to his soul. And when he spoke his in return, they were like that gold chain on her wrist. But they wrapped around them both, binding them in a way that he had not anticipated.

He had thought he knew what this meant.

Because that day he had discovered the sorts of treachery his father protected. That day that he had realized that the orders he had taken for years had been in service of an insidious plan, and nothing that protected or bettered his people, he had sworn that he would uphold a set of principles. That he would not be led by his heart.

That he would not be led by anything other than a code of honor.

But now he had made vows to another person, and not an ideal.

When it came time to kiss her, it took all of his self-control not to claim her utterly and completely right there in front of the roomful of people. He touched her face, and he exercised restraint he did not feel, kissing her slowly but firmly, making sure that she knew it was a promise of more. A promise for later.

He had been restrained these past weeks.

But it was over now.

The vows were made. His course was set.

There was no turning back. Not now.

Whatever would become of this. Of them... It was too late.

You chose this.

He gritted his teeth against the truth of it.

It had been easy to say that he had done it for Matteo.

That he was doing it to atone for the sin of taking her in the first place. But the fact of the matter was he was far too selfish to turn away from her.

The idea of giving her to another man had been anathema to him. An impossibility. Had his brother insisted on marrying her, he would have…

He would have betrayed him. He would have stolen her. Secreted her out of the country. Abandoned his post. Abandoned all that they had built.

The truth of that roared in his blood.

Like the beast that he was.

But there was nothing to be done about that now. She was his, so it didn't matter. She was his, so it couldn't matter.

He pushed it all away as he continued to kiss her, and when he was through, the congregation was clapping, and they were introduced.

But he didn't hear any of it.

There was nothing.

Nothing but the pounding of his blood in his veins, the demand that burned through his body like molten lava.

He would endure the reception for as long as he had to. For as long as he had to pretend to care about flowers and ice cream and all manner of things that were only stand-ins for what he had truly wanted all along.

He didn't care to touch the petals of an alarmingly soft purple flower. He wanted Violet. Her skin beneath his hands. He didn't wish to lick an ice-cream cone. He wished to lick her.

And he would play the game if he had to, but that was all it was to him. A game. A game until he could get to her. Because that was all that mattered.

She talked to her family, and he knew that he could not rush her away from them. She was speaking, even to her father, and though there was cautiousness between them, he wondered if she might make amends with him. Javier didn't know how.

He asked her that very question once they got back to their room. In spite of the fact that his blood roared with desire, he had to know.

"I don't know if it will ever be the same as it was," she said. "But it was never easy. It was never perfect. I can always see those sorts of tendencies in him. Those beliefs."

"But you will forgive him."

"Yes. I think sometimes… If you value your relationship with another person enough, you have to be willing to accept that they are flawed. I don't know that I'll ever be able to make my father see the world, or me, the way that I want him to. I can keep showing him, though. And in the meantime I can live my life. But cutting him out of it completely wouldn't fix the wound. It wouldn't heal anything."

"It might teach him a lesson," Javier said.

"I think having to watch me join with you might have begun to teach him a lesson," she said.

"What does that mean?" he growled.

"Only that you are a bit more feral and frightening than I think he imagined my royal husband might be."

"The beast, remember?"

"Yes. I think… We are husband and wife now. And I would like to know… Why?"

"Why what?"

"Why did you become the beast? The sins of your father. We talked about that. But it's deeper than that. I know it is. Because you changed when you found that little girl…"

"What do you think I was doing all those years before? I was seeing to his orders. Arresting men when he demanded that I arrest them. And women. Separating families as he commanded. And he would tell me it was for a reason. Because they were traitors. Because it was upholding the health of the country. But I realize now they were freedom fighters. People who wanted to escape his oppressive regime, and it was oppressive. That innocent people were put behind bars, tried and… I helped. I upheld his rule of law, and I regret it."

"You didn't know."

"Maybe not. But when you have believed so wholeheartedly in a lie, you can never trust yourself again. You can never trust in the clarity of your own judgment because you have been so fooled. Because you were a villain and all the while imagined yourself a hero. And you will never, ever be able to walk through life without wondering which side you're on again. You will never be able to take it for granted."

"It takes such courage to admit that. You are brave. And I can see that you'll never take the easy way. You can trust yourself."

He shook his head. "No. I can't. I love my father and I allowed those feelings to blind myself to his faults."

"Well. So did I with mine."

"Your father is not a maniacal dictator. As challenging as he might be."

"No. I suppose not." She put her hand on his face, and he closed his eyes, relishing the feel of her delicate fingers against him. "You saved that girl, Javier."

"But so many more I did not save. So many I harmed myself. Arrested. Sent to a prison run by my father, where they were undoubtedly tortured. There is no salvation for such sins. My hands will not wash clean. But I can use them to serve."

"I'm sorry, but I know you, Javier. You're not a monster."

"I must assume that I am," he said, moving away. "The better to protect the world from any harm that I might do."

"I don't think you are," she said.

"This is not a fairy tale. The things that I have done cannot be undone. I can only move forward trying to do right now that I understand. Now that I have the power. It is not about being transformed by magic. Such a thing is not possible."

She moved to him and she bracketed his face with her hands.

He had no chance to respond to that, because she kissed his mouth, and he was dragged into the swirling undertow of desire by the softness of her lips, the slow, sweet sweep of her tongue against his. She was inexperienced, his beautiful goddess, but she had a sort of witchcraft about her that ensnared him and entranced him.

That made him fall utterly and completely under her spell.

How could the magic fail here? Because of him. That had to be it.

She was made entirely of magic. Glorious soft skin and otherworldly beauty wrapped around galaxies of light. She was something other than beauty. Something more.

Something that made his heart beat new and made him want to defy a lifetime of commitment to honor.

He had devoted himself to believing only in a code. A list of principles that helped him determine what was right and wrong because he knew full well that his own blood, his own heart could lead him in the direction of that which would destroy him and all those around him.

His belief in that had been unwavering.

When he looked at her, his Violet, his wife, he knew that he could believe entirely in her. In her magic. In the way her soft mouth rained kisses down over his skin, in the way her delicate fingertips brushed over his body. The way that she undid the buttons on his shirt and tackled the buckle on his belt. Yes. He could believe in that.

He could drop to his knees and pledge his loyalty to her and her alone, seal his utter and total devotion by losing himself in her womanly flavor. By drowning in the desire that rose up between them like a wave, threatening to decimate everything that he had built.

And he didn't care.

Just like he hadn't cared that first time they had kissed in the ballroom those weeks ago, when she had belonged to another man and his loyalty should have stood the test of time but crumbled beneath all that she was.

She was magic. And she was deadly.

And now, just now, he did not have the strength to deny her. To deny them.

And so, why not surrender? Why not drown in it? She was his, after all. He had gone down this path weeks ago, and it was too late to turn back. He had made her his.

His.

And tonight he would make that matter. He would revel in it.

He stole the power of the kiss from her, taking control, growling as he wrapped his arms around her and walked her back against the wall, pinning her there, devouring her, claiming her as his own.

He had spoken vows, but they were not enough; he needed to seal them with his body. He needed her to know.

He needed her to understand.

The way that she destroyed him. The way that he was broken inside. So that she would know. And he didn't know why he needed her to know, just like he didn't know why he had been in the library that night they had first made love. Why he had been looking through that same book that she was, trying to read the same story and find some meaning in it.

To try to see through her eyes the way that she might see him.

And it shouldn't matter. It never should have. Because she had been his brother's and he had been toying with betrayal even then.

But she's yours now.

Yes, she was his. For better or worse.

He feared very much it might be worse. Because he hurt people. It felt like a natural part of what he was. That monster.

But perhaps if it was only this, if it was only lust, he could control it.

He wrenched that beautiful dress off her body. She was an Angel in it, far too pure for him, and it nearly hurt to look at her. Burned his hands to pull the filmy fabric away from her. But it left her standing there in white, angelic underthings. Garments that spoke of purity, and he knew that he was unequal to the task of touching them. Just as he had been unworthy of touching her in the first place.

But he had.

And he would.

He tore them away from her body, leaving her naked before him. Except for those jewels. The necklace glittering at the base of her throat, the cuffs heavy on her wrist, the chain wound around them. And the ring, his ring, glittering on her finger, telling the world that she belonged to him.

He had never had her in a bed.

He hadn't realized that until this moment. And tonight he would have her in his bed. Their bed.

She would not have her own room, not after this.

It was often customary for royal couples to keep their own spaces, but they would not.

She would be here. Under the covers, in his bed with him. Her naked body wrapped around his. Yes. That was what he required. It was what he would demand.

He picked her up and carried her there, set her down at the center of the mattress and looked at her. He leaned over, spreading her hair out around her like a dark halo, and then he stood, looking at the beautiful picture that she made. Her soft, bare skin pale against the deep crimson red of the quilt. She took a sharp breath, her breasts rising with the motion, her nipples beading.

"Such a lovely picture you make, My Princess."

"I didn't think my official title was Princess."

"It doesn't matter. You are *my* princess. *Mine.*"

He bent down, cupping her breast with his hand, letting it fill his palm.

She was soft, so delicate and exquisite, and it amazed him that something half so fragile could put such a deep crack in the foundation of what he was. But she had.

He lowered his head and took one perfect, puckered nipple between his lips and sucked all her glory into his mouth. She arched beneath him, crying out in soft, sweet pleasure, and it spurred him on. He growled, lavishing her with attention, licking and sucking, stroking her between her thighs.

His wife. His beautiful, perfect wife, who threatened to destroy all that he was.

How had he ever thought that it was possible to maintain superior connections to this country. To duty and honor when the marriage bed presented shackles that could not be seen with the human eye. Perhaps that was why the cuffs existed. Not to create a sense that they were bound to each other, but to turn them physical. All the better to remove them when one chose to.

Because the ties that existed in his heart he could not see, he could not touch and he did not know how to unleash.

It was supernatural in a way that he would have said he did not believe in.

It was strong in a way he would have told anyone such a thing could not be.

And he was linked to her in a way he would have said he could not be to another human being.

Because he had given those things away so long ago. Because he had pledged loyalty to Matteo and not love. Because he had pledged his blood to Monte Blanco, but not love.

And what he wanted to give to Violet was deeper, and he was afraid that she was right. That magic had always only ever been love, and that it could turn and twist into something dark and evil, just like magic.

All that magic that she was.

All that… He did not wish to give the word a place, not even in his mind.

And so he covered his thoughts with a blanket of pleasure, wrapping them both in the dark velvet of his desire, lapping his way down her body, her stomach, down to that sweet place between her legs. He buried himself there. Lost himself in giving her pleasure.

Got drunk on it.

Because there was nothing to do now but revel in it. Afterward… Afterward there would be time for reckonings and for fixing all of this. But not now.

Now was the time to embrace it.

The only time.

Here in the bedroom.

And maybe that was what the cuffs were for.

To create a space where the world didn't matter. Where there could be an escape.

And maybe for other men that would have worked. But not for him.

Because he didn't know how to create space.

He only knew how to be all or nothing.

How to be an agent of his father, or a war machine acting against him.

How to be a man, vulnerable and useless. Or how to be a beast.

But he had the freedom to be that beast with her. And somehow, with that freedom he became both. Wholly a man and wholly an animal in her arms, and she seemed to accept him no matter what. She shouldn't.

She should push him away. She always should have pushed him away.

But she had gone with him, from the beginning.

She had chosen to be with him.

And when he rose up and positioned himself between her thighs, when he thrust into her body, and when her beautiful eyes opened, connected with his, he felt a shudder of something crack through his entire body like a bolt of lightning.

She lifted her head, pressed her soft mouth to his, and he felt words vibrating against his lips. He couldn't understand them. Couldn't do anything but feel them, as the sweet, tight heat of her body closed around his.

She clung to his shoulders as he drove them both to the pinnacle of pleasure. And when she released, he went with her. Pleasure pounding through him like a relentless rain.

And then, he heard her speaking again, her lips moving against the side of his neck, and this time, the words crystallized in his mind.

The words that he had been trying, trying and failing, not to hear. Not to understand.

"I love you," she whispered. Her lips moved against his

skin, tattooing the words there, making it impossible for him not to feel them. He was branded with them.

"I love you. I love you."

"No," he said, the denial bursting forth from him.

He moved away from her, pushing his hands through his hair. Panic clawed at him and he couldn't say why. He was not a man who panicked. Ever. He was not a man acquainted with fear. Because what did he care for his own life? The only thing he feared was the darkness in himself, and maybe that was the problem now. Maybe it called to the weakness that he had inside of his chest.

The desire to sink into her. To drop to his knees and pledge loyalty to her no matter what.

Even if she asked him to mobilize against his brother. Against his people.

And it didn't matter that she wouldn't.

What mattered was losing the anchor that kept him from harming those around him.

What mattered was losing the only moral compass he knew how to read.

What mattered was Monte Blanco and it was becoming impossible for him to hold on to that.

"I'm sorry," she said. "You don't get to tell me that I don't love you."

"I cannot," he said.

"Why not?"

"Haven't you been listening? Haven't you heard anything that I've told you? Love is the enemy. You're right. Magic. And magic can be dark as easily as it can work for good."

"So why can't you trust that between us it will be good?"

"Because I cannot trust myself," he said.

She put her hand on his chest and he wrapped his fingers around her wrist and ripped it away. She stared at him, the hurt in her eyes far too intense to bear.

Because he did not have the freedom to be himself with her. It was far too dangerous. And he had been lying. Evidence of his own weakness if it ever existed.

That he had wanted to pretend that what he knew to be true wasn't. That he wanted to give himself freedom when he knew that he could not afford it. This woman was a gift that some men could have. But not him.

Yet he had been weak, far too weak from the beginning to turn away from her. He'd been given every chance. Every roadblock in his personal arsenal had been set up. She had been intended for his brother, and if that could not keep him away from her, then nothing could.

She was dangerous. Deadly.

A threat to his own personal code in ways that he should have seen from the beginning.

Because she had been eroding the foundation that he had built from the beginning. Just a touch. A kiss. And then he had stormed into his brother's office to tell him that Matteo could not marry her. To tell him that he could not see through the plan that he had to make their country better, because Javier had wanted Violet for himself. He had never wanted to let her go. He would have gone after her. That much he knew.

But his brother had given him options that he had liked, and so he had taken them. Made it easy to keep on going down that slippery slope.

So he had done.

And now... Now he was sitting here in the consequences of it. She loved him. He could not give her that love in return.

He had broken not only his own sacred vows, but in the end he would break her too. And that was unacceptable.

But he had married her. And that was done. Consummated. Presented before the entire world.

But they did not have to live together as man and wife. He could give her the freedom that she had wanted. But he could not give her this.

"Love is not to be," he said. "Not for me."

"I know that you don't trust it," she said. "And I understand why. But you have to understand that what I feel for you has nothing to do with the way you were manipulated into caring for your father."

"Was I manipulated? Or did I simply want to accept the easiest thing. The easiest reality."

"Do you think that I'm going to trick you into doing something wrong? Do you think that I'm secretly here to destroy your country?"

"No," he growled. "No," he said again. "It's not that. It has nothing to do with that. But a man cannot serve two masters. And my master must be my people. It must be my country. It must be to duty, and to honor. That is where I must pledge my allegiance, and I cannot be split between a wife and a nation."

"Then make me part of your people. Make me one of those that you have a responsibility to. Surely that can't be so difficult."

Except that he knew it would destroy her. It was not what she wanted. It was not what she deserved. And without it she truly would be in captivity for all of his life. And he would be her jailer. And so he was trapped. Between violating all that he needed to be for his country and destroying the life of the woman who had married him.

He reached over to her and unclasped the first bracelet from her wrist. He unwound the chain that she had wrapped there, and then unclipped the second bracelet.

Her eyes filled with tears as she stared at him, but

he knew that it would be a kindness. It was a kindness whether she saw it that way or not.

"What are you doing?"

"You are not my prisoner," he said. "And I will not make you a prisoner."

"Now you say this? Now, after we've been married? After I told you that I love you? That's when you decide to give me freedom?"

"We must remain married," he said. "That much is obvious. My brother would take a dim view on there being a divorce so quickly. It would cause scandal. And... I do not wish to undo all that you have done for my country. But you may go back to California. To your life. There is no reason that you must stay here. You do not need to be under my thumb."

"What if I choose to stay?"

"What you choose is up to you. But that will not alter my behavior. That will not change the fact that this place is my priority. That it is where my duty lies."

"I love you," she said.

She got out of bed, standing there, naked and radiant in the center of the room. "I love you, and you can't make it so that I don't. I love you," she said, like a spell, like an incantation, like she was trying to cast it over him, like she was trying to change the very fabric of what he was. Destroy him, then remake him using those words to stitch him back together.

As if she might be able to use them to take the beast and turn him back into a man.

"And I cannot love," he said. "It is that simple."

"You can," she said. "You can. But you're not a beast to protect the world from you, you have to be a beast to protect yourself from the world. You're afraid, Javier. You're afraid of being hurt again, and I understand that."

Her words lashed against something inside of him that felt tender and bruised. And he hadn't thought that he had the capacity to feel such a thing.

"You don't know what you speak of," he said. "You are protected. Even the betrayal that your father meted out to you was not one that might put you in peril or threaten your comfort in any way. He sold you to a king. That you might be exalted. You have no idea what I am fighting against. You have no idea what real suffering is. I have seen it. I have caused it. And I have to guard against ever causing it again. Do not give me your quick and easy sound bites, Violet King. I am not one of your internet followers. I am not impressed by quick, condensed versions of truth that are easy to digest. I have seen human suffering on a level that you cannot possibly understand. And I am related to the cause of it. If my life must be devoted to the undoing of it so that those in the future can simply live, then it must be. But don't you ever accuse me of being afraid."

And for the first time he saw her crumple. For the first time, he saw her bravery falter, and he hated himself for being the cause of that. He had plucked the woman from her office some weeks ago and taken her off to a land that she had never even heard of, and she had remained strong. She had remained stoic. She had an answer back for everything he had said. But not now. He had finally taken that from her. He had finally destroyed some of what she was.

And there was no joy to be had in that.

It was confirmation. Of what he was.

That spark of light she had placed in him was now extinguished in her.

She had said he was not a monster, but he knew that he was.

That he would destroy her only more as the years wore on.

He hurt people.

He had caused pain under the rule of his father, and under the rule of his own heart, he would cause Violet pain as well.

"If you think that's what I meant, if you think that's who I am, then you haven't been paying attention at all. I thought that we knew each other. I thought that our souls recognized each other," she said, her voice breaking. "You saw me reading the book… And I knew that you would be reading it too. I knew it. You know the library was the first place that I looked for you that night we first made love. Because somehow I knew you would be looking at the same story I was, trying to see if you saw us in there."

"You misunderstand. I wasn't looking for answers because I already have them. I understand that this was significant to you. That this was a first for you. But I have lived life. I have already had all the revelations I will have. Perhaps you can think of me as a lesson learned."

"What an expensive lesson," she said, her tone full of venom. "Wedding vows seem a little bit extreme."

"As I told you, the wedding vows can remain."

"Why would I stay married to you? If you don't want to have a real marriage?"

He gritted his teeth, fought against the terror that clouded his chest at the idea of losing her. He liked much more the idea of being able to keep her while keeping her separate.

"Do what you must."

He gathered his clothes and began to dress.

"Where are you going?"

"Out."

"I would never have thought that you would transform

yourself into a basic sort of man. But that is very basic. Just out. No explanation."

"Because I don't owe you an explanation. Because you got the explanation that you were going to get already. That you thought there was more is your problem, not mine."

He gritted his teeth against the burning sensation in his chest and he walked out of the room, closing the door behind him.

Closing the door on them. On temptation.

Whatever she did now was her choice.

But he had done his duty, for honor.

Whatever she said, that was why.

He ignored the kick in his chest that told him otherwise.

He ignored everything.

Because that was the real gift of having transformed himself into a beast.

When he had done that, he had taken his feelings away as well.

So why did his chest hurt so much?

CHAPTER THIRTEEN

VIOLET WAS STUNNED. All she could do was sit there in the center of their marriage bed, alone. She had known that he would have an issue with her loving him. She had. But she hadn't known that he would do this.

Why now? Why had it come to this now?

All this time he could have set her free. He could have made this bargain with her.

And suddenly she felt very alone. Her whole family had been here for the wedding today, but she hadn't had enough time to speak to them. Would she have found strength from them?

She could call her sister. Her mother. Her father even.

She knew what Minerva would say, actually. Minerva would want her to do what made her happy. But Minerva would also say that sometimes difficult men needed you to believe in them until they could believe in themselves. Because that was what had happened with Dante.

But no one had helped Violet up until this point. This had been the most independent she had ever been. Yes, it was somewhat enforced by the entire situation, but it was still true. She had to stand on her own two feet since she had been brought here. It had been difficult.

Difficult to face the fact that her relationship with her family hadn't been what she thought. Difficult to be thrown in the deep end of independence, when she had been so surrounded by the people that she'd loved for so long. The people that she had depended on for her entire life.

But all of this had been about choice. A lesson in it.

Ironic that she'd had to be kidnapped and dragged across the world to really face the fact that she wasn't her own person. Not that what she had built wasn't hers to some extent.

But she had been propped up for so long by her father, and then was angry about the fact that he had been controlling things from behind the scenes when she had…

She had been fine with it as long as it had benefited her.

Allowing him to invest money when she had needed it.

Knowing that he was there as a safety net.

But nobody was a safety net for her in this. Because her heart was involved, her emotions. And there was no one who could fix it but her.

Her and Javier.

But he had broken it, because he was afraid. Whatever he said, he was afraid.

She understood what he thought. Understood why he felt the need to protect himself so fiercely.

There might not be real curses in this life, but there was pain that could feel like a curse. Betrayal that could make you feel changed.

And there might not be magic spells or incantations, but there was something even more powerful.

Love was the magic.

And she was going to have to figure out how to make it work.

She didn't have a spell. Didn't have anything to make the fairy tale literal.

But then, the beast wasn't on the outside. It was inside of him.

And it wasn't made of the sins of his father, wasn't made of tainted blood. It was made of fear.

And love couldn't exist alongside fear. Because they would always fight with one another. Love demanded bravery, and fear demanded that you hide.

He was hiding.

He was the strongest, bravest man she had ever known, but in the face of love, he was hiding.

If she could understand that.

Because he had just taken her heart and flayed it open. And she had already known that love could hurt, because the betrayal of her father had wounded her so badly, and she had to make the decision to forgive him in spite of that.

Was that what she had to do here? Forgive and love until he could do the same?

She didn't know.

She found herself wandering to the library, because it was where she had found him before. It was where she had found some of the answers she had been looking for. Maybe... Maybe she would find them again here.

Because she wanted to understand. Because she had so many questions.

Why had he done this now? Why had he turned away from her now? Told her she could live a wholly separate life from him, go back to California...

He didn't do it until he was sure that you loved him.

That truth sat there, like a rock in her chest. He hadn't done it until he was certain of her love.

He had not done it until part of him was certain that she would stay.

And so that meant she had to, she supposed. Even if it was the hardest thing she had ever faced in her entire life.

The idea of staying with a man who didn't love her.

She went straight to the back shelf, but she couldn't find it. The book with their story.

The book was gone.

And that, above all else, gave her hope.

"What are you doing down here?"

Javier looked up from the book and at his brother.

"Where else would I be?" He asked the question somewhat dryly, and yet to him, it made perfect sense that he was here. To him, it made all the sense in the world.

"Not Dad's favorite dungeon," Matteo said. "But still, definitely a logical choice for somebody who is punishing themselves."

"Is she still here?"

"Who?"

"My wife."

"As far as I know."

"Are you certain?"

"Honestly, I didn't consider the whereabouts of your woman to be my responsibility. I thought that was one of the perks of flopping her off on you. What has happened?"

"She's in love with me."

"Obviously," Matteo said.

"It's obvious to you?"

"Well. Not necessarily to me. But my mouse may have said something to the effect."

"Livia said something about it?"

"Only that she thought Violet seemed quite taken with you. And that it was probably a good thing she hadn't married me, all things considered."

"She's a fool."

"*Livia?* She's the least foolish woman I have ever known."

"No. Violet. She's a fool to love me. Anyone would be a fool to love either of us."

"It's true," Matteo said. "I don't disagree with you."

"So you understand that I told her I could not esteem her over the fate of the country."

"Is it a choice that must be made?"

"Yes. Because if the choice for Monte Blanco's well-being is not my ultimate motivation, then something else will replace it. And that makes me vulnerable."

"Vulnerable to what?"

He spread his arms wide. "To this," Javier said. "This. To being just like our father. A man with a favorite dungeon. A man who harms others."

"Is that what you think? That a mere distraction could turn you from the man that you are into the man that he was?"

"Haven't we always said that we must be careful to turn away from anything that might make us like him?"

"We must. I agree. But I suspect that you loving this woman will not bring it about. I think it is loving yourself above all else that opens you up to such concerns. Do you think that sounds right? Because our father never loved anybody. None of his corruption came from loving us so much. Or our mother, who we never even knew because she was dead before you ever took your first steps. No. Love did not cause what our father did."

"But I have to be vigilant…"

"Against what?"

"As we discussed, it would be far too easy to fall into another life. After all, wasn't it so easy to believe that our father was good because we thought we loved him?"

"What's the book?"

"Something that Violet was reading. A beauty and the beast story."

"What do you suppose you'll find in there?"

"An answer. Magic. I don't know. Some way to change myself, because I don't know how else I might. To be a man for her rather than a beast."

"Maybe you don't need to change it all. Doesn't the Princess in the story love him without changing?"

"But she deserves better. She deserves more."

"What did she ask for?"

"Nothing," he said, his voice rough.

"Then why not offer nothing but yourself?"

"Because that is something our father would do."

"No, our father would take the choice away from her. Which is what… Well, that's what I did, in the beginning, isn't it? Our father would do whatever he wanted regardless of what she asked for. So why don't you go back to her? And find out what it is she truly wants. Listen. Don't simply follow your own heart. That's what men like our father did. Consider another person. See where it gets you."

"Maybe to disaster. Maybe to hell."

"How does it feel where you are now?"

"Like *hell*," he responded. "Like I'm a foolish man staring at a fairy tale asking it for answers."

"Sounds to me like you don't have any further to fall. And I need you to be functional. So sort yourself out."

"Are you advocating for love and happy endings now?"

Matteo laughed, shaking his head. "Hell no. The opiate of the masses in my opinion. But if you wish to join the masses, Javier, then I won't stop you. And if it is what Violet wants, then all the better that she didn't marry me. Because I would never be able to give it to her."

"Are you such a hypocrite that you would advocate for me what you don't believe you can have for yourself?"

"Not a hypocrite. Just a king. A word of advice. Javier, you were not born to be the King so don't take on the responsibilities that I carry. Take on your own. You're a warrior. And you were born to be. That is your position in this country. And the difference between you and our father was always compassion. It was the sight of that little girl being married off that changed you. That made you see. It was always compassion that made you better. It was always caring. Because a man who is in and of himself a weapon ought to have that sort of counterbalance, don't you think? In my estimation, love will make you stronger at what you do."

"And for kings?" Javier asked.

"A king should not be vulnerable." Matteo turned, then paused for a moment. "But it might be the only thing that keeps a beast from being dangerous. If you are so worried about hurting others, perhaps you should think about that."

And with that, his brother left Javier there, sitting in the bottom of the dungeon holding on to the book. And he knew that he would find no answers there. None at all. No. The only answers for who he was, who he might become, who he needed to become, lay with Violet.

If only he could find the strength in himself.

But perhaps, until then, he could borrow strength from Violet.

Suddenly the fairy tale made sense in a way that it had not before. His fingertips burned, and he opened up to a page with an illustration of the giant, hulking beast having his wounds tended by the delicate maiden.

Perhaps he was too focused on the transformation.

Perhaps he had not looked enough at what the story was really about.

As she said, almost every culture had a version of this tale. And in it, the beauty was seen by the reader to be the weak one. Put up against a dangerous beast.

But he was the one who changed. He was the one who transformed, because of the power of her love.

In the end, it was the beauty who held all the power.

In the end, it was her love that made the difference.

And so, he would have to trust in her power. Trust that, like in the story, she was more than able to stand up to the challenge of loving him.

He was the one who had to find his strength.

She had already proven that she had more than enough for the two of them.

CHAPTER FOURTEEN

SHE HADN'T GONE back to California.

Her social media efforts had begun to create more tourism in Monte Blanco, and she was working with the tourism bureau and local business owners on strengthening the market. She was still involved in her own company, with her VP holding down the fort on the local level back in San Diego.

She had begun spending more time in the city. She had rented office space and had begun working in earnest on her project to bring work to Monte Blanco. Specifically for women. She was in talks to figure out manufacturing, something that she was arranging with Livia, and she had already hired a few women that she had met at a local shelter to work on data entry.

She was having to do some training, and she had hired people to do that as well.

And all of it was helping distract from the pain in her chest, though it didn't make it go away.

She was still living in the palace. It was just that it was so big it was easy to not see Javier at all. And he had allowed that to be the case. He hadn't come to her.

She wouldn't go to him. But she was there.

Because part of her was convinced, absolutely, that she needed to stay. That he needed to know she was choosing not to run. That he needed to know that she was choosing this life. That it was not a kidnapping, not anymore. It was just a marriage.

And she wasn't the one not participating in it. That was him. He was the one who was going to have to figure out exactly what he wanted and exactly how to proceed. She couldn't do it for him. And that, she supposed, was the most difficult lesson of all. That no matter how much she wanted to, she couldn't force a transformation if he didn't want it.

He had to accept her love.

And right now he didn't seem to be able to do that.

She looked around the small office space, up in the top of the small, cobbled building. Above the ice-cream shop. It was so very different from all that modern glass she had left behind in San Diego. But she wasn't sure she even remembered that woman. The one who wanted things sleek and bright. The one who had been so confident and set in her achievements.

She still felt accomplished. It wasn't that she didn't know that she had done impressive and difficult things. It was only that she had found something she cared about even more. She had been so focused for so long. And it hadn't allowed for her to want much else. That had been a protection. She could see now. Because caring this much about something else, about someone else, was extremely painful. But it had also pushed her to find a strength inside of herself that she hadn't known was there. And so for that she was somewhat grateful.

Grateful, if heartbroken.

Because no man would ever be Javier.

She knew that she would never find another man she wanted in the same way. That she would never feel this way for another man. Because she hadn't. Not for twenty-six years. She had had chance after chance to find another man, and she had never even been tempted. And she wouldn't be. Not like this. Not again. But that didn't mean she couldn't thrive. It was just that she would never fall in love again.

Tears pricked her eyes. She didn't want to fall in love again anyway. She just wanted to love him. And she wanted him to love her back. Even facing the fact that it was impossible now didn't make it seem real. Because she hoped... She just hoped.

She wanted to believe in the fairy tale. But she was afraid that the real world loomed far too large. That the damage inflicted on him by his father would be the ultimate winner.

And she didn't want to believe in a world like that. But she had to face the fact that it might be all she got.

She went downstairs, stopping in the ice-cream parlor and getting herself an ice-cream cone, trying not to cry when the flavor reminded her of Javier. The owners of the shop hadn't asked her any questions about why they hadn't seen Javier. Why it seemed that she was always alone, the Prince nowhere to be found after the two of them had been so inseparable at first.

Plus, she had a feeling she just looked heartbroken. She was trying her best to get on with things, but it was not easy at all. She was strong. But strength didn't mean not shedding tears. Strength didn't mean you didn't mourn lost love. Or in her case... Love that could have been if it weren't for a maniacal dictator who had taken the love of a young boy and used it so badly. Made him think that he was the monster, rather than his father.

When she went back out onto the street, she stopped. Because there, down one of the roads, she saw a silhouette that looked familiar. And she flashed back to that moment she had been standing in her office. But she had imagined then that he was dangerous. And now... Now the sight of him made her heart leap into her throat.

"Livia told me I might find you here," he said.

"Livia is a turncoat," Violet said.

"She works for my brother. Her loyalty is always going to lie there."

"Well. *Well.*"

"I need to speak to you."

"Why?"

"I need to know... I looked for answers. I looked for answers that didn't have an enchantment or a spell. I don't know how to change."

"You don't know?"

"No," he said. His voice rough.

Her heart went tight, and she looked at his sculpted, haunted face. "Javier, it was never about the right spell. In all the stories, in all the lands, in all the world. It was never magic that changed the beast. It was love."

He shuddered beneath her touch. "I know. But I looked and looked at that book. At this story." He held the book up. "The beast isn't the strong one. It's the beauty. It's her love. And still I'm not... I'm not fixed."

"Yes," she said, moving toward him, her heart pounding hard. "But don't you know what changes him? It's not just her loving him. It's him loving her back. Love is the magic, Javier. We might not have sorceresses and spells, but we have love. And that's... That's what makes people change."

Hope washed through her as she saw a change come over his face, his body. As he moved into action, swept her into his arms and pulled her up against his body. "Is that all I have to do? Just love you? Because I do. Because I have."

"Yes," she whispered.

"What if I hurt you? I am afraid... I have caused so

much pain, Violet. All the years since don't make it go away."

"You have to forgive yourself. Because you're right, some things can't be undone. But people do change, Javier. You have. It doesn't wipe the past clean. But neither does a life of torturing yourself."

"If I hurt you... I am so afraid I will hurt you. More than I fear any other thing, more than I fear losing you, I fear hurting you. And that is what I could not accept."

"You won't," she said.

"You are so sure?"

"Yes," she said. "Because I saw the Prince beneath the beast the moment we first met. Even when I didn't know you, I trusted your word. You know the cost of selfishness, and you will never ask others to pay it. If you were your father, we would all know it by now. You simply have to believe it."

"What if I don't change?" he asked, the question sharp and rough. "What if love is not enough to change me?"

"I love you already. You're the only one who thinks you're a beast, Javier." She took a step back, putting her palm on his face. "*You* need to see the change. Not me."

"I love you," he said. "And I... You're right. I was afraid of what that might mean. Because I did love my father. Very much. But he was a monster. And I couldn't understand how I had been so blind to that. How I had seen only what I wanted to see. Because of how much I loved him. And I never wanted to be that way again. I never wanted to be vulnerable to making such mistakes. But I think... I think it is time for me to accept that I am a man, and no matter what, I will be vulnerable to mistakes. But with you by my side... You have a compassionate heart, Violet. And perhaps the secret is loving other people. Valuing their opinions. Not shutting yourself up in an echo chamber of your own desires so that nobody ever reaches you. So that no one can hold you accountable for what you do. Our love will make me better. Loving you… Matteo said something to me today. He reminded me that our father never loved anyone. That it wasn't love that made our father behave the way he did. It was the love of himself. The love of power above people. I trust that we will find right. Good. That you will help me."

The plea was so raw. So real. Straight from his heart.

"Of course," she said, resting her head on his chest. "Of course I will do whatever you want. I will be whatever you need."

"But what do you get from this? What do you get from me? I need you. I need you to be a moral compass. I need you to love me. I need you to change me. What I do, I do for you."

"You showed me my strength. You gave me the fairy tale I didn't even know I was looking for. And I became the heroine of my story in a way that I didn't know I could be. You are my prince. And you always were. Even when you were a beast."

A smile tugged at the corners of her mouth, and she kissed him. Deep and long. And when they parted she looked into his eyes. "And if am being honest. I quite like you as a beast. With cuffs and chains and the lack of civility. Because you've always held me afterward. Because you've always treated me with care. Because you know when to be both. A man and a beast. And I think that's better than just having one. It makes you perfect."

"I thought… I thought that my father had doomed me."

"No. The sins of our fathers might have brought us together. But they don't define us. It's about us. And it's about what we choose. It always has been.

"That's the real magic. That no matter where you end up in life… You can always choose love."

"I choose love," he said. "I choose you."

"So do I." She bracketed his face with her hands. "But I must warn you. I have a debt to collect, Prince Javier."

"A debt?"

"Yes. You owe me for the rest of my life."

"What is it that I owe you?"

"Only all of you. And I intend to collect some every day forever."

"Then you're in luck. Because I intend to give myself, all that I am, even the broken parts, forever."

"Excellent. I might still take you prisoner, though."

"I would happily be your prisoner."

"I shall have to figure out which of the dungeons is my favorite."

"Whichever one has a bed."

"Well. That I most definitely agree with. Did we break the curse?" she asked.

"I believe that we did."

"Magic," she whispered.

"Or just love."

EPILOGUE

"PRINCESS VIOLET," CAME a rich, deep voice from behind her. "I believe I have a debt to collect."

A smile touched her lips, and she looked down into the crib at her sleeping baby, a girl they had named Jacinta, then back at her husband, who was prowling toward her, a wicked smile on his face. Man and beast become one.

That was how he loved her. And it was how she liked it. Fierce and tender. Dangerous but utterly trustworthy.

"Do you?" she asked. "Because last I checked I was still the richest woman in the world, and a princess on top of it. I doubt I owe anyone a debt." She had continued to run her company successfully from Monte Blanco, and with the country having become the most photographed tourist destination in the world, a phenomenon and a craze in the last five years, her brand—now primarily manufactured there—had only become more in demand.

"This is not a debt that can be paid with money. Only with your body." A shiver ran down her spine. "And with your heart."

Javier was the best husband. The best father. He loved her even more now that they'd been married half a decade than he had in the beginning, and she never doubted it.

"I wanted a kiss earlier," he said, gruffly, nuzzling her ear. "You were too busy with Jacinta and Carlos."

"Carlos was eating paper," she said, in a voice of mock despair over their three-year-old son's taste.

"And I find I am still in need of my kiss."

So she kissed him.

"I find that is not enough," he said, and from behind his back he produced the jeweled cuffs. Anticipation fired in her blood.

"This is one debt I'm eager to pay," she said.

When she had paid—enthusiastically, and repeatedly— she lay sated against his body.

"You are right," he said finally. "You are magic. You have transformed me multiple times, you know."

"Have I?"

"Yes. From beast to man. Heartless to a man with more love than he can contain. You made me a husband. You made me a father. You made me love. You made me whole."

"Oh, Javier," she breathed. "This is the very best magic."

"Yes, My Princess," he agreed. "It is."

* * * * *

MILLS & BOON

Coming next month

CLAIMING HIS BOLLYWOOD CINDERELLA
Tara Pammi

The scent of her hit him first. A subtle blend of jasmine and her that he'd remember for the rest of his life. And equate with honesty and irreverence and passion and laughter. There was a joy about this woman, despite her insecurities and vulnerabilities, that he found almost magical.

The mask she wore was black satin with elaborate gold threading at the edges and was woven tightly into her hair, leaving just enough of her beautiful dark brown eyes visible. The bridge of her small nose was revealed as was the slice of her cheekbones. For a few seconds, Vikram had the overwhelming urge to tear it off. He wanted to see her face. Not because he wanted to find out her identity.

He wanted to see her face because he wanted to know this woman. He wanted to know everything about her. He wanted… With a rueful shake of his head, he pushed away the urge. It was more than clear that men had only ever disappointed her. He was damned if he was going to be counted as one of them. He wanted to be different in her memory.

When she remembered him after tonight, he wanted her to smile. He wanted her to crave more of him. Just as he would crave more of her. He knew this before their lips even touched. And he would find a way to discover her identity. He was just as sure of that too.

Her mouth was completely uncovered. Her lipstick was

mostly gone leaving a faint pink smudge that he wanted to lick away with his tongue.

She held the edge of her silk dress with one hand and as she'd lifted it to move, he got a flash of a thigh. Soft and smooth and silky. It was like receiving a jolt of electricity, with every inch he discovered of this woman. The dress swooped low in the front, baring the upper curves of her breasts in a tantalizing display.

And then there she was, within touching distance. Sitting with her legs folded beneath her, looking straight into his eyes. One arm held the sofa while the other smoothed repeatedly over the slight curve of her belly. She was nervous and he found it both endearing and incredibly arousing. She wanted to please herself. And him. And he'd never wanted more for a woman to discover pleasure with him.

Her warm breath hit him somewhere between his mouth and jaw in silky strokes that resonated with his heartbeat. This close, he could see the tiny scar on the other corner of her mouth.

"Are you going to do anything?" she asked after a couple of seconds, sounding completely put out.

He wanted to laugh and tug that pouty lower lip with his teeth. Instead he forced himself to take a breath. He was never going to smell jasmine and not think of her ever again. "It's your kiss, darling. You take it."

Continue reading
CLAIMING HIS BOLLYWOOD CINDERELLA
Tara Pammi

Available next month
www.millsandboon.co.uk

COMING SOON!

We really hope you enjoyed reading this book.
If you're looking for more romance, be sure to
head to the shops when new books are
available on

Thursday 15th October

LET'S TALK
Romance

For exclusive extracts, competitions
and special offers, find us online:

f facebook.com/millsandboon

🐦 @MillsandBoon

📷 @MillsandBoonUK

Get in touch on 01413 063232

For all the latest titles coming soon, visit
millsandboon.co.uk/nextmonth

JOIN US ON SOCIAL MEDIA!

Stay up to date with our latest releases, author
news and gossip, special offers and discounts, and
all the behind-the-scenes action
from Mills & Boon...

 millsandboon

 millsandboonuk

 millsandboon

It might just be true love...